MOONS' DANCING

MOONS' DANCING

THE CHILDREN OF THE ROCK
VOLUME 2

Marguerite Krause

and

Susan Sizemore

Five Star • Waterville, Maine

First Edition
First Printing: December 2003

Published in 2003 in conjunction with
Tekno Books and Ed Gorman.

Set in 11 pt. Plantin by Minnie B. Raven.

Printed in the United States on permanent paper.

Library of Congress Cataloging-in-Publication Data

Krause, Marguerite.
    Moons' dancing / by Marguerite Krause and Susan Sizemore.
        p. cm.—(The children of the rock ; v. 2)
      ISBN 1-59414-063-4 (hc : alk. paper)
      I. Sizemore, Susan. II. Title.
  PS3611.R377M655 2003
  813'.6—dc22   2003061828

To Jane and Mike, for putting up with us

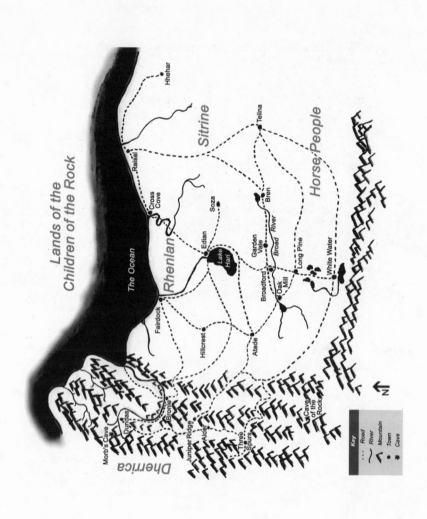

Part I

CHAPTER 1

"What are you doing?"

"Hush," Jordy whispered.

Vray hushed. In the three days since they left Broadford, she had already learned quite a bit about what it meant to be a carter on the road. Jordy and Tob had a well-rehearsed yet flexible routine for each day's activities. Since bringing Tob on his summer's journeys had effectively halved Jordy's work load, he claimed that adding another helper should make things even easier. He'd insisted on one and only one firm rule of behavior. When he spoke, Tob and Vray were to obey immediately. He would answer their questions, argue with them, and otherwise treat them as responsible young adults most of the time, but at moments of decision, his had to be the only voice.

Tob looked around from unharnessing Stockings. The sun was low in the west, about to disappear behind the distant purple mass on the horizon that marked the beginning of the Dherrican Mountains. Jordy, standing beside the wagon's front wheel, had reached under the driver's seat and pulled out a stone. His manner did not suggest danger, but Vray stopped rummaging in the back of the wagon for firewood and apprehensively tried to locate whatever had attracted the carter's attention.

Around them stretched mile after mile of gently rolling Atowa grassland. They had been crossing the almost featureless plateau for two days. Two days of similar travel remained before they reached the southern shore of Lake Hari. The road to the north was empty, straight, and unvarying all the way to the horizon. Just visible where the road passed over the southern horizon was the clump of pale green trees that marked the location of the little spring-fed pond at which they'd filled their water casks. A similar

9

cluster of trees was visible a few miles to the east of the road. With those exceptions, the expanse of new grass was unbroken. Vray could see no travelers other than themselves, no startled flocks of birds or fleeing herds of antelope that might warn of a pack of jackals or, worse still, a hunting phantom cat.

Jordy's attention was on a gentle slope less than a dozen yards from the wagon. He held the stone in his right hand, arm half-cocked. Vray, standing above and behind him in the bed of the wagon, had a fleeting glimpse of brown fur and tall ears before he threw. The little animal rolled over several times under the impact. Jordy turned at once, produced two more stones from under the wagon seat, and trotted up the slope.

Recognition came belatedly to Vray. "That was a rabbit!" she exclaimed.

"Shhh," Tob warned her. "There may be more."

Jordy crouched down as he neared the top of the slope, then threw his remaining two stones one after another, almost more quickly than Vray's eye could follow. He straightened and disappeared briefly over the top of the hillock.

"Your mouth's open, Iris," Tob teased her gently.

Vray recovered her dropped jaw and walked toward Tob. "He's fast."

The comment was inadequate, but she wasn't ready to try to explain the deeper layers of her unease. Every time she thought she had a firm grasp of just what the carter was capable of, he turned around and did something unexpected. It wasn't that she hadn't expected Jordy to be a skillful hunter. She knew his skill with a bow. However, for a few seconds, his intensity had made her expect danger rather than dinner.

He's only a carter, she reminded herself sternly. He and his friends might be plotting revolution, training the villagers to fight, but that didn't mean he knew the first thing about actually confronting a troop of Damon's guards. By the Firstmother, today's kills were only rabbits!

Jordy came down the slope toward them, two rabbits in one hand and one in the other; a satisfied half-smile on his face. Vray, annoyed with him for making her uneasy, folded her arms over her chest.

"I thought that's what the bow was for," she said, inclining her head toward the back of the wagon.

"That great thing for a beastie this size? Half the meat would be ripped away. Besides, it wasn't handy. That's why I keep throwing stones here." He laid the rabbits on the wagon seat, then reached underneath. With a sharp tug he slid out an entire tray of slightly jagged, palm-fitting stones. He looked over Vray's shoulder at Tob. "That reminds me, we saw grouse near here last summer, didn't we?"

"Halfway home from Edian? Yes, I think that was the night."

"I'll have a look. A bird or two will make a good lunch tomorrow." He slipped a few stones into his pockets. "Be sure to set up the tent. The wind's turning to the north, and that means rain. I'll be back in an hour."

"Right, Dad," Tob replied.

Jordy left. Vray returned to the wagon and gathered a bundle of firewood into her arms. She found the patch of bare, red-brown soil that marked the location of previous travelers' campfires and laid her wood beside it. Then she returned to the wagon for the cooking gear. Tob led Stockings out into the grass and hobbled her. Vray expected him to go around to the back of the wagon and begin unpacking the tent. Instead, he took the pack full of pots and utensils away from her, set it on the ground, and wrapped his arms around her. Vray responded willingly enough with a kiss. When she came up for air, however, he wouldn't let her go.

"Tob," she said. "We're supposed to be setting up camp."

"We've got plenty of time." He kissed the end of her nose, then began nibbling lightly over her cheek.

Vray's skin prickled pleasurably. "Tob!" she repeated insistently. "Not now."

11

"Why not?" He rubbed his hands lightly up and down her back.

"Our father . . ."

"Won't be back for an hour. He said so. Besides, it's not as if he doesn't know."

Vray stiffened in his arms. "What?"

Tob began kissing the side of her neck. "He's sired three children, you know," he said between kisses.

"General knowledge is one thing." Vray's eyes closed in spite of herself. "It's specific cases parents don't always approve of."

"He approves of us."

Vray pushed against his chest and tried to glare at him. "Approves of us? Of you and me together, us?"

"Sure."

"You told him?"

Tob finally reacted to the astonishment in her voice and paused in his caresses. "He asked. Actually, he guessed the morning after the Festival that I'd been with you." A blush reddened his already sun-darkened cheeks. "He said what I'd been doing was obvious."

"Mothers," Vray muttered. She cleared her throat. "He didn't mind?"

"Why should he? He's proud of you, Iris. I've heard him say so to Herri. The whole village likes you. You were pretty strange when you came to us last summer, but you've gotten a lot better." A hint of worry darkened the earnest blue eyes. "He knows I didn't just take advantage of you. I never would have suggested it, if you didn't really know what we were doing!"

That shattering sound, Vray told herself, *is the collapse of my sense of self-importance.* She had entertained doubts about the fairness of seducing an innocent Keeper boy. She had never thought to consider that Tob and Jordy might be concerned about her innocence. She took a deep breath. "Of course you'd never do that, Tob."

His smirk returned. "You're not embarrassed, are you? I suppose I could have said it was someone else, but Dad says trying to keep secrets only complicates life sooner or later."

"I'm not embarrassed." She fidgeted thoughtfully with the embroidery on the front of his tunic. "But, isn't it a little awkward? For Dad, I mean? With Mama being all the way back in Broadford, I mean."

Tob took her hands away from his shirt and slid them around his waist. "That's why we should do it now, while he's not here." He covered her mouth with his.

The kiss lasted a long time. When they stopped, Vray allowed her concern one last expression. "He'll know," she murmured against Tob's throat.

With one hand he released the nearest tarp from the back of the wagon. A flip of his arm shook it open. It was still settling to the ground as Tob lowered her onto it, the grass a soft mat beneath them. "He won't mention it if we don't."

The words freed Vray, and she reached out for the drawstring on Tob's trousers.

A glaring yellow pine cone the size of a small mountain skimmed gracefully through pink froth air. Aage did not interfere. A few ninedays passed, the moons zigzagging absurdly overhead. Aage left his head where it was and carried another with him to the top of the wall. Below, a few trout grinned at him, fangs glinting in the light of a nearby greenish star. Again he turned away. He knew them. They were rarely dangerous and never effective. Without eyes, he looked elsewhere for a threat. Without ears, he listened to babble rising and falling, approaching and receding. A flock of three-legged horses tumbled end-over-end in the distance.

Direct threat. Aage bent the power sharply, losing as he did so the odd images his mind produced when he wasn't busy. There was only the world, a fragile sphere suspended in night, enclosed in its protective web. Only himself, one strand pulsing with power. Only the Others, making yet another attempt to snatch the web and tear it away.

Aage fought, his concentration pure, effortless. He never

spoke of what he did, even to Morb. When Morb was present with him, no discussion was necessary. Later, when they resumed their bodies, no discussion was possible. At least not for Aage. He suspected that Morb, with his centuries of experience, was no longer troubled by a need to conceptualize what he experienced in physical terms. He never encountered bizarrely shaped sheep or clouds of shouting porridge.

Of course, he never heard the gods, either.

Aage became aware of their presence as his struggle with the Others reached its peak. They did not come every time he entered the realms of power, but they always came in the midst of battle. The first time he became aware of them he had thought them another hallucination, another distorted product of his mind's attempt to translate the totally alien into familiar terms. He quickly learned that the gods did not appreciate being dismissed out of hand.

He'd been taught that the gods spoke to certain Dreamers, especially at moments of crisis. Until it happened, he had never imagined it would happen to him. The other Dreamers, however, had gratefully accepted his messages from the gods. Soon he, too, was able to view the occasional communications as simply another manifestation of his power-bending gifts.

He continued to put all his energy into his struggle with the Others. In effect, he became two people: one, a wizard wielding magic against monsters; the second, a very normal, very flesh and blood Child of the Rock. The gods' presence was the warmth of friends standing close beside him on a cool evening.

Then he saw the vision. The ledge outside Morb's cave. Evening. Hot, sticky, midsummer. Golden Keyn-light revealed glistening perspiration on Morb's brown shoulders as he seated himself on his boulder. The power was surging with dangerous intensity. All three of the Dreamers on the ledge were aware of it.

Aage watched the third Dreamer duck into Morb's cave to fill his bowl with water. His. Not one of the Greenmothers. Another male Dreamer. A new Dreamer!

Aage waited eagerly for the young wizard to emerge. Who was he? He'd glimpsed dark hair. Not Forrit, then. Unless the blond Sitrinian boy was going to darken unexpectedly as he matured. As quickly as he thought it, he dismissed the idea. His vision-self knew this new Dreamer, knew he wasn't Forrit.

The vision faded. A mood lingered, reassurance and warning combined. This Dreamer's gifts were strong. He would bend the power, hold off intruders as well as, perhaps better than, Morb himself. The warning was that his strength would be needed. Dangers lay ahead.

Before the gods could recede, Aage called out wordlessly. *Why do you show this Dreamer to me? Who will he be? Will he need special attention to reach that moment on Morb's ledge?*

He will be there. You will be with him.

Who is he?

Present generation Dreamer child.

Aage's adversary was in retreat. With one part of himself, he bent the power to end the battle. Another part strained to retain awareness of the gods. *Please. Who is he? Which of the chosen Keepers' and Shapers' children?*

There was no immediate answer. A shiver of protest prickled at the back of his awareness. Not Damon!

Danger. In the instant that he completed his battle, another attack began. Aage's senses whirled as he made the transition from offense to defense. He had to abandon his interrogation of the gods. Visions of the future would serve no purpose if he allowed the world to be destroyed in the present.

The initial onslaught was fierce, but this Other lacked perseverance. Aage bent the power with more confidence. He pushed harder; the Other began to collapse. Then, even more abruptly than before, it swelled, doubled, tripled its strength. Aage narrowly evaded the trap. Once more he built his defense.

The voices came with no advance warning. *He is not a son of Damon.*

Aage did not feel ready to resume the conversation, but the gods obviously thought he was. Perhaps they knew his strength better than he did himself. Encouraged, he shifted his place in the power, stretching the web a bit, preparing a strategy he'd often considered but never tried for fear of the risk. As he worked, he addressed the gods. *Whose son is he?*

Yours.

A Dreamer child yes, but—

Your child, wizard.

He almost dropped the barriers he was so carefully erecting around the intruder. *My child? How my child? You made Dreamers infertile.*

Your child, wizard.

It's not possible!

Silence.

Is it?

Your child, wizard.

He tried to feel the gods' presence, gauge their mood. Failed. More of his energy drained into the battle. *My child?* he demanded. *With what mother?*

Silence.

What woman would have me? Not Savyea or Jenil. They're as infertile as I am. Perhaps, when I tell them that you said this to me . . .

They would not approve.

I don't understand. Who could be mother to my child? I haven't had time for a lover for three years. My only friend is the princess . . .

Princess.

This time the shock of disbelief worked in Aage's favor. The burst of energy drove his adversary back. *I should have a child with Jeyn?*

The Princess.

A twist in the strands of power marked Morb's arrival. In the presence of two wizards, the assault from the other universe collapsed. Aage knew without calling that the gods were gone, too. Morb ordered him back to the world.

The morning sun had just cleared the peaks on the other

side of the valley. The mountains tilted. Aage's head landed on Morb's hard shoulder. Morb's hands caught at him, preventing him from toppling off the boulder. Odd. The old wizard's hands seemed to be gripping some other person's body. The numbness spread rapidly, deadening sound, dulling vision.

Morb's voice reached him, faint, distorted. "What happened to you?"

A vision, Aage wanted to say, but he couldn't hear his own voice. *A vision I don't want to think about.*

He drifted into darkness, peaceful and quiet.

If he hadn't been terrified, he might have enjoyed it.

CHAPTER 2

Brownmothers were, in one way or another, connected with half of the buildings in Bren. As residents alone, they and their families would have been a noticeable presence in the town, but their influence extended far beyond the homes and shops they occupied. Brownmothers headed several dozen extended families that consisted primarily of apprentices to local crafters. Some were children who had come to learn trades not taught in their home communities. The rest were there because they had no other family.

Not one but two houses of healing fronted the village square. A different group of Brownmothers maintained the low, sprawling storage building erected on the outskirts of the town to house libraries salvaged from the homes of Shaper families destroyed by the plague. At present, only one of the Brownmothers working at the storehouse was a Shaper herself, capable of interpreting writing, so she worked alone at the task of keeping the collection organized, and left the important physical care of the records to other hands. On the opposite side of town, Brownmothers' herb gardens stretched along the lakeshore.

No one could spend an hour in Bren without being aware of the Brownmothers. Anything that affected them, affected the rest of the town.

Jenil acknowledged the shy waves of two children as she crossed the square. Her visits to Bren were always interesting. Midmorning activities filled the chill, early spring air with noise: the creak of wagons, the ring of metal from the smithy, people calling out to one another, neighs and bleats and clucks and barks. A few heads turned subtly in Jenil's direction as she passed. It wasn't because she was a stranger to the town. Savyea, although she visited less frequently, did not attract the same attention. Her visits were regularly spaced, and everyone knew the reason behind them. For over a decade she'd been training the cousins, the two young Dreamers-to-be, for the change that was now, gods willing, only a few years away. Jenil sometimes visited the children, too, but more often she had other motives for coming to Bren. People knew that, which was what prompted their curiosity.

Everyone treated her in a different way, a fact she accepted with a certain amount of amusement. The court at Edian viewed her with a mixture of fear and contempt. In small villages, people who saw her only in times of disaster, wielding great magic that protected their loved ones from death, met her visits with awed respect. In Garden Vale, her neighbors took her for granted. The healthy curiosity of the people of Bren was a pleasant change.

At the center of the square she paused. A flicker along the lines of power touched her senses. One of the other Dreamers had arrived. Savyea? Power quivered, near at hand. In the house of healing. Then it moved again.

Smoke materialized out of the bright, empty air. "Come to Morb's cave," Savyea said. "Bring all your dragon powder. At once." A second tiny cloud formed with her departure, overlapping the first.

Jenil transported herself away, giving the watching villagers a third wisp of smoke to marvel at. She stopped in her room at the Bren inn long enough to snatch up her bag, crossed the miles to Garden Vale in the space of another heartbeat, then lifted the knee-high jar of power-focusing powder from its corner. She settled the jar in her arms and took the final, mountain-spanning step to the ledge before Morb's cave.

The sun was more recently risen here than in Sitrine. Some of the relative coolness of the night still clung to the rock wall at the back of the ledge, but it was dissipating rapidly in the sunlight that streamed across the valley.

"Bring it here." Morb gestured to her from the dark opening. None of his usual good humor softened the ugliness of his features. He disappeared again without waiting for her acknowledgment.

Jenil entered the cave. Savyea knelt on the floor beside Aage. He was sprawled limply on his back, eyes closed, looking as though he'd been dropped and left to lie where he fell. Morb sat down at Aage's head, a bowl of water in his hands. Power bent around him and steam began to rise from the magically heated liquid. Jenil set her jar beside Morb and knelt quickly opposite Savyea. With one hand, she reached for Aage's throat. His pulse beat against her fingertips too slowly to provide much reassurance. She made a rapid visual inspection of his body, but saw no sign of injury.

"What's the matter with him?" she asked aloud.

Savyea, immersed in the power, did not answer. Morb set the bowl of water on the stone floor near Jenil and lifted the lid from the jar of powder. "He was fending off monsters. The first I knew of anything unusual was when his power began to fade."

"Was he trying to face too many of them?"

Morb cupped his hand and scooped one palmful of powder, then a second, from the jar into the water. "No. I went to assist him. There was only one Other present, and he had almost defeated it."

He hesitated, then added yet a third handful to the now fizzing water. Jenil watched uncertainly. Sparks of otherworldly color floated upward from the bowl, shifting and intertwining, though not a breath of air moved in the cave. A scent that was not a scent teased her perceptions.

The powder-laden water in that bowl, portioned a sip at a time to fifty Keepers or Shapers, would kill them instantly. Properly diluted, it would prepare three hundred or more for a healing. The Shapers would have to kill a dozen dragons or sea monsters, two dozen phantom cats, to replenish what was about to be used on a single exhausted Dreamer.

The question was, what had exhausted him?

Savyea opened her eyes. "I'll hold that," she told Morb. "You lift his head."

Jenil picked up the bowl and passed it to her. Even that brief contact made her hands tingle with sudden over-sensitivity. Savyea also reacted to the amount of energy that pulsated in and around the water.

Morb met her sharp stare, his gaze level. "You felt it. He's drained. Any less won't revive him. If we delay, the whole jar might not be enough." Without waiting for her reply, he pulled Aage toward him, the muscles in his bare arms and shoulders tensing as he maneuvered the limp body of the larger man into position in his lap.

Power writhed around them in aimless tendrils. Jenil caught Aage's lolling head between her hands and gently eased it back until the pale hair rested against Morb's dark chest. Savyea positioned the bowl just beneath his nose, not quite touching his lips, and waited.

With his next shallow breath, Aage inhaled glittering motes of magic. Steam drifted upward around his face. His next breath was deeper, and the one after that, a lung-filling sigh.

Not all of the power-enhanced vapor reached Aage. Jenil blinked against a sudden dizziness, as the air itself began to take on odd reflective properties. She knew stories of the centuries before the plague, when dragons and the Shapers who hunted them were far more plentiful, and Dreamers like Morb so numerous that they wielded their world-shielding power for only a few ninedays each year. The stories spoke of Greenmothers who brewed excess powder into an intoxicant headier than wine. Until recently, the number of dragons and similar creatures had been decreasing, which had made the powder too precious for other than utilitarian purposes. Now, however, she understood the wistful longing when older Dreamers had reminisced about the effect of the powder on their bodies.

Savyea's face had flushed a bright pink. Morb, close as he was to the fumes, was getting a glazed look in his eyes. Aage half-lifted his head, his lips parted. Concentrating, Savyea placed the rim of the bowl into his mouth and trickled a few drops onto his tongue. He swallowed. One of his hands moved fractionally. Savyea increased the trickle bit by bit, until Aage had finished every drop.

The bowl seemed translucent. So did Savyea's hands. Jenil blinked again and shook her head. The cave itself had lost much of its solidity. Lines of power moved and turned around them, far more real than mere stone. Jenil discovered that she had pressed one of her hands flat against the floor, as though to anchor herself in place. The powder had conveyed a great amount of energy, but little control.

Savyea trembled, swayed, and sank back on her heels. Aage did not wake. Jenil somehow put aside her giddiness and checked him with all her senses, physical and magical. To her relief, the alarming weakness was gone, replaced by a suffuse glow of energy that gradually spread throughout his body. By the time she emerged from her examination, the side effects of the powder had dissipated. The cave's rock walls safely enclosed her once more.

"That was interesting," Savyea offered with something like her usual brightness.

Jenil stood awkwardly. Sometime during the last few minutes her foot had fallen asleep. "What kind of monster did this?" she asked Morb.

"I've never seen him affected this way before," Savyea agreed.

Morb eased a pillow under the sleeping younger wizard's head, then got to his feet. He laced his fingers behind his neck and stretched. "Let's hope it doesn't happen again." His arms dropped wearily to his sides. "I've got to go."

As he left, Savyea leaned forward once more and gently shook Aage by the shoulder. "Aage. Aage. Listen to me."

Sluggishly, he turned his head and opened his eyes. The expression on his face was dreamy and unfocused. "Hello."

"We're going to Bren." Savyea spoke with exaggerated patience. "The Brownmother house, dear. Do you know where it is?"

There was a pause, then his right hand lifted languidly to point in a direction that was more south than east.

"Not quite. Pay attention, dear. Look with me. That's right."

The power bent, first around Savyea then, less gracefully, around Aage. Jenil found herself looking at two wisps of smoke, scented with apple and lilac.

She grimaced as returning circulation pricked the cramped muscles of her foot. Another crisis successfully resolved. Now that it was over, anguish swept through her. What if Aage had died? She feared for Morb, too. Old and strong as he was, he had not gone untouched by the unusual healing. She had little gift for holding off other worlds, but until Aage recovered Morb needed someone to whom he could turn for assistance.

Still shaking from the over-stimulation of those few breaths of powder, Jenil covered the jar and picked up the noticeably lighter container. She twisted the lines of power and transported herself out of the cave. Trembling, she located Morb in his vigil at the edge of the world. He accepted her offer, their communication as clear as it was wordless, and assured her he was in no immediate need.

Jenil chose her next destination and arrived in her room at Garden Vale. The house was quiet. It was not yet noon, and the Brownmothers had not returned from their morning's pursuits for the midday meal.

Jenil replaced the jar in its customary corner. She sat down on her bed long enough to pull off her shoes. Then she curled up on her side, pulled a blanket over her shoulders, and fell asleep.

After a day of rain, the weather became mild. Jordy, striding along next to the wagon hour after hour, was comfortable in trousers and tunic. Vray couldn't yet match his endurance. When she rested in the wagon for a few miles, especially if a cloud passed in front of the sun, she welcomed her cloak. The winds that swept across Atowa in springtime were cold.

She curled her legs more tightly under her and leaned against the roll of Cyril's rugs. Tob, sprawled on his back near the tailboard of the wagon, snored gently. They had reached the point where the road began a gentle curve to the east to skirt the tree-lined shores of Lake Hari. The first shoots of pale green grass covered the plateau as far as the eye could see to south and east. Around the lake, trees interrupted the view to the north. Overhead, the sky was a faded blue, liberally dotted with clouds.

Vray shaded her eyes with one hand and peered toward the west. At this distance she could not pick out the barns and fences of her mother's estate. She dropped her hand into her lap. Not that there was anything worth seeing. Except for the horses. She wondered if her mother had even noticed she was gone. Not that it mattered. If she did go back—when she did go back—it would be on her own terms. Perhaps with King Sene's help, if she could get a message to him. Perhaps she would speak to him in person, if Jordy went to Raisal this summer.

She realized she was still staring to the west when the carter dropped back to walk beside her. He gazed in the same direction. "Nothing to be seen this early in the year."

Vray tore her guilty attention from the horizon. "What?"

"The queen's horses." Jordy's attitude remained casual. He had one hand in a trouser pocket, the other swinging freely at his side as he walked. "Other times I've passed this way we've seen some of her trainers out running the two- and three-year-olds." He glanced up at her. "Beautiful animals. Have you seen them?"

"In Edian."

"Ah, yes. That reminds me. Would you like to visit your other family?" His eyes, mild blue to match the sky and his mood, regarded her steadily. "Where in Edian do they live?"

"No!" Vray said too quickly. The old terror knifed through her as though her year in Broadford had been only a pleasant dream. She forced the fear down and reclaimed control of her voice. "I'd rather not. They wouldn't want to see me."

"Your choice." A hint of disapproval tightened the carter's mouth. "Are they all that terrible, then?"

"Let's say you wouldn't want to meet my father."

His eyebrows lowered fiercely. "You have that wrong, lass. He would not want to meet me."

His protectiveness shocked Vray out of her first fear. It wasn't difficult to imagine Jordy facing the king. He had firm opinions regarding responsibility and parenting. He wouldn't hesitate to express them. It was an intriguing prospect. Tempting. Then she thought of Damon.

"Please, Jordy. I'm not ready yet."

"Aren't you?" His expression softened. "Ah, well, perhaps you're right. Such a serious confrontation should be perfectly timed, perfectly planned."

"My thought exactly," she agreed. "I won't hide from him forever."

"No, I can see that you won't." Abruptly he returned his attention to the road ahead of them. "Is it likely you'll be recognized in Edian? Even if we avoid your family, might we be seen by former friends or acquaintances?"

"I've thought about that. It's been a few years since anyone there has seen me. I've changed since then. Besides, no one will expect me."

"Not in a carter's wagon?"

"Not anywhere," she insisted. "By now, anyone who once knew me will think me gone forever, if they think of me at all."

"You still miss them."

"Friends, yes. Not my family." She didn't try to hide her bitterness. "I wish now I could pretend they had nothing to do with me, that I have no connection to them."

"You can't deny your past, my girl. It's part of you."

"I know. Just let me avoid it a little longer."

"You're old enough to decide for yourself. I'll try not to interfere."

"Thank you."

The road straightened out. Stockings, lost in whatever passed for thoughts in her limited brain, did not. Jordy leapt forward and took her by the halter. At his insistence, she reluctantly gave up her attempt to veer herself and the wagon off the road.

Vray resumed watching the distant line of trees. She couldn't make herself known in Edian. Damon would only send her away again. Everything she'd heard indicated that his power was greater than ever. She just wasn't ready to face him. Not yet.

Once Jordy had Stockings straightened out, he walked backward for a while, watching the girl. She was staring at the horizon again, unaware of his scrutiny. He turned around and glared at the uneven road surface, then urged Stockings to the right around a particularly deep depression. There was no excuse for such disrepair so close to a town the size of Edian! What was the king thinking of? Not the state of his kingdom, or the needs of his people, that was certain. Not much of a king. Not much of a parent, either. What he'd done to the girl was inexcusable.

Jordy was doing all he could think of to help her, but it was not enough. She should have been able to trust him by now. He gave her every opening he could. She must suspect that he'd guessed the truth. If she wanted to tell him, she could, but he couldn't just ask her. If he asked, he forced her to choose, and he was too afraid she'd choose a lie over the truth.

She knows I love her, he thought. Didn't she understand what that meant? He would accept her, no matter what. She had heard his complaints about Shapers. Maybe she thought he would reject her if he knew the truth. He wanted to be a comfort to her, not a threat. He thought she was growing fond of the family. She'd become fond enough of Tob, at least. Had she told him the truth? No. Tob would tell him something that important. The lad knew that Jordy wanted only what was best for her.

She was still afraid of Edian, not ready to talk about it to anyone. He supposed he couldn't blame her for being afraid. He just didn't understand why she was afraid of him.

Jordy tugged on Stockings's lead rope, bringing her back to the middle of the road. He trudged on, the sun warm on his face. Soon he'd have to start wearing his hat. His skin never browned as Tob's did.

His thoughts turned to the trading to be done in the next few days. With good weather they could have quite a successful round this year. The whole summer was ahead of them. He should have felt cheerful.

But he didn't.

CHAPTER 3

They spent two days in Edian. Vray wore a scarf over her hair and didn't bother to wash her face. Their wagon was one among many in the merchants' encampment, and strangers were too busy to pay any attention to one more apprentice carter. People who were acquainted with Jordy from past years welcomed her as his new, adopted child, there to learn a trade. She was accepted without question among the carters and traveling craftspeople, and never laid eyes on anyone she had known before her banishment. While Jordy worked through the marketplace, selling their cargo and arranging for the outbound load, she and Tob accepted the goods delivered to the wagon and secured the merchandise for travel. At dawn on the third morning, they were on the road once more.

In Edian, they had met with the first of many people who seemed to share Jordy's dissatisfaction with Hion's rule. To Vray's surprise, Jordy began discussing his plans for revolution with the man right in front of her. However, as the days passed, everyone they talked to, in marketplaces or inns or on the road, treated her as though she had been part of the conspiracy from the beginning. From their point of view, she supposed it was a natural reaction. She was the carter's daughter. She wrestled with the burden of their trust the rest of the way to Cross Cove.

Spring seemed to advance more quickly as they traveled farther north. Afternoons grew warmer. On their fourth day out of Edian, they came upon a slow, shallow river. It flowed from the southeast toward the sea, meandering back and forth across the plain in loops several miles across. The road continued its straight course toward the northeast. They forded the river several times, where the pebbly bottom provided a firm path for wagons, and the water barely covered

28

Stockings's hocks. At the final crossing, the river had deepened, and the road spanned it via a broad stone bridge.

The next day the land grew more broken. As the river straightened, its flow quickened, carving into the soil. In the course of a few miles the gully widened into a valley. The road veered north to follow it and they left the grassland behind. As the valley deepened, damp walls rose next to the stony road and returned echoes from Stockings's hooves. Ferns and scraggly bushes clung to the slopes, background to the subtle colors of early-blooming flowers. Gulls appeared overhead, drifting effortlessly on outspread wings.

The river ended in a waterfall, seventy feet in height from the lip of the valley to the ocean below. A few dozen yards before the precipice, the road turned to the right and cut a less direct route down the face of the cliff. Jordy drove the wagon along the narrow switchbacks while Vray and Tob walked behind.

The houses of Cross Cove clustered on the quarter-mile-wide spur of land that jutted into the sea and formed a natural breakwater for the harbor. Other structures clung to the cliff face, safely above the reach of storm and tide. Everything Vray could see—buildings, fences and quays—was constructed of stone.

Their road became Cross Cove's widest street. It passed through the center of town, first paralleling the harbor, then dropping toward it, then doubling back on itself. The traditional market square was not a square, but a street that extended from quay to quay all along the inner curve of the harbor.

Jordy guided the wagon into a space next to a basket weaver's stall and swung down from the driver's seat. He beckoned to Vray. "I have a few errands for you." Looking past her, he raised his voice. "Unload the nuts first, Tob. The chickens will keep where they are."

Vray barely heard Tob's answer. In the past few days she had reached a conclusion, and she didn't want to be distracted. "Jordy, about your plan to break the villages away from Shaper control."

He paused in the act of pulling off his driving gloves. "What about it?"

"I had an idea that might help." His hands resumed their motion, and she rushed ahead before her doubts could interfere. "You're looking for leaders in each village, aren't you? There's a woman here in Cross Cove you should see. Her name is Quardt."

"The paper crafter. I don't see her having much sympathy with a rebellion, m'girl. She works closely with the Shapers. Her prosperity is linked with theirs."

"She's also as eager as you are to see Damon's excesses held in check."

"No one here has recommended her."

Vray's back stiffened. Stubborn man! "I knew her when I lived in Edian. Her neighbors may not like her, but she's reliable and determined. Once she sets her mind to something, she'll do it."

In reply Jordy motioned toward the horse. "Hold her head."

Vray complied. The carter unharnessed Stockings as he continued to speak.

"I'll consider your suggestion. Now, about business. We'll be going east from here, then south through Sitrine before we turn back toward White Water and then on to Dherrica. Our stop here has to provide us with fish oil, agates, and, most importantly, dyes. The first dyer you're to see is Mees. He lives on the spit; ask as you go. He knows I'm expecting to take two barrels of his best purple dye. You need to tell him that I've brought last year's payment from Lone Pine and the crate of preserves he requested.

"When you leave his house turn right, then left at the second street until you see a flight of steps on your left, going down. You'll see a dye shop at the bottom. The owner there is Jenek."

He interrupted himself. "Lead her forward now." Vray urged Stockings away from the wagon.

Jordy came forward and stood on the other side of the horse, absently unfastening her bridle as he resumed his instructions. "Jenek will be difficult. I've only the one bundle of cotton for him. We can spare two of the linen as well, or the small chest of dried apple. The small, mind, not the large. Don't mention the extra walnuts. I intend them for Raisal. Now, do you have all that? Or would you rather write it down?"

"I don't need to write it down. I'm a Red—" Vray stopped in abrupt, but belated reaction to his mild words and her automatic response.

He took the halter rope from her limp hands, his voice a confidential rumble. "Now that was a slip on your part, Highness. The first, I'll grant you. Keepers don't write."

"Dad," Tob called from the back of the wagon. "What about the beech wood?"

"I'll be right there," Jordy called back. His steady gaze didn't leave Vray's face.

She swallowed the assorted angry, embarrassed, indignant, and panicked remarks that crossed her mind. From some hidden reservoir of poise she found a reasonable tone of voice and said, "We have to talk."

"I think it's time," the carter agreed. "After supper."

She backed a step away from him. "I'll go see Mees."

"And Jenek."

"Right."

"Good girl."

Vray ran off without answering Tob's cheerful wave.

"Tob, when you finish with that, come here."

Propping the black iron pot on top of a barrel to dry, Tob glanced around in his father's direction. Since they'd finished their supper, full night had descended. Jordy, his back toward Tob, was a black silhouette against the light of their fire. Opposite him, Iris was also on her feet, throwing her cloak round her shoulders.

Tob quickly took the bucket of wash water and placed it out of the way under the wagon. He dried his hands on the lower edge of his tunic as he joined the others by the fire. "What is it?"

"We're going for a walk."

"You are?" Tob looked uncertainly between his father and Iris.

"All of us." Although she said nothing, Iris seemed to understand what was going on. At Jordy's words, she started toward the street that led inland from the quayside marketplace. Tob hurried to catch up with her. Jordy followed behind at an unhurried pace.

"I visited Quardt as you suggested, lass," Jordy said as they left the waterfront behind them. "It seems you're right about her. Ivey passed this way a few ninedays back. Quardt had the news from him. Friendship with Ivey is as good a recommendation as I know. Quardt will be looking for a way to help, and for others who will stand against Damon."

The street wound between shops shuttered for the night and houses warm with lamplight and the muted sounds of conversation. Tob reached Iris's side and took her hand. Jordy came up on her other side. His old gray coat blended into the shadows and his voice floated, almost disembodied, through the darkness. "All right, Iris."

"I don't know where to start." Alarmed, Tob tried to peer in to her face. Why did she sound so bitter? She walked with her eyes on the ground, her hair hanging in a protective curtain around her face, and he could not make out her expression.

"Who sent you to Soza? Your father?" Jordy prompted her.

"He must have approved, but it was Damon. I defied him once too often."

"Over the execution of Emlie? We were in Edian the day you held the Remembering, Tob and I."

"The day she did what?" Tob demanded.

"No one is supposed to know." Iris tossed her hair back out of her face, her words aimed at the carter. "My brother nearly destroyed me at Soza. I admit it. But he didn't make me stupid. When Jenil rescued me, she said that secrecy was my only protection. I agreed with her then. I still agree with her now."

32

"What else did Jenil have to say?"

"Your brother?" Tob looked from one shadowed face to the other, wishing one of them would tell him what was going on. "What brother?"

"Prince Damon," Jordy said with a touch of impatience.

Impossible. His father had to be teasing. Except that Jordy and Iris both seemed completely serious. "But, that would mean she's the Princess Vray!"

She came to a dead stop in the middle of the street. "Is it that difficult to believe?" she asked, sounding more irritated than ever.

"Yes! No. That is, I don't know." He stared at her, seeing the truth in her face, yet still unwilling to believe. She was his Iris. Not the missing princess. She couldn't be. "You don't act like a Shaper."

"No," she agreed, almost inaudibly. "I don't. Or at least, not enough to notice."

Jordy touched her elbow. "I'll give the Greenmother that much credit. She was right to hide you. You've little chance of safety if your secret becomes widely known." He gestured forward, and they resumed walking. "Did Jenil intend you to hide in Broadford forever?"

"I don't know. Maybe she's forgotten me—the way she made everyone at Soza forget about me. Maybe she plans to come back for me when she feels the time is right."

"When the time is right for what?" They passed through a splash of light from the window of a nearby house. Jordy's eyes were narrowed thoughtfully. "What do you know of Aage's prophecy, m'girl?"

Her grip on Tob's hand tightened. He squeezed back, dizzy with the rapid twists in the conversation, wishing he knew why she needed to seek his reassurance at this particular moment.

"I've heard it," she told the carter.

"What prophecy?" Tob asked.

"My teacher in Edian said that Aage's prophecy was the result of the plague, not anything the Shapers had or hadn't done. She said that it wouldn't be possible for my parents' generation to have enough Dreamer children to replace those that had died, no matter what Aage said."

Tob clenched his jaw. "What prophecy?"

"The gods came to Aage in a vision." Iris gently withdrew her hand from Tob's. "They said that since the proper Shapers of my parents' generation did not fulfill their vows to wed Keepers and provide a new generation of Dreamers, selected members of my generation would be allowed to assume that responsibility."

"That makes no sense," Tob said. Both Iris and his father looked at him curiously. "Shapers and Keepers can't make babies together. Everyone knows that."

Iris looked troubled. "They can when it's time for a new generation of Dreamers."

"The time came and went twenty years ago! The new generation of Dreamers has been born already."

"Only two were born," Jordy said.

The street veered sharply left and downhill, to end in the yard of one of Cross Cove's smaller inns. Jordy paused. The faint glow from the inn and the even fainter reflections of light on the underside of the clouds that filled the sky provided no meaningful illumination. Where they stood at the top of the street, surrounded by dark, silent shop walls, Jordy and Iris were no more than bulky shadows in Tob's eyes, their features indiscernible. He groped to recapture Iris's hand. His fingers brushed the fabric of her trousers, but she made no response. She was still listening to Jordy.

"Are you going to hide in Broadford forever?" their father asked.

"I'm not in Broadford now, am I?"

"Because you said you felt you could be more than just the village Redmother. You implied that you would find carter's apprentice a worthwhile second role. Is this or is this not the extent of your ambition?"

Her voice was no more than a whisper in the darkness. "I haven't decided exactly what I'm going to do. I need to find out what's been going on in the world."

"You already know Jenil's ambition," Jordy insisted.

"And Aage's and the others. Dreamers are no different from the rest of us. They want children to carry on for them after they're gone. Think about that. That's why Jenil brought you to us."

"I've been careful. I may not know much, but at least I know my body's cycle."

Tob was grateful that the darkness hid his consternation. However, his throat betrayed him by tightening up as he spoke. "We could produce a Dreamer child! We haven't, have we?"

"No."

"You'd best consider the possibility," Jordy said. "Don't take offense, Highness. I'm not saying you and Tob aren't responsible lovers. But a fruitful union of Shaper and Keeper happens only a score of times in a century. It's not just a question of physical maturity and auspicious timing. The power of the gods is involved. Myself, I've never trusted the gods."

A round of singing began in the inn below. The murmur of the sea against the quayside a quarter mile distant continued; an inescapable background to everything that happened in Cross Cove. "Do you want me to leave?" Iris asked softly.

"No. I've not said that, have I? Just because I've no use for the Greenmother in some respects doesn't mean I'll ignore her advice when it's sound. You're safe with us. Your home is with us now. I'm leaving word as we go that I want to talk to Jenil. If she hears, and if she decides to come to us, we'll get some answers from her." His hand moved, a dim shape that reached out to pat the girl's shoulder. "Until then, you'll have what advice I can offer, you know that. But if there are choices to be made, you're the only one who can make them."

She moved suddenly, and gave the carter a hug so brief, so fleeting, that Tob would have thought he'd imagined it if not for Jordy's quick grunt of surprise. Then she was standing alone once more, her voice sweet and cool. "Well, I've already made one decision which I won't reverse. I

35

think the Keepers need to be able to protect themselves from my brother's excesses. Let's go down to that inn and foment rebellion."

"Let's do that," Jordy agreed.

It didn't take long for Jordy to lose himself in an intense, rather loud discussion in a corner of the inn's main room. Tob wasn't interested in arguments he'd heard a thousand times before. As soon as their father's attention was thoroughly distracted, Tob caught Iris's eye and nodded at the door. She stared at him thoughtfully, then nodded back.

They slipped out of the inn and walked down toward the docks. Without a word, Iris took his hand. Tob gratefully squeezed the slender, cool fingers. This was still Iris. He could talk to Iris.

"Do you want to have a baby?"

She tightened her hand around his. "Why? Do you?"

"Me? No!" He grimaced as his voice broke, squeaking its betrayal of his tension. "Wait. Don't take this the wrong way. It's not that I don't think you'd be a wonderful mother, and I do love you. But if Dad's right, and we could—"

The darkness of the path prevented him from seeing Iris's expression, but the sound of her voice was amused. "Dad's not right about this. He doesn't think enough about the gods to understand how they work. They'll give us Dreamers only when Shapers and Keepers cooperate, and that means trying when we're fertile. I love you too, Tob. That doesn't mean I'm ready to start a family with you." She hesitated, then added in a more gentle tone, "I'm not sure I'll ever be ready."

"You're not? That's good! Because I'm not, either." He stopped, and drew the tall girl into his arms. Familiar warmth flooded his veins, and he shook his head. "Why, Iris? Feeling like this, we should be sure. Shouldn't we?"

She answered slowly, "There's more than one kind of love."

He wanted to kiss her. Instead he waited, thinking about

her words. "True," he agreed after a moment. "We love, but we're not 'in love.' Is that what you mean?"

"I don't know. What do you think?"

He kissed her then. She responded, her body relaxing against his. He drew back to take a breath. "You think Dad will be annoyed?"

"No. He gave his advice. It's up to us what to do with it. I don't ever want to hurt you, Tob," she added fiercely.

"Same here." He caressed the side of her face. "You won't. You haven't. We'll always talk to each other. Right?"

"Right. So." She licked the tip of his nose. "What now?"

Tob slid his hand around her waist, under her blouse, feeling the heat of her smooth skin. He turned her up the street. "Let's go back to the wagon."

CHAPTER 4

"Captain, may I volunteer for duty with Corporal Janakol's troop?" Nocca asked.

Dael craned his neck to look up at his large little brother. "Why?"

"It's Peanal's troop, one of the five troops being sent to the border. I want to be with Peanal."

Ah. It's getting serious, Dael thought. "So you want to spend the rest of the summer doing nothing useful on the Sitrinian border?"

Nocca blushed, but admitted, "Yes."

"Go right ahead and volunteer. If you can't convince Janakol she needs you, you're not as much in love as you think you are."

Nocca bounded out and left Dael alone in the guardroom. Dael mused benignly about his brother for all of half a minute, before his official worries intruded once more. Five troops were going out on the roads this year. Last summer the prince had sent off three troops with orders to chase the horse people back to their side of Rhenlan's border. The guards promptly turned the assignment into an excuse for several bloody skirmishes. Damon had been pleased with the booty they'd brought back: horses, which he claimed would benefit the breeding stock for the king's guard.

Dael had no objection to widening a breeding pool, but the current method frightened him. The citizens of Edian never objected to any dispute with the horse people. Not as long as Rhenlan won. The horse people had been a threat since the last generation of Dreamers, long enough that no one remembered anything good about them. Their culture was too different, their goals at odds with those of the Children of the Rock. When Damon ordered troops to that border, the populace cheered them on their way.

People could easily fall into the habit of cheering troops on their way to battle. Battle with anyone. Dael rested his elbows on the table, dropped his head into his hands, and groaned.

"Captain."

"What?" Dael growled, then looked up. One of the castle servants stood uncertainly in the doorway.

"Prince Damon wants to see you."

"Coming."

He waited until the servant was gone, then pushed himself to his feet, straightened his tunic, and left the guardroom. Light rain was falling, glistening on grey stone and the blue slate roofs of the stables. One of the grooms, the barrel-chested Palim, watched him from the shadows. Dael hunched his shoulders and hurried up the stairs into the castle proper.

In the small audience chamber, Damon stood next to a reading table, a sheaf of paper in one hand. "Captain. Good. How soon will the first troops be ready to leave Edian?"

"Within a few days, Highness. Organization of provisions and equipment is underway."

"I have information that there have been troop movements on the northern part of the Sitrinian border. Prince Chasa could be using that as a distraction to enable him to cross our border. Again." Dark eyes cut into Dael across the high table. Dael stoically ignored the criticism. "Perhaps this time you'll be able to catch him."

Which meant he was being ordered to the border along with the troops. Was Damon that worried about the Sitrinian border? "I'll do my best, Highness."

"You always do."

"Yes, Highness."

"Send regular messengers. I want to be kept informed."

"Are we to do anything more than confirm their presence?"

"If they are on their own side of the border, no. Do

nothing to provoke a confrontation. However," Damon lay the papers down on the table, "I want it to be known that my captain of the guard is a capable man. I want it known that I am aware of everything going on around this kingdom, through you. If they offer violence, don't feel you have to avoid responding."

He thinks I want to kill people. He thinks he's rewarding me with this opportunity. Does he think he's using a madman to command his troops? Before his anger could surface, Dael inclined his head to the prince. "Yes, Highness. I understand."

Damon waved him away, and Dael gratefully escaped as quickly as he could.

Aage opened his eyes, a fine film of perspiration a clammy discomfort beneath his robes. Another nightmare. He never remembered details, knew only that he was not sleeping well. Savyea knew it too, but said nothing. She merely continued to tempt his body's appetite with lightly seasoned soups and herb tea, and listened noncommittally the few times he tried to stammer out his feelings.

The garden of the Brownmother house drowsed peacefully under a cloud-dotted spring sky. Aage sat up, brushing a few bits of dried grass from the back of his hand. The shadow of the building behind him had crept across his blanket as he slept. Another afternoon gone. He'd done nothing but sleep for days. Sleep and think.

It's necessary. Why do I dread it?

Gods. How do I ask her?

In front of him a flicker of smoke assumed the substantial form of Savyea. "I thought I felt you stir," she said. Aage met her assessing stare steadily. "You're getting stronger, but you're still not easy in your mind."

"I'm not," he agreed. Denying the fact would have served no purpose. A keen intelligence lay behind the firmly established facade of Savyea's unflappable maternal serenity. Aage respected that. Under the present circumstances he also feared it. Because the fear could betray him, he masked it with frustration. "Not much use, am I?"

"We need you, never fear."

He wanted advice. His dread, however, was stronger than the desire. If he found it so difficult to articulate the gods' command within the privacy of his thoughts—*make Sene's child pregnant, I should do this, with my Jeyn?*—he would never be able to present the idea to anyone else. Perhaps when he finally understood, he would no longer feel the need to justify the deed he contemplated. A Dreamer child would be justification in and of itself. He had to concentrate on that image: another little Forrit or Mojil, to grow up strong and confident and wise in the loving atmosphere of Sene's court. Sene would forgive a lot for his first Dreamer grandchild.

"Sitrine will need its autumn rains." Savyea's insistent voice pulled him out of his preoccupation. "Morb is going to be looking for your help. Soon, I hope, we'll need you to tutor our children, and there is always dragon powder to be processed and the wind demons to banish."

"I know, I know." Aage offered her a slightly apologetic, completely honest smile. "I've been cooperating, haven't I? Doing everything you and Jenil could think of to hurry my recovery?"

She pursed her lips. "Except sleeping well."

"I'll work on that."

"Now you'll turn sleep into work! Aage, dear, if we don't stop now, this is going to turn into an argument. Come up and have some supper."

She vanished. Aage tested the lines of power, and the response of his inner senses. All things considered, he was feeling stronger. With only a twinge of discomfort, he transported himself after her.

Perhaps the gods' prophecy would seem less daunting once he regained his strength.

Damon rode to his mother's house with only a small escort, two guards and Palim. As soon as they arrived, he sent the guards to their bunks and Palim to the stable. His mother did not make an appearance. Damon didn't care. She liked to pretend she disapproved of the man he had come to meet. Pretense only. Without her cooperation, he could not have arranged the meeting at all. He allowed his mother her games. While she thought to manipulate him, Damon quietly did exactly as he pleased.

Tonight it pleased him to see his uncle once more.

Damon went down to the stables. Palim had put the horses in their stalls and was waiting for him near the tack room. Under Palim's steady gaze, a large man paced the aisle between the stalls. The visitor wore battered boots and a threadbare cloak over mismatched clothes. Only one person in Edian had hair as red as his, and that was Gallia, the queen. His sister.

"Good evening, Uncle Soen," Damon said.

Soen whirled, his eyes darting swiftly around the stable. "This smells of a trap, boy." His rough red beard jerked stiffly with every word.

"No trap, Uncle. I have a proposition for you."

"Proposition?" The man paced away again, watching Damon out of the corner of his eyes. "What can your kind propose to me?"

"An arrangement for your benefit. An agreement."

"Ha!" Soen shouted. "That for agreements!" He spat on the floor. Damon noted with amusement that the oh-so-unflappable Palim had one hand on his knife.

"I chose the wrong word, Uncle. Let me rephrase it. I propose survival."

Soen stood still. "Not anyone's to propose, boy. You either survive or you don't. I survive without you."

"I will be king soon," Damon said. "Then, dear Uncle, you'll survive on my whim or not at all."

"No one threatens us. No one catches us."

"Dael does. My captain of guards. He'd kill far more of you if I allowed it. Perhaps when I'm king, I will."

"We'll leave Rhenlan. Borders mean nothing to us."

"Borders won't exist when I rule everything."

Soen laughed heartily. One of his front teeth was broken. "Will you, boy?"

"I don't believe in ruling by laws I don't like. For example, I might not like the law that commands us to kill Abstainers. I might create a new law giving Abstainers leave to take what they wish from certain villages. What do you say to that, Uncle?"

"You might do this. You might do that."

"You don't want promises, do you?"

Again, Soen laughed. "Gallia's sharp tongue. Hion never had wit like that. So, boy, what might Abstainers do between now and the moment you become king?"

"They might work for me; those who are able. The king's guard always needs experienced killers."

Palim didn't move, but the look he gave Damon was, by itself, almost worth the time and patience that Damon was expending. Soen resumed his nervous prowl up and down the aisle. "The guard? You control that captain well enough that he'll accept us?"

"The guard is growing. Captain Dael doesn't have the time to meet every new recruit. Tell your people, Uncle. Have them see Mother's groundskeeper. He'll guide them to Palim, here."

For a moment, Soen became calm. "Young fool." He studied Damon with flat, dead eyes, the soft menace in his voice far different from his usual blustering. "Have you learned nothing from your father the king? Abstainers recognize no authority. They're not my people."

"Tell them anyway. Tell them soon. I want to start forming the new troops while Dael is out of the way for a few ninedays. Did you bring a horse?"

Soen nodded suspiciously.

"Good. Palim has a couple of saddlebags of supplies for you. Good night, Uncle Soen."

Damon reached the stable door. Behind him, Soen said, "You're as mad as I am."

Pushing the door open, Damon glanced back into the stable. "Hardly, Uncle. Merely enthusiastic about my

43

life's work. Now, good night."

As he walked toward the guesthouse, Damon allowed himself to relax. Palim would take care of the man and make sure that he got safely away from the grounds of the queen's estate. News traveled quickly among Abstainers. Their ability to evade his guard patrols proved that. By the end of the nineday, Damon expected to see some early results from this night's work. Dear Uncle Soen. He didn't appreciate the potential, didn't recognize what could be made of Abstainer mentality. However, he'd see soon enough. They all would.

Won't Mother be surprised?

CHAPTER 5

Aage sneezed again as he removed another book from the case's top shelf. He cradled it in his arm and crossed the room to sit behind the desk. From the library door behind him came the sound of familiar laughter.

He gave Jeyn a quick, disgusted, look. "You've been moving things around in here again, haven't you?"

She took a step into the room. He decided that perhaps he didn't want to look at her after all. She was dressed in a clinging blue dress, pale hair pulled up and back to reveal her long throat. He didn't want to notice how beautiful she was. Knowing that a part of him was growing eager for what lay ahead only made it worse.

"I haven't been in here in a year," Jeyn informed him.

Aage put the book on the desk and began leafing through the heavy parchment pages. "Neither have I," he admitted. "But you still moved things around, didn't you?"

"I don't remember." Jeyn crossed the room and pulled the curtains all the way back from the windows just as the candle stub on the desk guttered and went out. Sunlight streamed in through the dust clouds raised by Aage's search. It was early morning. Aage vaguely remembered hearing birds announce the dawn some time ago.

"There." She came back to the desk. "Even wizards can't read in the dark."

He spared her another look, and this time kept his eyes on her. "We can, you know."

"Ha." Jeyn seated herself on the other side of the desk and propped her elbows on the wood. "You've been in here since you returned. Lorrs says he sent you breakfast but you returned the tray untouched."

"I'm not hungry." He returned to the task of deciphering the gray squiggles on the stiff, beige page of the book.

"Father wants to see you."

"I'll attend him later."

"There's weather-making needed in Port Town."

"I'll see to it tomorrow."

"Feather wants—"

Aage slammed the book shut. He had no interest in whatever Feather wanted. "Jeyn, I'm busy. Very busy."

His sternness didn't affect her. It never did. She smiled. "Besides all that, you haven't made time to talk to me since you came home. You've been gone half the summer! Make time now, Aage. You're getting pale." She waved a hand toward the door. "Let's go for a walk."

"I don't have time."

She dismissed the excuse with a frown. "You really don't look well. The king needs a healthy wizard. Keeping you healthy is one of my jobs. Would you have me shirk my duty?"

Aage rested his hands on top of the book, palms flat on the worn leather binding. He met Jeyn's level gaze. "I've been ill. Visions from the gods have a way of wearing me out. I have work to do. Very important work."

Her eyes rounded in surprise, and she sat up straight. "A vision? Another one?"

She sounded annoyed, as if visions were frequent inconveniences—and as if she suspected the gods of purposefully undermining her efforts to keep him well. Aage almost laughed. "The last was years ago. Before you were born. Little good it's done anyone," he added bitterly. "The gods speak and no one listens."

"Maybe this time will be different. What did they say? Have you told Father?"

Aage closed his fingers into fists, wishing he hadn't spoken of the gods' message just yet. Jeyn would have to know soon enough. He had to tell her, ask her, as soon as he found the correct passage in the correct book. He also wished, not for the first time since his awakening at Bren, that Savyea kept notes on fertility magic somewhere besides her head. If the gods were going to tell him to do something, they could at least give directions on exactly how to go about doing it. He'd made love often enough, to Shapers, Dreamers, and Keepers, but a simple act of sex wasn't going to be enough for him to make a child.

Jeyn rose from her chair, excitement bright on her face.

"No!" His voice halted her before she could move toward the door. "Don't be so eager to spread word of another prophecy. I haven't anything to tell your father just yet. I have to consult some old records first."

She looked at him over her shoulder, frowning. "Why?"

He patted the stack of books piled on the left of the desk. "Research. Not all magic is bending power with the will."

"The gods want an act of magic?"

He nodded. "I've done something like it once before, but it's been nearly twenty years and I don't remember the details. I wrote them down. Once I find them and adapt them for their new purpose, I'll let you know what the gods want."

Jeyn smiled. "You most certainly will, wizard mine."

"Yes, Highness. In fact, I promise that you will be the first person I tell."

She nodded emphatically. "Or I'll make good on my threat to bake you into a pie."

"You've been spending too much time with Feather."

She went to the door. "Do your research. I'll send your breakfast," she added, and left.

Aage stared after her for a moment. "The first and the only one to know, my princess," he said softly. "Until it's accomplished and there's another Dreamer baby to protect the world." He sighed heavily, ran his hands nervously though his hair, then opened the next book on the stack.

"The prince is right. There are troops here."

"They've been playing games for two days," Janakol replied. "Foot races yesterday; the day before that it was wrestling. All day." Dael looked down to catch a reminiscent smile on his corporal's face. "They have some very attractive men over there."

"Is that why they've come to the border? To seduce members of Rhenlan's guard?"

Janakol flushed, but said brightly, "Might make for a change. Some battles are more fun than others, Captain."

Dael laughed. "True. Too true." He gazed eastward, the afternoon sun behind him revealing the Sitrinian camp in every detail. Today's activity appeared to be a game of strategy. Grins and laughter suggested that they were enjoying themselves. "That still doesn't answer my question," he continued. "Why are they here?"

"It's their border?" She shrugged aside his reprimanding look. "Sorry."

"Who's leading them?"

Janakol spread her hands. "If you mean as a group, no one. We've counted nine troops, each with its corporal. They must have seen the rest of you arrive. They're just not interested."

"Well, I am. And I'm getting more interested every minute. Lengthen the sentry line, Corporal. Twenty-four-hour watch."

"Yes, sir."

"You and the other corporals report to my tent before sundown. We'll make further plans then."

Dael walked along the perimeter of their camp, greeting each sentry he met, then moving on. A hundred yards away he could see shadows passing in front of other campfires. Everything as it should be. The Sitrinian guard was as well trained and disciplined as his own. As well muscled too, he added with a reminiscent smirk for Janakol's earlier observation. They never did anything without good reason. By the Rock, what kind of diversion was this?

Diversion. Damon thought it had something to do with Chasa, but Dael didn't believe that. None of his scouts had reported any sign of activity along the border for ninedays. There were easier ways of sneaking into Rhenlan. Easier, and far less attention-getting, than the King of Sitrine staging a festival for their benefit.

It was a festival, wasn't it? A show of strength? No. Not a sword drawn or arrow loosed since the confrontation, if that was what it could be called, began. Not a distraction, at least not of any kind that Dael understood. The Sitrinian guards had only succeeded in drawing more of Dael's people to the border than would normally patrol here. There had been no sign of troop movement anywhere else, either, so it wasn't an attempt to force Rhenlan to spread its patrols too thinly.

Dael stopped walking and glared across the darkness at the other camp. *If this is Chasa's idea of a summer holiday, I'm going to throttle that boy. All they've done is attract our attention. Why would anyone want to do that?*

He resumed his silent patrol, allowing the slope of the land to lead him toward a small wood that straddled the border. Leaves rustled, their pale undersides glinting in the moonslight. Something clever was going on here. All right. His job was to figure out what it was, and then deal with it. Very well.

If I were in charge of that mob of Sitrinian acrobats, why would I have brought them to the Rhenlan border?

An owl called in the woods. In the Rhenlan camp, a horse neighed, and was answered by several others. Dael followed the sound of the owl into the shadows of the trees.

Enough diffuse moonslight peeked through the branches overhead to enable him to see where he was putting his feet. There was little underbrush to impede his progress. At the bottom of the slope, a stream gurgled along its stony bed. Dael went as far as the bank of the stream, which he judged to be near the center of the wood. He stopped, gazing across the stream to the other bank. He saw nothing, heard nothing.

He waited several minutes, then addressed the mild summer night. "If I was going to plan an ambush, this would be a nice spot. Isolated, shielded from both camps. Very well. I'm here."

"So am I."

The unfamiliar voice was on his side of the stream. Dael

turned quickly, and saw the gleam of moonslight on a bald head. "So I see." Dael didn't draw his sword, but his hand rested conspicuously on the hilt.

A deep, rumbling laugh answered him. "You're good, Captain. It's a pleasure to meet you at last."

The man stepped out of the shadows. He appeared to be in his late forties, broad-shouldered, fit, alert as a fighter should be. Dael looked for a sword, but the man's belt was empty.

"We're quite alone," the man continued. "I'm Sene."

"Oh." Dael took a half-step back in spite of himself as he absorbed the matter-of-fact statement. "What does the King of Sitrine want with Rhenlan's guard captain?"

"Just a chat."

"Major troop maneuvers along twenty miles of border, all to arrange a chat?"

The king of Sitrine nodded. Dael studied him for the slightest sign that he wasn't who he said he was. It was no use. Years of experience with Hion and Damon convinced Dael that he was in the presence of a ruling Shaper. On top of that, the family resemblance with Prince Chasa was too strong to ignore.

Perhaps a reckless disregard for personal safety ran through the bloodline, as well.

"An interesting diversion, Your Majesty." Dael continued to listen to the silence of the wood. They were still alone. No guards approached from either camp. Of course, he hadn't heard the king approach, either.

That was not reassuring, unless Sene had been hiding at this precise spot all along. "How long have you been waiting for me?" Dael asked.

"Three nights. There's a wide spot upstream that's good for fishing."

"That's where you were? Up the stream?"

Sene's head moved as he surveyed the surrounding trees. "There's no comfortable place here. It's not far. I knew I'd hear you coming."

"Fishing at night?"

"It's a knack I have. I've heard that you pursue other diversions after dark."

"Where do you hear about me?"

"From rumor. From traveler's talk. From my guards, and Ivey. You're quite well known."

"You know Ivey?" Surprise pulled the reaction out of Dael before he could stop himself. "How well do you know Ivey?"

"My daughter's going to marry him. Of course I know him. But," Sene continued before Dael could decide whether or not the king's comment had been innocent, "he was reporting to me for years before he and Jeyn started getting interested in each other."

"Reporting to you?"

"About events in Rhenlan. You know, who's in favor, what the royal family is doing, how your farmers and merchants are faring. That sort of thing."

"You're telling the captain of the Rhenlan guard that one of his friends is a Sitrinian spy!"

"Well, he is. Since he also works with you and Jordy that makes both of you spies too, I suppose."

Dael's mouth went dry. Damon had been right to fear Sitrine. Not because of the strength of their guard, but because of the razor-sharp intelligence of their king.

The thought crossed his mind that he should feign ignorance, proclaim his loyalty to Hion, and escape before the persuasive man in front of him could say another word. The lie died in his throat. "Not exactly. Jordy answers to no master."

"Very well. He's a revolutionary, not a spy. It makes no difference. I know what Jordy wants. Get all the Shapers to go away and leave him and every other Keeper to lead their lives in peace. That won't work, you know."

"A king would think that way."

"That does influence me, doesn't it?"

"This is a very interesting conversation." Dael gestured back toward his camp. "Somehow, though, I don't think you went to all this trouble just to have a chat."

"But I did. I wanted to see if you were as clever as the boy says you are." The king chuckled. "If Aage knew I think of him as a boy, he'd glower. He's my wizard. Have you ever been glowered at by Aage?"

"No."

"It's quite an experience."

"Not as bad as being glowered at by Jordy."

"I haven't had that pleasure." Sene gestured upstream. "Come on, let's walk."

"Not until you tell me why I didn't hear you."

"Hear me sneak up on you, you mean? Oh, that's just Aage." The king dismissed the matter with a shadowy wave of one hand. "One of his magic tricks. Involves sprinkling dragon powder on boot soles. Too wasteful to use very often, but this was a special occasion. Be flattered."

"I am." Unable to think of any other objections, Dael accompanied the king along the bank of the stream.

They came to a small clearing in the trees where the stream bent sharply west. At the outer edge of the curve, the waters spread into a wide pool and a flat boulder projected out into the placid backwater. Dael made out familiar shapes against the stone: several fishing poles and a low wicker basket. He looked at the man beside him. "You really have been fishing."

"It's better with lights," Sene said. "Still, it's been restful. Especially for the fish."

A laugh escaped Dael. At Sene's invitation he abandoned any last attempt at suspicions and sat on the edge of the boulder. "Would you consider hiring an experienced captain of guards? I would come highly recommended, if you cared to ask Hion about my abilities."

"We'd better not." Sene sat beside the basket, leaned back, and lifted the lid. "There's bread and cheese here. Hungry?" He pulled out a loaf without waiting for an answer, tore off a chunk, and passed it to Dael. "Not that I couldn't use you," he continued. "You'd find the work more satisfying than what you face in Rhenlan. But it wouldn't be right for me to tempt you away. Rhenlan needs a hero."

"I'm not a hero. I'm a guard."

"Don't sound so bitter. Not everyone can do what you do."

"Kill people?"

"Protect Rhenlan when her Shapers won't."

"Rhenlan's lucky her monsters are gone."

"Are they?"

Dael stared at the king. "The fire bears are dead."

"Have some cheese. Use your dagger." Sene handed the full piece to Dael. "I didn't bring one." He reached down into the blackness next to the boulder. "All I brought was this. It would be wasted on cheese."

Dael was on his feet the moment he saw the king pick up the scabbard. Without the effort of thought, his sword was in his hand.

Sene did not draw his blade. "Put that thing away," he said mildly. "I've brought you a better one." He held the scabbard toward Dael. "I hope it's the right weight for you. They look to be about the same size. Try it."

The point of Dael's sword dipped uncertainly. "You're not threatening me, are you?"

"I've got an army back there," Sene countered, pointing over his shoulder. "If I wanted to threaten anyone, I'd use them. This," he jiggled the scabbard, "is a present."

Slowly Dael sheathed his own blade. "I'm very confused." He took a deep breath and stepped forward. "Not too confused, however, to dismiss such an offer." Before the king could do anything else unexpected, Dael took the sword from his hands.

"It fits you," Sene said.

Dael hardly heard him. The sword was far lighter than he'd expected. He closed his fingers over the hilt. One gentle touch slid the blade smoothly out of its sheath. Keyn-light danced in yellow sparkles on one edge of the blade, while Sheyn-light brought out blue highlights from the flat. The green flicker that emanated from its entire length had nothing to do with moons.

Awe softened Dael's voice. "What is this?"

53

"Dragon powder in the steel. The only way to best a monster."

"We don't have monsters in Rhenlan."

"Not tonight. That's no guarantee you won't face one soon. Take the sword. The gods know somebody has to. Hion can't and Damon won't lift a blade in defense of Rhenlan's Keepers. You're all they have. I think you'll do well enough."

A warm flush of gratitude filled Dael. "Thank you, Your Majesty."

"You're welcome, Captain. I'd better take your old sword. Someone in your camp might find it a bit odd if you come back from your walk doubly armed. Does that one fit in your scabbard? It was designed to the Rhenlan guard pattern."

Dael drew his old blade again and laid it on the boulder. The new sword slid into the scabbard a bit roughly, but it did fit. "I'll adjust it when I get back."

"Good idea. Although that blade is stronger than most."

"Thank you," Dael repeated, feeling rather numb. Then his natural caution reasserted itself. "Now, what else do you want?"

"You are a distrustful young man. That's good. Several things. First, I want you to learn how to use that sword, and I know just the man to teach you."

"My time isn't exactly my own."

"This won't take long. You're on border patrol, aren't you? Well, you'd better inspect the border all the way to the sea. That's where you'll find him."

"Who?"

"Your tutor. The best dragon-slayer in the world. Pirse of Dherrica."

Dael shook his head, torn between disbelief and admiration. "Why am I not surprised? You do realize that King Palle's claim of blood-debt against the prince has never been answered. As a guard, my vows require that I bring anyone accused of lawlessness before the nearest law reader."

54

"Your vows also required unquestioning loyalty and obedience to Hion and Damon. If you can re-evaluate them, you can re-evaluate Pirse. That's another thing. I want you to watch yourself with Damon."

"I do."

"Good. I want you to remember that you have a friend in Sitrine. Me," the king added with an unnecessary jab of thumb to breastbone. "I want you to keep an eye on your friend Jordy. His ideas are unpopular in some circles—including mine. Don't let his extremism distract you from protecting your people. The danger is Damon, yes, but he won't stand still to be defeated by Jordy's open revolt."

"We don't want it to come to open revolt," Dael protested. "At least, I don't. I agree with you. Damon is too strong."

A chorus of neighs broke out in the Rhenlan camp. Sene glanced up at the moons. "Changing your watch already? We wait another hour. Well, you'd better be going. You're about to be missed, if your corporal is any good at all."

"She is. Thank you, Your Majesty. I'll consider what you've said."

"Good night, Captain. I look forward to our meeting again."

Dael walked away from the pool. Halfway up the slope, he looked back. Moonslight shimmered on the water, moving with the ripples that expanded as he watched from a tiny splash near the center. The line was invisible, but the rod was a straight black shadow projecting out from the boulder.

The king of Sitrine was fishing.

CHAPTER 6

"Something up ahead, Dad," Tob said.

"Just a minute."

Tob shifted forward on the driver's seat of the wagon, but did not check Stockings's speed. The road was level and straight, comfortable for trotting, and they'd been making excellent time. The morning sun was already hot; they had to start their days early in order to cover any distance before the long midday rest. They'd spent several ninedays traveling through the beautiful countryside of Sitrine. Iris had wanted to see King Sene during their stop in Raisal, but they'd heard in the market square that he'd gone off on patrol with the guard. When she asked after the minstrel Ivey, she was told he was dragon hunting with the prince. To Tob's relief she didn't try to leave a message. He wasn't ready for her to be talking to kings, and he didn't think Dad was, either.

The group of people spread across the road a half mile ahead of them evidently didn't understand the finer points of long-distance carting. As Stockings drew closer to them, Jordy climbed out of the back of the wagon and sat down beside Tob, wiping the harness oil from his hands with a rag.

From a kneeling position just behind him, Iris said, "They're not Abstainers. That's a guard camp."

Tob saw the cluster of neat brown tents on the left side of the road. "What are they doing here?"

"This could be the Rhenlan border," Iris said.

Jordy did not reply. He stuffed the rag in his back pocket. "That's no concern of ours. Just drive on, lad. Cover your hair, lass," he added to Iris.

Stockings trotted on, her hoofs sending up little puffs of dust, great muscles sliding easily beneath her sweat-dark coat. Tob's fingers remained still on the reins but his jaw muscles tightened. The guards were clearly visible now, five men and a woman blocking the road. As the wagon swept toward them one held up a hand and yelled, "Halt! In the name of the king."

Stockings didn't even twitch an ear. She was big enough, and slow-witted enough, to run over anyone or anything in her path and never notice the difference. If these guards expected her to behave like a normal horse and shy at a loud noise or waving arms, one of them was going to get hurt. Tob looked sideways at his father, and saw his ice blue eyes narrow appraisingly. He glanced back at Iris. Her hat covered her braids, and her expression was remarkably like Jordy's. Tob hardly recognized her.

"We won't risk it," Jordy said suddenly. "Rein her in."

Tob gratefully pulled back on the reins. After her usual hesitation, Stockings slowed and stopped with a few yards to spare. Two of the guards approached the wagon. Only then did Tob notice that two of the others, who stood closest to either side of the road, held drawn knives.

"State your business," the first guard said to Jordy.

"State yours," Jordy returned.

The first guard scowled. The second said, "Our business is the safety of everyone in Rhenlan."

"Is the road unsafe, then?"

"There's nothing wrong with the road," the second guard admitted.

"Good." Jordy nodded politely. "Thank you for your concern. We'll be on our way."

The first guard laid a possessive hand on the side of the wagon next to Tob. The woman stepped forward and grasped Stockings's bridle. "Not yet," the first guard said. "Not until you tell me where you're going and what you're carrying."

Tob waited. He guessed from the sour expression on his father's face that Jordy was considering and discarding replies to the guard's demand and not liking his options. Iris put her hand on his shoulder, her fingers tense. Finally

Jordy said, "You'll find nothing unusual in the wagon. Wool dye, spices, barrels of smoked fish and similar food-stuffs. A box of glassmaker's pigment. Personal supplies. As for where we're going, this road leads into Rhenlan."

"We know," one of the other guards answered sarcastically. "This is the border."

"Is it, indeed?" Jordy replied politely. "To think I've been coming this way for years and never noticed."

"A nice cargo of goods," the first guard said. "I'm surprised they're allowed out of Sitrine."

"Trade profits everyone," Jordy said.

"We don't need strangers crossing our land to the benefit of Sitrine and Dherrica."

Outrage made Iris's voice shrill. "We're not strangers! We're better Rhenlaners than you are."

"Not by the sound of him." The guard's wink was probably intended to be pleasant.

Jordy gave Iris a stern look before he turned back to the guard. "Part of this cargo is expected in Bronle, aye." He made no attempt to alter his way of speaking. "But the rest, along with whatever I acquire in Dherrica, goes to Edian. Nothing fine enough for the royal court, perhaps, but I've heard that the king values the taxes of even the lesser merchants. They won't do business and they won't pay taxes if you interfere with the arrival of their merchandise."

"Think of the time and trouble you'd save if you turned aside here and went directly to Edian."

"Half this cargo's not needed in Edian. We're on our way to Bronle."

"Half, you say? Take a look." At the first guard's command, two of the men went to the back of the wagon and threw aside the tarp. Jordy twisted in his seat, watching them. Anger smoldered at the back of his eyes, but he made no attempt to intervene.

"Keep still, lass," he whispered when Iris swiveled to face the intruders. Tob shivered, alternately terrified and furious. He made himself stare at Stockings's hindquarters, shutting out the noise of the men rummaging through their carefully packed goods. He envied the horse, oblivious to threats in the present or worries about the future. She shifted her weight to three legs, and her head drooped lower as she fell into a spontaneous doze.

"It's what he said," one of the guards announced. "Just weaver's supplies and a few barrels."

"What's this?" another asked. Tob turned his head to see one of the men lift a dark brown five-gallon barrel in his arms. "Ale?"

"In that small a keg?" another scoffed.

The first guard looked expectantly at Jordy. "Well?"

"Cinnamon," Jordy admitted.

There was a chorus of delighted whoops from the guards. The man holding the barrel shifted his grip and started to carry his find away from the wagon.

Jordy sat perfectly still. "It's not for sale."

"Well, we're not offering to buy it," the guard mocked. At Stockings's head, the woman sniggered.

"Consider it part of this year's taxes," the other man said, and grinned as he shifted the barrel to his shoulder.

"One of the nice things about serving Rhenlan," the first guard observed, "is that we're appreciated. Prince Damon understands how difficult border duty is. Lonely work. It can get dangerous, too. So far from Edian we have to rely on the available resources, don't we?" A ripple of amused agreement passed through the rest of the half-troop.

"If it's supplies you need," Jordy said, voice utterly calm, "I can spare a barrel or two of the fish."

The guard held up a warning hand. "I'll say this once, carter. This isn't the market square. Our choice won't change. Not unless you'd like us to choose to take more? No? What's your name and village?"

"Jordy. I live in Broadford."

The guard nodded. "Your activities will be reported. Be grateful the border hasn't been officially closed."

The woman stepped back with a disdainful look at the sleeping horse. The rest of the guards drifted toward the edge of the road.

"I won't forget your advice," Jordy told the first guard. He touched Tob's arm. "Let's go."

Tob lifted the reins. Stockings snorted loudly and shook her head. "Walk on," Tob called to her. Reluctantly, she leaned her weight forward and got the wagon started.

As they moved away, there was a short mutter of voices behind them, followed by a burst of laughter. Tob started to turn. Under his breath Jordy hissed, "Don't look back."

The back of his neck burned with shamed anger, but Tob obeyed.

Stockings gathered enough momentum to break into her steady trot. The road bore on in the same direction for another mile before finally veering north to skirt the edges of a small marsh. All sound of the guards had faded and the trees and high grasses of the patch of wetland completed the separation. Jordy gripped the back of the seat and stood, swaying with the motion of the wagon, to survey the road behind them.

"I hate king's guards," Tob said. "Every guard that ever was."

"Hate the Shaper who commands them," Iris said.

"Well, we're not being followed."

Tob glanced over his shoulder as his father climbed down amid their disordered cargo. "What will happen when we try to enter Dherrica?"

"I don't know. The same or worse."

"Worse?" Tob protested.

Jordy began repacking torn-open bundles. "I don't like it any more than you do. Borders. Border foolishness!" His words came sharp and bitter, punctuated by the jerky movements of his hands and arms as he sorted through their cargo. "Foolishness that interferes with our lives. I shouldn't be surprised that it's starting like this."

Iris asked, "What will we do when we have to cross the border again?"

"We'll think of something," Jordy said grimly. "If our load is light enough, we'll try leaving the road. We'll see what we find as we get close to Dherrica. You're going to have to be careful, Highness. These guards didn't recognize you, but others might."

"I know." Her expression was grim. "It's not going to be easy to be careful."

Tob could think of nothing else to say. He resumed watching the road and the horse and the passing landscape, and tried to forget the drawn knives and laughter.

He didn't succeed.

Jeyn hadn't been on the terrace or in her room or in the garden. Aage went to each spot in turn, taking nearly an hour as he lingered along the route of his hunt. He prepared to make his speech with each entrance, only to have to put it off again. By the time he bent the power to take himself out to the beach beyond the orchard, he had grown so annoyed he almost forgot what he wanted to say.

His irritation vanished as soon as he arrived on the shore. Jeyn sat alone on the group of boulders just above the sand, her cloak thrown casually back. She was outlined by strong moonslight, her pale clothes and hair shimmering against the dark backdrop of the sea. Her legs were drawn up, her hands clasped around her knees, as she stared out at the water. He studied her for a moment before he approached. Was it just the effect of the light, or did she really look lonely?

Jeyn's head turned toward him, and she sniffed. "Lilacs? You smell like Savyea tonight, wizard mine."

Aage climbed up beside the princess. "Do I?" Perhaps it was because his mind was on the same subject that occupied so much of the elder Greenmother's thoughts. He kicked a stray bit of seaweed out of the way as he reached the top of the rocks, then hitched up his black robe to let the cool sea breeze cross his bared legs.

She leaned against him. He put his arm around her shoulder, and they remained quiet for a while. In the familiar companionship that settled over them, he could almost forget why he'd come to her.

"Are you all right, love?" he asked at last.

She rolled her head against his arm. "Tired." She sighed. "I spent all day with Daav working on the plans for the new coast road. It wasn't the work; that went well enough. Dad's not going to like it when I suggest a new tax to pay for the road."

"Not the road. Not worried about a tax, either. What is it, then?"

"Daav. He doesn't argue with me anymore, but he still looks at me as though I've broken his heart. He's very good at making me feel guilty for not wanting to marry him. Guilt's tiring."

He answered with a grunt and a reassuring squeeze of her shoulder.

"What brings you out of your library?" she asked.

"You, Highness. I've something to tell you."

Jeyn slipped from his grasp and turned to face him. Her eyes lit with excitement. "About your vision? So, tell me! What is it the gods want?"

Aage's throat went dry. He swallowed with difficulty and looked past her to the sensuous roll of the water, then further out to the horizon to count the stars in a low-lying constellation. "You," he whispered, so softly that she couldn't possibly hear it above the sound of the waves.

"Aage?"

He cursed the gods. He had a reputation for being ruthless, though how he'd earned it he didn't know. He looked at Jeyn. "I'm to father a child. The gods have promised me a Dreamer son by a Shaper mother. That was my vision, Highness."

She sat very still, head tilted to one side, expression stunned. "How can you have a child?"

"The gods promised it."

She lifted her chin and looked him in the eye. "It's against everything we've ever been taught!"

"I know." He held her gaze. "The times are more desperate than ever before. The gods' first gift has been denied by most of the Shapers. They're giving us one more chance. A last chance, I think. A promise of a wizard so powerful he'll be able to protect the world from every outside attack. He'll buy us time for another generation to be born in the proper cycle. It has to be done, Jeyn." He shifted forward and took her hands in his. "We have to make the child, Jeyn. You and I, together."

"What?"

The hands he held were cold. "You and I," he repeated. "That's the message the gods sent me."

She shook her head in denial. "But, Ivey."

"This changes nothing between you and Ivey, love," Aage insisted. He didn't let her gaze break from his. "You'll have your life together, Dreamer children from him. I promise. But first, I need you. We need to make a Dreamer to protect what few youngsters the chosen will give us. A guardian, Jeyn. For our world, and for our children. I've seen it. Seen him."

"Seen him? Seen your son?"

"Our son, Princess. He'll be dark-haired like your father, just as sun-browned, with the same solid build. Blue-eyed, like me. I've seen him! I felt him bend the power, manipulate the web like he was playing a child's game with string. The gods showed him to me as a wizard in his prime, told me who his parents were." He inched closer to her. "I didn't want to believe, Jeyn. I didn't understand. I've been worried and frightened ever since I woke from the vision. I kept the knowledge to myself until I was sure the power could be bent to make it possible.

"I found a way to do it. The gods promised it, so of course I found the way." *I think I've found a way,* he added honestly to himself. *The gods want this. It has to work. Jeyn has to agree. Something has to go right, just this once!*

"The gods must be obeyed. Help me, Jeyn. Please."

She pulled her hands from his, rose, and turned her back on him. A cloud passed in front of Keyn, engulfing the princess in shadow.

Aage got to his feet and put his hands on the girl's shoulders. Would she believe him? Demand proof? No, not Jeyn. She shouldered every burden that duty demanded of her.

What's more, she trusted him. That didn't make it any easier to place this responsibility on her.

"Jeyn?"

"I . . ." She leaned back against him. "It frightens me, Aage."

"I know, love. Me, too."

"You're sure it's what the gods want?"

"It is."

"I have to tell Father."

"No. Not yet. Not until we've accomplished it. I don't want this to be another failed prophecy. When we know there's going to be a Dreamer baby, then we'll tell Sene."

She didn't argue. She did say, "I wish Ivey were here."

Aage thought it was better for now that the minstrel was away from Sitrine. He didn't answer her. He waited for her reaction to subside and practicality to reassert itself. He didn't have to wait long.

"Well, when do we get started?" she asked, still facing the sea.

He leaned forward to chuckle in her ear. "It's not so simple as a romantic night on the beach, love. There are preparations I have to make."

"Oh." She sighed, then turned to gaze into his eyes. "I almost wish you were ready tonight. I could use a little romance. I was feeling lonely enough before you brought me this news."

Aage stepped away from her, but held his hand out for her to take. "Let's go home. Your father and Feather could use some company. We'll talk about the child later."

"Soon?"

"Soon." She took his hand and they jumped down from the rocks together and started back toward the lights of the king's residence.

CHAPTER 7

A few hours after dawn, the morning had already grown warm. Vray sat up straighter, the sun hot on the back of her neck. She and Tob sat on the tailboard of the wagon, playing a game, as it rolled toward the northeast. A few more ninedays, a few more villages, and they'd be turning for home. The seemingly endless summer days were growing shorter. The circular route they'd followed, through Sitrine in the east, along the southern edge of Rhenlan, then up the winding roads of Dherrica, would end, too.

She had learned so much. Everywhere they went she had met people, listened to their concerns, argued courses of action far into the night with shepherds and Brownmothers and blacksmiths—and Jordy. Her adopted father's single-mindedness still disturbed her. What she needed was a way to coalesce her experiences into a single, concise answer to solve every problem. She regretted that she hadn't been able to visit the king of Sitrine. She wasn't quite sure how Sene could help her. At the time, she'd been half glad she hadn't had a chance to talk to him. However, she needed advice. She did not want to believe that Jordy's solution was the only way to handle Damon.

She tapped the game board with one finger. "This is taking too long," she muttered under her breath.

Tob looked up from the board. "I'm thinking," he protested.

"Not you, Tobble. Everything."

"You said you wanted to play Dragonrock."

"I did."

"Well? Pay attention. I think I'm about to get one of your princes."

Vray watched as Tob moved his small wooden dragon

from one ring of the board to the next. She scowled, her hand hovering in mid-air between the threatened prince and an almost equally vulnerable village. She made an exasperated noise. "Is it all right if I concede?"

"No. We'll come back to it later." He leaned his elbow on a barrel and propped his head on his hand. "Out with it. What's worrying you now?"

She mimicked his posture, still frowning. "I can't help thinking things should be moving faster. Damon's control is tighter than I thought. Something has to be done. Soon." She restlessly sat up again and swung her legs over the edge of the tailboard. In the distance loomed the last of the Dherrican Mountains, dark green slopes rising up like a wall across their back trail. "You can't just raise a rebellion piecemeal across the length and breadth of a kingdom."

"Why not?"

"You're worse than he is." She slapped at his knee, but he drew his leg up out of her reach.

"Be practical. What else can we do? I think Dad's made good progress. We talked to dozens of people last summer. This summer, it's been hundreds. There's not a village in Rhenlan that hasn't at least given thought to rejecting Damon. The Dherricans and Sitrinians don't see him as a serious threat, but when the time comes . . ."

"When does the time come? If the villages don't act together, this will never work."

"We will act together."

"Simultaneously? That's what's needed if you're going to stand against king's guards." What was needed was a Shaper leader, if this was going to work at all. What Shaper would agree to help them? Sene? Herself? Would she have to lead Jordy's rebellion? There had to be some easier way.

Easier to defeat Damon than defy Jordy? She gave a silent chuckle. She had changed, hadn't she?

"You'd be surprised how fast news can spread from one village to the next," Tob said.

"Not as fast as a king's messenger can ride."

"That's where we get most of our news."

She gave an exasperated sigh. "You inherited Jordy's stubborn streak, did you know that?"

He smirked at her. "Thanks."

The wagon lurched sharply to the left. Pieces from the Dragonrock board clattered to the bed of the wagon and Vray half jumped, half fell off the end. Tob twisted around, grabbing the sideboard to steady himself.

Stockings shied violently again, trying to push the shafts sideways across the road. Jordy was in front of her, both hands on her halter. She flung her head back once more, almost pulling him off his feet, but the carter allowed his weight to work for him. His steadying voice reached Vray's ears as a wordless murmur. The horse subsided and came to a trembling halt.

Tob started to get to his feet. "Dad?" he called. "Was it a snake?"

"Worse," Jordy replied, voice tight with anger. Tob hurriedly jumped out of the wagon, braced for some unguessable threat.

Vray gasped as she saw the source of their danger, a black-cloaked figure that had materialized at the side of the road.

Jordy ran one hand soothingly along the horse's neck and shoulder. "Hold her, lad." Tob ran forward and took the halter rope from his father. Jordy strode across the road, hair tousled and tunic grimed where Stockings's dusty shoulder had bumped against him.

"I can't believe I caused that." The black hood fell back, revealing the brown, very surprised face of Greenmother Jenil.

"Not you," Jordy growled, stopping in front of her. "Your smoke."

"Oh. My apologies, carter Jordy." She gazed past him. "Is that you, Vray?"

All summer long, she had continued to use the name Iris. A precaution, Jordy had called it. Suddenly she didn't feel like Iris anymore. "Yes, Greenmother."

"You're looking well. I'm pleased to see that life in

Broadford agreed with you."

"Why?"

"I beg your pardon?"

As Vray's indignation rose, her voice rose with it. "Why? Why are you pleased? Why Broadford? You've been manipulating my life and I think it's about time you told me just what you expect to happen now."

"You're not only looking well, you're quite your usual self, Your Highness." The Greenmother turned her attention on Jordy. "Her recovery is remarkable. You've surpassed yourself, carter."

"Explanations, Jenil," Jordy replied, his tone sharp.

"You're going back into Rhenlan, I see. Good. I'll walk with you."

Jordy turned his back on the Dreamer. His tight-lipped expression warned that the woman was severely testing the limits of his tolerance. At his father's peremptory gesture, Tob urged Stockings forward once again. Vray slipped between Jordy and Jenil as they began walking ahead of Stockings.

"Is that your answer, that you knew I'd be well taken care of?" Vray asked. "It's not enough, Greenmother. What did it matter to you whether I continued my mindless existence at Soza or became a healthy Keeper's daughter? Not that I'm not grateful, but then I'm not looking at the situation objectively."

"Naturally I prefer you whole in mind and body. I'm a Greenmother. I devote a great deal of time and energy to healing."

"Yet you refused to keep her and heal her yourself," Jordy said.

The Dreamer flicked his remark away with an impatient wave of one hand. "I heal the body. Her suffering was of the spirit. She didn't need someone to bend the power over her. Don't criticize my decision, carter. Not when it's so obviously worked out in her best interests."

"But why?" Vray nearly hopped up and down in frustration. "There must be a reason."

"Not necessarily," Jordy complained. "Aimless Dreamer interference, that's all."

Jenil's dark eyes glinted dangerously. "Never aimless. I have my goals. Incomprehensible, perhaps, to the short-sighted, but that's your loss, not mine."

The back of Jordy's neck reddened. Vray intervened quickly. "Advise us then, Greenmother. What did you anticipate my doing with this life you've given me?"

Jenil allowed herself to be distracted from her glower at the carter. "It's a good life, isn't it?"

"For a Keeper. I'm a Shaper."

Jenil performed an elegant shrug. "So, shape."

Vray bowed her head to stare at the hard-packed dirt beneath their feet. The road bent slightly toward the north, bringing them beneath the shadows of an aspen wood. Somewhere nearby a stream splashed over rock.

Jordy broke the silence. "Have you been in Edian recently?"

"The king still lives," Jenil replied. "The prince continues to strengthen his position. Vray knows what the court is like."

"I should be there," Vray said softly. She lifted her eyes and found that the Greenmother was watching her. "But how can I? My brother will only banish me again—or find an excuse to have me executed."

"You'd need to time your return. Make it very official, very proper, very public."

"She can't count on the king," Jordy said.

This time Jenil accepted his criticism with a gracious nod. "No, she can't. But the queen might do."

"You're joking," Vray said.

"She misses you."

"She doesn't know I exist."

"You're a piece of marriageable property." The Greenmother caught Jordy's eye. "Damon sent inquiries to Soza. They know she's gone."

"Stones! How long since they found out?"

"A few ninedays."

"I think you might have warned us!"

"You've been safe enough in Dherrica, and I've told you now, haven't I? Besides, they can't trace her. Not directly. Her only danger will be if she is seen and recognized."

"With all the guards on the road, that could happen," Vray complained. "No. I won't be fetched back to Edian like a stray sheep. I won't be made to disappear again, either. It will have to be Gallia."

"On your terms, lass," Jordy said. "Don't accept less."

"Never." She stopped and faced the Greenmother. "Is this what you wanted, Dreamer?"

The others stopped as well. Tob halted Stockings only an arm's length from the conversation.

Jenil said, "I won't know that, will I, until I've seen what you do in Edian?"

"Don't go if you don't want to, Vray," Tob said.

She smiled for the first time. "Oh, I don't want to go, Tobble. But I need to." She grew serious again and looked from Jenil to Jordy. "You realize I have no idea how to approach the queen."

"I'll go with you." The Greenmother cast a quick glance at the nearby range of mountains. "Not from here. Where is this road leading you, carter?"

"I'm expected in Atade. After that, we can swing south of Lake Hari easily enough, assuming the queen will be on her farm."

"She's never anywhere else," Vray said.

Jenil nodded. "You'll be two ninedays at least. I'll rejoin you somewhere along the road west of Hari." She took a step back from them and closed her eyes.

"Wait!" Jordy shouted. The Greenmother's eyes flew open. Jordy unceremoniously gripped her arm and urged her back up the road, past the end of the wagon. "Not from there," he concluded. "Here now, this won't alarm the horse."

Jenil's mouth twisted with displeasure, but she vanished without further comment. Her puff of smoke drifted down the road a few feet and gently dissipated. Stockings didn't notice a thing.

Jordy flattened his hair with one hand as he returned to the front of the wagon. "Well, we've wasted enough time for one morning. Giddup, girl," he said, and clapped Stockings on the rump. As she moved forward, he took the halter rope from Tob.

Vray came around to Stockings's near side. "May I take her for a while, Dad? I need some time to think."

"Come ride with me," Tob said to Jordy. "We can finish the Dragonrock game Iris and I started."

Jordy relinquished his place at Stockings's head. He and Tob stood back to allow the wagon to pass them by. She heard them swing onto the moving tailboard. Jordy asked, "Which side was Vray playing?"

"The villagers."

There was a thoughtful silence before Jordy said, "Perhaps it's time for a change of luck."

Before the plague, Atade had been the capital of a kingdom, home to one of the several dozen extended families of Shapers whose members governed distinct geographical regions. It had been a town equal in size to Bronle, Edian, Raisal—or Garden Vale, Bren, Dundas, Lone Pine, abandoned Hillcrest, or Three Spurs. The first of the smaller plague-carrying fire bears had been discovered in the broken land south of Atade. Forty percent of the town's population died in the first ten years, including three generations of the ruling family. Its wizard died fighting the fire bears. Its castle remained, doors barred and windows shuttered, halls and storerooms barren, overlooking the road that swept into Atade from the west.

"Sad place," Tob commented as they walked beneath the castle walls. The early afternoon was sunny and warm, which only emphasized the stillness of the melancholy scene.

"I've never taken you to Three Spurs," Jordy said. "Imagine one of the empty villages in the lake country, but ten times larger. Imagine houses with polished stone fronts and a deep mountain lake bluer than the sky, reflecting the castle and the white snow of the mountain behind it." He stared absently down the road, obviously seeing in his mind's eye a landscape markedly different from that of the summer-dry plain. "To have seen Three Spurs at Fall Festival, a great blue and gold pavilion set in the market meadow, and to see it now—" He broke off, embarrassed. "Aye, well, sad's not the word, son. Just remember that whatever you've seen in Bren or Lone Pine or here, there were other places that lost even more."

Vray had never heard the carter in such a reminiscent mood. That, or perhaps the fact that she'd been reflecting so much on her own past and future, emboldened her to take advantage of the unusual moment. "Why did you leave Dherrica, Jordy? You've obviously never stopped loving the mountains."

He looked at her sharply. "What on earth is that supposed to mean?"

"What on earth do you think it means?" She imitated his broad inflection and the way he rolled his r's, earning a grin from Tob and a grudging snort from Jordy. Reverting to her usual speech pattern, she continued, "You must miss it sometimes."

"You knew Three Spurs, Dad?" Tob asked.

"I couldn't say I knew it. I visited there when I was Matti's age." They were past the abandoned castle now, approaching the inhabited buildings of the town itself. The road curved out of view among the first houses and stables. Jordy coaxed Stockings slightly to the left so that they were no longer occupying the entire road.

"We don't choose the place we're born, the way we're taught to speak, any of our earliest influences," he continued. "Aye, Three Spurs, and the mountains, and Trumble are a part of me. But my home is Broadford."

Why did every conversation come round to questions of choice and responsibility? Vray pressed her lips together to keep the querulous comment from escaping. They didn't, of course. She was being irritable and self-centered. Just because she had been thinking of nothing else lately didn't

mean she was entitled to read her own preoccupations into
every casual comment she heard. She had asked the man a
simple question and he told her, politely, that he preferred
Rhenlan over Dherrica.

You should be flattered for the king's sake, Vray told herself. *Why?* another thought taunted her. *It's no reflection on
me, for good or ill. I didn't choose my parents, did I?*

Jordy caught her annoyance. He gave her one of his
more rueful half-smiles. "Sorry, lass, didn't mean to lecture."

"That's all right, I've gotten used to it." She intended to
accompany the words with a regal stare, but ruined the effect with an exasperated sigh. Jordy knew her too well. His
response was a completely unrepentant chuckle.

Tob interrupted them, pointing ahead. "What's going
on?"

The road had emerged from the cluster of buildings onto
Atade's market square. At first, Vray was not certain what
had caught Tob's attention. Two inns, four taverns,
smithies, stables, and shops ringed the close-cropped
meadow. Some were occupied, others showed signs of
abandonment, as was typical of towns and villages that had
lost substantial portions of their populace. The people who
stood in front of the one functional inn appeared to be well-
fed and well-dressed, and all around them the late afternoon was alive with the usual sounds of a healthy village:
the bleating of goats, the cackle of chickens, and children's
voices, some near at hand, some more distant and less clear.

Vray took a second look at the crowd gathered in front of
the inn as Tob lowered his arm. Jordy said, "That does look
unusual."

The wide double doors of the inn were blocked open to
catch the afternoon breeze. A woman emerged from the dark
interior and shaded her eyes with her hand to peer in their
direction. Other heads turned and several voices called greet-
ings. The woman grabbed a man away from his conversation
by the elbow. As soon as he saw the horse and wagon he hurried forward to meet them, the woman at his side.

"Jordy. We were beginning to wonder if you'd make it this year."

Once more, Jordy told how the early spring weather had slowed them and accepted the often-repeated comments on how Tob had grown. Then, with another intrigued glance at the people grouped around the inn doorway, he answered what would inevitably have been the next question before it was asked.

"This young woman is my daughter, and now apprentice. Iris, this is Tagara. He makes the green lacquer you admired on those goblets at Dundas inn. Dimin," the woman smiled her acknowledgment, "is innkeeper. Atade's version of Herri, you might say."

"Half his size but twice as charming." Apparently there was some long-standing joke behind the remark, for Dimin winked at Vray as she continued, "And a better cook. Wait until you try my five-bean pie."

"We're looking forward to it," Tob said with feeling.

Jordy tilted his head in the direction of the inn. "Not trouble, I hope."

"A problem, I'd call it," Tagara said. "At least it's our own, thank the gods, not something from Edian. Do you know we've had fifteen troops of guards through here since Spring Festival? I'll bet you a chicken to a gooseberry they're going to goad the Dherricans into something. Once the first fighting's over, you know where they'll come for replacement guards. Here, that's where they'll come."

"You'll find several people eager to have a word with you tonight or tomorrow, carter," Dimin added. "Do 'em good to get their minds off family squabbles."

"Serious?" Jordy asked.

"Only the future of the flour mill," Tagara replied. Tob looked impressed. "The father died suddenly last nineday and his youngest son insists he should be miller rather than his elder brother."

The problem began to interest Vray. "Where is your Redmother?" she asked.

"Gone to Fairdock," Tagara said. To Vray's dismay, the

slightly overweight little man launched into another digression. "Her daughter's due to be birthing twins. Your carter friend here tells us that's not so shocking these days, but this is her second set. Has a pair of girls not two years old, and now this. I wouldn't be surprised if it's because she visited the Greenmother at the Cave of the Rock when she was just a child while her mother was completing her Redmother training."

"The younger son," Dimin said firmly, retrieving the conversation, "doesn't think his father would have made a preference known to our Redmother. Says it would have embarrassed his brother." Dimin shrugged. "There'll have to be a full challenge, witnesses called, evidence gathered."

"The first born has his rights," Tagara said. "Trouble is, he's generally shown more interest in his farm than in the mill. A large number in the town favor Hankel because he's dedicated to the work. If opinion was less evenly divided, we'd have Dimin here and a few others hear the challenge. It's not good, the mill standing idle, but with the issue so sensitive, we'll probably have to wait for our Redmother's return."

"At least you have the choice," Vray said. She couldn't help thinking of her own Redmother training. Vissa had taught her that very few disagreements between Shapers were ever resolved in a private challenge before local interested parties. Shaper responsibilities tended to include far more than a single mill or even a single village. Quite often, one Shaper who wanted to challenge another would seek out not one Redmother, but three, to ensure that all aspects of the situation were thoroughly examined. When the matter involved the ruling house it had to be heard by representatives of all of the Children of the Rock: Keeper, Shaper, and Dreamer.

Vray's legs trembled so violently that she almost stumbled. The answer to everyone's problems had been hanging in front of her all along; it had no business coalescing so suddenly it almost made her faint! There it was, obvious, glorious, simple, terrifying. The specific details of how she should go about it flooded her mind with such clarity, such profusion, that she strongly suspected it must have been in the back of her mind already. Perhaps she'd ignored it because having an answer meant having to act.

"Choice?" Tob prompted her, puzzled. Dimin and Tagara looked on politely. She saw Jordy's eyes widen as he, too, was struck by the implications of the conversation. Controlling his initial surprise, he caught her eye, but said nothing. He knew they had both reached the same conclusion, and knew too, that she needed no warning that this was neither the time nor the place to discuss it.

"The choice of whether to wait for your own Redmother or make use of the services of a convenient visitor." Vray admired the steadiness of her own voice as she returned Dimin's polite smile. "I've been training as a Redmother in Edian and Broadford," she added in explanation.

"You have? Why, that's perfect!" Dimin exclaimed.

Tagara thumped Tob good naturedly on the shoulder. "Not that your father hasn't always been welcome here, but I think this young lady is the best cargo he's brought us in fifteen years!"

"I think I might be offended," Vray said mildly.

"I know I am," Jordy growled.

Tob stepped up beside her and put a protective arm around her waist. "You can only have her temporarily. Very temporarily."

Dimin urged Tagara toward the inn with a gentle shove. "Go and tell the others. They're surely wondering what's taking us so long." He moved away and she started off in the opposite direction. "We should be able to settle this before supper."

Jordy shook his head in disapproval and called after her, "Not until after I've stabled my horse!"

CHAPTER 8

For their last night's campsite, Jordy chose a level stretch of beach on Hari's southwestern shore. A stand of old oaks shielded them from the nearby road. In front of them spread the rippling surface of the lake. The far shores to north and east were invisible beyond the horizon. As dusk descended, a few lights marked the location of the Queen's house, only three miles away across the southern curve of the lake. With a reasonable start in the morning, they would meet Jenil at the southern entrance to the estate at midday.

Sheyn and Keyn, matching crescents, followed the sun below the trees. Stars reflected dimly from the surface of the lake. Jordy sat on a log near the fire, giving the harness leather a thorough inspection for signs of wear. A smile quirked his lips. There was no weakness in Vray's Redmother training, or so the citizens of Atade seemed to believe. She had settled the dispute over the mill with such skill and compassion that everyone went away satisfied. The younger brother had possession of the mill, and the elder would be compensated by an addition to his farm land and a guarantee of privileged access to his brother's services. The rest of the villagers were relieved to see the conflict ended so quickly, and made no secret of their admiration for Vray's good sense and efficiency in dealing with the matter.

If Vray could bring the same wisdom to bear on the problems in Edian, all of Rhenlan would benefit.

In the flickering light of the fire, Jordy used his hands more than his eyes as he continued to examine leather straps and metal buckles. The harness was in excellent condition and didn't really need his attention. By appearing busy, however, he gave the children the illusion of solitude they needed. They walked up and down in the darkness at the very water's edge, dark shapes against the background of glimmering water. Their voices, low and confidential, barely reached him over the gentle lapping of water on sand.

Jordy did not try to hear their conversation. They were not children, really—except to him. In their own eyes, he guessed, they were a man and woman confronted with a difficult separation. He hoped they weren't really in love. He was as sure as a parent could be that she was Tob's first lover, which could make it a uniquely intense relationship for him. Jordy had not been pleased to find himself interfering in their relationship by reminding Vray of her theoretically increased chances of getting pregnant. Not that his advice had mattered. Traveling together as they were, he was well aware that they hadn't stopped coupling. Given the girl's decision to try to resume her life in Edian, a summer's celibacy might have been wise. Surely it would have been easier to part as brother and sister than as lovers.

Tob walked up from the beach, his attitude subdued but not, to Jordy's relief, particularly troubled. "Need any help with that, Dad?"

"No, I'm almost finished."

"Right. I'll turn in, then."

"Good night, laddie."

Tob moved away from the fire, toward the bedrolls laid out in the circle of trampled grass near the wagon. Jordy began gathering the harness together. He looked up as Vray entered the circle of fire light.

"Jordy, I know what I'm going to do."

"Sit down, my girl."

She accepted the invitation without hesitation. With every day that had passed since she had acknowledged her true identity at Cross Cove, he'd seen less and less hesitation of any sort from the girl. He doubted that the change was conscious on her part. She was behaving more like a princess because she was feeling more like a princess.

"I'm going to take the throne away from Damon," she told him. "I know how you feel about Shapers, and I know

I've been doing my best to help you make the villages more independent. I'm not saying I don't still agree with you, up to a point." She sat on the very edge of the log she'd chosen, leaning toward him, her bright eyes catching and reflecting the firelight. "But I'm a Shaper of the ruling line of Rhenlan. The only way to fulfill my vows to the gods is to become queen. I doubt I can win the king's favor, but even without Hion, there are always factions in the court and town. I'll use them. To begin with, I'll get control of the king's guard."

Jordy stopped the enthusiastic gush of words. "The guards? How?"

"I'm going to get married."

He studied her demure expression with deep suspicion. "Aye, no doubt you are. You have someone specific in mind, I take it."

"Oh, yes. We're going to be madly in love, although he doesn't know it, yet."

"Will he find your confidence in him appealing or terrifying, Your Highness?"

"He used to think I was kind of cute."

She was, Jordy decided, well aware of the enormity of what she was about to undertake. "What do you want me to say?"

"What you think."

"I won't change my mind if you win the throne. Not simply because it is you on the throne. Our world is out of balance. I won't sit back and depend on one well-meaning Shaper to put it right. That said, I believe you'll do your best. Whatever happens, lass, you've my admiration, here and now, for being willing to try. Never forget that."

She stood up suddenly, and turned her back to the fire. "I won't forget." Her voice shook with intensity, or perhaps something else. She stared at the wagon, and at Stockings on her tether, before facing Jordy once more. "When I'm Queen, I'll invite you to Edian. Will you come?"

"You know when to find me in the merchants' square. Ask me there and I'll consider it."

"You mean it, too! All right, I'll do it. The first nineday after the first Spring Festival that I'm queen. Watch for me."

"I'll look forward to it."

"Pepper and Matti are going to be furious that I didn't say good-bye."

"So are several others in the village I could name," Jordy agreed.

She sat on the log beside him. "Everyone will wonder how you could come back without me."

"You're a grown woman. It's your decision whether to make your life in Edian or Broadford. They'll understand that."

"Making my home in Edian," she mused. "That's true enough. You won't tell them more than that?"

"Unless you're intending to tell Damon that you've spent the last year and a half with us."

"No!" Vray said quickly. "Jenil is going to take full responsibility for removing me from Soza. The people there don't really know how long it's been—she did something to their memories with the power when she took me. My brother's not going to be happy that she interfered with one of his plans. He can't cause any trouble for a Greenmother, but it won't do Broadford any good if he learns that I was sheltered there."

"I agree, lass. It's best for everyone if Tob and I keep the secret."

"It's not a complete secret," Vray admitted uncomfortably. "Ivey the minstrel has known all along."

"I guessed as much."

"Sitrine knows, too. The king, I mean, not the entire population." She paused, then concluded, "And all the other Dreamers, of course."

"Never mind, my girl. Who Jenil or Ivey took into their confidence is their concern, not yours. You told me when you were ready."

"I told you because you already knew."

"That's good enough."

"No. I should have told you sooner. I knew I could trust you. I just . . ." She stopped, groping for words.

He placed his hand over hers and squeezed gently. "You had a lot to worry about. We haven't agreed on everything, you and I."

"We agree on hardly anything," she corrected him.

"Just the need for change."

"I'll do my best, Daddy."

He got to his feet, draping the harness neatly across his arms. "Time we were asleep. See to the fire, please, Vray."

"All right."

He stood there, surprised at his unwillingness to end the moment. Considering her brother's habits it was quite possible that, after tomorrow, he would never see her again. He'd grown entirely too fond of her to be comfortable with that thought. If she'd been an average child going off to face the uncertainties of the everyday world, he would have felt more easy in his mind. Or would he? The attempt at self-deception made him smile ruefully. "Rest well, lass."

"Good night, Dad."

The woman seated at the table did not look up as Vray and Jenil crossed the room. The servant announced them, drawing an impatient wave of her hand, then closed the door as he left. Even the firm thud of the oak panel against its frame wasn't enough to draw the red-haired woman's attention away from the paper she was reading.

Vray had been nervous about this meeting. She certainly hadn't slept much the night before for thinking about it; what she was going to say, how she was going to deal with the queen. Seeing Gallia, and witnessing the woman's perpetual preoccupation with her own affairs, made Vray think fleetingly of Jordy's wife Cyril. The comparison did not flatter the queen. Cyril at least had an excuse for her preoccupation. The woman was not only mute but, Vray had decided, more than a little lost. She felt sorry for Cyril. With Gallia, the only emotion that stirred within Vray was annoyance.

"Mother!" She said the word loudly.

Gallia's head came up. Vray had often been told that she and the queen looked alike, but she had never noticed the resemblance until now. Even as a child she had sensed her mother's hard-held anger at life. She wondered if the queen had always been unhappy. She was certainly unhappy now. That, and anger, radiated the way light flared from a torch. As strong as they were, the emotions seemed impersonal and unthinking, not directed at any one person or event.

Gallia blinked. "Vray? You've grown."

"It's been four years."

"Has it?" Her eyes flicked to Jenil, then back to Vray, while a finger tapped slowly on the side of the table. "What brings you here, girl? I thought you were at Bren or Garden Vale or—"

"Soza," Vray cut in. "Didn't you ever ask Damon where I was?" She heard her voice begin to rise and took a deep breath. Fury would be wasted on her female parent. She needed Gallia's help and couldn't afford to antagonize her.

The queen gave another impatient wave of her hand. "What are you doing here?"

"I want to return to court."

"Well, go then."

"Father hasn't sent for me. He thinks I'm at Soza."

"No, he doesn't. He sent a guard here a nineday ago asking where you'd gone."

"Then you did know where I've been!"

The woman's eyes hardened. "Until you disappeared. Damon said it was for the best."

Damon. Always Damon. "For whom?" Vray demanded, although she knew the answer. For Damon, of course. Vray planted her hands on her hips, but Jenil touched her arm before she could say more. Vray bit her tongue and waited.

"For everyone," Gallia snapped.

"I found the girl at Soza in an appalling condition," Jenil told the queen. "I decided she'd been there quite long enough. A princess has duties best fulfilled at court."

Gallia laughed harshly. "Yes. We all have duties. I fulfilled mine to Hion—I gave him children. Now I expect to be left alone."

"Parental duty doesn't end with childbirth."

"I've heard this lecture before, Dreamer. Go back to court if that's what you want, Vray. You're a woman grown. You can take care of yourself."

"She can't return without your protection," Jenil insisted. "You must take her back to Hion, and talk him into restoring her rank at court."

Gallia's annoyed, angry expression didn't change. "I'll give her a decent dress, and the loan of a horse. That's the most I'll do to interfere with the king's affairs."

Vray hadn't been listening closely to Jenil. Her mind had been racing, searching for some way she could avoid having to beg this woman for help. At the mention of the word "horse," she had her answer.

Jenil started to speak again, but Vray shook off the Dreamer's hand. "Greenmother, leave us."

Jenil paused, surprised, then bowed her head to Vray. "Yes, Your Highness."

The Dreamer left through the door. Once it was closed, Vray faced the woman whose features so closely matched Vray's own. "Do you remember the horse fair in Edian when I was thirteen? Five years ago," she added, since the woman obviously had not kept track of her age.

"All horse fairs are alike," Gallia replied.

"Not this one. There almost wasn't a horse fair that year. I'm sure you remember." Vray enjoyed watching a little of the color drain out of the queen's face. "If there had been no fair, it would have been your fault. I remember. I'm a Redmother, I remember everything. I was in the stables and overheard you talking with that man. The red-haired one who shouldn't be alive."

"You weren't allowed in my stable," Gallia accused her. "Not after you almost ruined that stallion."

"I know. You have devious children. I was visiting one of your horses—the one I bought at the next day's fair, though you probably don't remember that, either—and hid as soon as I knew you were in the barn. Our confrontations were never pleasant."

"This one certainly isn't."

"It will be less pleasant in a moment." Vray smiled. "That man—Soen, your brother, you do remember him?— has no legal right to life. He certainly had no business speaking to the queen, no business being in Edian. The queen had no business plotting the theft of a great many horses with him. Not even horses you owned."

Gallia stared at her as though she'd never seen her before. "It was you," she said in a wondering voice. "You interfered. How?"

"The guards stopped it. That's what we have guards for, to protect us from Abstainers."

"You told the guards."

"Yes. I could have told the king. I still could tell him. In fact, I'm considering it. Should I tell him, Mother?"

"You should have stayed in Soza."

"It's a wonderful training ground. For blackmail, among other skills. That's the only way to get your dinner sometimes. Should I tell Hion about your dealings with your brother? Your exiled, insane brother? Should I, Mother?"

Gallia's jaw tightened. "What do you want?"

"A place at court. A Keeper husband. Your help in getting both. Not too much to ask in exchange for my silence."

"A Keeper husband." Gallia grimaced. "How foolish. You don't believe in that nonsense."

"It's a whim."

"Hion will never allow it."

"I know how to deal with Hion." *I hope,* Vray added silently.

"What sort of place at court?" Gallia asked.

"I'm a princess, though you seem to have forgotten that. A princess, and a royal Redmother. That's my place in the court. Can you think of any reason why I shouldn't have it?"

Vray knew she shouldn't be taking so much satisfaction from the queen's grimly set features, but she couldn't help it. She didn't let her satisfaction, or nervousness, show. She stood before Gallia with every appearance of haughty confidence. She was going to win. She had to win. She also was all too aware this was only the first of many confrontations she would have to win. The first, and maybe the hardest. She prayed to the gods that practice would make it easier.

Gallia twisted her hands together in her lap. Finally, she said, "I'll take you to Hion, and speak to him on your behalf."

Vray gave a gracious nod. "You have my gratitude, Mother." She went to the door, then turned back one last time. "We'll leave for Edian in two days. I'll need new clothes first."

"Yes," the woman said. "Of course."

Vray left to find Jenil. How odd, to call Gallia "mother." She had had more concern from a speechless woman of the horse people than she'd ever had from that woman who loved horses.

She found the Greenmother in an overgrown herb garden. Jenil was studying some leaves she'd plucked from a mint plant. Vray took a pleased sniff as she approached. "I love those brewed as a tea."

Jenil made a sour face. "Not unless they're blended. Not these, anyway. Who taught you about herbs?"

"No one. I don't know how to brew a tea unless it comes in a cheesecloth bag from the shop." She took Jenil by the arm and led her to a bench beneath a poplar tree. Once seated, she checked carefully to see that none of her mother's servants were about. Assured that they were alone, she said, "Tell me about your visits to Edian to treat the king's illness."

"Good morning, goldsmith. Timik tells me you have need of my wagon."

"Good day to you, carter. Gemstones from White Water." Loras got up from his workbench and gestured Jordy over to the display case on one wall. The two customers speaking with Deenit at the front of the shop paid them no attention.

"It'll be next summer before I return to White Water. I'm heading home after I've finished here."

Loras waved a negligent hand. "My order can wait until then. Advise me on what goods to barter for gemstones."

Deenit's customers prepared to leave with their purchase. Jordy said, "Citron is a valuable fruit in the south, and I know a man in Raisal who's always looking to improve his flock of chickens."

The bell over the shop door jingled. "They're gone," Deenit said.

Loras took Jordy's elbow and turned him away from the display case. "Come see Dael. He's in the kitchen."

Loras opened the door in the back wall of the shop and led Jordy through to the family's living quarters. The curtains were drawn over the kitchen windows, making the large room dim and uninviting. Dael, seated at the table, gestured Jordy toward a chair. Loras remained in the doorway.

"I looked for you at the inn on my last trip," Jordy began by way of greeting.

"I couldn't make it," Dael said. "It wouldn't have been safe."

Jordy scowled. "Safe? Has it gotten to the point in Edian that two men can't sit down and have a wee chat?"

"They can." Loras folded his arms and leaned his rangy body against the doorframe. "As long as they don't mind being watched."

"I'm losing track of Damon's spies and informers," Dael explained. "He knows there's some dissatisfaction among the merchants. I'm sure of that much. Whether he knows the true extent or any names is another matter." His wide shoulders lifted in a shrug. "We decided for everyone's safety that it's better if I keep my reputation unsullied."

Jordy gave an appreciative snort. "I'll take that as a compliment."

"You won't laugh if the king decides to restrict travel," Loras said.

Jordy glanced back at him in alarm. "Is that likely?"

"I don't think so," Dael said. "He's too anxious to build on his popularity with the merchants."

"You're the one who noticed his growing interest in travelers," Loras argued.

"We had trouble with border guards on our way out of Sitrine," Jordy said. "They stole from us, but let us pass."

Dael gave an unhappy nod. "I'm aware of those 'patrols.' Damon wants to hear about everyone who comes in or out of Edian."

"For what purpose?" Loras asked. "To control trade?"

"For information," Dael said. "He's a tactician. Knowledge is a weapon. The larger his spy network, the greater his strength. That's why he's starting to watch merchants and carters, minstrels and players—anyone who travels away from their home village. Especially anyone who travels from kingdom to kingdom."

"That's why we're in here," Loras concluded with a nod at the kitchen.

"I wish I had more positive news," Dael said.

"Never mind, lad. You keep your place in the court. Damon wants information? Well, so do we, and you're in the best position to get it."

"Not for a nineday or more."

"Eh?"

Dael shrugged apologetically. "A quick border tour. Five troops are leaving this morning. In fact, they should be ready now. I'll have to get back."

"What are your plans for the winter, carter?" Loras asked.

"Home. With as many trips to nearby villages as the weather will allow."

Dael rose. "Good journey, carter."

"And to you."

At the back door, Dael knocked twice. A young guard poked her head in. "Still quiet, sir."

"Let's go."

CHAPTER 9

How very interesting, Damon thought as he looked upon the group gathered in the great hall. *Here we all are together. A family. Parents, children, even a distant aunt or cousin or whatever relation Jenil is to us. How very annoying.*

The king sat on his throne. The queen and Greenmother stood before him. All three looked annoyed. Damon stood beside the hearth, ostensibly to warm himself, though neither the afternoon nor the hall was particularly chill. Vray stood alone in the center of the room, hands clasped before her, eyes downcast, a veil of deep red hair shadowing her face. Damon had an excellent view of his sister in profile and enjoyed running an expert eye over the pretty girl before him. She had changed in the years since he'd sent her away. She looked healthy, not wan and wasted by the ravages of Soza. Damon was glad of that, almost grateful for Jenil's interference. No reason to arouse sympathy from Father.

Yes, very healthy. Still a bit thin for his taste, but elegantly so. Her kittenish prettiness had turned into tempting sensuality, her coloring complimented by a tight-bodiced court dress in blue and gold. A few weeks on the road traveling from one Brownmother house to another seemed to have done the girl a world of good. He rubbed his hands briskly together. She looked so delightfully meek. *It would seem that Soza has done its work. She would make a very tempting gift to offer to the right man.*

He came forward and laid a brotherly hand on the girl's shoulder. She flinched admirably. "Welcome home, sister," he said in a voice soft but not friendly. "What shall we do with you?" She remained silent, passive under his hand.

He glanced toward the throne and watched his father's skin flush bright red as his already annoyed expression turned to rage. "No," the king said firmly to the queen. "I'll take the girl back, of course. She could have returned to Edian anytime she wished, Gallia. I don't know what she told you, but the idea was for her to finish her education. I won't hear any more of this exile business." He turned his wrath on Jenil. "And I won't hear any more of this prophecy nonsense. I will choose who, or if, the girl marries." Hion thumped his fists on the arms of the throne. "Am I understood?"

Damon stepped forward. "What's this about marriage?"

"The prophecy," Mother answered for the king. She pointed toward Vray. "Jenil and I have discussed the matter at great length, Hion." As usual, she spoke to the king as though she thought him an idiot. "We think it would be a proper gesture toward the Keepers if Vray were to have one for a husband. It would be a popular move," she added with a fond glance for Damon.

Damon returned the fond look, but said hastily, "I don't agree, Mother."

"Surely you can see the advantage, dear, of showing the Keepers your regard for them by having one in the family. It is traditional, after all, and many believe the prophecy. Whether it's true or not, the marriage would be diplomatic."

"It's a foolish tradition. Shaper and Keeper should keep to their own."

"My father was a Keeper," Jenil said. "My mother a princess. They loved each other very much, and they gave two Dreamers to the world." She looked at the king with what Damon interpreted as speculation. "Can the world do without Dreamers, Majesty? Can the world do without healers? Healers able to bend the power against serious injury and illness are rare. Only two of us remain, and Savyea can no longer be bothered to leave the Cave of the Rock. She's grown weary of the world, you know." She sighed sadly. "As have I. In fact, I believe this will be my last journey away from Garden Vale. I think it's best I keep my magic to myself from now on. It's obviously neither needed nor appreciated in your court."

Hion went from angry red to frightened white. He seemed to be grasping the chair arms with all the force in his body. "What are you saying, Greenmother?"

Jenil looked very sad, but very determined. "I am saying, Hion, that we are going to come to an agreement. Vray will marry a Keeper, or I will never return to Edian. Nor will you be able to find me if you come looking. I have been your healer for many years, but if you refuse me, I will never use my skill in your service again."

"This is outrageous!"

"Yes," the Greenmother agreed. "But if the Shapers had not grown so adamant about letting the Dreamers die, this outrage would not have become necessary. Well, Hion?"

The king sat back in his chair, glaring at the Greenmother. Damon watched with interest. He had never expected such a clever move from a Dreamer. It was nice to know they had some cunning. This was something he could understand. Something he could counter. He stepped closer to the throne and caught Hion's eye. "Do it, Father," he advised. "It really isn't such a bad idea. The people will be pleased."

"You think so?"

Damon nodded. His mother beamed proudly at him and he took her hand, kissing it. "We'll make quite a celebration of it." He looked to Jenil. "Will that please you, Greenmother?"

She nodded coldly.

"Good."

Hion looked relieved. "Do it, then. Find the girl a husband, Damon. Someone appropriate."

"Yes, Father."

Vray was not consulted, and Vray wisely kept quiet. Damon found himself very pleased with the girl.

Drops of moisture from the unseasonably cold rain clung to Dael's cloak and hair as he entered the passageway that led to the great hall. There would be a fire blazing in the hearth there. The warmth interested him far more than the formality of reporting road conditions to the king. The last few days had been uncomfortably damp. Gods willing, the weather would moderate in time for the Fall Festival.

Even before he entered the hall he could hear the voices and laughter of the gathered court. Many female voices, which meant Damon was in attendance. Unfastening his fur-lined cloak, Dael tossed it to the nearest servant, thanked the girl with a smile, and proceeded through the archway.

The room glowed golden with the flames from candles and the hearth that took up most of one wall. By comparison, the rain-diffused light from the high, narrow windows was insignificant. Hion was speaking with several older Shapers, and Redmother Vissa stood with four Brownmothers near the fire. Their voices were easily drowned out by the more vibrant conversations taking place beneath the central chandelier.

Dael noted that Damon was wearing scarlet and silver. The prince was in a good mood. Dael wondered who had died, then spotted the willowy beauty that stood close by the prince's side. That explained the prince's smile. Damon had made a new conquest.

Dael forgot the longed-for hearth and took up his usual place against the wall next to the archway. This might be his only chance to appreciate without being noticed. The girl was probably a Shaper, although he had thought himself familiar with all the Shaper families who came to court. The girl at Damon's left hand had deep red hair, worn thick and loose around her shoulders. Her silvery gray gown complemented the prince's apparel, as well as showing her slender figure to the best advantage. Nice, Dael thought. Not too skinny, not plump either. Just enough in all the right places. He liked her height. She was nearly as tall as the prince. Odd. Damon usually liked them fragile. She had the look of sunlight and fields to her. Maybe a wealthy Keeper's daughter? Dael knew most of the prominent Keeper families, or at least their daughters. Something about her was familiar, but she was not a local girl.

She had been carefully listening to something witty Damon was saying. Once the required laughter ended she glanced away, head turning gracefully above her white throat. Dael found himself looking at a spot at the base of that throat and licked his lips—just as her eyes met his. Almost as if she'd known exactly where to find him. Uptilted eyes and a wide, sensual mouth he hadn't seen in years. Of course, he hadn't thought the generous mouth sensual then.

"Kitten?" he whispered.

Dael hasn't changed a bit, Vray thought. He had his hunter's look on. Despite her youthful efforts, she'd never expected him to look at her like that. She almost laughed with delight as his lips unmistakably formed his favorite nickname for her. *He's just recognized me. I have changed.*

She couldn't spare too much time to admire the captain of the guard. She took in as much detail as the shadows where he stood would allow, then firmly turned her attention back to her brother. Damon was making an effort to be loving and cordial. She gave half her mind to being equally caring in return, while mentally reviewing what she'd seen.

She had thought perhaps that time and distance had caused her to idealize him—especially the way Matti and Pepper always teased her about him. She hadn't. He really was that tall. His hair really was as golden and thick as she remembered it. Even the lines around his mouth and eyes were there. A lived-in face.

If he was half as fast and strong and smart as she remembered, he'd do. She looked toward her father, then smiled back at Damon.

Dael would have to do. There was no other tool here she could trust.

"Captain." Damon came forward and put his arm around Dael's shoulder as Dael entered the private audience chamber, leading him toward a pair of chairs placed near the fireplace. "Let's talk as friends."

Dael accepted the unwanted contact for the few seconds required before he was able to sit down. Damon poured two cups of wine and handed one to him. This was a bad sign. What now? A raid into Sitrine? Set fire to a village whose residents had complained about their taxes? Dael had heard of no impending crises in the two days since he'd returned to town—unless it was a crisis to find Princess Vray once more in residence in her father's castle.

Years of practice allowed Dael to smile over the edge of the goblet. "I'm at your service, as always, Highness."

"Friends." Damon repeated the word with peculiar emphasis.

"I'm honored."

"That's right. You will be."

Despite his control, Dael's smile slipped. "Highness?"

Damon sat on the edge of his chair. "More than friends, in fact." The prince lifted his glass in a toast. "Brothers. King Hion will announce the betrothal in the morning, but I thought you deserved fair warning, and whatever meager advice I might be able to offer."

Betrothal. He'd heard the word before, but in the present context it made no sense. *Whose betrothal? Why do I need a warning? Advice?* "Highness?" he repeated blankly.

The prince threw his head back and shouted with laughter. "My dear captain, if only you could see your face! I've never seen you at a loss. This is delightful! The legendary Dael can be taken by surprise after all."

"I'm not getting married," Dael told the prince. "I don't know what you've heard—"

"But you are," Damon interrupted him. "It's all arranged. Don't tell me this is the first you've heard of it! You know that my father has agreed on a Keeper husband for the girl?"

"Yes." Not officially, but the rumor was all over Edian. Princess Vray would be given in marriage according to the old custom. An old custom for which Damon had no respect. Yet it was Damon who would choose whom the poor girl would marry—Dael's thoughts stopped. *Gods!*

"I've given the matter careful thought. She's benefited from her time away, but I still think she needs someone with a firm hand. Someone who understands my concerns for the future of the kingdom. A friend I can rely on."

Dael's mind raced frantically. Choice wasn't going to come into this. Never mind if he had no plans to take a wife. He was going to have a wife. A dangerous wife. Dangerous to him. Damon had no love for Vray. If he wanted her at all it was as a tool. A tool to be guarded by his loyal captain. Guarded until needed—or disposed of when necessary?

"We will be brothers. Brothers, with the best interest of the kingdom uppermost in our minds. For instance," Damon went on after taking a sip of wine, "this Dreamer business. Rhenlan has no need of Dreamers. You and I are agreed on this, I think."

None of Dael's inner turmoil disrupted the smooth demeanor he presented to Damon. "Of course."

"I don't particularly want any nieces or nephews cluttering up the castle. I don't want Jenil fussing over Dreamer babies. To be blunt, life will be much simpler if Vray never has children."

"So my duty as a husband is . . . ?"

"Is to leave my sister alone," Damon told him with another bright smile. "I'm so glad you understand."

Stones! Dael swore silently. Hasn't he looked at her? Not as an annoyance but as a woman? "She's very attractive, Highness."

"What of it? There are many beautiful women in Edian. You know most of them already. Surely you're not worried about being lonely?"

Dael chuckled. "No, Highness. Of course not. But I am a man. Must I keep my hands off my own wife?" He gave the prince a lecherous, conspiratorial smile. "There are many ways to control people, Highness."

Damon tilted his head to one side. "Love blindness?" He shrugged. "Why not? I've faith that you can persuade her to lead a quiet life, one way or another. Just as long as there are no children."

Easy to order; harder to ensure. Did the prince expect him to beat her child out of her? Keep her constantly locked away? Not for the first time, Dael resented his reputation. Allowing none of his feelings to show, he smiled coldly at his prince. "A quiet life," he repeated. "I'm sure I'll find it rewarding."

Damon nodded. "You will be my captain when I am king. Under my rule, your rank will bring you more power than ever before. Power and wealth. However, let's leave that discussion for the future."

"As you wish, Highness."

"Vray!"

Dael slammed the door behind him, startling Redmother Danta out of her chair. He glowered at her. "Out."

The woman asked no question, but retreated from Vray's sitting room through another door.

Vray remained seated by the window. She looked up and smiled demurely. "Captain." Her voice was soft, her expression gently inquisitive. "You seem upset. Is something wrong?"

He stomped across the room to stand in front of her high-backed chair.

"Please sit down." She gestured toward the tray on the table beside her. "Have some wine and cake. Please."

"Vray," he repeated. She smiled again. He sat. She handed over a full glass she'd already been holding. He drained it. It didn't help. She was still smiling when he handed it back and said, "We're getting married, you know."

"I know," she replied.

"Damon told you?"

"He didn't have to."

"Why me?"

"You are the most logical choice. Loyal to my father. Popular. A respected hero. Who else is there?"

He looked at her suspiciously. "How did you arrange this?"

"It was Damon's idea."

He ignored her denial. "You did arrange it."

She sighed. "Don't state the obvious too often. Someone may hear you."

"Vray!"

"What!" Her answering shout was nearly as loud as his.

"Why did you do this to me?" He sat forward and ran his hands through his hair. "Why?"

Vray got up and made sure both doors were closed and locked. She came back and took her seat once more. "Who else could I marry?" she asked.

For a moment her expression was as adoring as he remembered it. The face of a fourteen-year-old determined to seduce him. Only for a moment, but the possessiveness of the look infuriated him.

"You could marry anyone. Could have manipulated this any way you chose."

"No." She looked down at hands clasped tightly in her lap. "This has nothing to do with childhood fantasies."

"Doesn't it?"

"You were my friend. I was hoping you would still be my friend."

"Don't try the plaintive waif on me, Vray of Rhenlan!"

She raised her eyes to meet his. "It used to work."

"It never worked."

"True. I'd forgotten."

He sighed. He had meant to remain furious, but seemed to have lost some of it. He was still angry, but the impulse to strangle her had ebbed. "What of my life? What of my choice?"

"I've no choice either. I must marry a Keeper. Why not have one I cared for when I was young?"

"When did you decide you must wed a Keeper?"

"Before I returned to Edian."

"You chose me before you even came back?"

"Yes."

"Did it occur to you I might already have a wife?"

She looked shocked. "You wouldn't marry anyone else."

"No, I didn't . . . but . . ." Impatiently he tossed his hair away from his face. "That's not the point. The point is I have no choice. You've put us both in a very dangerous position."

"I'm used to it." The words carried the first hint of bitterness that Dael had seen in her since her return. "As for the captain of the guard, he has only to do his duty. What danger is there in that?"

She had been away. She couldn't know what had been happening here. "What am I going to do with you?"

"Marry me," she said with complete confidence. "It's the king's command."

He stood and bowed formally. "Always the obedient servant."

"That's not how I remember it."

"Some orders cannot be obeyed," he agreed. She was just as he remembered her. She had been thirteen when she'd first tried to command him into bed. At fourteen, she'd defied her father and her brother to do her duty as a Redmother. Was she still that strong? Why had she returned to face Damon? Had her exile been so terrible that dealing with Damon was preferable? Was she hoping that Dael could protect her? Was it her hero she remembered and wanted as a shield? Had he ever been that kind of a hero?

Her strength had survived the exile. So had her ability to scheme. Did he stand a chance of knowing all that she wanted? Once, he had. That was years ago. She was younger. Life was simpler. He was simpler.

"What am I going to do with you?" he asked aloud.

"You asked that already."

"I've been asking it since you were eight years old!"

"And I've been telling you. Maybe now you'll listen."

"Now I have no choice."

She jumped to her feet. "You keep saying that! Is having me so bad?"

She had grown, that was certain. They weren't eye to eye, but it was much closer than it used to be. Only a few inches separated them, then she leaned closer still. Or

97

maybe he did. One of them was moving, and if he didn't do something he was going to end up kissing her.

Why shouldn't they kiss? They were betrothed.

The velvet of her dress was soft to the touch. He slid his hands around her back, and felt a tug as she gripped the ends of his hair to pull his face toward hers.

She tasted of cakes and wine.

CHAPTER 10

The weather was hot for a Festival day. *I ought to have a word with Aage,* Sene thought. *He hasn't been behaving like a proper court wizard since his last visit to Morb.*

"Has Jeyn said anything to you about Aage?" Sene asked his companion at the table in the royal pavilion.

Ivey set his wineglass on the coral-pink linen tablecloth, next to the large bowl of apples, imported from Rhenlan for the festivities. No one else was in the large pavilion at present, although Dektrieb walked by every few moments, keeping a discreet eye on his king's dessert plate.

"Just that he's busy with some magical experiment," Ivey said. "Why?"

"It's too hot," Sene grumbled. "I don't want people uncomfortable. This is supposed to be autumn, after all."

"You're spoiled, Your Majesty."

"I know." Sene stabbed a single raisin and nibbled on it. "Tell me the news from Bronle."

"King Palle doesn't appreciate outsiders visiting his capital. It's the one place he thinks he controls. I was only allowed to remain within the town walls overnight, and there were guards present the entire time I was at the inn. I was allowed to play, but not sing. Couldn't even recite a humorous verse. I was told that my kind wasn't wanted in Bronle. Guards escorted me half a day along the road when I left."

"So what news did you manage to spread in spite of these daunting obstacles?"

Ivey offered a mostly humble smile. "A rumor I heard about Prince Pirse. A rumor that he is continuing the royal bloodline. A rumor that he plans to offer a life for a life. People were skeptical. I reminded them that Palle's accusations against Pirse have never been tested in front of a law reader. I got a few people thinking, at least."

"Did you tell anyone about the birth of Pirse's Dreamer daughter?"

"Not yet. Safer for little Emlie if she stays hidden in her mother's mountain village until the official policy toward Dreamers in Dherrica has improved."

"A good point. Well done, minstrel. What about the rest of Dherrica?"

"Stories of Pirse's heroism are already common throughout the mountains. Palle doesn't leave the castle, so he has no idea how unpopular he really is. The only contact Dherricans have with their king is through his tax collectors and the guards who accompany them. Pirse they see and talk to several times a year. They like him."

"They should."

"You want them to, Majesty. And what you want, everyone should want."

Sene glowered at him. "Am I that obvious?"

"Yes. That's all right. We trust that what you want is for the best."

Dektrieb came past the open side of the tent yet again. This time Sene waved him in. Pushing his chair back, he said softly to Ivey, "He's been wanting to clean up in here for an hour. Better let him get on with it so he'll stop making me feel guilty."

As soon as they left the pavilion, Jeyn appeared out of the crowd and took Ivey's arm. "Dad, he's mine now. Fair is fair. Come on, Ivey. There are several new musician apprentices waiting for you to hear them play. I think they sound like cats in heat. Perhaps you can make out if they've chosen the right profession."

Sene watched the two young people disappear into the throngs who meandered through the pavilions and scattered tables that filled the field. He turned in the other direction and wandered toward the racetrack. Many people, some of them friends and some only vaguely familiar faces from the town, nodded and smiled at him as he passed, but he didn't stop to talk. He was feeling lonely, but perversely not in the mood for conversation. Maybe it was because his back had been aching for a few days. For the first time in years, he wished a holiday would end and all these people would go home.

Years, was it? He was being melancholy. He wasn't used to that, and didn't like it. Waste of time. A man didn't have that much time to live that he could waste it being moody. Gods! Melancholy *and* morbid!

Everything was going well. What did he have to complain about? Maybe he should have followed Ivey and Jeyn, forced himself to enjoy the music. He ought to be cheerful, like the two young people who loitered near the racetrack.

They hadn't noticed him, and wouldn't notice him if he didn't linger, which he would not. He allowed himself one further look at the laughing couple who had caught his eye. Blond head and black were tilted together as Chasa and Feather exchanged some joke. Feather was perched on the rail of the saddling paddock, Chasa standing in front of her. In that position they were just about the same height. They were holding hands.

How nice.

They looked happy together. She used to smile at him like that. Sene truly hadn't realized why. Or that he had smiled back. Old fool. Perhaps he did love her. A little.

He missed the child. But it had been worth it, avoiding her for so long. Worth it to see the way she smiled at his son. Chasa deserved her.

And Sene missed her.

Vray considered a choice of cloaks. The maid held one on either arm while trying to conceal a yawn, waiting none too patiently for the princess to decide. Vray sat on the edge of the bed, aware of how early it was, aware of the coolness of the weather beyond her bedroom window, aware of the importance of the day. She was determined to take a walk around Edian anyway.

One of the cloaks was fine woven light blue wool, lined in white. The other was deep rust, the weave wider, the sturdy cloth slightly worn. She'd brought it with her from Broadford. In fact, she'd used the cloak to wrap the few belongings she'd taken from Jordy's wagon to her mother's estate. She slipped to her feet with a smile and took the old cloak from the servant. "Go back to bed, Teza. I don't want any help right now."

Teza shook her graying head. The woman had appointed herself Vray's personal servant the day the princess returned to the castle. Vray was aware that the position had not exactly been fought over by the staff. Most people were afraid of courting disfavor by associating with Vray, but Teza had volunteered her services, then rounded up a pair of girls to assist her. The girls were in awe, not of her, but of Teza. Vray was more amused than anything else, though she would have preferred the conversation of Matti and Pepper to the maids' shy efforts to impress her. It was Teza who noticed her work-roughened hands, complained about the freckles and tan from sun and wind on her face and arms; Teza who wasn't quite sure if she approved that the princess was lithely muscular instead of just plain thin. Vray hadn't yet decided if Teza was one of her brother's spies. Spy or not, Vray liked the middle-aged woman.

Teza stifled another yawn and began, "Highness, there's so much—"

"To do," Vray finished. "I know, I know. But I haven't been in Edian for Festival for years. I'm going to be too busy in the castle later in the day to take part in any of the town's celebrating. I've missed it," she confided to the sleepy woman. "You get some rest, Teza. I'll be back in an hour. Two at the most. Then I'll have a bath and you can do my hair and get me to the great hall in plenty of time."

Teza sighed. "Stubborn as ever and never doing what's good for you. Think you were still sneaking out to chase after the young captain."

Vray's cheeks reddened. "You noticed that?"

"Everyone did, Highness."

Vray adjusted the comfortable old cloak and ventured a persuasive smile. "A good man, Captain Dael."

"Yes, Highness." Teza's expression softened. Women's expressions usually did when discussing the captain.

"He'll make a good husband." Vray decided to embroider on the theme a bit. "Protective. Hard working. Competent."

"As you say, Princess."

Vray gave an emphatic nod and went out the door while Teza was caught in another yawn.

Vray's rooms were in the tower on the floor beneath her father's. She counted the worn stairs as she went down them, and glanced down the corridors that branched off the landings of each of the three floors between her room and ground level. The only thing new in the last five years was the presence of a guard at the entrance to each floor.

A babble of voices greeted her when she entered the corridor leading to the great hall. Vray paused and smoothed her hair. Every Shaper who was able had made the journey to Edian for Festival, as tradition dictated. This was courting time for young Shapers, one of few chances in a year when the widely scattered families got together. Vray could remember watching the intricate social maneuvering of boys trying to meet girls, girls trying to assess boys, and parents trying to impress one another. She had never participated in it herself. Hion and Gallia had never needed to impress anyone. Even if they had, they probably would not have thought of her as a marketable commodity. As for Damon, he had always made it plain that he controlled his own destiny.

Controlled it poorly, Vray thought as she considered the doorway of the hall. As much as she wanted to escape the castle for a while, she supposed she should go in. This was nothing like standing in front of a village as Redmother. These were Shapers, her own kind. Each of the dozen families were the leaders of the areas in which they lived. She had to win their approval, their respect—their friendship?— or else any attempt she made to take power, even with the backing of the Keepers, would end in violence. Shapers fight when they feel threatened. She didn't want Shapers fighting her, fighting and killing her people. Which meant she had to win them to her side.

Which meant she had to go into the room.

She handed her cloak to the door guard, smoothed down the skirt of her simple walking dress, and went into the great hall, carrying herself with all of the confidence she could feign. A few of her distant relatives looked up with varying expressions of interest and hesitant welcome at her appearance. Early as it was, trestle tables lined the walls all around the large room, servants standing behind them to serve the on going breakfast of Festival morning. Grown second and third cousins sat with their plates at the round tables in the center of the room, while a few people milled around, socializing. Harassed nurses followed a pair of small children as they explored their new surroundings. Vray smiled at the antics of the little ones, but decided to concentrate her attention on her peers. To be precise, the younger women. The young, marriageable women.

Vray wondered what Damon considered marriageable as she made her way into the group. How long had he been looking now? He was almost thirty-one years old. If he'd married at a normal age, his children would be entering their teens by now. She knew he'd never lacked for eligible females to choose from. He always had at least one lover living in the castle. One former companion had been sent to Soza before Vray, for demanding marriage, and was probably still there. Vray doubted anyone had pushed Damon since that incident, but the interest remained. He had to marry soon, if he wanted an heir. If he remained without an heir, her challenge of his right to rule would have more weight, which was fine with her.

Vray narrowed the field to four women, old enough but not yet married, all of whom were present in the hall this morning. Three, including absent Soen's eighteen-year-old daughter, were heirs to sizable lands of their own. All four had been friendly to Vray since their arrival. None of them had seemed to attract any notice from Damon.

My brother, Vray thought, *is strange. I've known that for years. I only hope I can use it against him.*

For an hour she played the gracious hostess to the king's visitors and accepted reserved good wishes on her marriage. She was polite to the few people she was sure were committed to Damon's plans for the future. Most, however, feigned indifference to anything beyond the affairs of their own lands. She participated in several conversations about crops and weather and animal breeding and improved conditions in a Keeper village. She was thankful that so many of Rhenlan's Shapers went about their business as Shapers had always done. Damon doubtless had plans for them once he was king, but they seemed oblivious to their danger. For now, she would let them stay that way. Time enough to raise the alarm before Damon actually tried to assume the throne. For the next nineday, she would simply work at getting to know everyone better. Later, she would keep in touch with each family, as the royal Redmother, and gradually see that they became aware that she was far more fit to rule than her brother ever would be.

At the end of the hour she retrieved her cloak and left the castle. She had already noted the increased number of guards around the castle, and a brand new barracks building where a stable had once stood. She was careful to give a friendly smile or nod to each uniformed person she passed on her route from the main building to the castle gate. She also meticulously noted each response, remembered each face.

It was a simple exercise, interrupted at the gate when one of the guards answered her nod. "Your Highness, a moment please."

The girl stood in front of Vray, directly before the open gate. The pair of them were immediately in the path of incoming foot and wagon traffic. Vray stepped out of the way of a cart. The girl moved with her, almost as if they were dancing.

"Yes?" Vray asked when they'd twirled around and were standing in the shadow of the inner wall. The young guard was an inch or so shorter than Vray, pretty, about the same age. Vray recognized her. "Peanal. You live in the same street as the goldsmith Loras. You've grown."

The pretty girl gave a bob of her head. "Yes, Highness. I've been waiting for you. I was going to come up to the castle, but I saw you leave the hall and decided to wait by the gate instead."

Vray crossed her arms underneath her cloak. "Waiting for me? Why?"

Spots of color appeared on the pretty girl's cheeks. Her right thumb rubbed back and forth across her dagger hilt. "Prince Damon has asked for a guard to be assigned to accompany you whenever you leave the castle. For your own protection."

Vray didn't try to embarrass the girl further by asking what she was supposed to be protected from. "I see," she replied. "I'm grateful for my brother's care."

"Yes, Your Highness. You looked like you were getting ready to leave the castle."

"I am. Or I was." Vray looked back toward the main building before addressing Peanal again. "If it pleases my brother, I'll certainly remain at home today."

"Oh, no, it's quite all right for you to leave," the girl told her hastily. "It's just that you shouldn't go out alone. Captain Dael assigned me to look after you," she hastened to add. "If you approve the choice, of course." Peanal gave her a friendly smile. "Do you approve?"

Vray began to relax. "I've never disapproved of one of my betrothed's choices." She took a step closer to the gate, Peanal close behind her. "Hardly ever," she amended.

They walked out into the road that led into the town. As she and Peanal descended the hill, they passed a pair of guards climbing toward the gates. Vray frowned at the thought of all the resources required to feed so many uniformed bodies.

"There was that girl at the Golden Owl," she said, returning to her earlier thought. "I considered her a very bad decision and told him so, quite firmly."

Peanal giggled. "Was that the time with the ale?"

Vray was delighted. "You've heard that tale?"

"From Nocca. Is it true?"

"Yes." The girl seemed eager to be a friendly watchdog. Vray was satisfied with Dael's choice.

"Where are you going?" Peanal asked.

"To visit my future mother-in-law."

"Oh, good," Peanal said. "The saffron cakes should be done by the time we arrive."

"I hope so. I've been dreaming about those cakes for years." Her own experiment with the recipe hadn't turned out anything similar to Deenit's masterpiece. Though everyone in Broadford greatly admired her efforts, it just hadn't been the same.

Together they turned onto the familiar street. When they reached the goldsmith's building, Peanal opened the front door for her. Vray took a deep breath to catch the rich aroma coming from the kitchen. They smiled at each other and followed their noses through the quiet shop, reaching the kitchen door just as Deenit set a fat yellow loaf on the table.

"Rose, dear," Deenit said, "I thought you were taking the baby to your mother's." She turned toward them. "Did you forget something?" Dael's mother stopped, and blinked. Then her still-pretty features brightened with a broad smile. "Your Highness! I was wondering if I'd see you before the wedding." She came forward and took Vray's hands. "You've grown."

"Yes, ma'am."

"Well, come in, come in. We haven't much time."

Within seconds, Vray had her cloak off and hung by the door and she and Peanal were seated with Deenit at the table, thick pieces of nutbread on plates in front of them. Vray took a large bite. It was warm and sweet and spicy and she sighed happily.

"Now I know I'm home," she said around the bread. "Thank you."

Deenit beamed. "Thank you. I'll remember to put a loaf

in the marriage basket. There's already one for Dael, but he hates to share."

"I know."

Deenit looked at her thoughtfully while Vray wolfed down her bread. "I just realized that the boy's actually going to be married. He's too old for you, you know. But then, you're not a child anymore, are you? Some honeyed tea might go good with that bread."

"No, thank you," Vray replied.

"Peanal?"

"No, thank you."

Deenit folded her hands on the table. She ran a critical eye over first one then the other of the girls. "You're both too skinny for my boys, but I suppose you'll do."

Vray gave Peanal a curious look.

"I've been trying to talk Nocca into settling down with her," Deenit explained. "They've been seeing each other for years. Ruudy and Rose have one baby and there's another one on the way, but it's taken them a long time and I'd like more grandchildren. Of course, I had my doubts that Dael would ever marry. He's been so fussy—as if he had to try out every girl in Edian first."

Vray threw her head back and laughed loudly. "At least I know how dedicated he's been to serving the citizens of the town."

"It hasn't been the same since you left," Deenit told her. "Not at all. Dael's been too serious and working too hard." She gave a maternally worried tsk. "You'll get him to rest and take care of himself and not run off every chance he gets."

Vray wiped crumbs off her chin, then tilted her head curiously. "Run off?" she repeated.

"Chasing Abstainers, riding the borders, training troops. He's always off somewhere, it seems." Dael's mother sighed. "Barely back in time for the wedding. What was he thinking, to go off to the border the day after the betrothal was announced? You keep him home and warm this winter and start a grandchild for me."

Vray considered her words with great interest. "Do you think we can? I'm a Shaper, after all."

Deenit seemed surprised. "Child, I was born in Raisal, the capital of Sitrine. I grew up knowing all about how Dreamer babies are conceived." She reached across the table to pat Vray's hand. "I'd like a girl, I think, if you can manage it. One with your red hair and Dael's blue eyes will suit, as long as I'm putting in an order."

"I'll try," Vray promised. She leaned back in her chair and studied the older woman. "Are you still Brownmother for this neighborhood? Will you be at the Mothers' table or seated with the family at the wedding feast?"

"With the family. No ugly black and brown robe for me this year. I gave up the post at Spring Festival. I thought I deserved a rest, but Gisah isn't doing a very satisfactory job—at least, people still keep coming to me and the law readers say I should help them when they ask. Perhaps I'll take the duties back next year if the neighborhood asks for me."

Good. Deenit had influence, but it wasn't official. Vray didn't want Damon noticing anything or anyone connected with her just yet. She shot a brief glance at the guard seated beside her, and decided to save talking about the town for some other time.

Vray got to her feet, and Peanal rose with her. "We'd better go," Vray said. "The bread was wonderful. Just the breakfast I wanted."

"Take some with you," Deenit offered. "It's hours before the feast. You don't know when you'll get a chance to eat before then. Or are you going to be a nervous bride?"

Nervous? A nervous bride? Vray blinked at the unfamiliar words. Without warning, her stomach gave a painful jolt; butterflies began to skitter around her brain. A thousand things she hadn't considered began popping to the front of her mind, things that had no connection at all to her ninedays of careful planning. She stared blankly at Deenit.

I'm getting married today, aren't I?

109

Married. Starting a new life. With the man she loved. Could it be true? She was getting married to a man she wanted to use. To use him, she needed to be married to him. She had thought that far ahead, but not far enough. When she told Jordy she was going to be in love, she was joking. Wasn't she?

She had thought herself in love when she was eight . . . and ten . . . and twelve . . . When she was fourteen she tried to seduce Dael. Actually, she had started planning it when she was eleven.

"You're thinking about him again," Matti and Pepper's remembered voices accused her.

She remembered a kiss, and Dael holding her. That had been nice. Very nice indeed. She had been thinking about Damon, about her duty, but had forgotten about her own emotions. About Dael's.

She had ignored everything Dael said. She didn't even remember what he said, and she was trained to remember everything.

She remembered being kissed.

Vray sat down so abruptly that it was almost like falling onto the bench. She clasped her hands in her lap and whispered, "Oh, dear." She felt like she was going to be sick.

Deenit came and knelt before her, taking Vray's hands in hers. "You're cold."

"I—" Vray looked into Deenit's concerned face, and saw Dael's features interposed on his mother's worried visage. "I'm getting what I always wanted." *May the gods help me!*

Deenit helped her to her feet. The guard slipped her cloak around her shoulders, and Vray pulled it close.

"Peanal," Deenit commanded, "get her back to the castle." Deenit stroked Vray's cheek and gave her a reassuring smile. "Don't worry, you'll be fine."

Vray nodded. "Of course," she murmured, but worry and confusion continued to chase around her brain. "I'll be fine. I have to get back." She managed a reassuring smile for Dael's mother. "Come along, Peanal," she said, and preceded the girl out the door.

CHAPTER 11

"Hand me that blanket, would you?"

There was no response. Doron turned, perplexed. She found her husband where she expected to find him, where he'd been since breakfast: seated at the table, one ankle propped on the opposite knee. The baby blanket was also exactly where she'd left it, folded neatly on the table at his elbow.

"Pirse!" She raised her voice. "The blanket."

"Hmmm?" He lifted his gaze and blinked at her. "What was that, love?"

Doron kept one hand on the wriggling Emlie. "Pass me the blanket," she repeated.

"Oh. Certainly." Without disturbing the large book propped open in his lap, Pirse handed her the blanket.

"I'm almost ready," Doron warned him as she deftly finished bundling up the baby. "You'll have to carry the stew."

Now that she'd caught his attention, Pirse cooperated willingly. "I'll get it," he assured her, closing the book as he stood. "Do you have your cloak?"

"Right here."

Doron, her hands full with the baby, did not notice until they were out of the house and sloshing across the yard that Pirse was carrying more than the pot of stew. "What are you bringing that for?"

He glanced at the carefully wrapped book tucked under his left elbow. "This? To read, of course."

"If I knew you were going to spend the entire day reading—Fall Festival day at that—I'd have left you at home!"

"It's a tale to be read to the entire village," he told her. "I'll close the book the moment I've finished."

She pushed the gate open with her elbow and held it for

111

him as he eased past her. A wisp of steam escaped from the
pot, making Doron's stomach rumble. She set a quick pace
toward Timik's barn and the feast that waited there.
"You've been teaching Redmother tales out of that book to
Hanig for the past four years. Why not let her recite it?"

"Not this one. I saved this one for last. She'll learn it
today, and add it to her memory for future Festivals."

"You're worried about something," Doron observed.

He gazed past Timik's barn, into the mountains beyond
the village. "There's never enough time," he said, a tinge of
bitterness in his voice. "I'm beginning to think that a band
of Abstainers leads a more settled life than I do."

"You know we've no choice. Your work takes you away
from Juniper Ridge." She hugged the baby. "My work keeps
me here."

"It's not worry. Not exactly," he admitted. "Everyone's
been most understanding. You're safe here."

"We haven't seen a troop of guards in two years. Even if
they do come, the last thing anyone would tell them was
that they'd seen you, much less that you'd fathered a
Dreamer here."

He somehow freed a hand to assist her in stepping over a
wide rill of water that cut diagonally across the road. "I'd
rather Palle believed that than jump to the other conclusion."

"What other conclusion?" Her footing once more secure,
she moved slightly away from him, until she could see his
face clearly. His expression was not reassuring.

"That she's a Shaper child. A threat to his throne." His
arm tightened over the book. "That's why I'm reading
today. In Dherrica we've forgotten a few important truths
about ourselves. I want everyone to know this tale, know it
in connection with Emlie."

Doron looked down into the sleeping face of her
daughter. "A tale of Dreamer children?" she asked softly.

"It's called the Story of Beginnings."

A wedding among Keepers is a private thing, Dael

thought as he finished plaiting the dark green ribbon into the thin braid on the left side of his head. He didn't know why bridegrooms always braided a few strands of their hair just so their bride could loosen them and take the ribbon. It looked rather like something the horse people would do, but it was the custom in Edian and had been for generations. Women who had been married for many years still frequently wore the marriage ribbons in their own hair on Festival days. Would Vray? Dael thought of how good the dark green would look against his bride's red tresses and found himself smiling. Green, the rich greens of pine forests and emeralds, suited her. Of course, that's why she had chosen it for her wedding color. A woman was supposed to be vain on her wedding day.

The mirror he was using was full length, set up in the bedroom of the quarters assigned for his and his wife's use in the castle. He had returned from patrol late, wanting only to rest, but Damon had been waiting at the gate to make a ceremony of showing him to these rooms. So he had slept here in the big, unfamiliar bed, thereby making the tower his official residence.

For any ordinary wedding, the sitting room of the suite would have been used for the ceremony. They could have exchanged their vows and gifts in private and announced their marriage at the Festival like everyone else. However, ordinary weddings didn't happen in castles. Dael could claim this place as his dwelling, but he and his wife had to start their life together in public. Live it in public too, probably.

Dael bestowed a frustrated glower on his reflection. The girl was up to something. Four and a half years away or not, grown into a beauty or not, he knew his Kitten. She was arranging lives, his included. Dael had just spent a nineday riding the borders, trying to stay angry at her high-handed arrangements. It hadn't worked. All he wanted to do was see her again, and be alone with her. Stones! It had been four years!

At least they'd get to return here eventually. After a

long, hard day. Then what? He adjusted his sword belt over the unfamiliar shape of the knee-length green tunic. He wasn't used to seeing himself in anything but his serviceable guard's uniform and found his reflection a bit disturbing. It wasn't just the tunic, or the braid. He was decked out in more finery than he liked, including a gold neck chain and wide garnet-studded gold wristbands that Nocca and Ruudy and Rose had insisted he needed. It was rather like looking at a complete stranger—or at one of the landowners or merchants who frequented the great hall, unaware of the guard captain who watched over their safety, unnoticed, in the shadows.

Would being married to Vray mean being constantly on display, rather than being effective in the quieter role he preferred? No, it would not. He had worked hard to maintain his quiet spot by the wall.

He squared his shoulders just as Nocca stuck his head in the door. "You're lovely," his tall brother told him. "Preen later. You're wanted in the barracks."

Dael turned on his brother. "Yes, I know. I'll be down in a few minutes. Better go inform the troops I expect to see them looking reasonably sober."

Nocca's wide face split in a grin. "It was a good party. Not every day our captain marries. Too bad you missed it."

"No, it isn't. The last thing I need today is an aching head. Go on."

He waited a few minutes before following Nocca, oddly reluctant to face the joking goodwill and congratulations from the guards who awaited his inspection. Deciding he had better get on with it, he opened the door and stepped into the corridor.

The first thing he saw was Vray, in a rust-colored cloak, standing near her elegantly dressed brother. One of Damon's ringed hands rested on her shoulder. With the thumb of his other hand, he stroked her cheek. Vray was pale. Damon wore the supremely satisfied look of a cat tormenting its prey.

"The fresh air does you good," Damon was saying as

Dael quietly approached. "But I'm afraid you'll find town life too exciting after the seclusion of the Brownmother house."

"You've given me a companion," Vray answered, her voice soft, her eyes downcast. "Someone to watch over me."

"Yes, I have."

Before the prince could add anything more, Dael stepped up behind Vray. He placed his hands on her shoulders and subtly tugged her away from her brother's touch. She moved back at once and leaned into the protective circle of his arms. Dael gave Damon an affable smile. "I trust I'll make a suitable companion. I can never thank Your Highness enough for your choice."

The amusement was gone from Damon's eyes, but his voice was as friendly as Dael's had been. "You're quite welcome, Captain." He waggled an admonishing finger under Vray's nose. "See that you're an appreciative wife."

"Yes, Damon," Vray replied meekly. "I will."

Dael gave the girl's shoulders a slight shake. "Time you started getting ready. You wouldn't want to be late for the ceremony." He released her and gave her a gentle push. "Run along."

Vray went without a word. Dael could only hope she wouldn't leave too many bruises for it later. The kitten he remembered had claws.

"I will care for her," he told Damon. "Just as you wish." *And if you put your hands on my wife again,* he promised silently, *you will deeply regret it.*

He gave the prince a parody of a friendly smile. "Excuse me, but I have to make sure everything is ready for the horsemanship exercises this afternoon. See you at the feast."

"Yes," Damon agreed. "We'll see each other later, Captain."

"The proper way to celebrate gatherings and festivals is in bed," Jeyn murmured contentedly into Ivey's shoulder.

115

Ivey lifted his head to look at her. "Your father wouldn't say that."

She gave a low chuckle. Outside her bedroom window, they could hear the sounds of nearly a thousand people entertaining themselves with more public pursuits than the one he and the princess had just enjoyed. Jeyn snuggled closer to him. "You only call him my father when you're feeling intimidated."

"Your father doesn't intimidate me. He harasses me."

"He wants you to get married."

"No. He wants you to get married. I'm only the intended consort. He wants to know your intentions toward me." *So do I.* "But since you're his darling daughter he doesn't harass you."

"He's been harassing me all summer," she replied. "It's your turn." She sat up, brushing her hair back over one shoulder. "Dad's very fair about such things."

Ivey smiled charmingly. "We could make him happy and announce our marriage today."

She didn't respond at once. Ivey noted the hesitation and reached out to tug on the end of her hair where it rested on the sheet beside him. Her bright smile, he thought, was nervous. "The announcements are over," she said.

"I'm sure they'd all come back to hear about the king's daughter."

She took the strand of hair from between his fingers and absently began braiding it. "I need to confide in you, Ivey."

Sitting up, he folded his legs and gathered the bedcovers around them. The afternoon had grown cloudy, and the breeze coming in the window was cool against his sweaty skin. He couldn't say he was surprised that there was something bothering her. She had been alternately too quiet and too teasing since his return to Raisal two days before. Dektrieb and Feather had warned him that she'd been agitated for several ninedays, but no one knew why. Feather had been relieved to have him back. She thought he would cure Jeyn's moodiness. He'd been willing to give it a try.

116

Stealing a few hours away from the public celebration had seemed like a good step, especially since this was the first chance they'd had to be alone together when both of them were rested enough to enjoy the privacy.

"I'm listening," he said. "Talk to me."

Instead of talking, she slipped out of the bed and plucked her under-tunic out of the pile of clothes they'd left on the floor. She pulled it on, then went and closed the shutters of the window. Ivey waited patiently, studying her pensive expression. Whatever she was about to say, she didn't think he was going to like it. He tensed as the obvious solution hit him. First the architect, now the minstrel? Who had she become infatuated with since he'd left?

"It's Aage," she began.

"What?" The word came out an unmusical screech. Jeyn stared at him. He swallowed and managed a more controlled, "What about Aage?"

"It's about a vision, actually."

"Aage's vision?" Ivey translated doubtfully.

"Well, who else has them? He's had a new one." She folded her arms, then paced away from the window, turned her back on him briefly, turned again, and finally said, "I'm sorry. I'm scared."

That did it. Ivey climbed out of bed and went to her, taking her by the shoulders. At least his fears of being replaced were unfounded. As close as she was to that wizard, Aage would never be a romantic rival. "Of what?"

"Of what the gods want."

"Want from Aage? Are you frightened for him?"

"Yes. No. He's all right now. He was ill for a while."

Ivey waited again, until his curiosity insisted that if he didn't prompt her, they'd be standing here until dawn. "Yes?"

She buried her face against his chest. "I have to do it," came her muffled words. "Aage is right. It's for the best. He will protect the others."

"Which others?"

"Aage and the other wizards."

"Then who will protect them?"

"Aage's son."

He tightened his grip on her shoulders, pushing her back until he could see her face. "Aage's son?" he repeated, doubt worming its way into his gut. "Why do I have the feeling that you don't mean just any Dreamer child?"

"I don't. That was the vision," she continued, tears in her eyes. "Aage is going to father a Dreamer."

"All right." Ivey refused to be awestruck. "What exactly frightens you about Aage becoming a father? Aside from the fact that such a thing has never happened before."

"The fact that the mother will be me."

No words would form in Ivey's mind. Jeyn stepped close to him again, and his arms went around her automatically. Her face against his bare chest was warm and damp, and the next thing he knew she was sobbing. Broken words came to his ears.

"I want to get married . . . have babies with you . . . he says we can't tell anybody . . . I can't keep a secret from you . . . I love him but not like that . . . but he saw our son . . . Ivey!"

Helpless, he patted her shoulder and cradled the back of her head. "He hasn't told anyone? Not Sene, or Savyea, or even Morb?"

She sniffed. "I think it was part of the vision. He's not supposed to talk about it. Not until it's happened."

"Why not?"

"I don't know! Maybe it has to do with the Others. The ones that Aage and Morb battle."

Ivey struggled with his confusion. What could he say? How could he argue against a vision from the gods? It might not be what he liked or what he wanted, but he couldn't deny that it had to be. If Aage had a vision, it had to be respected. Respected, and feared.

Jeyn had every right to be frightened. Terrified, in fact—which, Ivey realized, was exactly how he felt.

"What can I say?" he asked her.

"You won't tell Daddy?"

He took a deep breath. "No. I won't tell your father. Not until you tell me to."

Her voice grew softer. "You'll still love me?"

"Yes," he said. His throat tightened over any further words. All he could do was continue to run his fingers caressingly through her thick hair.

"Thank you for understanding."

"I'm glad you told me."

"I was selfish to tell you. Now you'll worry, too."

He had to smile at her. "You think I wouldn't have worried to find you pregnant some day and not know by whom?"

"There is that," she agreed.

He thought a moment. "Some day," he mused. "Some day soon?"

"I hope so. I want to get it over with!"

"You're not pregnant yet?"

"No."

"Not fertile tonight?"

"You know I'm not."

"Good." He tugged her back to the bed. "We have time yet before anyone will miss us."

CHAPTER 12

It's all a blur, Vray thought as she took another bite of food she couldn't taste. *I'm a Redmother. I'm sure I'll remember it all tomorrow, but right now I can't remember a thing.*

No, that wasn't true. She touched her throat. She remembered Dael's hands reaching into the basket that his father put on the table. There were lots of things in the basket, including a smell of almonds. Yes, she remembered that, and a glint of silver, and a line of pink embroidery on something. She remembered Dael's hands.

She looked sideways, aware of the servants who moved behind the long table, aware of people seated along its length. She was aware of other tables and other people and of the fire blazing in the great hearth and of a great deal of noise that was probably talking and laughter and toasts to the happy couple. Aware. However, she was seeing very little. She saw Dael's hands because she was looking for them. Her left hand rested on the linen-covered table. Dael's right hand easily covered hers. It was warm and heavy and the skin was rough. He wore a plain gold band on his right forefinger. He'd worn that ring as long as she had known him. Nothing about Dael had changed.

Except that now he couldn't send her away anymore, because he had just made a promise to live with her for all their lives. He'd made the promise as he reached into the basket. His hands had come back up holding his token of the marriage promise. From his fingers had dangled a simple gold chain. Hanging from the chain was a faceted emerald pendant the size of his thumbnail. Vray remembered his hands on her throat, fingers brushing the back of her neck as he fastened the clasp.

Vray touched the pendant that rested at the base of her throat, then the ribbon that tied back her hair. She found herself looking into Dael's eyes and smiling. He smiled back.

I must look like an idiot, she thought.

She had no reason to be so happy and she certainly shouldn't let it show. She didn't care. She couldn't help it. She was happy.

Even if it was all taken away from her in an hour, she was going to be happy now.

I don't think I have anything to worry about, Damon thought as he sat next to his sister and watched her besotted worship of her new husband.

The girl was dazed with lust. Damon turned his head and laughed loudly at some feeble joke Uncle Ledo had made. The king had departed an hour ago. For years now, Hion had made no more than a token appearance at the Festivals. In recognition of the importance of the wedding, he had actually witnessed the ceremony and listened to the congratulations of a few representatives of Rhenlan's other Shaper families. He had even remained for the first course of the meal. Probably no one but Damon had noticed exactly when he'd slipped away. A servant, used to the king's habits, had cleared his place.

Damon signaled to another servant to fill his goblet. He stood and waited the few seconds it took for everyone's attention to focus on him.

"It's been a long day," he said to murmurs from the diners. "Long and joyful. Especially joyful for my family. First," he went on, "I wish to officially welcome home my wandering sister. Dear Vray, you've kept yourself from Edian for too long." The suddenly attentive girl blushed and ducked her head demurely as voices called out agreement with Damon.

"However, you're with us now and we are happy to have you. We are happier still," he declared, gesturing toward Dael, "to celebrate our family's union with our dear friend Dael. There was a prophecy made long ago," he reminded the crowd. "You know my personal feelings about Dreamer nonsense. Nonetheless, the prophecy was that children could be born out of the proper cycle to this generation of Keepers and Shapers."

A low murmur of acknowledgment rose from the crowd. Damon gave an elegant and dismissive shrug. "That may be true, although it is hardly the real importance of today's marriage of Shaper princess and Keeper guard. The true purpose for us, the rulers of Rhenlan, is to honor a Keeper we truly admire, a Keeper who serves us well and who we are proud to call friend. By marrying my sister, Dael becomes one with the ruling house. He joins his strength to ours, and together we will all grow stronger. We will better serve the people of Rhenlan. I want it to be known that though this marriage will please the Dreamers, it was not done for them. Dael and Vray did not marry to grant the Dreamers another generation of their own kind. We have chosen that the captain and the princess wed for the sake of every useful person in Rhenlan, Keeper and Shaper alike." He raised his goblet and everyone followed suit. "I offer this final toast, then, to the bride and groom, symbols of the unity of the people of Rhenlan."

Damon drained his cup and waited until the applause built into cheers before taking his seat once more. The cheering continued as Dael led Vray through the room and out of the hall. Damon watched them go, slowly sipping his wine. There went the hope of every young Keeper from now on. It would be known that, if they served him well, they might be rewarded with Shaper daughters or sons—and the Shaper property attached to them.

He wouldn't be generous with such rewards, but the hope would be there. Hope was such a useful tool.

Thank you, cousin Jenil, for giving me this new way to manipulate the foolish.

The dance ended with a flourish from Timik's big drum. Laughing and breathless, Doron half fell away from Pirse. He caught her hand again to steady her. His shirt had fallen open with the exertion of the string of lively dances Timik had inflicted on everyone, and his black hair was mussed. Doron compared him to the sturdy, good-natured village men on either side, all equally disheveled, now leaving the center of the barn for the kegs and tables against the wall. They were fine, healthy people, but the prince—compared to the rest, Pirse shone with vigor and sensuality.

"All right?" he asked her curiously.

"I'd better check Emlie," she said, and slipped away through the crowd.

At this time of year one of the lambing pens was usually set aside for the smaller children. All had fallen asleep several hours ago. Doron bent over Emlie on her cot and adjusted the blanket that covered her back. How they could sleep through the talk and laughter, not to mention the thunder of booted feet on barn floor to Timik's enthusiastic accompaniment, no parent understood. Still, each Festival and gathering was the same, children underfoot far into the evening, until one by one they ended up in the secluded corner set aside for them, to be eventually bundled home by exhausted adults.

Doron wasn't exhausted yet, but she did need something to drink. She brushed her hair back off her forehead as she worked her way toward one of the beer kegs. Timik had already finished his rest and was picking up his drum, a calculating expression on his face as he surveyed the returning dancers.

"—could use your help," the tanner said as Doron finally reached the bench where the kegs were resting.

She looked up, alerted by something in the man's voice. Sure enough, he was speaking to her husband. Pirse, his back to Doron, replied, "Only if you can wait until mid winter. I've got to be away until then."

"Do you indeed?" Doron asked with venomous calm, her thirst forgotten. "And when are you leaving?"

The tanner excused himself and left quickly. Pirse said, "Can we discuss this later?"

"What happened to all that talk earlier, about how much you long for a settled life?"

"It wasn't just talk. You know that."

"Can you not spend even a nineday of the autumn at home? Emlie hardly knows you."

By this time he looked so thoroughly uncomfortable that she knew what he was going to say. "I was going to tell you in the morning. I have to be in Live Oak for the double half of the moons." He glanced around them, but they were alone. Everyone else had returned to the cleared dance floor. "I received word on my way here. It didn't work the first time."

"What a terrible hardship." Doron folded her arms over her chest, foiling his attempt to take her hand. "Another few days in Kamara's bed. I have such sympathy for both of you."

"Doron." Pirse spoke levelly, but there was a warning spark in his eyes that cooled her anger somewhat. "I refuse to argue about this. I admit Kamara is a fine woman, worthy mother to a future ruler of Dherrica. You and I both know that she is nothing to me beyond that. Yes, you do know it," he continued, "when you're not wrapped up in this childish jealousy." Abruptly, his voice softened. "I'm not Betajj. I'm not going to leave you."

"Oh, you're hopeless!" Her loud cry was covered by the first staccato beats from the drum. She stepped closer to Pirse, until she could stare directly into his eyes. "You'll come straight back?"

"By the time Keyn reaches full. I promise."

"Dance with me," she commanded, grabbing his wrists.

"One more," he agreed. "Then I take you to bed."

Vray pushed the lock firmly in place, then turned and leaned her back against the bedroom door. Dael sat on the edge of the bed wearing a linen nightshirt too thin for the autumn night. Her own nightdress was just as impractical. Both of them took the time to eye what they saw.

They both broke out laughing.

Vray crossed her arms beneath her breasts and said, "This wasn't quite how I meant to start."

"Meant to start what?" Dael asked with a teasing smile. He stood and stepped toward her. The unmistakable outline beneath his nightshirt showed exactly what he meant to start.

Making love to her husband was possibly the one thing Vray wanted most in the whole world. Unfortunately, Damon's little speech had brought her stunned thoughts back into focus. She had to say certain things to Dael before they could be together. Perhaps, after she was done speaking, he wouldn't want them to be together after all.

He placed his hands on her waist, but Vray ducked under his arm and put a table between them. He turned toward her with a smirk. "Shy?"

"I've never been shy about you, Dael. We have to talk."

"No, we don't. Even if we do—let's do it later."

"Sit down."

Much to her surprise, he obeyed. He crossed his legs and his arms and said, "All right. Talk."

Vray stayed by the table, nervously gripping the carved edge. She licked her lips and began. "When I arranged for us to wed, I didn't do it out of love. I didn't do it out of concern for you. I did it for Rhenlan and I did it for myself and I don't intend to apologize. I do intend to tell you the truth."

"Ah," he said, sounding not in the least offended. "I knew you were up to something. You told me as much when you first returned to Edian."

"I know. I just couldn't tell you everything. Not then. I need the guard," she went on. "I need the most popular man in Edian at my side." She felt her throat tighten with emotion and her next words didn't come out as sharp and ruthless as she had intended. "I need you."

He stood and slowly edged around the table, as though he was afraid she might run. He was right. From the moment they left the great hall, running had been an option that lurked very temptingly at the back of her mind.

"Why, precisely, do you need me?" Dael asked.

Because you're the only man I'll ever really love. The words caught somewhere deep in her chest. She felt tears begin to spill, but cleared her aching throat and managed to say, "Because I am going to depose my brother."

She swiped her eyes with one hand—a hand Dael caught and held between his.

"You're cold," he said. "Come to bed."

His calm response drove her to distraction. "Are you listening to me!?"

He nodded and stroked a hand through her hair. "You're going to depose Damon. Anything else?"

This wasn't how she had expected him to react. Why didn't he yell at her? Or threaten to denounce her? Why was he holding her—and why was she quivering like a complete coward? She had rehearsed this encounter over and over since she'd first worked out the details on the south shore of Lake Hari. It wasn't going at all as she had planned.

"Yes," she answered his question. "There is something else."

She didn't know quite when he'd picked her up, but she liked being carried by him. When he put her on the bed, she held on to him and pulled him down beside her.

"What?"

"I love you."

He kissed her temple. "I know. You've always loved me. Does it interfere with your plans?"

She shook her head. With a trembling hand, she touched her fingertips to his temple, then traced the outline of his face while her eyes looked deeply into his.

"I didn't think so," he said. "I suppose we'll just have to work around it."

"Dael?"

He smiled and reached to close the bed curtains. "Don't worry, Kitten," he told her. "I love you, too."

CHAPTER 13

"They said I'd find you here."

Dael stepped through the doorway of the guards' bathhouse. He was surprised to see his father standing in the dust of the training ground. "What is it, Dad?"

"I was just visiting your wife. Thought I'd stop by and see my son while I was here. Haven't seen you since the wedding."

"Right, Dad." It had only been three days. Loras was not one to break up his working day with casual visits to friends or family. Dael rubbed the already damp towel down his bare chest before tossing it onto the pile of used laundry. His muscles were pleasantly tired, but no longer sore after the long soak he'd enjoyed. The on-duty attendant appeared from the other side of the building and thrust a dry tunic into his hands. Dael pulled it over his head, picked his sword and belt out of the rack, pulled on his boots, and started across the courtyard. The afternoon sun was warmer than usual for the season and a few people lingered in the pleasant light of the courtyard. Loras accompanied Dael past the walls to the road leading into town.

"Vray looks as beautiful as always," the goldsmith continued idly. "I brought her a new pair of earrings. Tiny oak leaves with acorns. I think she likes them."

"Yes, Dad." They were well away from the castle gates by this time. "Now why are we talking, really?"

"A message from Jordy," was the succinct reply. "A village has asked for some swords. How many are still in stores?"

Dael sighed, and walked a little faster, leaving his father momentarily behind. Under his breath, he muttered, "Jordy, what are you getting me into?"

A few strides later he felt the familiar long-fingered hand

on his shoulder. "Dael?" his father said. "Nothing's wrong, is there?"

"Wrong?" Dael looked over his shoulder at the castle. Vray's tower window faced the town, not that she'd be gazing out at this hour. She'd be working at something, somewhere. Vray was already working at undermining her brother's power. Just as Jordy was enthusiastically working at undermining her brother's power.

No. Not just Damon's power. Shaper power. Stones!

"You look worried," Loras prompted. "About the swords? Can't you get them?"

"Oh, I can get them. The question is who they will be used against."

Loras frowned at him, honestly confused. "We're hoping they won't be used at all, remember? They're for defense, against Damon's troops."

"The king's troops," Dael corrected.

"No," Loras countered. "You are the captain of the king's guard. Your troops never misbehave."

"Guards serve Shapers. Ruling Shapers, Dad. My wife intends to be a ruling Shaper."

"She'll do a much better job of it than many others I could name."

"Dad, think. What are we doing? What does Jordy intend that we do? Overthrow all Shaper rule. All Shapers, Dad."

Loras looked doubtful. "Vray has nothing to fear from us."

"If she intends to be queen she does! Whose side am I on, Dad? A year ago it was so simple. I thought Vray was dead. I wanted Damon overthrown. I agreed with everything Jordy said. Shapers had gotten out of control. We could do better for ourselves. That's what I thought. Now, watching Vray, knowing what she is capable of, I'm not so sure. I admire her. I agree with her plans. The trouble is, I also agree with Jordy's plans." Not to mention Sene of Sitrine's ideas, which had given Dael many hours of contemplation. He kept that complication to himself. "What will Jordy do to Vray?"

"He won't do anything to her!"

"When she opposes him? All right, maybe he won't do anything, but he'll expect me to. She's going to be in his way, in our way. He won't believe that she'll just settle down to be my faithful wife, keeping my house and raising a family. Which she won't do. Will he expect me to lock her up?"

"What are you telling me?" Loras demanded. "You're not going to help us anymore?"

"Us. I'm a Keeper, too. That's my problem! Jordy's right. Vray's right. Neither of them will acknowledge that the other's right, and I'm caught in the middle!"

They walked slowly down the hill, silent for the space of a dozen strides. At last, Loras said, "Right now the thing to concentrate on is that Damon is wrong. I understand your concern, but I think Jordy and Vray would at least agree that Damon is the most important threat. Whichever one of them prevails, it'll be better than Damon. Who knows? Maybe they won't ever have to meet."

Dael gave him a skeptical look. "Right, Dad."

The road entered the north square, uninhabited except for a few dogs and people gathered near the well.

"Can you get those swords or not?" Loras asked.

Dael kicked at a pebble with his toe. He had to get back to the training ground. "I'll get them. How many?"

After a morning of hard work in the practice yard, Chasa stopped in his rooms on his way to the bathhouse. He found the shirt he was looking for and was almost out the door again when a timid voice stopped him.

"Chasa?"

Feather sounding meek? Feather was never meek. Rather alarmed, Chasa went through to their bedroom. His wife stood, pale and wide-eyed near the window. In the same odd, guilty-child voice, she continued, "I threw up."

Chasa frowned. "Was there something wrong with breakfast? I ate the same things you did, and I feel all right."

"I threw up yesterday, too."

"It could be an illness. Do you want me to send for a Brownmother?"

"And two days before that," Feather went on.

"Feather—"

Her voice became even quieter than before. "The night of the double full, remember?"

"The double full," he repeated. He knew what she meant. A few ninedays ago, Sheyn and Keyn had both been at the full together. The phase of the moons which governed Feather's body cycle.

She was still talking. "My bleeding hasn't started yet, either. It always starts within the second nineday after the fulls. I've always been regular before and—"

Chasa's whoop of joy cut off her nervous babble. "My lovely Filanora!" he crowed. "You're pregnant!" He swooped down on her, scooped her into his arms, and began dancing around the room.

"We're going to have a baby! We're going to have a baby!" he sang, fitting the words to one of Ivey's livelier melodies and swaying in time to his own beat.

"You smell and I'm going to throw up on you," Feather declared. She loosened her clasp around his neck long enough to yank hard on one of his ears. "You really are going to make me sick again," she yelled over his singing.

He stopped and set her—gently—back on her feet at once. He grabbed her hands instead and squeezed them. "I won't do it again," he promised. "I won't do anything you don't like. Are you feeling all right? Would you like to sit down? Can I get you something?"

"You are a prince," she informed him. "Isn't there some rule against a prince acting like an idiot?"

"I don't think so," he replied, grinning idiotically and enjoying every moment of it. "Haven't you noticed that people make all sorts of allowances for about-to-be-new parents?"

"Parents?" Her pale, wide-eyed expression—which he now recognized as panic—returned. "I'm not ready. I don't know how to be a mother."

"You'll be wonderful."

"I don't know anything about how to be a mother. I don't remember my own mother. I was raised by a Greenmother. What kind of training is that for raising a— oh."

"You grew up in a Brownmother house. Mothers everywhere. Besides, Jenil did all right with you. Spoiled you, but turned you into a passable person. Come on. Dad got back from the border last night. We've got to tell him!"

Ignoring her squeaked protest, he kept a tight grip on his wife's hand and started searching for the king. Feather had to trot to keep up with his quick strides as they hurried from room to room. Sene wasn't on the terrace, which had been Chasa's first guess, or in the library, but two of his map rolls were missing, so they went to the large meeting hall.

The maps were set edge to edge, spread to their full extent on the smooth tile floor. A large book lay nearby, pen and ink pot next to it. Sene stood at the other side of the maps, arms folded and chin on his chest. He didn't notice them until they were all the way into the room, breathing quickly from their rush through the building.

"You're filthy," Sene said to Chasa. "Now what are you two up to?"

"We're going to have a baby," Chasa announced.

His father's expressive face displayed a giddy succession of emotions, from incomprehension to exultant delight, all within a matter of seconds. Sene's smile creased his entire face. "My boy," he said, and strode forward to envelop Chasa in a bear hug. "I am proud of you." He stepped back. "More than proud. I don't know what to say." He turned to Feather, still brimming over with happiness.

"No swooping." Chasa's warning stopped his father's enthusiastic step forward. "Or swinging. She's got morning sickness."

"Oh." The king restrained himself to a warm hug, then kissed the top of Feather's head and stepped back again. He searched first Feather's face, then Chasa's. "A baby," he said with wonder. "You really did it."

"We really have," Feather agreed.

"Who else have you told? No one?" Sene rubbed his hands. "Let's see. Who else should know? Well, everyone should know, but who shall we tell first? Do you mind if I tell some people? It's your news, after all."

Chasa laughed. "Go ahead, Dad. You've been waiting for this for years. Tell anyone you like. We don't mind. Right, Feather?"

"You're only enjoying this," she accused Sene, "because you won't be the one getting up with the baby in the middle of the night."

"Ah, but that's because I've already been through that with my own children—and I had to deal with twins."

"With two wet nurses and a nanny to help you," Chasa teased him.

"True. Aage can play nanny to this baby. Still, I did my share with my own children. Now I get to be the grandfather, which means I'll enjoy all the pleasures of a young child with none of the work." His cheerful voice softened. "Grandfather. I'm going to like that."

Chasa waved him toward the door. "Well, if you're so excited about it, go tell someone."

"I'll do that." Patting their shoulders as he passed, he strode out into the hallway. A rich, booming, "Dektrieb!" floated back to them.

Chasa wrapped his arms around his wife. "Well, he's happy."

"Yes. Are you?" she asked softly.

He hugged her. "Yes."

"You know what?" She hugged him back. "So am I."

"What are these?"

Vray looked up from her book at the appalled voice. Teza stood before her, expression full of distaste, a pair of soiled gloves pinched between thumb and forefinger of her right hand.

"Gloves?" Vray answered hesitantly. The servant glowered. Vray tried a friendly smile, and tried to think of an explanation. "Gardening?"

Teza shook her head, braids swinging. "Indeed? They'd be more suited to driving a wagon. Smells like horse sweat, if you ask me. How did they get into your belongings?"

Vray closed the book carefully. Leaving it on the table, she stood and snatched the gloves away from the offended woman. The familiar scent of Stockings's sweat recalled her brief apprenticeship on the road. "They are mine. I didn't ask you to look through that bag. Those are my private possessions." Had the prince set her to snooping? It would be a shame if Teza turned out to be one of her brother's pawns. She really liked the woman.

"I was putting your private possessions in your cedar chest. The place where you've always kept your private possessions," Teza reminded her. "I had it brought from storage. I have to keep this place organized, don't I, Highness? Do you want those smelly old things in with your dolls and storybooks? And what about that leaf collection? I was going to ask if you wanted that thrown out. Or those locks of Captain Dael's hair. You collected some every year from the time you were nine until they sent you—" Her rush of words stopped and she blushed. "The rumor among the guards is that you were at Soza. Were you really? With no one to look after you? You, a Redmother and a princess. I wouldn't credit such a story, except that your hands are rougher than any kitchen maid's, and your elbows and knees are a disgrace. It's a wonder the captain will have you in his bed."

Vray's cheeks burned as she became more and more bemused and embarrassed. "All right, Teza. We've known each other for a long time and I do appreciate your efforts. I'll take care of these. You can toss the leaves on the fire, but I'll keep the hair, thank you. Just put it in the chest." She smiled with more sincerity. "My old cedar chest? Who put it in storage after I left?"

Teza looked cautiously around the room, then took a step closer to Vray, almost close enough to whisper in her ear. "I think we have to be careful around Sedri. She's a good girl, but thinks Prince Damon fancies her. I've told her he never takes Keepers to bed, but she's after his favor. The other maid's from a country village the guards raided for supplies and recruits a few seasons ago. She came to Edian so her family wouldn't starve. She's all right. I've noticed you being cautious with all of us. I approve. But those gloves! I don't know why, but to me they're evidence you've been up to something you couldn't do in Soza. Seems to me I remember seeing a girl about your size and shape running errands for a carter in the square last spring. She reminded me of you at the time, but I didn't see how that was possible." Her face went very pale and Vray knew her expression had given her away. "It was you, wasn't it?"

"Have you told anyone else?" Vray grabbed the woman by her shoulders. "Will you tell anyone else?"

Teza's surprise gave way to indignation. "I most certainly have not and will not! They thought you were in Soza. You weren't. Good for you. Now, calm down. You've got more important things to think about than whether or not your servants go running off to tell your brother every little detail of your life. Your brother finds out exactly what I want him to and no more."

Vray stared at Teza. "Why should you be loyal to me?" she asked. "My brother's favor is more valuable than mine."

Teza's eyes glittered. "For now, perhaps. What about in the future? I have grandchildren. I want them to grow up in a law-respecting kingdom. I knew the minute you forced the king to obey the prophecy that you were going to challenge your brother."

Vray cleared her suddenly dry throat. "I didn't force anyone to do anything."

"Not force," Teza amended with a knowing smile. "You influenced His Majesty in the best interests of the kingdom. People appreciate that. You'll see. Keep it up, Your Highness." Gently, she retrieved the gloves from the floor where Vray had dropped them. "I'll toss these on the fire, too.

You can remember your carter friends without any mementos, I think."

Feeling a bit overwhelmed, Vray sat back down by her book. "Very well. Thank you, Teza. Did you have any other questions?"

"When are you two going to have a baby?" the servant asked, then stomped off before Vray could think of an answer.

CHAPTER 14

Palle said nothing during the short walk from the great hall to Damon's private audience chamber. He hated visiting Edian. He hated everything about the expedition. He never liked traveling, and he positively loathed the windswept, monotonous road across the Atowa Plateau. Every time he opened his mouth he attracted curious glances. No matter how carefully he chose his words, the inflections of Dherrican speech attracted attention. Most of all, he hated the fear that drove him to Damon for assistance.

The Rhenlan prince was issuing orders, calling for quarters to be prepared for the King and his party, food and wine to be served in the audience chamber, certain troop corporals to present themselves at the central guards' barracks, and a groom to be found and sent to the castle. When the last messenger was dismissed and they were finally alone, Damon faced him and said, "You have five minutes. What has really brought you here?"

Resentfully, Palle said, "I did not lie to your father. I want the boy. I want him challenged, and his interference in Dherrica's affairs ended."

"Such urgency. Why Palle? Why now?"

Urgency was not the word Palle would have chosen to describe his position. The word was too mild, the circumstances far more desperate. "There are rumors that Pirse has fathered a child."

"A child?" Damon snapped. "An heir?"

The Rhenlaner's open concern pleased Palle immensely. "Any direct descendant of Dea would have that right, yes."

"Don't patronize me. How certain are you? What sort of rumors?"

"Recurring rumors. A child exists somewhere, Highness. The claim that Pirse is its father is accepted without question as true. My attempts to learn more than that have failed. Too few people will talk to my guards. You have followers skilled in gathering information. I had even hoped you would have heard something of this already."

"I haven't been looking for information about children." Damon clasped his hands behind his back and paced the width of the room, scowling. "If this is true, even if you bring Pirse to justice, you will have only secured the throne for this unknown and its family. You would be regent, no more." He stopped, glittering eyes fixed on Palle. "There can't be that many possible mothers for such a child. I thought you had the other Shaper families of Dherrica well in hand."

"I have! As soon as I first heard this rumor, I checked to see if there had been any recent births, any young women gone from their homes under mysterious circumstances."

"And?"

"Nothing, Highness."

With savage sarcasm, Damon said, "I understand you have no direct experience in this matter, but believe me, no child can exist without a mother."

"Once it is born it can," Palle replied, stung into sharpness. "Pirse respects the danger I present to him, never forget that. He hides this child from me, just as he hides himself. With a suitable wet-nurse it could be anywhere in Dherrica. Or," he suggested darkly, "in certain neighboring villages."

Abruptly, Damon's expression relaxed, and a condescending smile touched his lips. "You were correct to tell me about this. We'll face the danger together, you and I. Allow a nineday for my people to reach the mountains. Within the nineday after that, they will bring word to you in Bronle."

"Bronle? I was not intending to return so quickly." He had counted on a long stay with the Rhenlan court as compensation for the rigors of his cross-country journey. He was Rhenlan's neighbor, a king equal in rank to Hion. He deserved banquets in his honor, and gifts from Edian's merchants, and he wanted to see a demonstration of swordsmanship by the famous Captain Dael.

"I would if I were you. I would not have left in the first place."

Damon's nonchalance unsettled Palle. "Why not? I could not have entrusted such a delicate matter to a messenger, could I?"

"Perhaps you should have. Or perhaps your guard, the citizens of your town, are so loyal you don't have to worry about what they would do if, in your absence, Prince Pirse returned to the castle and proclaimed himself king."

Palle's hands grew clammy. "He couldn't. He murdered the queen. Everyone knows that."

"You're right. It would be an incredible risk. I wouldn't even mention it, if it weren't for the popular support he seems to have among the more ignorant residents of Dherrica."

"He's no threat once I catch him." Palle conquered his nervousness. "My request to your father still stands. Help me locate him, and we'll worry about the child later."

"As it happens, I have a fairly recent report on Pirse's movements. We'll confirm it when we speak to the corporals, if you like."

"Where is he? Is he near?" Palle asked eagerly. The entire wretched trip would be worthwhile if it led him to his nephew.

"He spent the early part of the summer dragon killing," Damon said. "For the past few ninedays however, my sources assure me, he has not moved from the mountains of southern Dherrica."

"Rock and Pool," Palle whispered, shock bringing the boyhood exclamation to his lips. "He might be only four days from Bronle. He might be there even now."

Politely, Damon enquired, "Shall I tell the king you won't be staying after all?"

"Yes. Absolutely." Palle moved toward the door. "My escort. I must notify my escort at once. We'll need fresh horses."

"Of course, Your Majesty. Anything we can do to help."

Palle stopped listening. Let the prince laugh at him. It didn't matter. He was going back; back to Dherrica where he belonged.

Nothing would matter unless he kept Pirse out of Bronle.

A strong wind howled across the town. It blew away the afternoon warmth, pushing heavy clouds across the sky to bring the night on sooner. Vray felt resentful of the wind and the stolen light. Resentful, but not afraid. She'd long since stopped quaking at the sound of wind. She stood by her window, one hand holding back the heavy curtains, and watched dots of light flare to life in the town below the castle. Her thoughts were restless but unfocused.

She didn't turn when she heard the door open behind her, or at the sound of a familiar tread on the carpet, or at the touch of a warm hand on her shoulder. She did say, "Dael," and take a half-step back to lean against him. He smelled of straw and horses. It made her think of Stockings, and Jordy's well-kept barn.

Her restlessness focused. She was homesick.

Dael sighed and said, "Vray." He sounded hesitant, troubled. She turned to look at him. He looked troubled, too, and there was a bruise on his left cheek.

Vray swallowed a smile, which then came out in her voice. "Have you been fighting?"

He touched the fresh bruise. "Yes."

She put her fingers over his. "Someone actually managed to hit you?"

He slipped his fingers out from under hers and put both hands on her shoulders, turning her to face him fully. "It happens. I trained Maric, and he's good."

"What condition did you leave him in?"

"Unconscious." He sighed again. "Vray?"

"Yes?"

He paused for the space of a dozen heartbeats. "I should have asked this before. Where were you, those years you were gone?"

139

Vray thought about her answer. She remembered herself in Broadford at this time last year, teaching Pepper to bake, Matti playing by the fire, the click of Cyril's loom, Tob bringing in firewood, Jordy joking with the visiting Canis and Herri. *I was home,* she thought.

"At Soza," she said, giving her husband part of the truth. The part of the truth he'd just been dealing with, from the look of him. "Was Maric stationed there?"

He nodded, mouth tight with anger.

"If he said he had sex with me, he probably did," she went on. "Several guards did, in the years I was there."

The fingers on her shoulders tightened painfully. "Soza? Four years at Soza? That's where I send guards as punishment."

"I know."

"Why didn't you get word to me?"

The questions, "How?" and "What could you have done?" were considered and put aside. "I was sent there by the king. I was sent there for the same reason other difficult people—children or guards—are sent there. To learn discipline."

"You did nothing wrong!"

"A law reader would disagree with you. I defied my father and older brother. The punishment was legal. Besides, I did learn discipline. I could have run away, maybe. But what good would it have done?" She shrugged off his hands.

A sudden howl of wind filled her head with vivid memories of Soza. She paced away from the window and Dael. When she turned, she saw that his hand had gone to the pommel of his sword. "There was nothing you could have done. Do you imagine I didn't think about it?"

Temptation rose in her. She could tell him of the nights spent lying awake, listening to the wind, imagining elaborate escapes, imagining Dael coming to her rescue. She could, but she would not. There was no reason to make a burden of guilt for him out of the dreams that had been her only comfort.

"If I had run away I would have been declared an Abstainer," Vray told him. "Your duty would have been to hunt me down. I would have died—and Damon would have won an even greater victory than he already had."

"You could have died at Soza!"

There was a great deal of pain in his eyes. Vray tried to lighten it. She held up her hands, still work-roughened despite so many ninedays back at the castle. "I learned to cook," she told him, "and clean, and how to weave, a little. I'm proud of those skills." She also learned patience. Deception. How to use every little advantage. How to survive. Damon sent her to Soza to teach her a lesson. She learned. Without the years there she would not have learned the skills she needed to defeat him.

She smiled at Dael. He relaxed a little, still troubled, but no longer suffering for her. Another deceit on her part. She showed him only the smile, not the cold, hard reason for it. He deserved comfort, not one more thing to worry about. "I'm almost grateful for Soza," she told her husband, and stepped forward into his warm embrace.

"I don't think I'll come to the Remembering," the old man told Dael. "I have cases to hear."

"You'd be forgiven for postponing them this once." Dael put a comforting hand on Law Reader Oskin's thin shoulder.

Vray watched the pair as she walked beside them, away from the burial ground. The morning was uncomfortably cold. Thick clouds overhead promised that the afternoon Remembering would be equally unpleasant. She was grateful that she was not the Redmother who would have to stand out in a cold wind, above a crowd of mourning friends and neighbors, her head bared to whatever precipitation might fall from the sky. She shivered. There was nothing worse than cold ears.

"I don't want to postpone them," Oskin complained. "Life goes on."

"Who will witness?" Vray spoke up. She hated to be dif-

---

ficult, but they had just buried Oskin's regular witness and her grandson apprentice. The two had died within hours of each other, victims of a severe fever that was causing much sickness in one of the lakeside streets. So far only these two had died. The Brownmothers were frantically working to assure that no others would follow.

Oskin shrugged listlessly. "I'll find someone." He looked sideways at the tall guard captain. "Dael. You've stood by me before."

"Not today," Dael said. "I'm sorry."

The old law reader's shoulders drooped. Old, Vray thought. Old and bird-boned, a fragile, dried-up man. Also one of the sharpest, most compassionate minds in the kingdom. His scrupulous fairness over the years had not endeared him to Hion or Damon. So far he had not attracted their open displeasure, mostly because he concentrated his intellect on judging Keepers, and didn't involve himself with anything to do with royal policies.

It was time to change that. Vray cleared her throat.

"I'd be pleased to attend you today, Law Reader," she said.

Dael looked at her suspiciously. Oskin merely looked surprised. "You? Why?"

"Yes," Dael echoed, "why?"

"It's important that I reacquaint myself with Rhenlan, remember?" she told Dael with a sweet smile. "Everything concerning Rhenlan. Law Reader Oskin hears cases from all over the kingdom. I could learn a great deal from working with him."

Oskin dismissed her suggestion with an irritable snort. "You'd get bored within the first hour. I need a dedicated Witness, not someone amusing herself on a whim."

"Hardly a whim. You forget. I'm a Redmother. I know how to listen. I know how to remember. I even," she added decisively, "know how to write."

"She does have some useful skills," Dael said. "Perhaps you should make use of her."

"I will be happy to come every day until the

Brownmothers have located another witness for you," Vray told the old man. "Your work is important, Law Reader. Let me help you."

Oskin's eyes had black circles of weariness and grief under them, but he managed a frosty smile for her. "Every day, Your Highness?"

"For as long as you need me."

"That would be interesting. All right." He walked more quickly up the street. "Come along. I'll have to show you the record books, and familiarize you with today's cases."

Dael bent down to kiss her and whispered, "Whatever you're up to, good luck."

"Thanks." She squeezed his callused hand and hurried after Oskin.

CHAPTER 15

"We must be far enough."

"A few more minutes. The moons are just rising."

"I know. Please stop, Aage. We're miles from anyone."

"Don't tell me you're nervous?"

"My brother loves sailing, not me."

"This is a nice little boat."

"Little is too generous a word." Jeyn nudged him with her foot. "If the wind doesn't change, we'll never get back before dark."

"The wind will change. I'm good with weather, remember?"

"You know what you're doing," Jeyn agreed. "I know, I know. I'm nervous. But I'm not panicking," she added quickly. "If I didn't trust you, wizard mine, I'd have jumped overboard and swum for shore hours ago."

"A man couldn't ask for a more sincere compliment."

"You probably say that to all your lovers before they drown."

Aage tilted his head back, measuring the shadows cast by mast and sails. Sometime in the last half hour the sun had reached and passed the zenith. Therefore, Sheyn and Keyn, invisible behind the midday glare of blue sky, were above the horizon. The moons were in the same phase together, first quarter, and double first quarter was the phase of Jeyn's fertility. If she didn't become pregnant this time, they would have to wait half a year before another occasion arose. Aage didn't intend to let anything interfere with this chance.

Watching him, Jeyn prompted, "Now?"

"Now." He brought the prow into the wind and Jeyn rose gracefully to her knees to furl the sails. Aage set the sea anchor and secured the boom and tiller against the gentle rocking of the sea swell. The mild sea was matched by a cloudless sky: clear, serene, benevolent. Confidence growing, Aage reached into the storage locker for the supplies he'd brought.

Jeyn came aft to help. The two of them could sit side by side in the bottom of the boat, but it was a tight fit. When they lay down, their feet would be resting below the tiller and their heads nearly touching the well of the centerboard. Not a spacious bed, or a comfortable one, but the privacy could not have been equaled anywhere else.

Aage finished preparing the first goblet and handed it to Jeyn. "This is the bitter one. You'd better drink it as quickly as you can."

She finished the contents in a few gulps, then made a terrible face, letting her tongue hang out of her mouth. "Bleacch," she said. "What a horrible thing to do to perfectly good wine."

"That's the worst of it, I promise."

She regarded him suspiciously. "I thought you said there was a second dose. Something I have to eat."

He reached into the locker and brought out a small bowl containing three small, seed-coated balls. "Yes, but it has to act more slowly. I put it in this honey-crunch candy. You won't notice a thing."

She licked her lips, still looking unhappy. "I hope you're right."

Aage leaned forward and gently kissed her, his mouth open, his tongue caressing her lips. What she considered a bitter aftertaste was a tingle of subtly crafted power that penetrated his skin. He opened his eyes again, searching her face. He saw no hesitancy or fear. A trace of embarrassment, perhaps, but mostly affection and trust. He stretched past her to put the bowl of sweets next to the centerboard, then gathered her into his arms for a second, more thorough, kiss.

The tiller creaked and water lapped against the hull, delicate accompaniment as they gradually undressed one another. For a few sweet moments, Aage relaxed into the rhythm of their foreplay, closing out every sensation except the touch of her sun-warmed skin against his own. Those minutes ended too soon. He was finding pleasure and giving it, but that was not why they had come together. He used the experience she had teased him about, set his hands to continue drawing her toward greater and greater physical arousal, but stopped paying conscious attention to what his body was doing. He needed his concentration elsewhere.

Bending the power, he tested the progress of the elixir through Jeyn's body. Carefully, he began to adjust the process, pulling the power inward here, directing it away there. As the balance improved, he began to experience the pulsing of the power as another level of pleasure, compatible to the forces that moved within his body, but much stronger.

He pushed harder. The web brightened, coming into his awareness, growing more tangible second by second. The moment came and Jeyn stiffened, eyes flying open as she became aware of the lines of power that now touched within her body.

She was tense, on the edge of fulfillment. Her hands had been urging him to enter her, but she paused, staring past his shoulder. Her lips whispered, "Aage?"

He raised his head, rediscovering the vision possible through his eyes. Fleetingly, he saw what she saw, what any Keeper or Shaper would have seen had he and Jeyn been incautious enough to have attempted this coupling anywhere near Raisal.

The boat was englobed by a thousand pinpricks of light. They glowed with the eerie intensity of a phantom cat's eyes, pulsated in a way that tugged at the stomach and made the head spin. Aage had never seen a phenomenon quite like it before, but then, to his knowledge, no one had ever bent the power in quite this way before.

Jeyn's arms went around his neck, dragging him down so that she could bury her face against his shoulder.

"Close your eyes," he whispered, nuzzling her hair. "Don't look."

He entered her, and her hips lifted to welcome him. He gasped as physical sensation and bending power assaulted him on more levels than he had known existed. Despite Jeyn's renewed, eager squirming, he held still long enough to fumble the pieces of honey-crunch out of the bowl and feed them one by one into her panting mouth. She chewed and swallowed each quickly, more interested in his kisses than in the sticky sweetness, oblivious to the new thrust of the power as her body absorbed the carefully prepared dragon powder.

They moved, bodies establishing a rhythm; Aage no longer sure that he was in control of the power that coursed around them in ever-tightening spirals. In the last instant, he opened his eyes one more time. The sparkling globe had tightened around them, purple-black darkness filling everything between the points of light, holding them suspended, out of touch with sea or sky. Even the boat and its bed of rumpled blankets were lost somewhere beyond the web. He was alone with her, their two bodies the only remaining evidence of a world whose existence he could hardly remember.

The ecstasy of release swept all thought away. Aage felt Jeyn's body respond with his, the familiarity of writhing arms and legs almost lost in a shock of power that flashed like lightning against Aage's Dreamer senses. In the distance he heard Jeyn cry out. Then there was nothing.

The sea lapped against the hull of the boat. Aage's knee hurt. He shifted his weight slightly and looked down next to Jeyn's body. The end of one of the sail lines lay in the bottom of the boat. He'd been kneeling on it. A red line marred his skin.

"You're dripping on me," Jeyn commented softly.

Aage carefully rolled to one side. "Sorry," he murmured and wiped his face with one hand. Sweat trickled off him. It glistened as well, in a fine sheen, all over Jeyn's body. "You're looking a little warm yourself, love."

She stretched languidly. "That was unique. I'm not sure yet whether I enjoyed it or not."

"No one ever appreciates the things I do for them," Aage pouted.

She smiled, but it was tentative. "I'll massage your ego some other time. Right now, I'm still feeling a little strange. You were right, though. I'm glad we sailed this far out. I'll need time to catch my breath before we get back home."

"Plenty of time," he assured her. "A nice, leisurely day of sailing. We'll both be well rested by the time we see the king."

"Do you think it worked?" she asked softly.

He placed a satisfied, loving kiss on her forehead. "How," he asked, "can you doubt it?"

"I was afraid I wouldn't be able to come at all," Vray apologized to Deenit. Her mother-in-law took her damp cloak and led her into the goldsmith's kitchen. The room was warm from a log fire, and smelled wonderfully of a day's worth of cooking. Outside, the afternoon light had grown faint. Wind drove a cold, sleet-filled rain down the streets.

Deenit hung her cloak with many more on pegs by the door. "What happened?"

"The prince. He wanted me to recite a whole list of trade agreements between Rhenlan and old Atowa. I never thought I'd get finished. I hope I'm not too late."

"I told her not to worry." Peanal closed the door behind her as she followed Vray into the house. "Parties here go on till dawn."

"Yes, something Rose always complains about. She threatened to go home to her mother again."

Deenit led them up the stairs to the family's common room. Brightly colored rugs from southern Sitrine covered the floor, now mostly hidden by myriad pairs of slippered feet. Vray left her fatigue on the landing. The moment she stepped into the crowd, her wide mouth curved in a charming smile. If Damon had had his way, she'd still be reciting useless facts into an inattentive silence, while he busied himself with reading the midwinter estate reports. He was very conscientious regarding the estate reports; his knowledge of the other large Shaper families' business affairs accounted for a large part of his control over their lives.

Brownmother Lamsi waved merrily from the food-laden table against the far wall. "You're late, Highness!"

Vray made her way toward Lamsi and her large husband, the woodworker Brenn. "Don't tell me there's nothing left."

"Would Brenn be standing next to an empty table?" Nocca asked. The tall guard emerged from one of the bedrooms. Loras came out behind him, his grandson tucked within the circle of one arm.

"The table is empty?" Loras asked plaintively.

Deenit came around the back of the table and put a full plate in Vray's hands.

Vray looked around. "Where's Dael?"

"Waiting for you." Nocca gestured her ahead of him toward the group gathered around the fireplace.

Deenit took the baby from her husband. "I'll take him. You don't have to work on your birthday."

Dael stood up at Vray's approach, tugging at his blue wool uniform tunic to straighten out the creases. "Good— you're here. Now we can do the toasts."

Vray wondered if they'd waited for her because she was their princess, or because she was the last family member to arrive. Knowing Loras, he would have more regard for her as a daughter-in-law than as a member of the ruling house. She accepted a glass of wine from Ruudy. The family's set of goblets was renowned in Edian for its fine gold work and inset precious stones. Except on such special occasions as this, they sat in the locked display cabinet in the shop. The pair she and Dael had received as a wedding gift, similar in shape but with a different design, stood in a place of honor in their living quarters in the castle.

Half of the prominent merchants of Edian gathered closer to wish Loras well on his birthday. Dael, as eldest child, gave the first toast. "Health and happiness, Dad," he said simply.

Everyone drank. Nocca took over the task of filling glasses as Ruudy stepped up on a chair. "To another prosperous year!" The journeyman goldsmith's toast earned a round of good-natured applause.

The toasts continued through all of the family and into the gathered friends, making Vray grateful that the wine was well watered. Many of the later toasts had to do with either suggestions for Loras and Deenit, or unveiled hints regarding further grandchildren. Amid a great deal of laughter and good cheer the ritual was completed, and people drifted away toward the food or into small conversational groups.

Vray circulated through the room, grabbing Dael's hand to pull him along with her. She greeted each merchant, each Brownmother, by name, and took a few minutes to inquire after each person's concerns. Since her marriage, she had been making a point of spending as much time as she could in town, getting acquainted with the citizens and discovering what was important to them.

From the Brownmothers she learned about problems in need of solutions: a well that was going dry on the east side of town, three orphaned children who had to be sent to Garden Vale, and the sorry state of several of the fishing piers on the lake. While Damon concentrated on his grand schemes, Vray was making herself useful in every quiet little way she could find.

With the merchants she used a different approach. Her summer on the road had given her insights into the commerce of the three kingdoms. At the beginning, she had watched and listened to Jordy as any apprentice was supposed to do. Being a Shaper, she soon began to see ways that things could be done differently. She took notice of products that might be profitably traded elsewhere, surpluses and needs that a single carter was unable to balance, and new markets for goods that no one had considered yet.

Now, firmly settled in Edian, she allowed Loras to introduce her to his friends at family gatherings. On such innocent occasions, she could make casual but helpful remarks, to which the merchants politely listened. In the last few ninedays, some had begun to come to her with specific questions, seeking her advice. She was ever aware of the danger of encountering one of her brother's spies, always careful to allude to travels with Jenil as the inspiration for her ideas. She hoped it wasn't too obvious that she was doing her best to make herself indispensable to the people of Edian.

Brenn cornered her to discuss her order for new clothing chests for their bedroom. Deenit called Dael to help her bring something up from the kitchen. As he left, Brenn said, "That woodcarver you recommended, the one in Broadford?"

"Kessit," she supplied.

"That's the man. The Brownmother who took Bisra's children to Garden Vale stopped to talk to him on their way down. He gave her some small samples of decorated paneling, which she brought by my shop last nineday. It's nice work. Come spring I'll send word to him that I want his partnership on some large commissions."

"I'm glad." Vray smiled. "It would be nice if the roads could be repaired enough for larger shipments. I'm sure we can count on that eventually." Not for the sake of trade, unfortunately. Damon would need improved communication, speedier passage for his troops into Dherrica and Sitrine if the present rumors in the court about his plans to take over those lands were true. So far, battles had been fought in the level borderlands of the Atowa plateau at the foot of Dherrica's mountains, or with the horse people on the plains to the southeast. However, if Damon truly intended to control as much territory as Vray thought he did, he was going to need roads.

Ivey's long-ago suggestion that she should travel and see the world had proven amazingly educational. She had a much better idea of how to take over the other kingdoms than her brother ever would. Jordy was lucky she didn't have such interest.

Brenn wandered off in search of his spouse. Vray decided she'd done enough work for the evening. Following Brenn's example, she did the same.

CHAPTER 16

Still snowing, Dael noted as he left the warmth of the stables. Snow lay several inches deep on the wide flagstones of the courtyard. A half dozen young boys, loosely supervised by an old servant bundled up to the ears in a red scarf, were wielding shovels and brooms in an effort to keep the yard clear. He admired the effort, but thought it useless as he leaned into the stiff wind that entered through the open gates. It was midday; many of his guards were crossing the courtyard between duty shifts. Dael joined a straggling group that was headed for the mess room.

He heard her voice, carried on the wind, before he saw her. She was sheltering in the archway between the kitchen and the courtyard wall. Vray's hair was hidden under her fur-lined hood, the sapphire blue cloak billowing around her boots. She was talking brightly to a couple, a guardsman and a young woman.

"I'll certainly speak to Cook about your sister, Amal. There are several feasts planned and she's been complaining she doesn't have enough help for her normal duties. I'm sure she'll be glad to take on an apprentice." She gave the guard an encouraging pat on the arm. "I'm glad to be of help."

Of course you are, Dael thought. *Every little favor counts, my princess.*

After the brother and sister heartily thanked Vray, they hurried toward the castle gates. Vray watched them go, arms crossed under the cloak, her expression hidden by the hood. Dael turned into the archway. His hot meal could wait.

"Hello, Captain," Vray greeted him. "I was just talking to one of your men."

"I heard. You've been talking to a lot of my people."

She looked up, eyes still shadowed by the fur rim. "I've noticed you noticing. You haven't tried to stop me."

"You're the princess. It's not my place to stop you doing anything."

"Ha!" Her laughter rang out, hardly muffled by wind or falling snow.

"Glad to be amusing, my helpful wife." He put a hand on her shoulder and guided her deeper into the seclusion of the archway. "You are being careful?"

Vray shook fox fur out of her face. "Peanal told me Amal was a good man. I trust Peanal for a lot of advice."

"Good. That's why I sent her to you."

"Amal spends most of his summers on the Sitrinian border," she continued. "I could use news of Sitrine. Most of the friends I've made so far find me easy to talk to."

"You are easy to talk to." He looked down at her sternly. "If you wanted a spy system in the guards, why didn't you talk to me about it?"

"Because neither you nor I know how many of your spies also report to Damon. We need a second, or third, independent source of information."

"You're being clever."

"I'm being a survivor. Besides, I don't want to get you in trouble. One of us has to stay on Damon's good side."

"I know. That's my place."

She stamped her feet. "It's cold out here. Have you eaten yet?"

"No. Have you?"

"Not yet. I've got to talk to Cook and you're supposed to be eating with your guards. I'll see you at suppertime."

Veiled by shadows and snowflakes, they kissed before they went their separate ways.

Downstairs the musicians were beginning their last set of dances. Most of the families with some distance to travel on a cold winter night had gone home early. Villagers from nearby farms lingered downstairs, finishing their conversations, while the remaining young children slept in their parents' laps. Tob watched from the top of the stairs. He was glad Herri had organized the village dance, but he wasn't happy about having to hide up here through most of the party. "I hate being lectured."

"I know." Jordy stood near the banked hearth, partially hidden in the shadows of the otherwise deserted upper room of the inn. He didn't look at Tob, because he was concentrating on keeping six apples rotating through the air. "Canis misses Iris."

"But why is she still angry at us? She's been like this all winter. Why doesn't she just accept our answers?"

"She doesn't like our answers. Iris is a mature young woman. She gave the matter careful thought, asked my advice, and chose to make a life for herself in Edian. That's all anyone needs to know," Jordy recited the same explanation he'd been stubbornly repeating for many ninedays, the same explanation that he and Tob had given to the village at Fall Festival, and to the upset fisherwoman every time they saw Canis. She, and others who'd become fond of Iris, weren't satisfied with Jordy's seemingly unmoved acceptance of his daughter's decision.

"But she was happy here!" Tob protested, echoing the arguments he'd had to listen to time and again. "When people ask me why she would choose Edian, I don't know what to say."

"You say you don't know."

"People think I'm supposed to know."

Jordy put a little extra height on the whirling apples, then deftly caught them, one by one, as they came down, tucking the first few into the crooks of his elbows and beneath his chin to free his hands for the rest. Smiling in spite of himself, Tob went over and helped him deposit the fruit on the bar. "Because you're her brother," Jordy commented, "and her lover."

"Right," Tob agreed glumly.

"Then I'm afraid you're just going to have to put up with appearing stupid." Jordy shrugged. "Just as I'll put up with being called an irresponsible parent, among other things.

But not tonight." He put a hand on Tob's arm and urged him toward the stair landing. "Is she still out there?"

Tob looked down into the main room. Canis remained firmly established near the door. She was talking with one of her neighbors, but her eyes regularly strayed over the thinning crowd.

"She's still there."

"Stones. It's late, lad. Off home with you."

"Not without you."

His father came up behind him. "Should we risk it?"

Tob regarded his father doubtfully. "It's not that late."

"Maybe not."

"She can't stay all night. Herri will chase her home."

"Aye."

"Let's play Dragonrock. There's a board behind the bar."

"Good idea."

Jordy moved a table closer to the hearth. Tob, relieved, went to find the game.

Dael ran up the tower stairs, long legs spanning two steps at a time. Teza opened the door of their rooms as he reached the landing.

"Is she here?" he asked, without pausing to wait for the servant's answer. The sitting room was empty, the door to Vray's room shut, but the door to his room was slightly open. Dael hesitated, then turned to Teza. "I want some privacy."

"Giving you trouble again, is she?"

"Out."

She shrugged and left, closing the hall door behind her. Dael crossed to his bedroom and pushed the door wide open.

"What are you doing in here?" he asked before he even saw her. An instant later he located his wife, kneeling on the floor at the foot of his bed. The chest was open. He wondered how she could have unlocked it.

"I stole the key last night," she said before he could ask.

155

"You're early for supper." Then she lifted her arms, in which was cradled a long, leather-sheathed object. Her expression was as sweet as honey and brittle as glass. "Where did you get this?"

"A gift from the king." A king, at any rate.

"From Hion?" his maddeningly thorough wife wondered.

"Put that down! Don't touch it!"

He was used to being obeyed. Vray merely stood, her hands carefully wrapped around the hilt. "I know better than to touch a dragon sword."

He walked forward and took the sword out of her hands, then pulled the blade a few inches out of the sheath. It glowed with its own lemon-yellow light. "Did you know this was here, or were you just breaking into my belongings for the practice?"

"I was curious. Who made it for you?"

He pushed the blade firmly back into its covering. "I don't think we should discuss this."

"We'll only discuss it until you tell me where you got that sword."

"Why? It's not important."

"My husband, the captain of the royal guard, has a sword that could have only been made for him by a wizard. Only one king I know of has a wizard. Doesn't that sound important to you? I think I should know who you've been dealing with."

"When you put it that way, it does seem important." *And if I can't trust you, Kitten, I'm a dead man anyway.* "King Sene. We met on the border last summer. He liked me. I liked him."

"Everyone likes him. I've never met him, but I intend to some day. He cares. Everything he does is for the good of the Children. He's what a Shaper should be." She stared thoughtfully at the sheathed sword. "This could be interesting. I wonder why he took an interest in you and gave you a dragon sword?"

"So I can kill monsters. That's what they're for, right?"

"When they're used properly. Did Sene teach you how to use it?"

"Not directly."

She lifted her gaze, eyes narrowed. "A dragon sword isn't just another blade. Without proper training, you'll be more of a menace than any monster."

"I didn't say I wasn't trained." He put the sword back in the chest and held out his hand.

Vray relinquished the key. "All right—you've been trained, but not by Sene. Let me guess. Prince Chasa."

Dael sat on the edge of the bed and tried to keep his expression wooden, but the effort was useless. His too-perceptive wife tilted her head to one side and regarded him with her most calculating expression.

"Not Chasa. Oh, dear. When you set out to do something behind my brother's back, you make a thorough job of it, don't you? You've been seeing Pirse of Dherrica."

"You make it sound like he's part of my daily schedule. Breakfast, guard inspection, weapons training in Dherrica."

She shook her head. "And you've been worried about me being careful?"

"My . . . indiscretions took place far from any prying eyes. You take your risks right under Damon's nose."

"I haven't done anything as risky as associating with an accused vow-breaker!"

"Good. See that you don't." He patted the bed next to him. "That's settled. Now come here, woman. We have to talk."

"We already are talking." Despite her protest, she settled obligingly at the head of the bed and leaned back against the pillows.

"Yes, we are. So is everyone in Edian. About me."

Her eyes widened in polite interest. "Really?"

"More specifically, they are repeating the things you have been telling them about me."

"I've merely been reciting the history of the town over the last nine years or so. That's a Redmother's duty." She folded her hands in her lap. "Now that I think of it, your name does come up quite frequently."

"It wouldn't if you didn't keep bringing it up. You're embarrassing me! Why should anyone care now about that fire, for instance? It happened years ago!"

"You saved lives. It's still important to those families. You also saved property. That's important to any merchant." She reached out and nudged his thigh with her foot. "You are important to the entire town."

"By the great crumbling Rock, woman, you're turning me into a figurehead!"

"You're clever, too."

"I don't want to be a figurehead," he growled. "Damon won't like hearing all these stories."

"Damon doesn't listen to Redmother tales."

"His spies do." The more his name was mentioned in the town, the greater the chance that his association with the malcontents of Edian would be found out. He understood what Vray was doing. She was setting him up to be consort when she became queen. A good plan—except that he had plans of his own.

Maybe he should tell her. No, not yet. Not until he talked to Jordy. The carter might not come to town before Spring Festival. After, then.

Rock and pool, I have to keep her from getting me killed before summer!

"Yes, but what do they report to Damon?" Vray asked, still talking about Damon's spies. "That his captain of the guards is well-liked? Respected? All I'm telling is the truth about what you've done for Edian. I make sure it reflects well on the royal family."

"But I'm still the hero."

"If Damon worried about being a hero he'd go out and kill some dragons. He doesn't worry about that. That's why he keeps you around. That's also his mistake. He thinks of you as his well-trained, safely leashed dog. You and I—and the king of Sitrine—know better. The citizens of Edian need to know better as well."

Dael hung his head and ran his hands through his hair.

She was as crazy as Jordy—and there was no stopping either of them. Gazing at his empty hands, he said, "I'm a man, Vray. Not a figurehead."

She slid down the bed until she was kneeling behind him. "I know you're a man." She spoke quietly, her hands rubbing his shoulder blades. "The man I love." After a pause, she added, "I'm sorry if I embarrass you."

He turned his head and looked at her. "You just want to get even for that time with the girl and the pitcher of ale."

"That story I haven't told!" she protested at once. "Well, not here. Not to anyone who'll repeat it."

"Keep it that way."

She wrapped her arms around his neck and kissed his ear. "I have to leave."

"So do I. I just came back to yell at you. I'll see you at dinner."

CHAPTER 17

Feather left the terrace as soon as she was finished with her supper. Her husband, father-in-law, and a guard corporal were deep in a discussion of troop movements and border strategy. Only Chasa acknowledged her departure, his smile distracted.

Feather was happy to be able to slip away. Each report from Rhenlan was worse than the one before. For the first time, there was open speculation about the state of Hion's health, and discussion in even the smallest villages as to whether he would have to step down from the throne in favor of his son. Troops of King's guards were more visible and more restless than ever. Sene's sources in the market square informed him that travel between Raisal and Edian or Cross Cove had been growing difficult even before the winter storms limited movement.

Somehow, Jeyn was involved too. Feather hadn't yet discovered the connection. All she knew was that for the past few ninedays Jeyn had been worried and withdrawn. Making a decision, Feather turned into the short hallway that led to Jeyn's rooms. Reaching the half-open door, she knocked softly, then stepped inside.

The princess was seated on the clothes chest beneath her window. The sea breeze stirred her hair and caused the lamp flame to flicker, casting odd shadows on the walls. Jeyn turned away from her contemplation of the dark night. "Oh, hello, Feather."

Feather entered and sat uncertainly on the edge of the chair in front of Jeyn's dressing table. "I missed you at supper."

"Dad didn't say anything, did he?"

"No. Felistinon was there with his report. More border worries."

Jeyn seemed to relax a little, but the way she said, "Good," gave Feather an unpleasant idea.

"Something's going on between you and Sene. Is that why you've been skipping meals?"

"I've been busy."

"That's not it."

"I haven't been hungry."

"If it's none of my business, just say so," Feather told her. "I'd rather hear that than a string of excuses."

"Oh, Feather." Jeyn gave a shaky sigh. "I miss Ivey." She stood up and gazed out the window. "Dad's not involved in this. I don't want him involved. The trouble is, he's too clever. Sooner or later he's going to know. Probably sooner. Aage didn't take that into consideration. Dreamers can be so impractical."

"I don't have any idea what you're talking about," Feather admitted when Jeyn paused. "I'll listen if it'll help."

"No. I'd have to ask you to keep a secret, and that wouldn't be fair."

"A secret from the king?"

"From everyone."

"Even Ivey?" Feather asked gently.

"I had to tell Ivey. He's going to be my husband someday."

"It's not someday yet. I'm your sister now." Jeyn turned toward her, and Feather held out her hand. "Ivey won't be back until late in the spring, will he? If you need a friend before then, remember I'm here."

"I need a friend now." Jeyn grabbed Feather's much smaller hand and squeezed it until Feather winced. "I never thought I'd feel this odd this quickly."

Feather looked up into brown, troubled eyes. "You're not feeling well? Have you seen a Brownmother?"

"I don't have to. I know what it is."

"Oh." Feather searched for the properly vague phrase to fit the game they seemed to be playing. "Do you know what to do about it?"

"No."

That wasn't it. Try another. "You can't tell your father?"

"No."

"Why not?"

"Because Aage is right. It goes entirely against tradition."

Feather pounced on that admission. "You can talk to Aage?"

"The trouble is, he's not always here. He has to work for Dad, when he's not off with Morb for ninedays at a time. I don't want to be left alone."

"You'll never be alone," Feather protested. "Besides, I can't believe you would do something that's really so wrong."

"Oh, it's not wrong. Dad will be proud of us."

Feather eyed her. "Yet you can't tell him?"

"Not now. It's too soon. If you needed to get away, Feather, where would you go?" Jeyn asked abruptly. "Where can I be safe?"

Feather held back her immediate answer. If she ever became as unhappy as Jeyn was now, she would flee to Garden Vale—but Jenil was her guardian, not Jeyn's. Besides, Rhenlan was the last place for a Sitrinian princess to go. Still, Garden Vale had other things to recommend it besides the Greenmother. Sitrine had its Brownmother houses, too.

"Go to Bren," Feather suggested.

"Bren?"

"You've heard of the place." Feather wasn't used to Jeyn being so vague. The unusual behavior was getting on her nerves. When Jeyn just looked at her, she forced herself back to patience and added, "The Brownmother house. That's the safest place I can think of."

Jeyn paced in silence, head bowed for a moment. "Of course, there's the library," she murmured at last.

"Jeyn?"

The princess looked up. Determination had masked, if not replaced, her earlier fear. "You're right, Feather. Bren is perfect. I should have thought of it. You can tell Dad I decided to go work with the books for awhile."

"Tell him? Me?"

"Oh, Feather, you've got to. If I go to him now, he'll ask too many questions. Please. Just until Ivey comes back. He'll deal with the king then, somehow. I'm sure he will."

"When will you go?"

"Tonight." Jeyn stopped at the window and gazed toward the sea. "Now, while the king is busy."

"Not alone."

She looked around, smiling tiredly. "I'll take a guard or two as escort. I do know how to travel." She grew serious again. "Don't tell him until morning, Feather. Please? Say I was restless. Say I was disgusted with this border nonsense. That's all true."

An unfounded, ridiculous, irrational thought entered Feather's mind. "You're pregnant," she announced. For an instant her own audacity embarrassed her, until the other woman crossed her arms protectively over her abdomen.

"It can't be obvious yet. You're just guessing."

"I'm right."

Jeyn nodded bleakly.

Feather thought back over the recent ninedays. "But Ivey hasn't been here since—Jeyn, you're supposed to have Dreamer babies!"

"It is a Dreamer baby."

Feather hesitated. "You changed your mind about Ivey?"

"No."

"Then who—?"

She barely breathed the name, "Aage."

"That's not possible." Feather waited for the princess to change her story, but Jeyn met her gaze without flinching. "You're serious. Rock and Pool."

"No one must know," Jeyn insisted.

"You did tell Ivey?"

"He knew we were going to try. When he gets back, ask him to come see me in Bren."

Feather ignored all the implications of Jeyn's disclosure. She intended to keep ignoring them for as long as she could. Jeyn had trusted her. She could keep her silence for now. For a while. This was Jeyn and Aage's crisis. Best to let them deal with it.

Even if it turned the world upside down.

"I hope you know what you're doing," Feather said. "I hope Aage knows what he's doing."

"We do. It will work. Really. You'll see."

Feather sighed and stood. "All right, I'll tell Sene that you decided to go to Bren to work in the library. He'll expect progress reports about those old books."

"I'll write something for him every nineday. We'll send messengers back and forth. He expects that whenever Chasa or I have to be away from Raisal for a time."

"Better hope he stays too busy to spare time for a visit."

"Aage and Ivey can worry about that."

There seemed nothing else to say. "Come on, then," Feather said. "I'll help you pack."

"Wolves!"

The shouted word, accompanied by thunderous pounding on the door, had Tob scrambling into his clothes before he was fully awake. Even Matti, sound sleeper that she was, stirred and mumbled. Pepper's nervous whisper reached him through the darkness. "Tobble?"

"It's all right. Go back to sleep."

Light filtered up from the room below as Jordy went to open the front door. The curtained opening to the girls' part of the attic remained still, with Pepper for once doing as she was told. Tob jammed his feet into his boots and dropped more than climbed down the ladder into the main room. They'd been very late coming back from the inn. He didn't think he'd been asleep long.

One of the lamps from his parents' room was perched on the wood box beside the door. Lim, the lower half of his legs caked with snow, leaned against the wall, hands on his knees, struggling to catch his breath. Jordy slung his quiver on his back. "Did someone go for Kessit?"

Lim nodded.

"Then we'll go straight there. Rest here as long as you need to, lad," he added with gruff kindness. "You've done your part tonight."

Tob grabbed a pitchfork from the stable and followed his father down the hill and out of the yard. Sheyn was a dim lopsided blotch high in the sky behind a thin layer of cloud, confirming what Tob had already suspected; dawn was still four or five long, dark, hours away. Fortunately the road into Broadford had been well packed down since the last nineday's snowfall, so they weren't hindered by the virtual uselessness of the dim light cast by the little moon. Tob matched Jordy in a half walk, half run that quickly warmed him despite the bitter cold of the air. Tob assumed they were going to the inn until his father turned toward the river on a path well east of the square. He caught up with Jordy and asked, "Where are we going?"

The question earned him one of his father's sharp, exasperated, over-the-shoulder glares. "Tob."

"I didn't hear Lim say where the wolves were," he explained hurriedly. "Or how many there are or if—"

"One of the fishers saw an entire pack crossing the ice, heading down stream. Both Jenk and Shar have flocks in their fields."

An entire pack. That was bad. It was common this late in the winter for hunger to drive the occasional lone wolf onto farmland in search of food. This year the weather had been unusually harsh. There had been talk around the village that deer as well as the smaller wild animals had become hard to find. Whether they had drifted north and east to escape the worst of the cold, or whether they'd simply died ninedays ago hardly mattered. Wherever they were, they obviously weren't sustaining the wolf population.

Panicked bleating led them to Shar's farm. The flock of goats was huddled in the corner of the fenced pasture nearest the house. Tob and Jordy waded through snow already disturbed by many booted feet and clambered over

165

the fence side by side. Halfway across the field the blue-tinted snow was marred by several dark lumps. Tob shifted his grip on the pitchfork and ran forward, but the three wolves were already dead. Jordy joined him and took off his glove long enough to run a quick hand over one of the carcasses. He grunted. Tob, peering more closely at the shaggy back, saw the protruding shaft of a broken arrow.

Jordy straightened and started for the river. Tob couldn't hear anything—the terrified goats behind them were making too much noise—but he followed anyway. They climbed another fence and cut through a small wood before they found the rest of the pack.

The rest of the residents of Broadford were there, too, or so it seemed at first glance. Everyone who could wield pitchfork or bow had come out in defense of the village. A very effective defense. Not a single wolf remained alive. Those with bows were already unstringing them. Herri caught sight of Jordy and beckoned him over.

"Too slow, carter. You see the price you pay for living so far from the square."

"I see you hardly needed my help," Jordy replied, smiling.

Tob went to help Haant and Heather drag the wolf carcasses into a line in the snow. He hadn't been keeping track of just how many people had taken archery lessons from his father during the past few years. Clearly, a pack of wolves was no longer a threat to Broadford. He saw, really saw at last, what his father had done. Not only in Broadford, but in so many other villages and towns. Jordy had made them strong. Strong beyond the traditional cooperative feats accomplished at harvest time or after storms or floods. If they could fight together as well as this, could anything—or anyone—threaten them?

The subdued manner of the archers told Tob that they, too, were stunned by what they had accomplished. Kessit dumped a large gray wolf on the snow near Tob, then walked toward Herri and Jordy.

Kessit said, "This is your doing, carter. We've dealt with

wolves before—but never like this."

"You were protecting your families," Jordy said gruffly. "You didn't need me to tell you to do that."

"Self-defense is one thing. This was a slaughter!"

"It would have been different," Herri said, "if they'd been king's guards."

"Would it?" Jordy demanded. "Aye, we'd like to think it would. We can hope that if it comes to that, a troop of guards will see reason, avoid a fight they can't win." He raised his voice and the people of the village stopped what they were doing to draw closer. No sound came from the frozen river a few yards behind them. The bleating of the goats in the next field had stilled. "What harm had any of these wolves done to you? Canis, whose flocks suffered losses?"

The fisherwoman removed her knitted hat and scratched her head. "Losses? None. We saw the pack before it crossed the river."

"Then why this?" Jordy gestured around them at the bloodied snow.

"You know very well why," Jenk snapped. "It's cold. Make your point, carter."

"I know why," Jordy agreed. "But do you? All of you? You killed these wolves not for what they did but what they threatened to do. Their presence here tonight threatened losses to your flocks. Though what are a few goats and sheep more or less to a village like Broadford? We have food and to spare."

"Not to spare for wolves," someone in the group exclaimed.

Jenk's arms were folded belligerently across his chest. "It's not one night's losses. If a pack like this fed well here once, they'd be back. That's where the danger lies."

"That and the danger to our families," Shar added. "We have small children to think of."

"Exactly."

Tob, watching his father closely, was surprised to detect a grim, almost bitter edge beneath his satisfaction. Jordy liked to win arguments. He liked to be right. Yet he didn't seem to be getting much pleasure from it this time.

"Which is why if the day comes, and we all think it will, that a king of Rhenlan sends his guards to raid our flocks and fields, you won't hesitate. You'll fight, as you fought these poor beasties tonight. The threat's the same," Jordy said. "A threat to the food you put on your tables. A threat to the safety of your families. You have to fight against that."

"Must we kill other Keepers?" Kessit's protest was quiet, his voice strained. "Keepers like ourselves? That's what we'll face, isn't it?"

Jordy didn't answer for a moment. When he did, the emotion that roughened his voice made Tob's throat tighten in sympathetic response. "By the Firstmother, it shouldn't come to that. A guard should consider his Keeper's vows before his orders, whoever they come from. He has to be willing to answer for his own actions regardless of what anyone else is doing. I've talked to so many guards and their families, all across Rhenlan." He looked at Kessit. "As you say, they are Keepers like us. It shouldn't come to killing. I'm convinced there are few troops like the one who came to take Pross away." The oaks flamed and crackled again in Tob's memory. "Even so, we have to be ready. Keepers keep. To keep our homes, our families, our lives, we have to be ready."

No one had a better answer. Tob looked around the loose semicircle of villagers. Right or not, it wasn't the answer for him. He couldn't fight this way. He had known it for years, as long ago as when Pross was taken away. He would never be able to harm people. All he could do was run his father's errands, and hope a real battle never came.

Herri's large hand rested on Jordy's shoulder in support, or, the odd notion flickered through Tob's mind, in comfort. The next moment the innkeeper stepped forward and clapped, the sharp sound rousing them from their somber mood.

"Who'll stay and help with the skinning?" he asked.

"Some good fur's to be had here."

With some grumbling and a few exaggerated yawns, most of those present pulled out knives and set to work. Shar built a fire. Herri took several others back to the inn to fetch food and drink for everyone.

Tob turned resolutely to the nearest carcass, pulled out his knife, and concentrated on thinking about the boots and hats and gloves that Haant and the tanner would soon make from the many hides.

CHAPTER 18

"One day without rain," Pirse grumbled. "Is that too much to ask?"

None of his companions chose to reply. Pirse didn't blame them. At this time of year, the rain forest of northern Dherrica lived up to its name.

They had tracked and killed a dragon that had been hiding in a cave on the coast, then turned south in response to rumors of a band of Abstainers in the valleys between Bronle and Dundas. Throughout the expedition, they had been subjected to day after day of gray days and clammy nights that left clothes, bedding, and supplies damp at best, soaking wet at worst. Pirse expected no better of the lowlands in winter, but many of the members of his escort were used to the milder climate of higher elevations.

His escort. He was almost ready to call them a troop— one of several that he had formed during his years of exile. They would never be as well trained as guards who spent half a year at a time sharpening their skills. Still, they were strong, determined, and, most of all, good people. They had come to him not out of greed or fear, but because they truly felt he was a leader they could respect.

For the past four years, he had taken such people wherever he found them, and taught them as much as they were willing to learn. Most were not only willing, but eager, to memorize everything he had to offer, including Redmother stories of the past, Dreamer lore, and, best of all, tactical advice on how to defend their herds, property, and loved ones. They needed to protect themselves not only from wild animals and Abstainers, but also from the ravages of Palle's overzealous tax gatherers—without attracting attention or retribution from the Bronle guard.

By midafternoon, the rain had given way to a dismal,

penetrating fog. Darkness was already falling as they climbed the last hill into Dundas. Pirse's companions dispersed to their homes, leaving him to ride to the inn alone.

As he dismounted in front of the stable, he noticed a piebald mountain pony dozing in the first stall. Forgetting the discomfort of his soggy boots, Pirse hurried up the steps into the common room of the inn.

"Pirse!" Ivey's schooled voice was as distinctive as his pony. He rose from a table in front of the hearth. "This is perfect! I hoped to find news of you, and now here you are."

Pirse stopped in front of the minstrel. "Have you been through Live Oak?"

"I have indeed." Ivey clapped his shoulder, grinning from ear to ear. "Kamara is pregnant. Savyea confirmed it this nineday past. A son, she says."

Pirse gripped the back of a chair for support. It was too early to feel the joy or wonder of a birth, yet the surge of emotion almost swept him off his feet. Part of it was gratitude, to Kamara for her cooperation, and to the gods for answering his prayers—and the rest was immense, incomparable relief. "We did it."

"You did it," Ivey agreed. He sat Pirse down in the chair. "Kamara has already picked out a name—Farren. It's a good choice."

"I can't go see her." Pirse stated it as a fact.

"Not with the way Palle is watching every Shaper family in Dherrica. Any contact between you and Kamara now would be sure to attract his attention." Ivey walked over to the cabinet in the corner of the room and helped himself to a bottle of wine. He brought it and two goblets back to the table, and poured for himself and Pirse. "Don't worry—her family is wonderful. I've even found a woman in the village willing to act as Redmother at the birth. Nothing open, of course. That would make a visiting guard troop suspicious. I'll teach her a few more tales every time I pass through, and she's taken an apprentice. When the time is right, Farren will be known as he should be."

"Ivey, you're a wonder. You'll be taking the news to Sene?"

"Eventually. I want to be in Edian for Spring Festival, and after that I owe Broadford a visit." The minstrel's expression grew more somber. "I have other news, as well."

Pirse sat straighter. "Such as?"

"Rhenlan. I told you that the Princess Vray has returned?"

"Aye. You mentioned it when we met before midwinter. She married Captain Dael."

"That's right. I haven't been able to talk to them, but the mood in town suggests that people are happy to have her back."

"Is that a problem?"

"That depends on whether Damon views her popularity as a source of support for his own power—or a threat. I'll be interested to hear what Sene thinks of the situation."

"He can't be too concerned about Damon being jealous of her power, or he wouldn't have given that dragon sword to Dael."

"The sword is still a complete secret in Edian. At least, I didn't hear even a whisper of a rumor about it. If Dael has used it, he's managed not to let anyone else catch him in the act."

Pirse twirled the stem of his goblet between his fingers. "The first time he uses it, people will know. It's a beautiful blade, unmistakably magic. Even my uncle would recognize its power."

"Can a Keeper control that much power?"

"This Keeper can." Pirse poured more wine into the worried minstrel's cup. "If you don't trust my judgment, trust Sene. It was his idea."

"Sene hasn't seen Dael handle the sword. You have."

"I've seen that he's a better swordsman than I am. Better than anyone living, Shaper or otherwise. Even Hion, in his prime, would have found a challenge in this guard captain of his."

"High praise, on the basis of two lessons."

"Three, actually. His technique is above criticism. All he needs now is some practice with the tactics necessary for each monster. Perhaps next summer he can get a few dragon hunts under his belt."

"I wouldn't count on it." Ivey drained his wine and folded his hands around the base of the goblet. "I don't like the look of Hion. This past half-year he's been involved less and less in the affairs of the kingdom. Damon is taking advantage of that fact to tighten his control. This fall he placed troops up and down Dherrica's border. From what I saw when I crossed, Palle seems to be trying to match Damon guard for guard. Unobtrusively, of course. I suspect much the same thing is happening on the Sitrinian border. I don't like it."

"I don't like the thought of Dherrica depending upon Palle for protection."

"Not promising, is it?"

"It seems I'd better go to the border," Pirse said with a sigh. "About time I tested my system of messengers, I suppose."

"Be careful, Highness."

Pirse shifted in his chair, rested his elbow on the table, and extended his feet toward the fire. At once, steam began to rise from his damp boots and trousers. So much for his plans to spend a nineday in Dundas, perhaps followed by a visit to Juniper Ridge. A day or two to replenish supplies and make plans, and then he would have to be on his way. If the situation in Rhenlan was as volatile as Ivey suspected, they didn't dare sit back and see what Palle would do at the moment of crisis. For all they knew, the show of Dherrican guards on the border was merely for the sake of appearances, and Palle would give up his kingdom without a fight.

Not his kingdom. Not for long.

"A son," Pirse said. He scowled at the fire. "Will Doron accept him, do you think?"

"Far better," Ivey said fervently, "than she accepted Kamara."

Pirse decided he would have to be satisfied with that.

★ ★ ★ ★ ★

"I like hunting."

Dael sighed. "You want to come along then."

Vray held up her bow and adjusted the strap of the quiver where it crossed her shoulder. "I want to come along. I'm tired of target practice. I keep beating Peanal."

"Fine. Let's go."

He had been going to spend the day by himself, Dael mused somewhat sullenly as he and his wife mounted their horses and rode away from the castle stables. He hadn't had a day to himself since the woman re-entered his life. He certainly hadn't told her of his plan to go hunting.

"Who told you I was going hunting?" he asked aloud.

She gave him an enigmatic smile. She was looking altogether too enigmatic today. "I have my ways," she replied.

"You have your spies," he corrected her.

Outside the gate, they turned west and followed the market road down toward the square. A few people noticed Vray and waved, calling cheerfully to her. She smiled and waved serenely back. Dael looked the other way. He supposed she had a right to feel smug. She was becoming increasingly popular with the staff, the guards, some members of the royal court, and the citizens of Edian. This was good. It was also dangerous, although he hadn't caught her in a single act of carelessness. She was always, in everything she said or did, first and foremost a loyal daughter, sister, and Redmother. That she had her own, private system of informers was to be expected of a member of the royal family of Rhenlan.

"It's a lovely day," Vray commented as they crossed the square and took the shortest road toward the countryside. There had been a warm spell for the last few days, thawing what little snow had been on the ground, but it had grown colder before the roads and fields had a chance to turn to mud. "Do you really mind my company?" She licked her lips. "I have such a taste for stewed rabbit. Cook promised to fix it for supper if I could bring her the meat." When he didn't answer she turned to study him. "Do you mind my being here?" she repeated.

"Not exactly."

"Good. Of course, if you were planning on visiting a girl-friend I could go hunt by myself for a few hours."

"I don't do that," he growled. "You're my wife."

"What has that got to do with it?"

He wanted to say something about one woman like her being more than enough for any man to handle, but she didn't seem to be fishing for entertaining banter. He studied her back, and said, "The only woman I want is my wife. That's you, if I remember the ceremony correctly."

"Damon encourages you to see other people."

"Damon asks a lot of me. I don't do some of it."

"Good," she said again, and the small smile returned to her lips.

The town ended abruptly. Fields and orchards spread toward a thin belt of trees. Dael led the way along a bare hedgerow. The morning sun cast long shadows ahead of them. He twisted in his saddle, watching his wife. She was gazing southward, so that the sunlight made her normally dark braids almost coppery. She caught him staring at her, and tilted her head inquiringly.

"Yes, Captain?"

"Are we really going hunting, or are you planning on taking me into the woods for a different sort of sport?"

"That might be nice, but it's a bit cool. I'm hungry, Dael."

"This does nothing for my reputation."

"You're a married man. You don't need to have a reputation."

At the edge of the trees they dismounted, and Dael tethered the horses. Then they strung their light hunting bows, nocked arrows, and began moving quietly along the border that separated field and woods. Vray paused and raised her bow. Dael looked in the same direction, saw the pair of rabbits snuffling through the dead grass a few feet from the protection of the next hedgerow. He smoothly lifted his bow.

Vray drew the arrow back toward her ear. "By the way," she said softly, voice barely audible over the whisper of wind, "I'm pregnant."

Both arrows flew. One rabbit leaped in the air and fell to its side, to lie motionless. The other vanished with a flash of its white tail.

"You missed!" Vray exclaimed as he rounded on her. "That's never happened before!" Her eyes were wide with mock astonishment, her grin teasing.

"Your fault!" he snapped.

"It takes two to make a baby, you know. Surely your parents told—"

"Vray!"

"Yes, husband?" She leaned her bow against her leg and folded her hands in front of her, waiting.

"You're pregnant? You're really pregnant?"

She nodded, the serenely self-satisfied smile returning once more.

He swept her up in his arms and whirled them both around in a dizzy circle. "We're pregnant!" he shouted happily.

Arms wrapped around his neck, she beamed down into his face. "That's what I said. And this is why I brought you out here to tell you."

Still smiling broadly, he hugged her once more before he set her back on her feet. Keeping his hands on her waist, he quickly grew serious. "You're right. No public displays of rejoicing. Damon is going to be very angry with both of us."

"Not until he knows. Which won't be until after we've made sure that all of Edian is looking forward to the birth of a new Dreamer."

"Exactly how are we going to manage that?"

"It's very simple. We'll use Jenil. She's been coming to see the king more and more this winter; I've told you how sick he is. She hasn't done any healing in the town for years, thanks to Damon's disapproval, but with my encouragement she's going to get out and about and show just how useful Dreamers really are. Meanwhile, knowledge of

Aage's prophecy has to become more widespread. All those lovely old Redmother stories have to be retold. Ivey can help with that, and he's promised to stay through Spring Festival."

"You have it all arranged," Dael said, impressed.

"I have to protect our baby."

"Our baby." He stepped back to look at her. He had never intended to have children. It was too dangerous for him to have children. Bleakly, he asked, "What if this child turns out to be like me?"

"Handsome, brave, wonderful?" she suggested. "Blond? I hope so."

"A killer. I'm that, too."

"So am I. There's nothing wrong with you, Dael, except that you think like a Shaper. Shapers know how and when to kill—and when not to. That sounds like you to me."

"I'm not a Shaper!"

"Well, the baby won't be, either!"

"Oh. Right." No matter what he said, she was going to remain pleased, wasn't she? Pleased, and radiant, and desirable. She was as slender, as beautiful, as she'd ever been. Instinctive worry made him ask, "Shouldn't you be taking special care of yourself? Doing whatever it is pregnant women do?"

She stepped away from him and walked toward the hedgerow. "I am," she called back to him. "I'm satisfying my craving for rabbit stew."

"I'm feeling old," Jenil said.

"Nonsense, dear. You're only one hundred and seventeen," Savyea replied.

Only one hundred and seventeen. Jenil felt each and every year hanging over her, poised to come crashing down. It was the season. She'd come into her power on a late winter day. That made this her one hundred and seventeenth winter. The day was clear; not too cold, and Garden Vale's square was almost half full. There had been talk that with the population growing, next year someone would have to open up the second inn.

"Eight new Brownmother apprentices arrived for mid-winter," she said aloud. "Added to the six who came to us this summer, the house is full."

"Maybe you should offer to reopen the inn," Savyea said calmly.

Jenil looked sideways at her companion. Savyea's head was bent slightly forward, gaze intent on her knitting. The eldest, most powerful Dreamer of them all was working five needles and four balls of yarn to produce a multi-colored pattern of birds in flight on the sweater yoke slowly taking shape beneath her hands. Very slowly. From past experience Jenil knew that Savyea would spend half a year or more on a single knitting project.

Savyea looked up and smiled sympathetically. "You'll enjoy them when they're born, and the next generation *will* be born. Trust me. We've set it in motion and it will come to pass. I remember when you and Aage were born. And the others. How we watched you grow, waited for the day when the knowledge would come and suddenly you would be there, bending the power. We were so eager to see which of you would show skill for our specialties. Exciting days." Her smiled slipped a little. "You'll see."

"We won't lose any of them," Jenil said fiercely. She thought of Mojil and Forrit, the young Dreamers-to-be, busy with their adolescent concerns in Sitrine. They were only mildly interested in the new Dreamer babies. They couldn't understand yet how narrowly they had escaped a terrible loneliness. Perhaps it would not have been as bad for them as it had been for her and Aage. If they had grown up as the only two Dreamers of their generation, their present isolation would have seemed normal to them. Instead, she and Aage remembered what it was like to have peers, the many others born in their generation, the many babies Savyea had loved, had taught, and had watched die one by one. Terrifying years, as the web of power grew quiet, as fewer and fewer survived to bend the lines, to touch the world.

"They'll be hopelessly spoiled," Savyea said. "The princess of Sitrine and Ivey should be married by now. Her twin's wife is expecting, and if someone as stubborn about getting married as our little Feather can do her duty, so can Princess Jeyn. Of course, it isn't her fault if the man goes wandering away from her bed. What's Ivey doing in Garden Vale when he should be in Raisal with Jeyn?"

"He's not here now, either. He left for Edian a few days ago. A hard ride, but he thought he should check up on Vray. He should be back in Raisal by spring. I'll try to visit him then."

"Excellent."

Jenil reached over to lift one tiny sleeve of the sweater in Savyea's lap. "Who's this one for?"

"Feather's child, I think. I really have to go through what I have stored at the Cave. It wouldn't do to slight one of them."

"Of course not." Not that there was any chance of that. Savyea knitted slowly, but then she'd been preparing for these babies for half a century. None would ever lack sweaters, blankets, scarves, or socks. Jenil still had one of the blankets from her childhood. Its pattern remained beautiful, although the years had made it too fragile to use. Savyea had her annoying habits, but she never neglected her children.

Jenil's spirits lifted. The years didn't matter, did they? There was more to motherhood than giving birth.

She wriggled her toes against the soft warmth of the socks Savyea had given her that morning. No. Years didn't matter at all.

PART II

CHAPTER 19

"So, when can I tell Mom?" Dael asked.

"We can't tell anyone yet," Vray said as they walked up the stairs inside the law reader's house arm in arm.

"You said that last nineday, and the nineday before that," Dael reminded her. He thought he was being reasonable, but his wife gave him an impatient look.

"I'm going to keep saying it. Until we've re-established some respect for Dreamers in Edian, I'm not going to risk it."

She was right. Dael didn't want her to be right. He wanted to watch his parents' eyes light with joy when he told them they were going to be grandparents again. "You're just lucky you haven't been morning sick."

"True."

Dael opened the door at the top of the stairs and escorted her into Oskin's rooms. The high stool in front of the Reading desk was empty, and from next door they heard the sound of water splashing. A moment later the old law reader stepped into the doorway, wiping his hands on a towel.

"Been spilling ink again?" Vray teased him, her tone gentle.

Oskin's lined face twisted unhappily. "No one knows how to make steady bottles anymore. What time is it?" he continued crankily. "Is my apprentice late? You weren't supposed to be here today."

"I enjoy coming here, Oskin," Vray said as she began to straighten papers on the desk. Dael stayed out of the way, leaning against the doorframe, content to beam fondly at his wife from a distance. "However, I didn't come this morning to help you. I came to ask you to help me."

Oskin dropped the towel on the edge of the desk, removed a book from her hands, and thumped it down randomly on a shelf behind him. "I owe you that. You witnessed for me most of the winter, and don't think I don't know that you had a hand in finding young Morlcrom to take on the job permanently."

"I did what I could." She picked up the towel and carried it to the other room, tossing it through the doorway in what Dael suspected was the general direction of the laundry basket. "I thought I had brought some order to this place."

"You did." Oskin sat down, watching her with gruff affection. "I'm only just getting it back the way I like it. Now," he said, folding his hands on the table, "what help does my princess need from a law reader?"

Vray was still for a moment. Then, looking at him steadily, she said, "I need to know the exact precedents for challenging a royal heir's right of inheritance. I need to know how to organize my approach, what evidence I'll need to present, and what Damon can do to counter my claims. Will you help me?"

That was blunt enough, Dael thought. Every muscle in his body tensed, but he managed to keep his hand away from his knife. Vray always ended up being the most blunt when she thought she was going to be subtle—at least with people she really cared about. Oskin was a good man. She was right to trust him. At least, Dael hoped she was right.

Oskin breathed out in a loud whoosh. "Is that all?" he demanded. He would have sounded testy if he'd kept better control of his voice. As it was, he sounded rather frightened. "A legal challenge? Have you given this careful thought, Your Highness? Prince Damon isn't known for having a high regard for any law that obstructs him. What makes you think he'll even hear a challenge?"

"That's part of why I need you." She leaned her hands on his desk, as earnest and persuasive as Dael had ever seen her. "I need to know how to present the challenge so that he can't afford to ignore it. If he does ignore it, at least I'll have respected the Law."

From his silent observation point, Dael admired the way that she said nothing about the revolution she was plotting if the challenge went wrong. She wasn't going to put Oskin in any more danger than she had to.

Just as Dael wasn't going to mention the revolution that Jordy and he were plotting, which would go into effect if his Kitten's plans failed.

Oskin pursed his lips. "Respect for the Law," he repeated. "Can't argue with that. All right." He beckoned Dael toward him. "The books we need are up there." He pointed to a shadow-shrouded shelf near the ceiling. "Even if you can't read, you're tall. Get me the first three on the left, then find your wife a chair. This will take a while."

Pirse rode into Juniper Ridge an hour past sunset. Doron would be annoyed. She would just be putting Emlie to bed and would complain about having to fix a second supper just for him. She also complained if he spent a single day more than necessary on his visits to the nearby villages. He could just imagine what she would have to say when he described his recent scouting expedition along the Rhenlan border.

Well, he'd grown used to never quite pleasing his wife. The thought of the bed that he hadn't seen in too many ninedays brought an anticipatory smirk to his features. He'd please her there, wouldn't he?

He had just past Timik's barn when a voice hailed him from the darkness. Pirse drew rein, peering toward the shepherd's house. He heard Timik's footsteps on the gravel of the yard, then made out the dark figure hurrying toward the fence. "Working late?" Pirse inquired as the man reached him.

"Watching for you, lad. There's been trouble."

"Here?" Pirse dismounted. "The guard, I suppose. What did they take?"

He was disgusted, but not surprised. Palle might have put most of his guards on border patrol, but not all. Over the past few years, Pirse had become familiar with conditions in the mountain villages. Most were isolated enough that he had been able to encourage new Redmothers and Brownmothers to take vows in each community, without attracting any notice from the guard troops that visited once or twice a year. Pirse had also served as a law reader would to settle disputes, when he wasn't working with the villagers to improve the defensibility of their houses and farms. He hadn't forgotten that Juniper Ridge was as vulnerable to injustice as any other village—but they had enjoyed a blessedly long stretch of peace, and the thought that some of Palle's greedy followers had disturbed his friends and neighbors made Pirse's hand drift toward his sword.

Timik placed his hand on Pirse's shoulder. "They took your family."

For one merciful moment the words made no sense. "Took?" His body stiffened. "Not Doron."

"And the baby." Timik's grip tightened, but Pirse scarcely felt it. He swayed, his vision blurring, and fought not to lose the sound of the man's voice. "At first we didn't know they were guards. They asked after Doron as if they were weavers who knew her dyes. They carried her off that very afternoon. Put her astride one of their packhorses while one of them carried Emlie. They knew, lad. Knew that Emlie was your daughter."

The first shock passed, leaving Pirse utterly calm. No urge for uncontrolled violence threatened him. He knew exactly what he had to do. The certainty left no room for emotions. "When did this happen?"

"Four days ago. Your uncle's counting on you following them to Bronle."

Pirse nodded curtly. "Then I think it's time I obliged him."

"You won't go alone," Timik assured him.

"I never intended to. It's time, Timik. Time I claimed the throne. Find messengers who'll go to Alder and any other village that can spare a few people. They'll have to hurry. I want to gather as many as I can before we start."

Timik released him and stepped back. His slow voice

held a note of surprise. "Yes, Sire."

Pirse mounted and rode down the hill. One flurry of commands was only a start. Other friends and neighbors would also have cause to be surprised before this night was out. With good reason.

None of them had ever witnessed the construction of an entire king's guard.

"I'm glad you've come," the Brownmother said to Feather as they walked through the quiet corridor of Bren's main healing house. Sunlight streamed through wide windows set at intervals along the outside wall, causing the warm yellows and oranges of the floor rugs to glow cheerfully.

"If you don't know what is troubling her," Feather protested, not for the first time, "I don't see what you expect me to do." All she knew was that Jeyn had not sent any messages since she'd come to Bren. The first word about Jeyn had come from the Brownmothers—and it had come to Feather, not the king.

"She's your sister. She may trust you more than she trusts us."

Feather touched the Brownmother's sleeve, drawing her to a halt. "Why? Isn't she letting you treat her?"

"She's obedient. Outwardly she's the picture of health. But we fear for her. Please, see what you can do."

Feather allowed herself to be led to the end of the corridor. The Brownmother knocked gently on the door, then ushered Feather inside and left her alone with the princess of Sitrine.

Jeyn seemed unaware of her arrival. She sat beside a table loaded with books, her embroidery stand immediately in front of her. Jeyn ignored both to stare out the window at the house's winter-empty garden.

"Wake up," Feather teased, refusing to worry yet. "You've got company."

After a terrifying pause, Jeyn turned her head. "Feather. Hello."

"Hello." Feather found a chair and carried it over to the window, where she placed it comfortably near Jeyn's. "How are you? Feeling homesick?"

"Homesick? No."

"The Brownmothers are worried about you," Feather said bluntly. "Brownmothers are terrible once they start to worry. I know, I lived in a house full of them for years." She paused, waiting for a response to her humor, or perhaps an objection from Jeyn that she was fine, that there was no need to fuss over her. Neither came.

"I worry, too." Jeyn studied her own hands, folded in her lap, with eerie intensity. "Feather, I feel odd."

"Have you told the Brownmother?"

"Told her what? I feel fine."

Perplexed, Feather reached out and touched the other woman's face, catching and holding her gaze. "You just said you feel odd."

"I do." Jeyn blinked rapidly. "That's the trouble. Everything's fine."

"I don't understand."

"Lots of women have fears when they're pregnant," Jeyn declared, pulling back in her seat.

"Is that what this is? Fear?"

"I've been dreaming while I'm awake, seeing colors that don't exist, feeling a touch against my arm when I'm completely alone. Can a Brownmother cure that?"

"That must be distressing," Feather said, but knew the words were meaningless as she said them. "I'd offer to send Aage to you, but I can't. He's gone to spend a few ninedays with Morb."

"I can't wait ninedays. I'm not sure I can wait hours. Feather, I've got to get rid of this feeling!"

"You're not just sick?" Feather tried for the last time. "The Brownmothers could change your diet, or—"

"That's not it. I'm healthy."

She looked healthy, but her eyes drifted away again, forgetting Feather's presence to watch a sunbeam. Feather studied the princess for a few moments, considering what to do. "We could send a message to Garden Vale," she said at last, though Jeyn didn't appear to hear her. "There are ways around the Rhenlan border patrols." Feather raised her voice. "Shall I send a messenger?"

Jeyn's gaze came back to her face. "Garden Vale? Aage wouldn't want me to tell Jenil."

Feather pressed her lips together in annoyance. "Aage isn't here."

"We need Dreamer babies. Jenil understands that," Jeyn murmured. "I'll go to her, Feather. Go to Garden Vale. Yes. I've always wanted to travel more. You're right. Thank you."

"That wasn't what I meant," Feather said, alarmed. "We can send for Jenil. You really shouldn't travel. You certainly can't travel through Rhenlan."

"Why not? I'm healthy." Jeyn stood up, the picture of alert self-confidence. "I need to be out, doing something for myself. Don't make such a face, Feather. I'll be fine."

"I came down here to see how you were feeling, not get you in worse trouble. You can't go to Garden Vale!"

"I won't tell anyone who I am. Spring's coming. Travel will be uncomfortable, but not impossible. I will go," she said decisively. Jeyn took Feather by the hand and tugged her out of her chair. "Come with me. We'll see the Brownmothers together."

Feather refrained from arguing with the princess. Maybe she was right. Maybe she needed some control over the situation. It was her baby, her body. Maybe she should go to Garden Vale. Maybe it wouldn't be all that dangerous.

Maybe Sene and Chasa wouldn't be too angry when Feather brought the news of Jeyn's travels back to Raisal.

Feather gave a short, sarcastic laugh, and let Jeyn lead the way out of the room.

CHAPTER 20

Vray woke to the brush of a kiss across her lips. She opened
her eyes. Dim pre-dawn grayness revealed her room's contents as vague, half-familiar shapes. The nearest, a dark
shadow looming over the bed, was her husband.

"I'm going," Dael said softly.

"Hmmm," Vray agreed. "Have breakfast with me?"

"Lunch."

"Fine."

He departed, closing their bedroom door quietly. Vray
pulled the bedcovers back over her ears. His scent still lingered on his pillow, but the spot he'd occupied beside her
was cool. Vray tried to drift back to sleep, but it was too
late. Too many mornings she'd wakened at this hour or earlier to the crowing of Cyril's rooster. She missed that
rooster. *But not often,* she admitted, remembering Dael's
kiss.

"Enough daydreaming," she murmured. Throwing back
the covers, she rose and quickly dressed.

For over an hour she worked at her Redmother records,
first by candlelight, then in the red glow from the rising
sun. She put the books aside when Teza appeared with her
breakfast on a tray.

Eventually Vray emerged onto the landing outside her
rooms, well fed and presentable to Teza's critical eye. She
smiled at the guard who stood next to her door. Being one
of Damon's personally chosen men, he did not smile back.
His straight-ahead stare did not even acknowledge her presence. She looked up toward the landing that led to the
King's rooms and saw another of Damon's favorites in position beside that door.

Vray paused, face tilted up, one hand resting against the
wall as she prepared to start down the staircase. Next to the

guard stood the king's personal servant, not at all where she was supposed to be at this hour. The woman noticed Vray. She snuck a furtive look at the guard beside her, then took three quick steps to the edge of the landing and beckoned to Vray with a fluttery gesture.

Vray had no desire to talk to the king, but something in the woman's manner stung her to action, and she ran lightly up the stairs before the guard at her door could react. The guard on the king's landing made a half-hearted move to block the doorway.

"Do you have orders that I am not permitted to see the king my father?" Vray demanded.

"No, Your Highness," the guard admitted.

Vray brushed past him, the old servant at her heels. The king's sitting room was unoccupied. The servant hurried around Vray and went to a doorway in the right-hand wall.

"This way," she urged.

Vray hesitated, her brash confidence waning. For as long as she could remember, Hion had been fanatical about maintaining his privacy. She cleared her throat nervously as she entered the bedroom. "Your Majesty?"

The servant pointed to the bed.

Vray took a few steps into the room. The place smelled of sickness, the air heavy. "Your Majesty?" she repeated.

Hion did not reply. His gaze was locked straight ahead, his eyes focused on something other than his surroundings.

"How long has he been this ill?" Vray asked quietly.

"I am not to speak of it." The servant would come no farther than the foot of the bed, her expression filled with fear. Her voice was a mere whisper. "He'll be angry."

"Not today." Vray touched Hion's flushed, fever-hot face. She looked again at the woman. "What's your name? You can tell me that, can't you?"

"Lily."

"Lily, do you know Brownmother Ausin in the town?"

"I'm not allowed to leave the castle."

"Never mind, then. You stay here. I'll get help."

Vray left the king's rooms and descended the stairway,

191

moving as quickly as she dared. No one in the castle would notice her going briskly about some errand or another. They would, however, notice her if she panicked.

To her relief she found a guard she knew and trusted about to enter the great hall, and called to him. "Stirik!"

"Yes, Your Highness?"

"Come here. I have an errand for you." She took him by the arm and led him toward the courtyard, away from listening ears. "Go to Captain Dael and tell him this: the king is ill. He is to send for Brownmother Ausin and Greenmother Jenil. Prince Damon also needs to be informed. I will stay with Hion until the Brownmother arrives. Do you have that?"

"Yes, Highness."

"Go."

Stirik ran for the guard barracks. Vray hurried back to the tower.

"Highness?"

Damon wrinkled his nose and pushed his plate away from him. "This had better be important, Palim. You know how I feel about the stench of the stable intruding on my meals."

The groom came directly to the table, a light of excitement in his usually dull eyes. "Princess is giving orders."

"What sorts of orders?"

"Sending for healers for the king."

Elation and indignation warred within Damon. "At last. But why did she hear of it first? Never mind. Which healers, Palim? Have the messengers gone yet?"

"One's gone into Edian. Other's saddling up for Garden Vale."

"Well, it's too late to catch the guard going into the town. Delay the Brownmother on her way here. I'll issue orders to prevent her entering the castle. We have to keep Jenil out of this. Does the court know yet?"

"Don't think so."

The door opened and a guard stepped in to announce,

"Messenger from Captain Dael, Your Highness."

Damon stood up, waving Palim away as the messenger entered. "Thank you, Palim. You may go. Yes?"

Damon listened to the messenger's report of his father's illness, and let his impatience serve as a believable substitute for the urgent concern the messenger would be expecting. By the time he dismissed the messenger, with a stern warning to speak to no one else, and left for the stables himself, Palim had several minutes' head start.

None of the servants or guards he encountered gave any indication that they'd heard the disturbing news. His sister was not making Hion's illness a matter of general knowledge. How discreet. Not that the facts needed to be hidden. Damon was simply looking forward to the satisfaction of making the announcement himself.

Damon beckoned to two of his guards, who followed him to the side door of the stable. "Tell me who's inside," he ordered one.

The man entered, returning within seconds. "Stirik. Just mounting. And two stable boys."

"Tell the boys they're wanted at the gate house, now." Damon pointed at the second guard. "You. Meet them there with something to keep them busy for an hour or two." The man ran off. To the first guard Damon added, "Once you've sent them away, meet me back inside."

Damon gave the guard a moment or two, then followed him into the stable. Stirik was about to unlatch the front doors. Damon walked toward him. "You! Just a moment."

The guard turned, one hand holding the horse's reins. "Your Highness?"

"My sister tells me you're to be our messenger to Garden Vale."

"Yes, Highness." Stirik waited, attentive and completely unsuspecting.

Damon came up to the man, gazing into his face with great seriousness. "I hope you understand the importance of this errand," he said. He drew his long knife as he spoke and stabbed upward through the guard's abdomen into his heart in one efficient thrust.

Damon stepped to the side as the body toppled forward. The horse snorted at the smell of fresh blood and shied back. Damon strolled back to the side door. His guard came up the center aisle of the stable, glancing curiously at the loose horse, the still-closed main doors, and what lay in front of them.

"Stirik won't be returning from Garden Vale. Take the horse to the queen's estate. If her groom questions you, tell him it's a gift from the prince."

The guard nodded. "And that?" He jerked his thumb at the body.

"Bury it." Damon glanced around. "In the dung heap," he suggested, and left.

Vray sat on a chair beside the king's bed. She and Lily had coaxed him into taking a few sips of water. Soon after, his eyes had closed and he'd drifted into a light doze. Vray sent Lily to meet Brownmother Ausin at the gate and hurry her along.

Hion moaned in his sleep. The low, pain-filled sound drove Vray out of her chair to pace back and forth between bed and window. "Why are you doing this to me?" she asked, hugging herself tightly. "All our lives, everything you've ever done has been for Damon's benefit. Just this once, couldn't you have considered my needs? And what about your kingdom? You've been Rhenlan's only protection against your son's appetites. How dare you throw that responsibility on me? You've never given me anything before."

She stopped. There was no more reaction from the unconscious man to the abrupt silence than there had been to her angry words. "Ignored again," Vray muttered. "I should be used to it." Coming close to the bed, she raised her head proudly and addressed the king in a clear, even voice. "I never could make you listen to me." Old memories stirred, and she rubbed the back of her right hand across her cheek. "This time you're not going to stop me from saying what I want to say. You're wrong. You've always been wrong in how you've ruled Rhenlan. Maybe I could have disagreed with you, but still respected your opinions if you'd ever explained anything to me. I could have respected you if I'd understood why you abandoned so many of the old ways. But you never spoke to me; not about anything." A tight knot formed behind her breastbone.

"Do you know what I resent the most? All those years I spent under your roof, all those years when you should have been one of the most important people in my life, and I look at you now and feel nothing. It's not something lacking in me, either. I worry about lots of people, about all of Rhenlan. I know what it is to experience love and joy and indignation. For you, I can't even find pity."

She gazed down at the king. Her head ached with tension, but her eyes were dry and her voice steady.

"It's not something missing in me. It's something you stole from me. That's what I resent."

A noise in the outer room disturbed her and she fell silent. A moment later Damon entered, a mask of polite concern on his face. After taking a second look at Hion, he turned suspiciously in place, inspecting the rest of the bedroom.

"Odd," he announced. "I distinctly heard conversation."

"You heard me thinking aloud," Vray said.

He accepted the explanation with a smirk. "Talking to yourself? A reaction to worry, sister?"

"A way of passing the time."

"You find waiting tedious? I don't. Anticipation provides a special pleasure all its own."

"Are we anticipating the same event?"

"The conclusion of Father's illness, certainly. Has he spoken to you at all?"

Vray resumed her seat at the side of the bed. "No. Perhaps his condition will improve, once Ausin brings something to break the fever."

"Ausin has never seemed a very reliable person to me. She might not answer your summons."

Vray carefully kept herself from showing any outward sign of tension. She gazed at the sick face of the king rather than looking at Damon, and wondered if Dael was aware that the messenger to Ausin had been intercepted.

"As for a useless Dreamer like Jenil, she's never had any respect for our authority. I have a strong feeling she won't come to Edian at all."

He meant to let the King die. Vray felt herself going cold. He was so sure he was close to the final triumph, a breath away from the throne he'd been hungering after for years.

"I pray you're mistaken about the Greenmother," she said, her words more plea to the gods than defiance of her brother's opinion.

"Not this time, little sister. I think that unless—or, let's be hopeful—until a healer arrives, one of us should remain with the king. He may have concerns about the way Rhenlan will be ruled. He may have advice to pass on during his illness." Damon sighed regretfully. "Unfortunately, as much as I'd like to be here, I simply can't be spared. The honor rightly falls to you, anyway, Redmother Vray, as the family chronicler."

"We both have work to do." Vray offered her counter-suggestion cautiously. "Like you, my place is at Court."

"At Court, supporting me. Very loyal, but unnecessary today. No, Vray. A dying king needs a Redmother at his side. You've always been concerned that Remembering be properly done."

"He's not dead yet!" Outrage put more force behind Vray's words than she'd allowed herself to express since her return to Edian. Suspicion flickered across Damon's face, but it was too late to salvage her pose of humility. That was a game she didn't need to play with him anymore. She didn't have time for it now, either.

However, she did try to make herself sound distraught rather than dangerous. "I'm sure he can recover if Ausin arrives in time."

"I'm not. This has been coming for years. Overdue, in fact."

196

He took one more cool, measuring look at Hion's sunken figure, then turned away. "Notify the guard if there's any change. He'll send for me." Without waiting for her to acknowledge his orders, he left.

Vray remained where she was for five minutes. She calmed herself, then tried to decide whether the King's breathing really had grown more shallow and labored since Lily had left. When she was as calm as she was going to get, she rose and went into the other room. She tried to push the door open so that she could look down the stairs. The door would not move.

Vray pushed on the door again. It felt as solid as the adjoining walls. She pounded on it with closed fists and shouted for the guard.

The guard's voice sounded distant and clear. "Yes, Your Highness?"

"Open this door."

"No."

"Why not?" Stupid question. She knew what he would answer.

"Prince's orders. The door is to remain locked."

Of course it was. Vray leaned her back against the door. She could think of nothing else to say. No healers allowed in. No troublesome princesses allowed out. Damon was being very thorough.

She wouldn't be meeting Dael for lunch, after all. If she knew her brother, she wouldn't survive the king for very long, either.

The secret, Damon noted with approval, was still safe. He passed the entrance to the great hall and beckoned to one of his guards to follow him. The woman left her post by the doors, eyeing him attentively.

"Yes, Highness?"

"Find Captain Dael. Send him to my audience chamber at once."

"Yes, Highness."

He continued down the corridor, listening to her

bootsteps recede in the other direction. *Hurry along, girl,* he thought pleasantly. *Everything must be in order before I notify the court of Father's sad condition.*

At his worktable, he unlocked the center drawer and lifted out his personal ledger. He flipped through the volume until he found the section he wanted. Hidden among some weather records were the notes he had been making for the past five years, for the speech he hoped to give tonight. He carried the book to his reading stand. He had updated the speech regularly. Most of it was already memorized. All it needed were a few specific details, which the next few hours would provide.

At the sound of a knock he closed the book and said, "Enter."

"You sent for me, Highness?"

Damon studied the captain of the king's guard. Over the years he had stopped noticing how truly heroic Dael could look. The man seemed every inch the hero today, dressed in rugged winter uniform, his hair slightly wind-mussed, his expression, as always, serious. Damon needed this man as his captain of guards. Dael had never given Damon reason to doubt his loyalty, until recently.

Until I gave him Vray.

Damon hoped what Dael felt for his sister was only lust. It had to be that. The man was no fool. Still, Damon couldn't afford to take risks. Not today, of all days.

"I've had disturbing news, Captain."

"Highness?"

"Sitrine. Troops moving, more than ever before. I fear for our border. I know you've posted your best corporals there. I know Sene would be mad to provoke an incident, but I can't ignore my sources. You're to leave at once."

The fair brows drew together, the frown a troubled one. "To inspect the border, Highness?"

"Inspect it carefully, Captain. Personally. Take a couple of troops with you, the best of your people that can be spared from castle duty. I want your preliminary report back by the end of the nineday. By messenger. You should plan on remaining out there until we're sure the threat is unfounded—or eliminated."

"You alarm me, Highness."

"I intend to. This could be the most urgent errand I've ever given you. Can you leave before midmorning?"

"Your pardon, Highness," the man said slowly, "but I understand that your father is ill."

"Well? What of it?"

"I dislike leaving you at such a critical time, Prince Damon."

"I value your concern. But you can serve me best at this very critical time by ensuring that our borders are safe."

"As you command, of course, Your Highness."

"You'd better get started at once."

"Highness." The man bowed, and left.

Damon stood quietly for a moment after Dael had gone, his fingers tracing the letters on the leather cover of his book. "RHENLAN," they proclaimed, "under Hion, father to Damon." He'd get to start a new book soon. A new book, with a new title. Hion was in his hands. So was his difficult sister. His sister's husband would be gone shortly, after which Damon could take charge of the court.

By the time he allowed Dael to return, his power in Edian would be secure. If the man objected when he learned that his wife was dead, Damon would be prepared to replace him.

CHAPTER 21

The messenger found Damon in the great hall, standing at one end of the hearth a few minutes after he finished informing the court of the king's illness. The murmuring, anxious voices of relatives and counselors stilled, then resumed as the messenger was identified as a guard rather than a member of the household staff.

Damon left the hall without looking back. He'd let them enjoy their relief. They would learn what was expected of the new court, his court, soon enough.

Palim waited for him in the isolated audience chamber, his damp cloak steaming slightly. Rain mixed with snow had swept into the town from the north during the night. As the morning progressed, the lowering gray skies were contributing nicely to the somber mood in the castle. Palim, however, showed no sign of strain. He greeted Damon with his usual appraising stare and expectant silence.

"Well?" Damon asked as soon as the door closed behind the departing guard.

"Messengers are ready to ride."

"Good." Damon paced the length of the room once. He'd been waiting for this for years, training himself and his followers for this moment. Desire to give the command, to take charge at last, was a physical ache. Still, he had to wait. "You resolved that little dispute?"

"Men still say it's a waste to worry about a village that size. Everyone wants in on the action here."

"They'll get their pick of positions once their first assignment is completed."

"They understand. Got three men for it, like you wanted. Clever boys, looking to profit once they're sent east."

"There'll be profit enough for all of us, never fear."

Away from the constant scrutiny of the crowd in the great hall, Damon clapped his hands and rubbed them together in eager anticipation. "You've put a lot of careful organization into this, Palim. It won't be forgotten."

The big man dipped his head briefly, politely. "Highness."

"One more thing. Captain Dael is going to the Sitrinian border for a few days. He should be gone before midday. Report to me if there is any delay. If the king dies before he has left the castle—well, come to me the moment you hear, and we'll decide if additional action needs to be taken."

Palim looked dubious, but shrugged his acquiescence.

"You may go."

Damon gave the groom a half-minute's head start, then followed him into the corridor. He proceeded to the great hall, whose occupants remained immersed in their insignificant speculations. A few faces turned toward him as he proceeded at a properly subdued pace across the large room. Those brave enough intercepted him to offer nervous, meaningless words of support and condolence. Damon ignored them all. They were his father's court. Some were his sister's friends. All were assuming, or at least hoping, that they would be welcome to serve the new king in some similar capacity.

Like the people of Broadford, they were in for a rude surprise.

Dael chose two troops of guards and made the necessary preparations for leaving Edian. Within the hour, they were out of the castle. Dael set riders to lead the column east and called the two corporals to ride with him at the end of the line. Owners of shops and homes watched with concern as the two troops, heavily laden with supplies and weapons, passed by.

The corporals had concerns of their own. "What's it all about, Captain?" one asked. "Abstainers showing their faces at last?"

"Not that I'm aware of," Dael said. There had been a

conspicuous absence of Abstainer raids since the end of last summer.

"Just a patrol," the other said. "That's all right, then. The Sitrinians are never a threat."

Dael looked at the backs of the two guards who rode fifteen yards ahead of them and listened to the creak and jangling of tack, the thud of trotting hooves, the calls of conversation and laughter that rippled up and down the line of riders. No one would overhear his conversation with the corporals. "I agree. You'll have nothing to fear from Sitrine, unless Edian sends further orders."

The corporal on his left glanced at him, puzzled. "What sort of orders?"

The time had come to voice his suspicion. "Orders to attack Sitrine."

"Attack?" the first corporal repeated blankly. "You mean start a fight? Why?"

"If it's the king's orders, do you need any other reason?" Dael asked.

The corporal on his right, voice rising slightly in question, said, "No?"

"You should," Dael told him.

A thoughtful silence followed. They had left the town itself and were moving into adjacent farmland. Dael had given them all the time he could. "This is where I leave you," he said. "Take your position on the border and wait."

"But you're supposed to be going with us!"

"I'm needed in Edian more. You've got your orders. Patrol. And these are my orders. Think before you take any action."

Dael reined his horse in and let the corporals pass by. Then he turned and began cantering back toward the last farm they had passed.

Damon had to be mad to think that he'd leave Edian now. Leave his wife—his pregnant wife—to face the crisis alone? After all these years, Damon had finally asked the impossible.

Before Dael could reach the entrance to the farmyard,

another horseman appeared around the bend in the road. As soon as he saw Dael, he halted. Only a dozen yards separated them. Dael stared at the uniform of a member of the household staff, the familiar face. It was Palim. Damon's chief informer only left the castle on the prince's business. Evidently something on this road was more important to Damon than the events occurring in the castle.

Dael spurred his horse toward the startled groom. Palim reacted, turning to flee, but Dael galloped down on him before the groom's horse could get started and grabbed Palim by the collar, dragging him from his saddle. The next instant Palim's knife was in his hand. Dael jerked his face back from the slash, released Palim, overbalanced, and toppled to the ground two strides after he dropped the groom. Both horses bolted.

Dael rolled to his feet, drawing his sword. Palim stood in the center of the road, knife ready. The man didn't seem to be aware that he was hopelessly outmatched. Dael took a step toward him. "You were following me."

"I didn't think you'd leave." Palim's face twisted in a condescending sneer. "Only a fool crosses Damon. He never believed you were a fool. I knew better."

"And you're going to go back and tell him so."

"That's right."

"I can't afford to let him know I'm still here."

"Think you can pay me to keep your secret? I might, if I thought you could win. You can't. Your father's gold wouldn't do me any good once the prince found out."

Dael lifted his sword. "I don't want to buy your loyalty." He began walking forward.

"Stop." Palim tensed. "Kill me, you're finished. Who'll protect your pretty wife? I can watch her for you. Maybe even put in a good word about this desertion. Prince relies on me. He'll listen to me." He took a step back, knife coming up in a defensive position as Dael loomed closer. "What about the law? Guards have to uphold the law. Kill me, it's murder."

Dael swung his sword. The blade cut cleanly through

Palim's knife arm and sank into the side of his neck. With a
jerk Dael freed his sword and watched the dead body
crumple to the ground. "I know," he replied.

Loras turned away from his conversation when the interior door of the shop opened, expecting to see his wife.
"Dael?" he asked in surprise.

"Trouble, Dad." His son, breathing heavily, crossed the
room and locked the front door. His guard's uniform was
gone. Instead he wore a farmer's shirt and baggy trousers,
and a ragged-hemmed gray cloak in place of his Rhenlan
blue. He acknowledged Ivey with a grim nod, but showed
no other reaction to the presence of their unexpected visitor.

"Good," Dael said. "I was going to send for you."

"What happened?" the minstrel asked. "You were seen
leaving town with a couple of troops."

"I'm supposed to be on my way to the Sitrinian border.
We've got to keep my return quiet."

"Sit down, son." Loras put down the pin he'd been
working on. "You know this finishes you with Damon if the
word gets out. Why risk that now? Vray is going to need you
more than ever, and sooner than we expected."

Dael pulled a short stool to the other side of the workbench where he was out of sight of anyone passing the
window. "He's up to something, Dad, but I don't know
what."

"You were sure he'd wait for Hion to die before making
his move."

"Word is that he's ill," Ivey added. "The town's been
seething with gossip since midmorning."

"He's ill," Dael confirmed, voice brittle with strain.

Loras liked the day's news less and less. "Dael, what do
you think Damon might be planning?"

Ivey smiled cynically. "Aside from leaping onto the
throne the instant his father dies, that is."

"I don't know!" Loras flinched at the anguish in his
son's voice. Dael's hand closed, white-knuckled, on the hilt

of his sword. "I've just been to see Brenn. His wife works in the castle. He spoke with her, and she got to a few of my guards. Vray hasn't been seen since breakfast. The king's room is locked, and only Damon's favorites have been allowed near. First thing this morning, before I was ordered to Sitrine, I sent a messenger for Jenil, but she may not return in time. I've got to know what's going on in that castle!"

"We'll find out," Loras said firmly. "Remember, we made plans for something like this. Give me a few hours and I'll have some information for you. Meanwhile, you've got to keep out of sight. You did get to Brenn without being seen?"

"Almost." Dael folded both hands on the workbench and stared at them. "Just after I turned back I found out I was being followed."

"Damon's people," Ivey guessed.

"The groom, Palim, followed us out from Edian. He would have reported straight back to Damon. So I killed him."

Loras kept his voice level. "Good." Dael's head snapped up, his expression incredulous, but Loras refused to allow his son's regrets or second thoughts to complicate matters now. "What did you do with the body?"

"I buried it under a haystack."

"That's all right, then."

Ivey got up. "I'll go see if there've been any new official announcements."

Dael watched the door close behind the minstrel. When he faced Loras again his expression was still pain-filled. "But, Dad!"

"Go change your clothes, those are dusty. I'll tell your mother you're home for lunch."

Hion woke several times during the course of the day. Vray called it waking because he opened his eyes and was able to swallow a little of the water she offered him, but he gave no sign of being aware of where he was or what was happening. The fever never abated. When he grew restless enough to move his head against the pillow, or to shift an arm or leg, he groaned with such pain that Vray's muscles tensed in unavoidable sympathy. Each motion was more feeble than the last. His breathing grew more erratic as the hours wore slowly on.

Vray gave up pacing and sat continually beside the bed. She had to be that close to see the weak rise and fall of his chest, to hear the whisper of air entering and leaving his body. "Do you know what you are?" she asked, voice subdued by the unwelcoming stillness. "You must be the last victim of the plague. That's fitting, I suppose, part of how you should be Remembered. For most of the Children, the way you met and conquered the fire bears will be the most important part of your story. Hion the Valiant, Hion the Successful."

A breath sighed out of him. Vray waited, watching, then she began to count the seconds. She stood and leaned over him, touched his face. "Your Majesty?" she whispered. Finally, she pushed the bedcovers aside and put her ear to his chest.

Feeling a little light-headed, she wandered aimlessly into the sitting room. Most of its contents were unfamiliar. The king had never invited her here. Their confrontations had always occurred in more public places. She recognized a few books that spent part of their time in the castle library.

The king was dead. She wondered how Damon would arrange her death. A fall down the tower steps would be the easiest to explain. A broken neck could be accounted for as an accident on a staircase. She could hear Damon's grieving speech to the townsfolk at the Remembering, Hion dead of an old injury, the Princess Vray's unfortunate fall. Damon gave lovely speeches. There would be a great many tears for the dead Shapers, an outpouring of love and sympathy for the new, deeply grieving king.

Vray growled in inarticulate anger and frustration. She had come so close to challenging the prince, but Hion had robbed her of the time she desperately needed. She would die. Her unborn child would die. Dael would die. There would only be Jordy's group of obstinate Keepers left to fight Damon.

The key turned in the lock. Vray shivered with fear as she turned, expecting the guard, or Damon, coming to check on the King's condition. She knew there was no way to keep them from discovering the truth. All she could hope for was a chance to escape. She looked desperately around the King's room. Where was his sword, his dagger? Even a belt knife would do.

The door pulled open to reveal Teza, peering cautiously toward her. "Your Highness? Is this a good time for you to get away?"

Vray ran onto the landing and helped Teza push the door shut. She almost laughed with relief. "Yes!"

Teza indicated the closed door with a tilt of her head. "How is he?"

"Where's the guard?" Vray countered.

"He went to relieve himself. Lily came to me when she was told she could not return to the King's chamber," Teza explained as they hurried down the stairs. "She gave me her key and I've been watching the guard ever since." They reached the empty landing in front of Vray's door. "Our guard left hours ago," Teza concluded.

"Where's Dael?"

"Ordered out of town."

Vray considered briefly. Every action she took now had to be the correct one. She had no time for mistakes, and no Dael to rely on. "King Hion has just died. My brother doesn't know it yet, but he was certain the end would come today. He's probably downstairs right now, preparing to assume the throne."

"While you were locked away in the tower?" Teza protested. "I knew he'd try something of the sort."

Vray gave the servant a wry smile. "For now, let's just call it an oversight. You had better return that key to Lily. Tell her it would be best to disappear for a while. Before you go down, please bring me my cloak."

Teza regarded her uneasily. "What are you going to do?"

"I am going to find Vissa and Danta, of course," Vray said. "And stay with them in public from this moment on." She was pleased to hear that her voice sounded serene and unafraid even though the fourteen-year-old child in her past was quaking with terror. "We have a Remembering to prepare."

Standing alone in the great hall, Damon stretched languidly. All in all, it had been a very busy day. Successful, for the most part. The important elements had finally been set in motion. He frowned briefly. He hadn't expected Palim, of all people, to disappoint him. The groom had last been seen helping Dael and his troops prepare for departure. He had not reported that departure to Damon, as he'd been ordered to do, nor had he come to the throne room after the announcement of Hion's death. The delay in dispatching Palim's chosen riders had not been significant. Damon always had reliable messengers at hand. Whether Palim's unexpected desertion was significant remained to be seen. It had to be desertion. But why today?

Damon dismissed the question. Nothing for him to do now but wait and reap the benefits of his planning. He stepped onto the dais and took the chair that his father no longer needed. "At last," he sighed, then leaned back and laced his hands behind his head.

Only one thing left to do. He supposed it could wait till morning. With the captain out of the way he didn't have to hurry. Maybe he would do it himself. He savored the thought. The girl had been nothing but an inconvenience since she was born. Mother had no use for her. She had made such a pest of herself this past year, sneaking around and trying to be clever. Possibly costing Damon the best guard captain he was ever likely to have.

So, how would she pay? Damon had planned on having her smothered, with the princess found lifeless beside the king's body. A painless death for her, and a useful tragedy to present to the town. Grief in the royal family would be wonderful for provoking sympathy. It was a pity she got away. Then again, the Remembering would be useful. He would let her play the Redmother for a few days. He could wait until his chosen time.

I think I'll make it knives, Damon thought. He would give the task to Cousin Vrain. Vrain had brought his sons with him to Edian, and they all had known Vray at Soza. They would enjoy getting reacquainted first. Later, Damon would hold the death over their heads to see that they continued to serve him well. Yes, that would do.

As for his captain, the Abstainers Dael was not expecting to find on the Sitrinian border were looking forward to dealing with him, if necessary.

Damon gazed down the length of the huge, empty chamber. The double doors at the end were closed, the few torches near the throne barely able to cast their dim light that far. Beyond the doors, the other residents of the castle would be moving numbly to their beds. An era had ended today. Many were still stunned by the finality of their loss. Some were even grieving.

One was going to die.

CHAPTER 22

On the few occasions that Doron had visited Bronle, she had found the houses too drab, the streets too narrow, and the castle perched above it all a distraction from what might otherwise have been an attractive view of the nearest mountain peaks. This time, she was also tired, hungry, in need of a bath, accompanied by strangers she feared and despised, and worn to a frazzle by Emlie's fretting. Seen in the gray light of an overcast morning, she found Bronle uglier than ever.

Few people lingered in the streets to watch their small procession pass. Lack of curiosity? Doron doubted that. Once or twice she caught a glimpse of faces peering furtively around corners once the guards' backs were turned. The expressions were suspicious, unfriendly. The unfriendliness was not directed at her.

Emlie tugged on her, wanting to nurse. Doron absently hushed the child, holding her more tightly as the horse lurched up the steep street toward the castle. Emlie began to whine unhappily.

The gates were open when they reached the castle. One of the guards trotted ahead, while another dismounted and began to confer with the gatekeeper. The third, holding the guide rope of Doron's horse, remained mounted and alert. Doron snorted under her breath. As if she would be fool enough to try to bolt from the courtyard of the castle itself. She wouldn't attempt such a feat on her own, let alone with a baby clinging to her. The caution of the guards, like so much of their behavior since dragging her and Emlie away from Juniper Ridge, was ludicrous.

Taking advantage of the momentary quiet, Doron readjusted her clothing and held Emlie to her breast. The child sucked greedily and Doron forced herself to relax. At least

210

she'd been given enough to drink to keep Emlie satisfied. The guards hadn't actually mistreated either of them, beyond forcing them to leave home, that is, and aggravating Doron by refusing to answer her questions.

A door opened at the top of a flight of stairs. The absent guard returned, followed by a man richly dressed in dyed leather, brocade, and a fur-lined cloak. Graying black curls framed his face, and an escort of three well-armed courtiers remained a watchful step behind their master. Doron had never seen him before, but she recognized him an instant before the guard's proud declaration confirmed her guess.

"Your Majesty, this is the woman."

"Clear the courtyard," Palle commanded. His personal guard moved away at once, shouting orders that sent people scurrying for doorways. Palle pulled the fur collar of his cloak up around his neck. A fitful wind moaned around the castle walls, blowing tatters of cloud down from the thick layers that enveloped the peaks of the mountains.

"Where's the child?" the ruler of Dherrica asked in a querulous voice. "Hold her where I can see her!"

Doron drew her cloak more firmly about the two of them. "What have you to do with my child?" she snapped.

Palle stopped a few steps above the courtyard. "I don't know you," he stated. "Is your entire family hiding in Juniper Ridge?"

If she had expected anything of Palle it was threats, not riddles. "Hiding?" she repeated.

"I thought I knew all the Shaper families of Dherrica and Northern Rhenlan. Yet, here you are. Do you have brothers or sisters?"

"A brother," Doron replied without thinking. Of course she wasn't thinking. He took her for a Shaper! The idea astonished and offended her—and gave meaning to the guards' treatment of her and Emlie. Because, if she had been a Shaper, mother to Pirse's child, then Emlie would have been their queen!

"Where is he now?" Palle demanded.

"What?" Doron asked, somewhat dazed.

"Your brother!" The arrogant snap in the words did much to clear the fog from Doron's mind. This was a dangerous man she faced. Whatever Palle's status in most of the country, he ruled Bronle with iron control. Defying him here, now, would accomplish nothing.

"In Rhenlan," she answered him. It was the truth. Telling it would do Ivey no harm and Palle no good.

Palle nodded sagely. "He has been Pirse's link to that country, no doubt."

Doron lowered her eyes. She didn't dare smile. "You know all about us."

"Show me the child," he demanded once more.

Emlie was almost asleep. Gently, Doron disengaged the warm, wet mouth and drew the child out from under her cloak.

Palle's mouth worked for a moment as though he were tasting something bitter. "She's his, all right," he said at last. He turned to the guard who had observed the whole conversation with ever-widening eyes. "Take them to the west wing and remember what I told you about visitors."

"Yes, sir."

"We'll speak again," he told Doron.

She watched him retreat back up the stairs and disappear into the castle. "Don't hurry on my account," she muttered after him.

"Greenmother! Greenmother! Where are you?"

Jenil rose from her stool and stepped quickly away from the bedside of her sleeping patient. "Shhh," she hissed sharply as she pushed through the curtained doorway into the corridor outside. "You know better, child," she told the young Brownmother who hurried toward her. "I won't have my healing undone by a lot of uncalled-for noise." The woman bit her lip with an anxious glance toward the room behind Jenil, but gave no sign of calming down. "All right, what is it?" Jenil relented.

"King Hion is dead." The Brownmother blurted out the words as though she hardly believed she was speaking them.

"Ah." Jenil exhaled sharply. Her first emotion was one of relief that the man's pain was finally ended. "When did it happen? Where's the messenger?"

"Gone, Greenmother."

"What?" Irritation sharpened the word. "Who dismissed him so quickly?"

"He didn't come here," the young woman hastily explained. "He only stopped at the smithy to replace one of his horse's shoes. He's on his way to inform the border troops."

"When did the king die?" Jenil demanded.

"Three days ago."

The last vestiges of Jenil's sorrow vanished, burned to nothing by a flash of outrage. Three days! She should have been summoned at once! It was all too evident that Damon was beginning as he meant to go on. He had said often enough that he had no use for Dreamers. Well, this was the first consequence of his attitude. Instead of being present at court as tradition dictated, she was left to gather whatever news chanced to pass through the village.

"Who else has been told?" she asked.

"I think by now everyone knows. People are wondering what will happen next. The messenger would not say what orders he carried for the border, but with Damon in command it could be anything."

"He wouldn't attack Sitrine." Or would he? This was Damon they were discussing. "Take over for me," she instructed the Brownmother. "I'll return as soon as I can."

With a practiced twist she left Garden Vale and re-emerged a heartbeat later in the main room of the inn at Broadford. Canis and Lim were engaged in a game of darts. Herri came out from behind the bar with a welcoming smile. "Jenil! We weren't expecting you."

Taking his arm, she led him back into the kitchen. "Have you heard the news from Edian?" she asked quietly.

"No. Not if it's something recent."

The voice of the dart players continued uninterrupted in the next room. Jenil said, "Three days ago Hion of Rhenlan died. We have a new king. Garden Vale heard it from a guard messenger on his way to the Sitrine border."

"Rock and Pool! The others should hear this. Will you stay awhile? We just finished supper. I can offer you a wedge of pie."

In answer, Jenil returned to the main room and took a seat at the nearest table. She was hungry and tired, and, she suspected, a little bit in shock. Sene deserved a warning. Knowing the man's talents, he probably didn't need one. One of his many sources of information might well have gotten the news to him already. She would definitely have to visit Vray. The girl would need help in organizing her support. Now that the crisis had come, was her husband proving to be an effective ally or not?

Herri sent Lim off to find Jordy and the others. He brought Jenil her promised pie, then went next door himself to fetch the smith.

Jordy watched Pepper polish the old harness strap. "Rub it in, there's my girl. A dry section can develop cracks and eventually break."

His daughter bent closer over the piece of leather, small hands working diligently. Jordy leaned back against the wagon, hands in his trouser pockets, and gazed fondly at her bent head.

Cool air drifted in with the opening of the stable door. Lim stepped in, breathing quickly, face flushed. "Excuse me, carter. Tob said I could find you out here."

Pepper looked up at the young man critically. "Could you please close the door?"

"What can I do for you tonight?" Jordy asked as Lim hastily drew the door closed.

"Herri says he'd like you to come to the inn. Greenmother Jenil has just arrived."

Jordy straightened. "Has she, indeed?"

"He's also sent for Jenk and Kessit. I saw the Greenmother. She looked solemn."

"Jenil is always solemn," Jordy complained automatically. *And Herri never over-reacts,* he added silently. "Ah, well, I'd best go down. Thanks for telling me, lad."

Lim left on his next errand. Jordy sent Pepper to the pasture with a few carrots to catch Stockings while he went to the house to tell Cyril where he was going. When Pepper returned with Stockings, he allowed her to help him strap the riding pad across the horse's broad back. Squinting up at the sky, he judged that the evening's clear weather would continue all night and that the coat he was wearing would be warm enough.

Stockings, well rested from several days' idleness, carried him to the inn in good time. Kessit was only just coming down the path from his farm. Jordy left the horse in a loose box in the stable, then went inside, where he found Canis and Lannal already talking with Herri.

Jenil remained quiet while they waited for Jenk. Lim had not misrepresented her mood, nor was it the self-important solemnity that so grated on Jordy's nerves. She was worried. She was also sitting in his favorite chair. He sat across the table from her and talked archery with Canis.

When Jenk arrived, Jenil waited until everyone had found seats and the beer jug had been passed once around before speaking.

"The minstrel Ivey visited me in Garden Vale several ninedays ago," she began. "On his way to Edian. At that time, things were very tense along the Rhenlan-Dherrica border."

"Define 'tense,' " Canis said.

"Guards on both sides questioning travelers, searching merchants' wagons, establishing camps near bridges and crossroads."

Kessit lifted his mug in Jordy's direction, the gesture earning several nods of acknowledgment. "Jordy told us that sort of thing has been happening all over Rhenlan."

"Your news, Greenmother," Herri suggested.

Jenil refused to be hurried. "The tension, in Ivey's opinion, is the result of uncertainty. This has been Dherrica's problem for years, but since the end of the summer conditions have also worsened in Sitrine and Rhenlan. The king's guards of Rhenlan are more numerous than ever. In Sitrine, Prince Chasa himself is patrolling the border."

Jordy leaned toward her. "Stop delaying, woman. What news?"

"The messenger reached Garden Vale at midday. Hion is dead." She looked into each of their faces. "Three days ago."

Too soon, Jordy thought, and acknowledged part of the source of the Greenmother's grimness. She understood how sorely the lass had needed time to prepare her challenge.

Lannal said, "You might have warned us, Greenmother, that Hion was dying!"

"He's been dying for years," Jenil snapped. "Even the power couldn't heal him, and it certainly couldn't predict when he'd die. My interest now is in Damon's plans. You tell me, carter. Ivey's concerned about the guards. What does Damon intend? Why are the messengers so slow in reaching us? You've seen none here in Broadford?"

Jordy looked away from his friends. The inn windows were squares of blackness, shielding them from the wide world with reflections of warm wood and candlelight. A very wide world. Darker and more threatening than it had been since the plague. Since before the end of the plague, in a way. The fire bears had been dangerous, a serious problem, but a problem with a straightforward solution. No solution to the problem Damon represented could be considered straightforward. The problem was too complex. Damon was too complex.

Now he was king.

"But not for long," Jordy muttered under his breath.

Next to him Kessit turned his head. "Eh?"

Jordy raised his voice. "Now that we do know, there are steps we'll have to take. We haven't got much time."

"We might get snow in the next nineday," Herri agreed. "We can't say the same for Edian. Spring comes sooner there. Isn't that right, Jordy?"

Jordy wasn't thinking about weather. He rubbed one hand over his eyes, then focused on the Dreamer woman. "You know Vray can't have been prepared for Hion's death."

"None of us expected it," Lannal said, confused.

"Not emotional preparation," Jenil explained tiredly. "Strategic preparation. The girl has every intention of becoming queen."

"It's time they know," Jordy told her. "Time all Rhenlan knows."

The Greenmother's robes whispered as she tucked her hands into the sleeves. "Don't you think she should make that decision?"

"I think she's going to have to act quickly or miss her chance. The same goes for us." He took a long swallow of beer before facing his friends. "Let me tell you about our Vray."

Herri blinked his surprise. "Our Vray?"

"We called her Iris."

Jenk choked on his beer. Herri patted his back, unaware that his own mouth was gaping.

"Iris, the princess?" Canis struggled with the revelation for only an instant, before making the connection most important to her mind. "You left that poor child in Edian to live in that . . . that castle?!"

"It was her choice!" Jordy argued once more. "She knew what she was doing—what she is doing, right now! What we all should be doing: preparing to protect ourselves against the injustices that will result from Damon's kingship!"

"She plans to be queen?" Lannal asked, picking up on Jenil's remark. "Hion named Damon as heir years ago."

"She'll have to challenge him," Canis snapped. "That's the only solution with a brother like that." However, she wasn't finished being angry with Jordy. "What I want to know is how, for one minute, you could even have considered leaving her to deal with Damon alone—"

"An inheritance challenge?" Herri glumly shook his

head. "Not a simple matter. Not when the ruling house is involved."

"Damon's held authority for years. Everyone in Edian knows him, but who knows the princess?" Lannal asked.

"—after having been abandoned once at Soza, to be dropped off and forgotten like another bolt of cloth—"

Jordy briefly rested his elbows on the table and cupped his hands over his ears. The gesture elicited a startled silence from the people crowded around Jenil. He straightened once more. "Plans," he told them. "This may be our only chance."

Canis pressed her lips together and sat back in her chair. The rest looked at one another, then burst into renewed speech.

This time, Jordy joined in.

"No word from Palim?" Damon asked impatiently.

"None, Sire," Brooksen replied, and shifted uneasily from one foot to the other.

Damon turned his back on the nervous guard and paced away along the top of the castle wall. In the town below, lights were being extinguished as the good citizens of Edian went to their beds for the night. No eyes to see the noble king, watching over his people as they slept. Damon smiled in the darkness. He liked it this way. No one watching over him, wanting explanations, questioning his choices. No eyes to follow his movements, except those of his guards. The king's guard. It would be that now, in more than name. Just a few more hours. One ruler, one force of guards, in a single, unified land.

"I want Palim," he said over his shoulder. "Check the stables again. He may have returned since you were last there."

"Yes, Sire."

"And Brooksen," Damon called, before the guard could move more than a few paces.

The footsteps stopped. "Sire?"

Damon leaned on the wall, looking out. "You'll be going with Vrain tonight?"

"Yes, Sire."

"Good. I'll want to see all of you later. To thank you personally for your service to the throne." He glanced over at the man, saw greedy speculation cross the torchlit face.

Brooksen lowered his head humbly, stepping back into shadow. "Thank you, Sire."

"First, Palim."

"Yes, Sire."

"Go."

The guard went. Damon relaxed against the wall. He wanted Palim. But he didn't need him. Not any longer. The work was done.

CHAPTER 23

Palle came awake at the sound of muffled tapping on his bedroom door. With a groan, he sat up. Beside him, his mistress murmured in her sleep and reached for him.

"Shhh," he told her. "I'll be right back."

He swung his feet over the edge of the bed and reached for his tunic. The bedside candle had lost no more than an inch since their lovemaking. Who would dare disturb him in the middle of the night? The sentry would have some explaining to do.

The man who stepped into the room as soon as Palle had unfastened the latch was not the sentry, nor were any of the three men who followed him and pushed the door closed behind them. The leader looked vaguely familiar, but Palle did not remember his name.

"Well?" he demanded. "What is it?"

"The end of your reign, Palle of Dherrica."

Palle fell back a pace as the leader's sword slid smoothly out of its sheath.

Behind the swordsman, the door crashed open again and more men poured into the room. The first guard through grabbed the swordsman's right arm and spun him around. A dagger glinted in the candlelight; the swordsman gave a grunt and crumpled, dead before he hit the ground. The other guards sprang upon the remaining three strangers. Their cries and scuffles woke Palle's mistress, who sat up with a squeal of terror.

Palle scrambled backward toward the bed. "Silence!" he snapped at the woman. She ignored him, and punctuated the battle with her shrieks. The room was too small for proper swordplay. The strangers fought viciously, but the guards had taken them by surprise. With fists and knives they overwhelmed the invaders, killing two of them outright and leaving the third crouched on the floor, clutching the stump where his hand had been.

Breathless with fury and relief, Palle turned and slapped the woman, hard. She stopped screaming and, face white with outrage, retreated under the blankets.

Palle turned to the first guard. "Well done! What is your name?"

"Thisben, Sire."

"That was too close. The sentry on duty is going to answer for this."

"He's dead, Sire." Thisben gestured at the strangers sprawled around the room. "There were only six of them, but they have accomplices all over the castle. Your Majesty, I don't think it's safe for you to stay here."

"What are you talking about? Of course I'm safe." Even as he said it, Palle leaned helplessly against the bed. The bodies on the floor proclaimed the absurdity of his statement. "It's your job to keep me safe."

Two of Thisben's followers had opened the door and were watching the corridor. Thisben himself kept his sword in one hand and knife in the other. "Yes, Sire, it is. That's why I strongly recommend that we get you out of the castle."

Indignation rose in Palle. "It's my cursed nephew, isn't it? How dare he spread his evil influence into the very heart of my household!" He started toward the last surviving stranger, but the floor beneath his bare feet was sticky with blood. He stopped where he was and pointed an accusing finger at the man. "You are a vowless Abstainer, and the servant of an Abstainer! Admit it!"

Thisben rested the point of his sword against the man's back. The man flinched, but said nothing.

One of the guards in the doorway glanced into the room. "They don't serve the prince, Your Majesty. At least, not directly."

"Explain yourself!"

"They're Rhenlaners, Sire." Thisben indicated the dead leader with a jerk of his chin. "That one escorted Prince

Damon on all of his visits. Everyone knows him. That's how they passed the gates."

Betrayed! Trapped!

A distant clash of swords echoed down the stone corridor and goaded Palle to action. He pulled clothes, weapons, and boots from the chest at the foot of the bed and threw them on top of the covers. The yowl of complaint that rose from the mound of blanket was unimportant, a mere nuisance heard, then forgotten.

"The Rhenlaners had accomplices, you say." Palle dressed as he spoke, straining to make sense of the sounds of battle that drifted through the castle. "Surely they are outnumbered by those who remain loyal."

"I wouldn't count on that, Sire."

"Gods!" Palle buckled his sword belt and snatched up his cloak. In the doorway, he paused as a new suspicion assailed him. Pirse's brat was in the castle! Had Damon and his nephew formed an alliance against him? The babe and its mother had only just arrived, but Pirse was rumored to have spies everywhere.

Thisben crowded close behind him. "We must hurry, Sire."

"Lead the way, Corporal." No time for regrets. Damon, or Pirse, or both of them together could have the castle, and the child, too, for all the good it did them. He, Palle, was the true king of Dherrica. He would gather his forces and return—and all who had turned against him would pay for the outrages of this night.

The last guard in the room pointed at the wounded Rhenlaner. "What about him?"

"Kill him," Palle said, and strode after Thisben.

There was a storm brewing out at sea. The thunder of the surf carried clearly on the still night air. Sene put the latest report from Chasa down on the table. He pushed back his chair, rose, and crossed the verandah, pulling his cloak tightly about him. It was the middle of the night. There was no wind, but the air was chill, even if spring was coming on. What would his dear daughter-in-law say if he caught a chill? In the privacy of the terrace he allowed himself a fond smile. He knew exactly what she would say. If he couldn't go to sleep at a decent hour, at least he could go indoors where it was comfortable.

He rested his hands on the railing and gazed out toward the sea. The sky was thick with stars all the way to the northern horizon. Whatever storm was driving that pounding surf, it was still too far away for its clouds to be visible. He breathed deeply, willing the crisp air to invigorate him. He was not indoors precisely because it was too comfortable there. This was no time for him to be lulled by comfort and security. He knew with utter certainty that the crisis was at hand. Damon would not hesitate to act, and act decisively, the moment his father was dead. Hion would not last much longer, according to the word Ivey had sent from Edian. Chasa's reports from the border confirmed that Damon was preparing some show of strength. His precise intentions remained to be seen.

The hoof beats that approached from the west grounds were almost masked by the sound of the surf. Sene stared at the two riders who appeared around the corner of the palace and cantered toward the terrace. They rode like guards. Sene knew his own troops. These were unfamiliar. One raised a javelin, ready to throw.

The railing beside Sene creaked. He whirled, ducked away from the man leaping toward him with knife outstretched, and dove for his chair. A second man vaulted over the railing behind the first. Sene snatched up the chair and swung it, legs forward in front of him. It shuddered under the impact of the javelin. The second man to come over the railing drew and swung his sword. Sene pivoted. A chair leg, sliced cleanly through, spun away and clattered against the back wall.

"Guards!" Sene roared. "To me!"

The door leading into the dining room opened. Two more unfamiliar men came through, swords drawn. Sene gave a wordless yell and charged toward the swordsman from the railing. He thrust the chair toward his face, forcing him back, then lunged unexpectedly and knocked the knife out of his first assailant's hand. The man leaped toward him barehanded. Sene grabbed him and pulled him close, and the man screamed as one of his companion's swords sliced across his back. Sene pushed him into the cursing swordsman. He spun as another blade descended toward his head. The chair splintered in his hand. He tossed the last fragment at the third swordsman's head and ran for the railing.

One of the horsemen had dismounted. He was in a vulnerable position, one arm supporting him as he vaulted over the railing, the other gripping a javelin, momentarily out of balance. Sene smashed into him before his feet had cleared the railing and knocked him back the way he had come. As he fell, Sene grabbed for the javelin, caught it, and turned again to confront the swordsman.

Something pushed him violently from behind. Sene staggered forward two steps and fell to his knees. The three swordsmen lowered their weapons. Sene looked down. A javelin point protruded from his chest just to the left of his breastbone.

His last thought was one of bewilderment that he felt no pain.

Jordy reined Stockings to a walk as they approached the turnoff into the yard. The bushes along the roadside and the rise of the hill blocked his view of the house. Still, he didn't need to see it to know there would be a light glowing in the window and Cyril waiting up for him behind it. He would give Stockings a thorough rubdown when they reached the stable. Perhaps that would give him time enough to cool his temper and order his thoughts before going in to face his wife.

A figure stepped out of the bushes, directly into Stockings's path. "Carter Jordy?" the man's voice inquired.

"Aye," Jordy replied. He heard a familiar tinny chink of metal on metal and was diving out of the saddle to his right before his mind consciously identified the sound. A sword stabbed across Stockings's back from her left, piercing the space which, split seconds before, had been occupied by his body. He ducked his head as he hit the ground on his shoulder and rolled a few feet, coming up into a crouch at the very edge of the road. Stockings, dependable as always, shied belatedly at the sword that was no longer over her back and jumped forward just as the swordsman was trying to go around her. She caught him squarely with her broad chest and sent him sprawling on his backside in the rutted road.

The second guard, the one who had stepped out of the bushes to challenge him, now drew his sword and started toward Jordy at a fighter's smooth lope. Jordy straightened, dug his hand in his pocket, drew out a rock, and whipped it at the man's head, all in one continuous motion. The rock struck between the guard's eyes with the solid thwock of cracking bone, and he toppled face-forward in mid-stride, dead. Stockings disappeared eastward along the road with a clatter of hooves and a flick of her tail.

Jordy stooped and snatched up the first weapon that came to hand, a bit of dead wood not quite the length of his arm. As the first guard got his feet under him and reached to retrieve his sword, the branch flew end over end to strike the side of the guard's face. The guard yowled in pained surprise and Jordy dashed past him, grabbing the sword.

He was still moving and slightly off balance when a third guard sprang out of the bushes. Jordy swerved desperately out of reach. Pool and pond! Still two against one? He had never been that good a swordsman! The fallen guard clutched his torn face with one hand as he fumbled his knife out of its sheath with the other. Jordy leapt toward him, kicked the knife away, then placed the tip of the sword against his chest and pressed him back against the ground.

"Back off if you value his life," Jordy warned the third guard.

"I don't." The man kept coming, featureless in the darkness, sword raised. Jordy feinted a stab at the supine guard's heart, changed it to a quick slash through the neck and sprang back, once more evading his assailant's thrust by a hairsbreadth. Then the guard was across his companion's corpse and Jordy was forced to meet him sword to sword.

Jordy found himself answering the first flurry of blows with reflexes he'd thought long lost. The guard tried a few less standard thrusts and Jordy parried those. He had the fleeting satisfaction of seeing the guard step back, hesitant for the first time. Then the guard passed his sword from his right hand to his left and sprang forward.

Jordy wanted to take to his heels, but he refused to lead this man to his house. No help was closer than the inn. He blocked the first swing awkwardly, ducked a jab to his head, and staggered as the guard's sword sliced solidly into his right arm just below the shoulder. Metal grated on bone as the guard followed through, driving Jordy to his left knee, his own sword falling as his right hand lost all strength. Jordy's left hand touched metal on the surface of the road.

The guard disengaged and stepped back, cocking his sword for a beheading stroke. Jordy got his hand under the hilt of the second guard's knife and tossed upward.

King's guards carried excellent weapons. The well-balanced knife crossed the few feet that separated Jordy and the guard and buried itself at the base of the man's throat. The guard dropped his sword, clutched at his neck, gave a low, gurgling moan, and collapsed.

Still kneeling, Jordy swayed. *Anyone else?* he thought fuzzily. They'd find him an easy target. He hadn't the strength to lift one more weapon, even if the gods shoved it into his hand. The night around him, however, had fallen empty and silent. His attackers must have left their horses some way away. Even Stockings was no longer audible.

An owl sounded its questioning call as Jordy got stiffly to his feet. He tried to wrap his left hand around the gash in his arm, but his hand wasn't large enough. His coat and tunic sleeves, cut half-through already, tore off readily when he pulled on them. He folded the cloth one-handed into a pad and pressed that against the wound as best he could. It didn't hurt. He began to walk toward the yard, an odd detachment threatening to distract him from his goal. The road was a blur of pale gray in the starlight. The sound of the owl was drowned out by the rapid patter of his pulse in his ears. His right arm, his entire right side, was warm with blood. He felt nothing beyond an indescribable weariness.

From the foot of the hill he could look up across the yard and make out the yellow patch of life which marked the window of the house. He leaned forward and began to climb.

The carving would not come right. Tob set his knife down on the table and turned the little wooden dog over in his hands. Matti was a perfectionist. He had promised her a wooden sheepdog, and she would expect a wooden sheepdog down to the last detail of leg feathers and tufted ears.

He lifted his head as his mother put aside her knitting and leaned forward to adjust the lamp wick. The oil level was low, too. Dad was really late. Tob looked at the carving again and yawned. Maybe he'd go up to bed after all, and hear about the meeting some other time.

As he fastened the cover on his knife, footsteps thudded on the porch. His mother went to the hearth to get the cider pot. Tob turned his head toward the door as it swung open.

He hadn't seen that much blood on someone's clothes since the first time he'd been allowed to butcher a goat by himself. "Dad?" he said in an uncertain whisper.

Jordy leaned heavily against the doorpost. "King's guards," he said hoarsely. "Tell Herri." His eyes drooped closed.

Tob scrambled off his bench as his father's legs began to buckle. Somehow, his mother got there before him. She caught Jordy as he sagged forward and held him until Tob could add his support. He felt his father's muscles tense as he made a belated effort to catch himself.

"King's guards? What king's guards? Where are they?" Tob asked.

"On the road. They're dead."

With their help, Jordy made it to the table, where he sank onto a bench. He leaned forward, resting his forehead against the table. A clear, lightly accented woman's voice said, "Get Jenil. Quickly."

Tob's head jerked up. His mother was at the cupboard, pulling out bed covers. She grabbed a lightweight summer blanket, hurried back to the table, snatched his knife out of its half-closed cover, and nicked the edge of the cloth in several places. Her eyes met his as she began ripping the blanket into strips.

"Get Jenil," she repeated. "Now, Tob."

Tob backed away from the table. Impossible. Everything was impossible. His mother didn't talk. His father didn't come home from a meeting pale and bleeding. It was a nightmare. He had fallen asleep at the table.

He clenched his fists and felt the stickiness of blood. His mother's impatient stare demanded obedience as clearly as her words had done. More clearly. Hadn't he devoted a lifetime to interpreting her expressions?

Tob turned and fled from the house. Stockings was nowhere in sight, so he took off down the hill on foot, stumbling and sliding in his haste. He rounded the hedge that bordered the road and nearly tripped over a body sprawled on the hard dirt. Two other dark lumps lay nearby, motionless. Tob avoided them, hugging the side of the road until he was past, then ran again, heart pounding in his throat.

He left the road and took the shortcut through the blacksmith's kitchen garden, causing the dog to bark sleepily from its place on the porch. Then Tob was out on the road again as it made its last turn into the village square. Chest heaving, he threw himself against the front door of the inn and began pounding on it with both fists.

The window shutters of the main room were flung open. Lamplight spilled out, illuminating Herri's bearded head as he peered around the edge of his window toward the door. "Who's there?" he called.

"Tob. We need Jenil."

Herri ducked back out of sight. A moment later the door was pulled open and Tob stepped into the inn. The Greenmother was a black shadow standing in front of the embers of the hearth fire. Herri put his hand on Tob's arm and drew him forward. "What's this, boy? Who needs Jenil?"

Tob tried to get his breathing back under control. "There are three guards on the road. Dad said to tell you." He looked from his father's old friend to the watching Greenmother, struggling with his confusion. "They're dead. I think he killed them."

Herri's hand dropped.

The Greenmother said, "Jordy was injured?"

Tob nodded mutely.

Herri's deep voice rumbled a barely audible, "Rock and pool, no!"

"I'll go at once." The Dreamer closed her eyes and vanished, leaving behind nothing but a crackle of power and a wisp of green smoke.

"By the gods, there might be others nearby!" Herri said suddenly. "Did Jordy say nothing else?"

"Only to tell you."

"I'll wake the village." The innkeeper glanced briefly at the door. "I'd like to go back there with you, Tob. Not that your mother needs a stranger underfoot."

"You're not a stranger," Tob protested, voice tight with fury.

The innkeeper looked at him curiously, but all he said was, "You're shaking, boy. Do you want to spend the rest of the night here?"

"No! I've got to get back!" Tob fumbled the door open and forced himself out into the night once more.

CHAPTER 24

Tob trudged up the hill and across the yard. Sheyn had risen, bathing the wall of the stable in his blue light. As he stepped onto the porch the door opened and the Greenmother stepped through.

"Well?" Tob hardly recognized his own voice, but the Dreamer understood him.

"He's too stubborn to die," she replied. Somewhere behind the acerbic words there was relief. "Do you know where they fought?"

Tob indicated the road with a jerk of his head. "Follow the path out of the yard. You can't miss them."

"You might want to clean up a bit before your sisters wake in the morning." With that parting advice the Greenmother stepped off the porch. Her black cloak made her difficult to see despite the moonslight, so that she seemed to fade rather than walk across the yard and down the path.

He went into the house and shut the door. The lamp on the table had gone out, but a fire burned on the hearth, providing adequate illumination as well as heating something in a large pot. The state of the room was worse than he'd expected. The cupboard doors were ajar, the pots were askew on their shelf, the contents of one of the herb jars were strewn across one corner of the table, and there seemed to be blood everywhere. Tob wrapped his arms around himself in silent misery. Jenil was right. The girls didn't need to see this.

He looked up at the closed attic door. Unless they'd seen it already? No. If they had been disturbed they would have climbed out of bed and lifted the door to peek downstairs and Pepper, at least, would have panicked. Therefore, they were still safely asleep.

Unsure that he was ready for anything else, but unable to stop himself, Tob crossed the room and paused in the doorway to the other half of the house—the private, secret half of the house, though he had never thought of it that way before. He couldn't see much of his father, just a brief glimpse of sandy hair and several layers of blankets on his parents' large bed. He could hear breathing though, slow but steady. Then his mother was in front of him, pressing him back through the curtains and into the main room.

He noticed for the first time that he was taller than she was. He braced himself, refusing to back up any further. "I want to see him."

She stopped pushing at him, but left her hands resting lightly against his chest. Her hair was unkempt, stiff in spots, her face streaked with dirt and damp, her tunic stained. Her expression, patient but not entirely comprehending, which had always evoked feelings of warmth and security in him, abruptly made him so angry that his vision blurred with tears.

He choked words out around the lump in his throat. "You're going to go back to ignoring me, aren't you?"

Her inhalation was no more than a breath of sound. "I never ignored you, my son." She took his arm, and this time he allowed himself to be led to the hearth. She sat him on a bench, then sat beside him, holding his hand.

He wiped the back of his other hand across his eyes and sniffed once before facing her. "I don't understand!"

"It is a personal matter," she said, voice low. "It has not changed. I will not speak before others."

"Only me? I'm the only one who knows you can talk?"

"Jordy has always known." She looked at him solemnly. "He is part of me."

Tob's anger threatened to return. "And your children aren't?"

"I cannot change what I am."

His hands itched. He rubbed them on the knees of his trousers and watched bits of dark brown flake off and flutter to the floor. He was wasting his anger. He'd said it himself.

He didn't understand. Didn't understand her. He had more urgent matters to think about now.

"I'm going to the king," he said.

Her grip on his hand tightened. "You can't."

"I'm not letting this go. Those were king's guards, Mama! I'm going to claim blood debt."

"No, you can't!"

She sounded so thoroughly frightened that Tob offered a hesitant smile. "You're worried about me? I won't do it alone. I'll get Herri's help. Vray is in Edian—Iris, that is, you remember her—along with lots of Dad's friends."

Tears welled out of her eyes and followed the planes of her face, redefining the streaking of earlier crying. "I will not allow it. You have no right."

"Blood debt, Mama? Who has a better right than a man's son?"

She shook her head. "You are not Jordy's son, Taubbelichena."

He could only stare blankly at her. The words from the not-mute woman made no sense. "What?"

"You are not his son. You cannot claim blood debt, by your laws or mine. Please, Taubbeli."

"I don't believe you! You're just saying that to keep me here!"

She nodded her head toward the bedroom. "He knows. Herri knows. You must know yourself. Look at you. Where do you see Jordy in you?"

Tob jerked his hand away from her and jumped up. So he didn't look like Jordy. What did that prove? Immediately his mind supplied other inconsistencies. He couldn't throw like Jordy, either. Or shoot. Or juggle. He couldn't tolerate gray beans, or strawberries, foods which the rest of the family, including Cyril, loved. His sisters had always teased him that he was the only one in the house who snored.

Sisters? Or half-sisters? Or had his parents adopted him the same way they'd adopted Vray? If they had, wouldn't the whole village know? Wouldn't he know?

He didn't know anything.

He glared down at his mother. "I wish you'd never spoken to me!" His heart tore inside him. "I can't even pretend you did it because you cared about me!"

"For your sake I should have kept silent," she agreed softly. "For Jordy's sake, I had to speak."

Tob had never felt so useless. So many feelings churned within him: anger, fear, confusion and loss, with no focus for any of them. He stared at the hearth and the now-steaming pot. Numbness settled over him, freeing his mind to retreat into consideration of habitual, petty concerns.

"Water?" he asked. His mother's eyes confirmed his guess without her having to speak. "I'll clean up in here," he told her.

He waited until she rose silently and returned to the other room. Then he dug the bucket and scrub brush out of the bottom of the cupboard and went to work.

Jenil bent the power and whisked toward Dherrica. As much as she tried, she could not believe that the attack on Broadford's carter was an isolated incident. Yes, he was a troublemaker. Damon might have learned of his existence, and chosen to eliminate the threat he represented. But Jordy was not the greatest threat to the new king.

Who else would Damon choose to eliminate? Hion had been dead for three days. Broadford was three days' easy journey from Edian.

Trained troops, riding hard, could cross half the world in three days.

She became solid on the ledge in front of Morb's cave. Behind her, lines of power pulsed around Aage, who was seated on a boulder, oblivious to her arrival. She walked past him and ducked inside the cave.

Morb rolled onto his side on his low bed and knuckled his eyes. "Jenil?"

"I need help. Something is happening in the kingdoms."

The old wizard got his feet under him and padded to the pool of water at the side of the cave. "Don't waste time explaining. Urgent problems. I understand." He squatted down and filled his hands with water, then emptied them over his head. Jenil lifted the hem of her robe away from the splattering droplets.

"Thank you, Morb. We need to take warnings to at least twenty towns, maybe more."

"Not me." He straightened. Power flickered around him, kindling flame in the lamps on the walls. "Aage knows about plots and plans, queens and kings. I'll take over for him in the web. Is it Rhenlan?"

"Hion is dead. I fear what Damon may do. He has already attacked one of his own Keepers."

"What do you want from Aage?"

"He must warn Sene, then Pirse, if he can find him. I'm going to Vray in Edian. She must make her challenge now, before Damon can do any more damage. Tell Aage I'll be in Broadford, waiting to hear from him."

"I'll tell him."

Satisfied, Jenil twisted herself into the lines of power once more.

Dael hovered soundlessly at the foot of the stairway, watching the changing of the guard in front of his and Vray's room. The original guard, one of Damon's favorites, went off to his supper, passing only a few inches in front of Dael's shadowy hiding place. His replacement smiled as Dael bounded up the stairs. "Good to see you, Captain," he said quietly.

"Thanks," Dael replied without stopping.

Vray's expression as he entered was welcoming, more or less. Her first words were a defiant, "I told you not to come."

"You're not ready?"

"I'm not going. Not yet."

Dael interrupted the argument long enough to kiss his wife thoroughly. When he opened his eyes, he found Peanal watching them with amusement.

He motioned the girl out. "Wait for us by the gate." As she left, he gave Vray another squeeze. "Now get your cape," he said.

Vray didn't move. "Did you talk to the law reader?"

"I've done nothing but talk for three days now. Nocca says you've had all my messages. It's going to take time, and you can't stay here."

"I have to. Don't you see, Damon is playing games, but I don't know what they are. I can't leave now. If I give up my place at court I'll lose all I've worked for. I can't bring challenge as a fugitive."

Dael didn't argue that point. "You can't bring challenge if he locks you up again. I'm not leaving without you, Kitten."

The puff of green smoke appeared in the center of the room a split second before the crackling sound reached Vray's ears. A black-robed mother took form rapidly, huge bundles of something at her feet. Dael's knife was in hand at the first indication of an intruder. As the fragrant smoke dissipated, Jenil pushed her hood back, and Dael slid the knife back into its sheath.

"Greenmother," he complained, "it isn't polite to appear in someone's home without warning. In my home, it also isn't safe."

Vray stepped up beside him, her attention on the bundles. "Jenil, what are you doing abroad at this time of night?"

"I believe these are yours." The normally gentle Dreamer voice was too smooth, too controlled. Dael felt a chill of anticipation as he knelt beside the bundles and lifted a flap of cloth.

"A guard." He drew the cloak farther back. "Mine, according to the uniform, although I don't recognize the face. Dead?"

"Dead," Jenil confirmed. "Three of them." She turned to Vray. "What does your brother think he's doing?"

"How did it happen?" Dael demanded. He dropped one cloak and lifted another, soaked with blood from a knife wound to the throat. "Were they fighting among themselves?"

"No. They tried to kill a man. He fought back, and I was

called to repair the damage. If this is how Damon plans to control his kingdom, hundreds more will die, villagers as well as guards!" Jenil pointed an accusing finger at Dael. "No more waiting! You must take control of the king's guard, now, before anyone else is threatened."

Dael stood slowly. "Greenmother, it's not that easy. Right now it might be impossible. I'm not even supposed to be in Edian."

"What man?" Vray asked suddenly. "Who did they attack? Where? We know Damon is aware of some of the people who oppose him. Is the man all right?"

"He'll live," Jenil answered. "Vray, dear, the man they tried to kill is Jordy."

Vray sat down abruptly on the edge of the nearest chair. Dael was at her side an instant later, one hand on her shoulder, holding her up, even as his own gut tightened with helpless anger at the thought of his friend's danger. "Vray, are you all right? Do you know Jordy?" He raised his voice and bellowed, "Teza!" at the closed door of the inner chamber. He turned to Jenil. "She knows Jordy?"

"He adopted me," Vray said in a small voice.

Dael stared at her. "He never told me!"

"Neither did I. We thought it safest, for Broadford." Her face paled. "Damon! He must have found out! This is my fault!"

"No." Dael squeezed her shoulder. "Maybe Damon knows more about the Keeper conspiracy than we thought."

"Then we'd better not reveal any more." Jenil gestured at the dead strangers and told Dael, "I'll take care of these. You take care of Vray." She vanished, taking the corpses with her.

Teza emerged from the other room and came directly to Dael. "You called for me, Captain?"

"More about the Keeper conspiracy?" Vray asked. A little color returned to her cheeks. "You know about that? Wait just a minute. What do you mean, Jordy never told you he knows me? Since when do you know Jordy!?"

"Let's concentrate on Damon for now, all right? He's gone too far, too fast."

She glared at him a moment longer, then nodded. "Too far, yes. He's done my work for me. No one will oppose my challenge now."

"Jordy might." Mention of the carter reminded Dael of how much Vray had kept hidden from him. "Just when did you have time to get adopted?"

"After three years at Soza!" she shot back at him with equal heat. "Did you really think I came back here healthy and sun-browned thanks to my cousin Vrain's loving care?"

"What else could I think? You didn't tell me anything!"

"You didn't tell me anything, either!"

The door slammed back on its hinges and a guard, sword in hand, burst into the room. He was halfway to Vray before he saw that she wasn't alone. A roar of combined fury and fear left his throat when he saw Dael, but he did not swerve from his intended target. Two more men ran in from the hallway, Vray's cousin Vrain behind them.

Dael didn't have to think about drawing knife or sword. They were in his hands as he leapt in front of his wife. Vray knew enough to flip a table on its side and duck behind it, dragging Teza with her.

The four men fought him together, quiet now except for their heavy breathing and clanging blades. Dael killed them swiftly, before the uneven odds could tire him. When his last opponent fell, he leaped to the doorway and peered up and down the stairs, listening. Dael spared a glance for the friendly guard, sprawled dead on the landing. Above, Hion's chamber was empty and still. Below, to all appearances, the rest of the castle slept.

He turned back into the room and gestured to Vray and Teza as they emerged from behind the table. "Come on. You can't argue about leaving now."

Vray came to him, pale but not the least bit hesitant. "Where?"

"My parents' house. We can't do any more here. Not until we have a better idea of the extent of Damon's control."

"I'll stay," Teza announced. "You may need friends in the castle."

"Are you sure?" Dael asked.

The woman glanced at the carnage, shuddered once, then lifted her face, her expression smooth. "I was in the servants' quarters all night, sir. I didn't see a thing."

"All right," Vray said. "Just be careful!"

With a nod, Teza slipped out the door and was gone.

Vray accepted the dagger Dael handed her and followed him onto the stairs, stepping over the dead guard. Her final protest was a strained, "The resistance! If it's not organized, we'll lose before we've begun!"

"We're organized," he assured her. "Don't worry. Your people will rally around you, even if you're somewhere other than this castle. Now, hurry!"

There was no guard at the foot of the tower. No doubt the man who'd been given this duty post was one of the corpses upstairs. They raced across the Sheyn-lit courtyard, flitting in and out of blue-tinged shadows. At the gate, Dael's sharp command silenced the guards before they could speak. Vray swept past them, head high, skirt fluttering around her. Dael ordered the gates closed and bolted, watched until his command was carried out, then pelted down the hill after his wife's departing figure.

Aage flicked across the landscape, away from Raisal, numb with horror. The smell of blood stayed with him, and the sound of Feather's hysterical anger. If the last of the assassins had not finally been killed by the household guards, the girl would have done it herself. She was distraught, surely mistaken in what she'd shouted about Jeyn. She had to be mistaken.

He arrived at Garden Vale to be told that the princess had only arrived a few hours before. The Brownmother who told him sounded worried. He hurried into the room she indicated. A single candle lighted it. Aage stood inside the doorway and let his eyes adjust to the dimness until he could make out the chair beside the window.

Jeyn didn't turn. He cleared his throat and came up behind her, putting his hands on her shoulders. She did not react to his touch. For a few seconds he couldn't speak. Power swirled up around her, but it felt wrong, unfocused.

"Jeyn, love," he said.

His voice caught her attention. She tipped her head back. "Hello."

Her dark eyes were empty. Aage flinched away from her. This was worse than Feather had guessed. He came around in front of the chair and made himself kneel next to the young woman. It was difficult to take her hand. "Jeyn. Can you hear me?"

"Hello," she said again.

"Ah, Jeyn," Aage groaned. He couldn't tell her. She couldn't be queen. Everything was wrong. Gods, why?

Jeyn tilted her head at him. "I need to talk to Aage. Do you smell apples?"

He stumbled to his feet. "I'm sorry, love. I'll be right back." After he saw Jenil. Too much was happening, too fast. Perhaps it was the gods' mercy that made Jeyn oblivious to the horror that filled his soul. Sene was dead, murdered in a perfectly planned attack. Who else was dying as he lingered here, wallowing in grief and guilt?

No one. He would find Jenil, and rouse Savyea as well. Between the three of them, they could carry warnings to every Keeper and Shaper in the three kingdoms who might be in danger. If Jenil did not know where to go, they would seek out Vray, or Ivey.

"No more death," he whispered to the gods. "Please."

As he bent the power to leave, the last thing he saw was Jeyn folding her hands over her abdomen. She didn't look in his direction as she commented, "I really must talk to Aage."

CHAPTER 25

The arrival of a rider roused the camp just before dawn. She reached the entrance of Chasa's tent, where four troop corporals waited in uneasy attendance. Chasa stepped outside, pulling a cloak close against the chill air. He would have done without the cloak if, in exchange, he could have had some protection against the foreboding he was feeling. He didn't know what he feared. The gathering of troops of Rhenlan guards along the border guaranteed trouble, but they were ready for that.

Overhead the sky had begun to lighten to a rich blue, although clouds lingered in the west, blotting out what stars might otherwise have remained visible. The rider, flexing her stiff hands, turned toward him as soon as he exited the tent. "Highness," she said. "The Rhenlaners attacked just after midnight, near the Great Road. Fighting is spreading as fast as their troops receive the order. I may be only minutes ahead of their messenger."

"Ready the guards," Chasa said to his corporals, who immediately scattered. "What else?" he asked the woman.

Her voice in the darkness held a suggestion of dissatisfaction mingled with pride. "I've outrun any other news, Highness. If your night watch has anything warm cooking over their fire, I'd be grateful for a portion and a fresh horse before I leave."

"You'll have them." Chasa directed her toward the pickets, then beckoned to a passing guard and sent him to find her something to eat.

Bands of lavender and rose were widening along the eastern horizon as the messenger set out toward the next troop encampment five miles to the south. Chasa put her out of his mind and wished that the sun would hurry. Standing at the edge of camp with the light growing behind

240

him, he could just make out a stirring among the Rhenlan troops a half mile across the border. It was a shapeless sort of motion, gray and indistinct. He set his four troops of guards in defensive positions just to be safe. Once the light grew, they would know more.

Soft yellow eggs. A piece of toasted bread, cream and brown and liberally spread with bright raspberry jam. A slice of sweet melon, the pale green of spring leaves in Garden Vale. Feather had to admire the artful arrangement of her breakfast plate. Brownmother experience taught that the most tempting foods had to look attractive as well as smell delicious. The cook was doing his best. What a pity that she had no appetite to tempt.

She put her hand on the edge of the undisturbed plate and pushed it away. "I'm finished, Dektrieb. Thank you."

"Yes, Your Highness." The servant limped to the table and began clearing dishes. Feather watched him, her hands resting on her rounded abdomen. Duties awaited her, but for the moment she was too exhausted to move. The baby was kicking restlessly and her back ached. Dektrieb worked slowly, hampered by splints on two of his fingers and a swollen elbow. The staff had been involved in the battle with the invaders and few had escaped without some injury. A terrible waste. Such loyalty. Such sacrifice. They'd been too late before they'd started.

"You should have stayed home today," she told Dektrieb as he balanced the tray on his good hand.

"This is where I need to be," he contradicted her gently. He looked around the lonely dining room, at the untouched clutter of maps in one corner, the bare spaces once occupied by now-broken furniture. The torn window blinds had been replaced temporarily with remnants from a previous set. They didn't match the rest of the room, but they fulfilled their function of blocking Feather's view of the terrace.

She didn't want to see or set foot on that terrace ever again.

★ ★ ★ ★ ★

There was something odd about Rhenlan's side of the battle. Every time Chasa tried to count their opponents, he came up with a different number. Forty-one was his best guess, more than three troops but less than four. That, and the reckless abandon with which some of the Rhenlaners fought, just wasn't right.

With difficulty, Chasa and his people held the border through the early morning, until the Rhenlaners broke off their most recent skirmish and both sides withdrew a quarter mile to regroup. Chasa counted three of his guards dead and at least five seriously wounded. The Rhenlan troops had suffered similar losses. Everyone else was bruised and tired.

Chasa paced restlessly along the western edge of their camp between one guard post and the next. This was such a waste! Surely the Rhenlaners would prefer to be at home. He knew he would. He could think of a dozen better ways to spend a day than supervising a few dozen Keepers as they pushed one another back and forth across a gully. That neither he nor his father had begun the violence, but were only reacting to the aggressive behavior of Hion and Damon, did not make Chasa feel much better. As much as he respected and understood his father's insistence on the necessity of patient, subtle manipulation of people and events, it wasn't easy to be patient at the battle line. It wasn't easy to be subtle with sharp-edged steel in your hand.

The puff of smoke that announced Aage's arrival was a welcome sight. Chasa stopped and stood waiting while the black-robed wizard took form a few feet in front of him. As soon as the Dreamer's face became clear, Chasa's momentary pleasure at the presence of his visitor evaporated.

"Aage?"

"Your Majesty, forgive me."

For a long, precious, interval, Chasa didn't understand. When he finally made the connection between the wizard's words and appearance he whispered, "No."

"I'm sorry. The King was killed last night. It doesn't

seem possible, but it's all Damon's doing. Somehow. He's king now, you see. Hion died four days ago. Jenil believes Damon intends to make himself king of the entire world. Guard yourself well, Majesty."

Grief choked him. Furiously he rubbed at the tears in his eyes and cleared his throat so that he could manage a broken, "I'm not King! You should be telling this to Jeyn!"

Aage looked, if anything, more ill. "She can't rule. She's not well. Forgive me, Majesty. I've failed Sene, I've failed Sitrine. I've failed in everything."

Chasa did not want to deal with a wizard's self-pity. "What are you talking about? What's troubling you—the fact that you were away from Raisal last night? Even a Dreamer can't be everywhere at once. At least you're here now. You can help me. What's wrong with my sister?"

Aage closed his eyes briefly. "Forgive me," he repeated. "I must go."

"Wait! Aage!"

"Be careful." In the blink of an eye the wizard was no longer standing there.

"If Dad's gone," Chasa shouted to the empty air, "and I'm here, who's governing Raisal?" He turned toward the northwest, toward distant Edian. "You're throwing everything into chaos, Damon! Is that what it will take to satisfy you? All three kingdoms out of control?" No answer came to his shouted challenge. His voice broke. "Dad, I'm not ready for this. What am I going to do?"

Aage bent the power until the Brownmothers' complex in Garden Vale took shape around him. Too much travel in too short a time. He put his hand out to the nearest chair, pulled it toward him, and sat quickly before his legs could buckle beneath him.

In the gray predawn light, Jeyn walked in a tight circle in the center of the room, her head tilted at an odd angle, eyes staring intently at nothing.

"Jeyn," he called softly. His dizziness began to abate as his physical strength slowly returned. Magically, he was de-

pleted to the point of pain. His Dreamer senses, an exten-
sion of his flesh and blood body, were over-sensitized by
exhaustion, and every muscle ached in sympathetic response. The flickering of bent power that emanated from
the child in Jeyn's womb had increased even in the few
hours he'd been gone.

Pushing himself out of the chair, Aage put himself in the
path of the Princess to stop her pacing. She bumped into
him, took a step back, and stared.

"Are you Aage? What are you doing there?"

With effort he kept his voice firmly under control. "Yes,
Highness, it's me. It's Aage. I'm back." He took both her
hands in his. "Everything will be all right."

She seemed to see him. "I think I'd better go home now.
Let's tell the mothers I want to go home. I want to see
Daddy."

He swallowed painfully. "It's a long way to Raisal, Jeyn.
I don't think that would be a good idea."

"But I feel fine."

The words were spoken calmly, a gentle reprimand from
a wise ruler to a well-meaning but misinformed follower.
The next instant she was staring at their joined hands, all
her fear and confusion back. "You're holding my hands but
I can't feel you touching me. Why can't I feel you touching
me? What's wrong with me?"

Aage interrupted quickly, before her agitation could in-
crease. "There's nothing wrong with you. I told you. It's
just the baby's magic. You're not used to the touch of
magic, that's all. We'll find a way to control it. Then you'll
feel more yourself again."

It was a lie, but he said it bravely, searching frantically in
his mind all the while for inspiration. He had to offer her
something. Something besides vague reassurance and the support of his company. He didn't lower his gaze when she
looked into his face again. Power bent around her in a pattern
invisible to any but Dreamer eyes. He couldn't tell her that his
refusal to run away was the best gift he could offer. He
couldn't tell her how terrified he was that she would go mad.

"What are we going to do now, Aage?" she demanded. As a five-year-old princess she had sounded like that, convinced that her wizard had all the answers and was merely being difficult by refusing to indulge her.

"What can we do?" he whispered. Gods, there had to be something. Too much traveling in too short a time had drained him. It would be hours before he could bend the power again, possibly a day or more. This was the price they paid for his secretiveness, the price they paid for his sense of duty. If he had been willing to risk the censure of the other Dreamers, they could have had the benefit of Savyea's consultation from the beginning. If he had not wasted so much energy running errands, he wouldn't be stuck here now unable to transport himself to Savyea in the mountains and ask her assistance. He could not even reach Jenil, only fifteen miles away.

If he didn't think of something, he would have to sit here, helpless, and watch Jeyn lose her mind.

Fifteen miles away. He turned the thought over in his mind. Two villages, Garden Vale and Broadford, connected by fifteen miles of road along the bank of the river. He could send a Keeper with a message for Jenil, asking her to come to Garden Vale. No, that wouldn't work. She, too, had done great magic, first in healing the carter, then in transporting herself from kingdom to kingdom, as he had done, throughout the night. She needed as much time to replenish her energy as he did. If she bent the power to come to Garden Vale, she would have no strength left to heal Jeyn. They needed her presence and her talents both, not one or the other. She couldn't transport to Garden Vale, he couldn't transport Jeyn to Broadford . . .

"Self-centered fool!" he exclaimed. Jeyn, her attention drifting, did not react until he released her passive hands and stroked her cheek instead. "Your Highness, would you like to go for a ride?"

"Yes," she murmured. "I'll go riding with Daddy. That's a good idea. We'll ride up to the beach." She turned her head vaguely. "Have you sent someone to saddle the horses? I want to take Dewdrop. He needs a good run."

Aage guided her toward the door of the room. "Yes, Your Highness." He hoped the delusion would last long enough to see them out of the village. He hoped she was as physically strong as she seemed to be, so that the journey itself would be no danger. He hoped that by evening, Jenil would have recovered enough to be of help.

Most immediately, he hoped that someone in Garden Vale would loan them a horse.

"Tobble. Tobble, move. You're on my shirt."

Small hands were shoving at his shoulder. Tob opened his eyes. Matti's face hung over him, clear in the dawn light that washed through the attic window. As he sat up, Pepper stirred and poked her head out of her blankets.

"What are you doing in our bed?" she demanded sleepily.

"He's on my shirt," Matti told her sister.

"I have to tell you something before you go down." Tob waited for Pepper to sit up, keeping his control of Matti's clothes.

"I'm cold," Matti complained, and tugged at the shirt.

"Just listen for a minute," he insisted. "You're going to have to take care of yourselves today. Dad's been hurt."

Matti frowned and Pepper looked worried. "Where's Mama?" she asked.

"Taking care of Dad. They're in their room," he added, anticipating Pepper's next question. "You can't bother them. We've got to get our own breakfast as quietly as we can, then go out and take care of the chores."

Pepper was hardly satisfied. "But what happened?"

Tob took a deep breath. "You know how Dad doesn't like the king's guards, and always says they're not to be trusted?" Both girls nodded. "Well, three of them came last night to fight with Dad."

Pepper's eyes grew round with shock. "They came here?"

"Who won?" Matti demanded.

"Not here to the house. Out on the main road. Dad won. The men are gone now."

Matti was looking at her brother as if she did not quite believe him. "If Dad won, why did he get hurt?"

"That's what happens when you fight with king's guards," Tob replied shortly. "Come on, and be quiet. We don't want to wake them up."

They dressed in silence. Tob was the first down the ladder into the kitchen. He examined the room quickly by daylight and was relieved to see that he hadn't missed anything in his cleaning. The girls went out to the privy. Tob raided the cupboard for the makings of a cold breakfast, and when they came back he handed each a plate full of food and a mug of tepid cider, then escorted them out onto the porch.

It was still early enough that the bird song from the woods across the road was loud and varied. The rooster answered the twitterings with his own raucous crow. Two of the stable cats came trotting across the yard, tails held high, looking for handouts.

Matti swallowed a mouthful of bread. "How late are they going to sleep?"

"I don't know."

"When will Daddy be feeling better?" Pepper asked.

"I don't know."

"Will Mama fix us lunch?" was Matti's more practical concern.

"Look, I don't know. We'll just have to wait and see. Right?"

He turned his head to discover Pepper staring at him solemnly. "You're scared, aren't you?" she observed with her usual uncomfortable perceptiveness.

"Just worried," he lied. He scanned the yard, hoping for inspiration. What could he pretend to be worried about that wouldn't needlessly scare the kids? He found it almost at once. It wasn't pretend. "Stockings!"

Matti looked around, puzzled. "Where?"

Tob put his hand to his forehead. "She didn't come

home with Dad last night. I should have gone to look for her."

"You're in trouble," Pepper agreed.

"Maybe she's just down the hill." Tob jumped up. "Finish eating. I'll be right back."

He loped down the hill. The entrance to the yard was empty. No Stockings, nor any trace of her. No corpses either. He walked from one bush-lined edge of the road to the other. There wasn't the slightest trace of a struggle. The Greenmother's magic at work again? He cupped his hands around his mouth.

"Stockings, Stockings! Come here, girl. Stockings!"

After a few minutes he went back to the house. He made sure the girls got properly started on their chores, and promised to come and check on them shortly.

When he went inside the house, his stomach churned, but not with hunger. No sense putting it off. He walked over to the curtain, lifted it aside, and stepped into his parents' room.

A lamp on the low table beside the bed was still burning, its glow all but lost in the morning sunlight. Tob approached the bed. His mother was asleep, seated on the floor, her head and arms pillowed on the foot of the bed. Jordy occupied the center of the bed, head and shoulders supported by pillows, his right arm heavily bandaged from the elbow up, lower arm lying limply on top of the blankets. He wasn't asleep. He turned his head toward Tob and lifted his left forefinger to his lips with a meaningful glance at Cyril's dark head.

Tob obediently kept his voice low. "I think we've lost the stupid horse."

Jordy dropped his left hand to his chest. "She didn't come home?"

"Probably can't find her way."

"Unless she wandered over a cliff. Have to consider that possibility," Jordy said. "Everything else all right?"

Tob suddenly couldn't find his voice. Pepper had been right. He was scared. He felt lost. Everything had changed.

Jordy was lying so still, new lines of stress etched into his face, his voice weak. Yet he'd had the strength to kill three men.

By the Mother of us all, Tob thought desperately, *I don't know him. I've never known him.*

He swallowed the dry ache in his throat and said, "You're not my father."

Jordy absorbed the words slowly. "So I didn't imagine it," he said at last. "She spoke to you."

"She's lied to me every day of my life by pretending to be something she's not!"

"Don't fault her, lad. You aren't in her place."

"What about you?"

Jordy's left hand clenched on the blanket. "We've lived our lives as father and son, Tob. That's what matters."

"Then it is true."

"It's true I didn't sire you. There's more to family than bloodlines, Tob."

"Who did? Do you know?" He couldn't bring himself to look at his mother. "Does she?"

An edge crept into Jordy's voice. "It wasn't like that. His name was Reas. He was my best friend."

"Oh, that explains it," Tob said caustically. Cyril's head lifted and she raised one hand to shove the hair back from her face. She sat up, and her worried gaze went immediately to her husband.

Her motion was the release Tob had been waiting for. "I'll go look for Stockings."

"Tob, come back! We're not finished."

He paused at the curtained doorway. "That's just what we are," he said, and got out of the house as fast as he could.

CHAPTER 26

Doron stood in the middle of her room, swaying gently from side to side. The motion originally had been intended to soothe Emlie. Now she continued it out of force of habit, although the child nestled against her shoulder had long since gone back to sleep. The castle was quiet once more, but it was not a quiet Doron trusted, not after the shouts and cries and metallic din of swords that had been coming and going all day. The first outburst had startled her from a sound sleep in the middle of the night, and set the baby wailing in surprise and outrage. She had cuddled Emlie against her, then picked her up and paced the room, murmuring calmly, ignoring the rushing footsteps in the corridor outside their locked door, pretending that she wasn't worried by the level of uproar that penetrated the thick glass of the window.

The noise had stopped almost as abruptly as it began, leaving Doron with quiet but no peace. She could see nothing out her window save an empty corner of the courtyard and the featureless gray of an overcast afternoon sky. They hadn't been given breakfast, and the guard who had brought them lunch had refused to speak to her. She told herself she had nothing to fear. Anything terrible that happened in the castle of Bronle boded ill for its master, not for her. Anyone who made trouble for Palle, she would count a friend. Hopefully.

She tried to be cynical, or at least realistic, and imagine something that would have caused the fighting she had heard and still be to Palle's advantage. The effort was fruitless. All she could think of, as often as she banished the image, was Pirse storming the castle in a truly heroic rescue.

He was fool enough to try it, too. Which was exactly

what had her worried and kept her holding Emlie when she should have let the child take her nap in peace.

Just how long did a successful rescue take?

For the first time in several hours, footsteps sounded beyond the locked door. Doron stopped swaying. Several people spoke together in the corridor, their words unintelligible through the solid oak of the door. She didn't hear Pirse, which was a disappointment. She also didn't hear Palle, or the sharp sarcasm of his weasel-faced guard captain, so she allowed herself a remnant of optimism.

An exclamation of satisfaction preceded the opening of the door. It swung wide to reveal several young people in the colors of Dherrica's guard and one highly unlikely sight: a plump matron, head thrust forward in the manner of the extremely near-sighted, draped in the folds of a traditional Redmother's robe several sizes too large for her. In fact, Doron had to look twice to be certain of the red embroidery. The robe was not only ill-fitting but also faded and frayed with lack of care, or age, or both. The only Mothers, Red, Brown or Green, that Doron had ever seen had been on her few trips outside Dherrica with Betajj. Even so, the cut of the garment and the distinctive red trim were unmistakable.

One of the guards took a diffident step into the room. "Excuse me," she began. "May we speak with you for a moment?"

Feeling more dazed by the second, Doron reacted automatically and placed a hushing finger to her lips. The guard nodded her understanding and turned to give a sharp look to her companions in the corridor, who fell silent.

Doron retreated to the corner of the room and carefully tucked Emlie into the bed, piling blankets and pillows to either side of her to help muffle the impending confrontation. When she turned back toward the doorway, neither the guards nor the Redmother had moved.

More confused than ever, Doron suggested, "Won't you come in?"

The girl, evidently the leader, complied, followed by the

Redmother. Three other guards leaned in at the doorway without actually crossing the threshold and watched with hopeful expressions. The girl began to pull her tunic straighter, noticed a rent along one side, and, with an embarrassed grimace, tucked the offending flap under her swordbelt.

"Stop fidgeting, Tatiya," the Redmother said.

"I mean no disrespect," the guard said the remark to Doron. "But I don't suppose Court rules apply today. You are the woman from Juniper Ridge?"

"Yes," Doron said warily.

"Well, we're not certain, but we think you might be Queen."

"Would you tell us why Palle brought you here?" the Redmother added. "We've heard only a few rumors, you see."

Doron stared at her expectant audience. "Where is Palle?"

"Ah, where's your sense, girl?" The Redmother's peering gaze became critical. "Gone, of course. How else could anyone dare to be seen in a Mother's robes?"

"He snuck away, we think," Tatiya said before Doron could grope for the words to ask. "A half-troop of Rhenlaners arrived last night, and entered the castle under pretext of friendship. Some of them tried to kill Palle, while the others seized partial control of the guard."

"Partial control?"

"They had allies in the castle. Bronle is full of factions." Tatiya shrugged off the distasteful state of affairs with a scowl. "Palle found out how little loyalty he has inspired over the years."

"Palle no longer holds the castle?"

Tatiya glanced back at her companions with a grimace. "To be honest, I don't think anyone is in complete command of the castle. When the fighting started, some of the guards rallied to Palle, others supported the Rhenlaners, and a third group opposed them both."

"Who do you serve?" Doron asked.

"We don't respect Palle, but that doesn't mean we prefer Damon." Tatiya's dark eyebrows drew stubbornly together. "We serve Dherrica. Please, tell us why you're here?"

Doron chose her words slowly. "I don't know, exactly. I'm not sure whether Palle intended to use me against Pirse, or against Damon."

"Things were not well between Palle and Damon," Tatiya said. "The Rhenlan prince knew more about Dherrica than our own king did."

"Neither of them knew the truth about Emlie," Doron said.

The Redmother inhaled sharply. "Emlie?"

Doron pointed to the cot. "She is Pirse's daughter. Pirse and I married at the Spring Festival after she was born."

"That's what I thought," Tatiya said with a decisive nod. "You are rightful ruler here."

The Redmother said, "Temporarily. And as regent, children. Not queen. Pirse has never answered the challenge or the blood debt claimed against him by his uncle. There are one or two other Shaper families with connections to the royal line who might choose to claim the throne."

"Not today," Tatiya insisted. "We need leadership today."

A new set of unknown dangers threatened to crowd into the space vacated by the hazards Palle had presented. "I'm not a Shaper!" Doron protested.

Tatiya stared at her. "Then the prince did not father your child."

"He did! Have you heard of the wizard Aage?" Doron appealed to the little Redmother. "I don't suppose you know how Dreamers are born?"

The woman lifted her chin. "I'm not ignorant. I know all about chosen Keepers and Shapers of every third generation—which is not Pirse's generation."

"The gods changed their minds," Doron said. "It's a long story."

"I'd like to hear it."

"We don't have time!" Tatiya interrupted them. She

faced the Redmother. "Is it possible that she's telling the truth?"

"With the gods, anything is possible."

Doron said, "Whatever you believe about Emlie, I still don't know anything about castles and guards and politics."

"Maybe not," the Redmother said. "No one will ask you to decide battle tactics. However, people need to know that they're fighting for something tangible. In this case, the just and rightful ruling family of the kingdom. From the eastern wall you can see fire in the city. Palle and his followers must be holed up somewhere, and who knows what the Rhenlan troops on the border are doing."

"Those sound like matters for the captain of the guard," Doron said.

"She sided with the Rhenlaners," Tatiya said. "Anyway, she's dead."

"Serves her right. Vowless dung-eater," was the not-at-all-matronly comment of the little Redmother.

"Understand me, Doron," Tatiya continued. "If there was only the guard to worry about, I could take command of the majority right now. My father was Cratt, Captain for Queen Dea, and my brother Karn is with the border patrol. I know what I'm doing, and most of the guards know me. If I tell them there is an option to following Palle, they'll take it. That's not the problem. It's the rest of Bronle, and all of Dherrica, I'm worried about . . . we're worried about." She included the others with a gesture. "The next nearest Shaper lives thirty miles from here. I'd bet my sword that the senior merchant of Bronle and most of his friends are under Rhenlan influence. Other things will have happened last night. That's why we came to you."

"It's not me you need. It's Pirse, though only the gods know where he is." Doron sighed deeply. "I suppose I'm the next best thing." She took another skeptical look at the matron's rounded face. "Are you really a Redmother?"

"My mother was, and she trained me—as well as was allowed, that is." The woman tried to adjust the over-long sleeves, but they quickly slipped back again. "I admit I was never presented before a Festival gathering. You know what Dherrica's been like. But I have the memories, or most of them, and I know the duties."

"Then remember this. The first official act of Regent Doron. Tatiya, daughter of Cratt, I name you Captain of the Guard. Here are your orders." She took a deep breath. "First, we'll need a proper guardian for Emlie. Is there someone in the castle who'll qualify as a nursemaid?"

One of the men in the doorway spoke for the first time. "Cook's daughter?"

Tatiya nodded. "Good idea."

"Fine." Doron looked around at the walls of her prison, her confidence growing. This wasn't the rescue she'd been expecting, but it had promise. "Send for her. Then let's get out of here. We need a proper conference room if we're going to get this kingdom organized."

"Another messenger, Highness," Brownmother Thena said from the doorway.

Vray looked up from the rough map on the kitchen table. She had been sketching lines and buildings on Deenit's largest bed linen since dawn. "Yes?"

"Our guards have taken the first street south of the market square. The fighting at the inn by the lake hasn't stopped. The captain is going there next." Thena's brown cheeks warmed with unease, but she kept any words of commiseration to herself. "Damon's guards are firing the lakeside district."

"Too late," Vray responded critically. "Loras will have warned everyone away from that end of town by now." She made another notation on her map. Large sections of Edian were still represented by blank space. Of the remaining areas, perhaps half were firmly under the control of the king's guard. The other half, consisting of a dozen scattered districts of homes and shops, had chosen to resist Damon.

Some of that was Dael's doing. In the hours before dawn, he had set himself to rouse people who already trusted him and convince them that the crisis was at hand.

Vray had consulted with Deenit and sent word to Edian's Brownmothers. Reaction had been slow. Too much shock, too much disbelief that Damon could have gone so far. Barely enough off-duty guards had gathered by daybreak to stop the first attempt by one of Damon's troops to penetrate the street above Loras's shop.

The streets surrounding the goldsmithy had been the first to bar passage to guards who had been sent out to demand the return of the absent princess. Rebellion had sprung up spontaneously at three other locations assaulted by overly aggressive search parties. Some people might have accepted threats and unpleasantness without thinking to challenge the guards themselves. They would have taken their complaints to the law reader after the excitement was over. However, Damon's troops had almost immediately gone beyond words to actions.

Perhaps the townspeople would have had difficulty deciding between Damon and herself, had it remained a matter of her word against his that he intended ill toward her and all of Rhenlan. Under the circumstances, they had no difficulty deciding that they would prefer anything to having their premises invaded, their possessions destroyed, and their neighbors, friends, or family members interrogated and abused in the name of King Damon.

Now the doubting was over. The people of Edian were taking sides.

"Thank you, Thena," Vray said.

After the woman left, Vray gazed down at the linen on the table and pretended to concentrate. What a joke. She wasn't fooling anyone, not even herself. The map was important—to a tactician, at least. Not that her beloved Keeper husband could read it. She would have to read it out to him, interpret what he saw as mere decorative black squiggles. He would listen politely, having already heard the reports himself and memorized all the relevant details better than she could draw them. Vray could just hear him suggesting that she shouldn't have wasted one of his mother's best bed linens.

Gods, if I imagine our conversation clearly, he'll have to come back to participate in it, won't he? He can't die if he's got to come here and annoy me.

She straightened her arms and pushed away from the table, flattening her spine against the back of the chair. She ached. Her head ached from staying awake all night. Her stomach ached from lack of food. Worst of all was the ache in her throat. Acknowledging it strengthened her need to cry. She felt her chin begin to quiver and inhaled shakily. *I don't have time for this! I refuse to be afraid for Dad. There's nothing I can do for him now. Nothing I can do for Dael, either—except organize the resistance against Damon, which I can't think about if I'm busy feeling sorry for myself.*

She pulled air into her lungs, an almost soundless sob. Tears spilled out of her eyes and trickled down her face on either side of her nose, running together in a warm line under her chin. She let them come for a few moments, a controlled indulgence.

Another deep breath, and she reached up to swipe the dampness away from her face and neck with both hands. She blinked, clearing her eyes.

Drying her hands on her skirt, she picked up the quill and leaned over the map once more.

Two troops of guards fought sword to sword in the center of the street in front of a bakery. The baker, bleeding from a shallow gash on his forehead, was hastily nailing planks across his shattered doorway with the help of several neighbors. As Ivey sped past, he caught a brief glimpse of upended shelves and ruined food within the bakery before he was in the next lane and out of sight of the destruction. He did not consider stopping to help. The same was happening everywhere in Edian. The king's guard—Damon's part of the king's guard—was using its search for the princess, her husband, and their "known associates" as an excuse to loot and steal among any of the townspeople they deemed uncooperative. Dael was organizing protection for the people of the town while trying to keep himself in hiding, and it wasn't easy. Ivey turned up another deserted lane, dim and shadowy in the late morning light. The sky was overcast. Dark would come early this afternoon. That, at least according to Dael, would be to the benefit of the rebels.

Ivey scowled as he slowed to a brisk walk, his breathing deep and rapid, legs aching. He didn't like the terminology even if it was accurate. As a storyteller and poet, he understood the multiple meanings of words. Legally, Damon was king and by rights the king's guard was his. By that standard, the guards who did his bidding were loyal. Dael's behavior was disloyal, rebellious. That he was right to rebel was not a concept that found its way into the emotional definition of the words. Traditionally, loyalty was always good; rebellion was, at best, of suspect value. Yet today in Edian, it was the loyalists who smashed windows and terrified the community and the rebels who strove to protect the weak and keep order.

Ivey turned the corner and found himself nose to nose with a guard. A voice growled, "Grab him!" and a hand caught at his clothing. He hit, kicked, and twisted. So did the guard. The guard, with the help of several friends, won. Ivey was dragged to his feet, one arm wrenched behind his back. He tossed his hair out of his face, intending to glare at the troop corporal. Instead he gaped stupidly.

"I know you! I saw you last summer in Cross Cove at Quardt's house!"

"You see a lot." The corporal examined him stoically. "The minstrel. Wasn't smart to leave you wandering loose. The king'll be glad to talk to you." He nudged the nearest guard with a bony thumb. "Take him to the castle."

The four guards bustled Ivey up the lane. He was too astonished to struggle. How many others in the group in Cross Cove had lied about their intentions? Were other villages in danger as well, because one or more of their people was actually in Damon's service? Just how much did Damon know? Had the struggle been lost even before it began? Would all the fighting be for nothing?

Being captured by Damon's people was the least of his worries.

"What are you doing here?" Vray demanded.

Her husband pulled the door closed behind him. His gaze strayed to the product of her morning's work. "Is that one of Mom's bed sheets?"

"It's a map."

Dael's mouth tightened. A streak of blood discolored one side of his face, and his hands and much of his clothing were filthy with dirt and gore, but as far as Vray could tell he was uninjured. He didn't give her any time to appreciate the fact. "We don't need maps. We need a reason to keep fighting. He's got the advantage, Vray."

"Then change the odds!" She stood, coming around the table toward him. "We have a few advantages of our own."

"True." He came forward, expression solemn. "We can't give up. Not as long as there's hope of beating him. That's why we've got to get you out of the city."

"What?"

"It's not safe for you here."

"It's not exactly safe for anyone!" Vray shouted in disbelief.

"You're not just anyone!"

"You can't be serious. I've got to be here. These are my people!"

"All Rhenlaners are your people. You've got to look ahead, Vray. We'll need you later, when it's all over."

"Dael, I am not leaving Edian! I'm not leaving you."

"You're not doing any of us any good by staying. How can you serve your people if you don't survive?"

"You'll protect me."

"That's exactly what I'm doing. I've made my choice. I want to be captain of the queen's guard. You're leaving."

"Where am I supposed to go?"

"South. I'm not the only one you can depend on. There's a safe place for you with Jordy. Knowing that, I can't allow you to risk your life here."

"Jordy," Vray repeated coldly. "Let's talk about Jordy."

Dael started to turn away from her. "We don't have time for a fight now!"

"Well, we're going to have one anyway." She caught his arm. "Why didn't you tell me you knew Jordy?"

With a sigh he stood still. "Why didn't you tell me?"

"I was protecting him!"

"So was I!"

"You knew I was working against my brother!" Vray shouted. "That I needed all the help I could get!"

"I know that Jordy has no use for Shapers!"

"I know. I'll deal with that later."

Dael's eyes widened. "How?"

"With your help. That's beside the point." She shook his arm to emphasize her words. "The point is, why didn't you tell me?"

"With you gone, Jordy's ideas were the only hope any of us had of a better future. Even after you came back, I couldn't be sure you'd prevail. What Jordy has done may be the only hope the villagers have now. And it's helping you, too."

"I know that. I helped him organize it," Vray snapped.

"So did I!" Dael scowled. "We're all on the same side. So what are we arguing about?" He paused. "Oh, right. About your leaving."

"Dael!"

He started to place his hands on her shoulders, then changed his mind and folded his arms instead. "Vray. Princess Vray of Rhenlan," he said firmly. "Listen to me. Not as your husband, but as an advisor. I believe we can take the town, but it's going to take time. Meanwhile, you owe it to the rest of us to stay safe. Unless of course you agree with Jordy that we'd be better off without any Shaper in charge."

"That's not fair," Vray said through gritted teeth.

"You know I'm right."

Silently she counted to ten. Then she folded her arms and demanded, "Where?"

"Where your brother won't look for you."

"Then why are you suggesting Broadford? Dael, he knows about Jordy."

"He also thinks he killed him. But you're right, Broadford's not safe. The Brownmothers recommend that you go to the Cave of the Rock."

"All that way? It'll take days!"

"There'll still be snow on the ground in the south, and there are no villages nearby to shelter you," Dael agreed. "It's idiotic to go there, when you could much more easily try for Sitrine and the help they could offer. Which is exactly why Damon will never figure out where you've gone."

Vray dropped her hands to her sides. "You're impossible to argue with when you know you're right."

"Your escort's outside. I told Nocca to pick out a good horse. Peanal helped Mom pack some clothes for you."

Vray plucked her cloak off the back of her chair. Dael helped her into it, and walked with her as far as the front door where Nocca, Peanal, and the horses waited.

Nocca held her mount's head and Dael boosted Vray into the saddle. Then he stepped out of the way. "Hurry," he told his brother. "The south edge of town may not be clear much longer."

Nocca nodded. As the horses began to move she turned her head for a last glimpse of Dael. He saw her, but didn't wave. He simply stood there, erect and motionless, in front of his father's shop, gazing after her.

Then they followed a bend in the street, and Vray couldn't see him any more.

The sound of a masculine voice in the next room dragged Jordy back to awareness. He focused blearily on the window nearest the bed. The pattern of light and shadows in the trees behind the house told him that it was still late afternoon. Interminable afternoon. He listened to the one-sided altercation for a few more seconds, then gathered his strength. "Cyril," he called.

The curtain over the doorway was jerked aside. Cyril stepped far enough inside to frown darkly at him. "That's

Herri, isn't it? Let him in, woman."

The expression in Cyril's eyes warned Jordy that she did not intend to humor him for very long, but she did leave the doorway, and a moment later Herri's bearded face, solemn with worry, poked through the curtain.

"Jordy? I won't disturb you if you're resting."

"Come in, come in."

Herri helped himself to the stool beside Cyril's loom and brought it over to the bed. As he carefully settled his large bulk onto the slender stool he said, "So that stupid horse of yours has lost herself, has she?"

"You've seen Tob?"

"No. He's been to everyone else in the village, though. According to Kessit he's been at it all day. Imagine he doesn't want to come home until he's found something one way or another."

"No."

"Maybe I should come back tomorrow." Jordy forced his attention back to the innkeeper, who was regarding him uneasily. "You should be resting," Herri said.

"I'm not tired, and I'm not feverish," he added for Cyril's benefit as she came through the curtain, a mug held between her hands. He saw a flash of alarm cross Herri's face. "Don't start looking like that. The wound's clean. Cyril's watching it."

To his annoyance, Herri stood. "Still, I won't stay."

Cyril reached the side of the bed. Jordy stopped her with a glance. "Wait," he said to Herri. "One thing you can do for me."

Herri replaced the stool by the loom and turned. "Anything, of course."

Jordy fought down the desolation that had been growing in him all day. "If you do see Tob, will you have a word with him?"

"About what?"

"I had to tell him about Reas."

"Pond and Pool, man, as if enough hasn't happened! Why?"

262

Jordy closed his eyes. "Because he was going to claim blood debt against the king." When that brought no response, he opened his eyes again to find Herri shaking his head in dismay.

"That's a nasty shock for a boy his age."

"To learn your father's a liar? Aye."

Herri stroked his beard. "You didn't tell him everything?"

"He wasn't ready to listen."

"I'll do my best," Herri promised. "And now I am going."

Cyril waited for the front door to close behind the innkeeper before she sat lightly on the bed beside Jordy. She rested a cool hand against his face. "You worry yourself overmuch."

"It's Damon I'm worried about," he complained. "What is he doing?"

"Forget him. Today he is someone else's problem." She held the mug to his lips and put one hand behind his head to steady him. "Drink."

He swallowed, the taste more of medicine than of cider. By the time he finished, a numbing warmth was already beginning to spread from the pit of his stomach outwards. He managed to find Cyril's face still hovering over him.

"If Tob comes home, talk to him?" he asked.

"We will take care of Tob. We will take care of everything. Now sleep."

Vision faded as Jenil's drugs took effect. So did the pain of his arm, retreating until there was nothing left but an empty, inviting void. Without any real chance to make a coherent decision one way or another, Jordy slept.

CHAPTER 27

What a waste. The entire day gone, and what had he accomplished? Nothing. Tob emerged from a footpath and stepped onto the eastern road, thoroughly disgusted. He had trudged the length and breadth of Broadford and its neighboring areas, through fields and orchards, around the fisher cottages, up to the top of the ridge and a mile northward along the familiar road to Edian. He did not find Stockings. He did not find anyone who had seen or heard of a stray horse in the area. He was more certain than ever that she was lying dead in a gully somewhere.

Habit forced him to glance up at the sky. If he walked quickly he would just reach home before full dark. Broken clouds drifted overhead as they had throughout the day. Some clear sky in the direction of Broadford allowed a few rays of sunlight through to touch the willows along the riverbank with a hint of reddish gold. The wind would hold from the northeast for perhaps another day, keeping the weather mild. Perhaps.

If the weather was going to turn unpleasant, that was too bad for Stockings. If she was stupid enough to get lost, then she deserved the consequences. It wasn't his fault if he couldn't find her, anymore than it was his fault that his parents had lied to him all his life. Parents. Ha. Parent and pretender. Poser. Hypocrite.

Tob started along the road, kicking aimlessly at occasional pebbles. It hadn't done him any good to be alone with his thoughts for a day. If anything, he felt worse. Their behavior was incomprehensible, inexcusable. They'd get what they deserved if he stopped caring. Standing on the northern road a little after midday, he had seriously considered keeping on, losing himself in one of the little villages that dotted the plateau west of Lake Hari. Only responsibility, he told himself, his vow to search for the stupid horse, had stopped him.

Deep in his brooding he did not immediately hear the sound of approaching hoof beats. When the unexpected cadence finally caught his attention, he whirled round, listening, alarmed. It wasn't fair. All day he'd been hoping for sight or sound of a horse, but it was a particular horse he wanted. Stockings's familiar, easy, clop, clop, not the complex, multiple hoof beats approaching. Complex and quick. Two or three horses, cantering. The only riders in Tob's experience who traveled that way, light and quick in a group rather than alone, were king's messengers. For an instant he saw the table at home, smeared with blood. King's messengers—king's murderers. His stomach heaved and he swallowed bile.

If he'd been quicker, the tangle of willows along the riverbank would have provided a hiding place. Dread and loathing were not emotions that inspired quick thinking. He was still standing in the middle of the road when the riders appeared over the crest of the hill that had hidden them from view. He'd never seen the woman before, or her chestnut mount. The man, wearing what looked like a mother's black robes flapping around him, was equally unfamiliar. The same could not be said for the animal he was riding.

"Hey!" Tob shouted, fear forgotten, waving his arms indignantly. "Hey! You there! That's our horse!"

The woman reined to a halt a few yards short of his position. Stockings didn't need any encouragement from her rider. The moment she heard Tob's voice, she dropped into her lumbering trot, throwing the black-robed man forward against her withers, and came to a determined stop. Tob ran forward to meet her. Her dark coat was streaked with the gray of dust and dried sweat, and her muscles quivered. She rolled her eyes and almost succeeded in catching his hand between vicious yellow teeth as he reached for her halter.

"I don't blame you," he told the indignant animal as he

evaded her lunge and caught her head. "What do you think you're doing?" he continued to her rider. "Anyone can see she's not built to be run like that!"

The stranger pushed himself upright on the riding pad. "I'm sorry. There was need. The young woman is very ill."

Tob privately thought that it was the man who looked gaunt and ill. The woman seemed quite comfortable, sitting patiently on her horse a few yards down the road. "That doesn't explain why you're using our horse."

"We found her grazing at the roadside five miles back. A gift sent by the gods. We really must hurry. Are you from Broadford?"

"That's right."

"My name is Aage. I must find the healer Jenil immediately. Do you know her? Can you tell me where to find her?"

"I know her. I think she's staying at Herri's inn."

"She might not be there. She was called last night to the home of a carter named Jordy. Can you lead me there first?"

The words, *Of course, he's my father,* echoed mockingly in Tob's head and remained unspoken. He said, "Slide forward," and flung himself onto Stockings's broad back as soon as the wizard had complied. Tob had often heard of the powerful Aage. Met face to face, he wasn't very impressive, a bony man with too much forehead, who radiated exhaustion and worry.

"You can find the carter's house?" Aage persisted.

"I'd better be able to. This is his horse." He raised his voice. "Giddup, girl."

Stockings walked forward with no more than her usual reluctance. Aage called to the woman as they passed her, urging her to follow. Her delayed reaction was disturbingly similar to the sort of dull incomprehension Stockings displayed. Maybe she wasn't well after all. Under Tob's urgings, the horse increased her pace to a trot.

A light rain accompanied them as they came to the outskirts of Broadford. Tob left the wizard standing beside his companion and her mount at the foot of the track while he led Stockings into the yard. Matti, sitting on the porch with her chin in her hands, squealed and jumped up when she saw him. Pepper popped out of the chicken coop and pelted across the yard.

"You found her! Where was she?"

"Halfway to Garden Vale. How are things?" Tob replied shortly.

"Oh, not too bad, except that Momma let Herri in to see Daddy, and she won't let us."

Matti joined them. "It's not fair. We can be quiet, too."

"I doubt it." Tob's response was automatic. Before Pepper could become indignant, he continued, "Anyone else visit?"

"The Greenmother is here," Matti said.

"Momma let her in, too."

"We're supposed to be patient. That's what Herri said."

"Oh, stop being so perfect."

As they squabbled, the girls continued to trail after Tob, who led the weary Stockings into the stable. He hitched her to the grooming stand and snatched up a brush, which he shoved at the irritable Pepper. "Here. Stop complaining and give me a hand. The Greenmother is here now?"

"Yep. She walked. I asked could she really disappear in a puff of smoke and she said not today."

Tob went outside. Aage and the woman were already coming up the hill. Tob met them halfway. "She's inside."

The wizard nodded. "I know."

When the woman dismounted in front of the house, Aage immediately wrapped a supportive arm around her shoulders. She was far less steady on foot than she'd been on horseback. Tob tied the animal's reins around the porch railing. Aage, without waiting for an invitation, guided the woman up the steps and in through the door. Tob entered unobtrusively behind them.

Jenil was standing at the hearth, a mug of cider at her lips. She stared at her fellow Dreamer, then at the woman, and slowly lowered the mug to the table. "Gods and mothers!" she exclaimed. "What have you done?"

"Please." The wizard's voice was very quiet. Desperate, Tob thought. Or guilty. "Help us."

The curtain over the inner doorway was pushed aside by Cyril. A petulant, "Well, what's happened?" came clearly from the next room.

"How can I?" Jenil asked in response to the wizard's plea.

"I don't want to hear about your disapproval." Aage's brittle calm snapped, and he took a step away from his charge. "You're a healer. Jenil, she needs you. They need you."

"I understand that," the Greenmother snapped back. "How can I fix something that shouldn't be at all? Aage, the power can't be bent to do what you've done!"

His chin lifted wearily. "You're wrong. I bent it. The gods gave me a vision. The proof is there."

"The proof is dying."

Cyril, who had been observing the conversation cautiously, darted forward, startling the two Dreamers. Tob saw what had alarmed his mother and was there a split-second before her, catching the strange woman as she began to fall to one side. He was heartily sick of people collapsing in their house. Aage and Jenil crowded round as they guided the woman to a bench at the table.

Jordy pushed through the curtain, looking wan, rumpled, and exceedingly annoyed. "Who in the world is that?" he demanded. If he was surprised to see Aage, he didn't show it.

"Jeyn, Sene's daughter," the wizard replied.

"Queen of Sitrine," Jenil said.

Aage met Jordy's skeptical gaze. "She's ill."

"She's pregnant," the Greenmother corrected sharply, and sat down next to Jeyn. "By him."

Jordy scowled throughout the rapid exchange. "I didn't think that was possible."

"It's not. That's why she needs help." Jenil placed her hand close to the young Shaper woman's abdomen, but did not quite touch her. Her black robes, voluminous as they were, could not conceal her shudder from Tob, who stood close behind Jeyn's place on the bench.

Jenil spoke to the woman without her usual acerbity. "Your Majesty? How are you feeling? Can you hear me? Do you know where you are?"

Tob retreated a few steps from the table. None of the adults paid him any attention. The Dreamers were concentrating entirely on the princess, or queen, or whoever she was, and Jordy was watching the Dreamers. Cyril, as though she were alone in the room, picked up Jenil's mug from the table and tidied the hearth. Tob, knowing the truth, took another step toward the outside door. His mother had fooled them all for years; friends, neighbors, children. They had accepted her as a person impaired, incapable of communication. How could they have been so stupid? Had no one really looked at her? Or had they looked without seeing?

Tob could see now. He saw the Shaper woman, who was definitely, truly, ill. Aage had seated himself across from her and was massaging her hands while Jenil continued to speak to her, trying to coax some response from the blank features. Seen in comparison with the queen, there was no mistaking the comprehension and awareness that infused Cyril's every movement. There was nothing wrong with her. She was a self-centered liar who just didn't care about other people. But there was nothing wrong with her.

He forced himself to look away from his mother, and found his eyes going automatically to Jordy for reassurance before he remembered that there was no comfort for him there. The house was overfull. Too many people and too much pain. He had to get away.

"She wasn't this bad a few hours ago," Aage said worriedly. "Jenil, you must have some idea, some suggestion."

She did not answer him immediately. Straightening from her examination of Jeyn, she turned instead to the waiting carter. "She's in great danger. If we have to waste time traveling to Herri's, we might lose her."

"She's dying?"

"Not immediately. She's going insane."

"No." Why he bothered to protest Aage couldn't say. He knew it was true. He just couldn't believe it was permanent. Jenil would help her. Jeyn didn't need the pity evident in the carter's measured gaze.

"It's just the strain," Aage insisted.

"You'll stay then," Jordy said to Jenil. He looked past her to catch the young man who'd been edging uncomfortably toward the door. "Move the bed in our room nearer the fire, Tob. Be quick, now."

Aage didn't participate in the ensuing bustle of activity. He was peripherally aware of Jenil putting something herbal to heat on the fire, of the broad-shouldered boy passing several times with bundles from the attic, of Jordy retreating to the other room to return mostly dressed, grumbling as he struggled to ease his useless arm into its sleeve, of the simple-minded wife rousing from her inattentiveness long enough to make her husband comfortable in the chair at the end of the table, and of the two little girls who at some point slipped in from the yard and made much of their father, until he set them to doing something useful. None of this interested Aage. He remained where he was, holding Jeyn's hands across the table, speaking quietly to her whenever she showed any sign of awareness.

The power bent irregularly around the unborn Dreamer, an invisible sparkle, an inaudible crackle as far as the Keepers were concerned. Jeyn showed no direct response to the fluctuations taking place in and around her body. The indirect response, her increasing mental dislocation, continued to grow stronger.

A sharp clunk of wood on wood marked the appearance at Aage's elbow of a bowl of stew. Startled, he glanced away from Jeyn. The Keeper woman set a place for Jenil, deposited a bowl in front of the carter, and circled the table to place Jeyn's portion directly in front of her. Jenil sat down, a steaming mug that smelled of spice and bitter herbs held between her hands. The children, responding to a wordless gesture from their father, picked up bowls and spoons for themselves and followed Cyril and the stew pot she carried through the curtain into the other room.

"What are you going to do?" Jordy asked from his chair at the end of the table.

Jenil set the mug on the table. "You're not going to understand."

"Don't accuse me of ignorance, woman. Not on the subject of broken minds."

Dread stalked Aage with an image of an older Jeyn vaguely puttering, just like the carter's wife. He forced the thought away. Jenil pressed her lips together and said nothing.

"It's something to do with this pregnancy," Jordy continued relentlessly.

Aage swallowed against the tightness of unease. "The magic's come too soon—to the baby."

"To the baby?" Jordy asked. "We are taught that Dreamer children have no magic, that you acquire your abilities in adulthood."

"This is not a Dreamer child," Jenil stated, her voice flat and cold. "It is a wizard's creation. Pride and power exercised with no regard to duty or sense."

"The safety of our people is our duty!" Aage cried. "I had to try. Only four of us remain, Jenil!"

"This smells good."

The anger in the room evaporated as they all looked to the queen. The tension did not.

With a wrenching effort of self-control, Aage resumed his calm facade. "Have some, love," he suggested.

"Thank you. I believe I will." Jeyn smiled at him, blinked slightly unfocused eyes in Jenil's general direction, and picked up her spoon.

"We're in Broadford," Aage informed her.

Jeyn nodded, chewing.

Tentatively, Jenil said, "Hello, Jeyn."

"Hello, Jenil," the girl replied. She took another mouthful of stew.

Jenil gestured down the table. "This is Jordy. You're staying in his home tonight."

Jeyn swallowed. "Hello, Jordy," she said politely. "Ivey knows a Jordy." After regarding him for a moment longer, her eyes sought Aage once more. "Am I finished yet?"

He couldn't stop the frown. She waited, head beginning to tilt to the right, spoon poised over her bowl. "You haven't finished your supper," Aage told her gently.

"Not that." Jeyn's manner was patient, reasonable. "Am I finished with the baby?"

The carter looked away.

"Not yet, Jeyn," Aage said.

"Yes, she is."

Jenil's cold contradiction stung him. "Don't say that."

"Is it time, Aage?" There was no longer any illusion that she was actually seeing him. What little contact she'd achieved with the solid reality of the farmhouse was slipping. "I'm very tired. Why is it taking so long?" Her lips moved for a few more seconds, but no further words were audible.

"You see my choice, carter Jordy," Jenil said.

Aage took the spoon from Jeyn's limp fingers and carefully placed it in the bowl before turning to Jenil. "Choice?"

"It's impossible, wizard. She knows it, even if you don't. The pregnancy must be ended."

"No."

"Don't you see?" She grabbed his arm. Her day's rest had partially replenished her strength, physical as well as magical. Lines of power bent between them, tingling against Aage's still-overused senses. "Even if she could carry it to term, what would be the use? There will be no Dreamer child to grow and prosper, Aage. You must have felt the truth. It's already insane."

Aage jerked away from her touch. "It's just the shock. We can't expect an unborn babe to understand the bending of power. Once we teach him, he'll be fine."

"Teach? When? Five months from now? Six? You're telling me a newborn will be capable of comprehending?

Even assuming that this child could survive the womb, which I seriously doubt, what do you imagine the power will do to it during the time required to teach the necessary understanding? Look what it has done to your princess, a mature, secure, personality."

"You did this on purpose?" Jordy glared furiously at Jenil. "Bad enough if it were some tragic, careless accident. This is an example of responsible Dreamer behavior?"

"Not now, carter," she said without taking her eyes off Aage. "You came to me for help, wizard. You know I'm right. Savyea would agree. Accept what has happened and help me, or leave."

Aage shook his head once. "There has to be another way."

"Do you care nothing for this woman?" There was a dangerous edge to the carter's voice. "You heard what she said. Her time has come. Not the way you hoped, but that's the price you're paying. The price she's paying. If a Greenmother says she can't save a baby—a Greenmother, man!—then I believe her. If she says she can save the mother, she should try. So either stop arguing or get out of my house. Or, by the Rock, I'll throw you out myself!"

Aage found himself on his feet, staring down the length of the table at the coldly angry carter. "Care for her? Care for her!?" he cried. The accusation, the entire situation, was so unfair that it left him speechless. He could never hope to explain the depth of his love for Jeyn. By the gods, who did this Keeper think he was to dare to challenge him?!

Jordy hadn't actually moved, but there was a tension in the lines of his body as he sat there which assured Aage he'd meant every word. He might detest Shapers and distrust Dreamers, but evidently at some point during the past few minutes he had set it in his stubborn mind that Jeyn needed his protection. If that meant bodily evicting a wizard, he'd do it. How he thought he'd do it, ill as he still had to be from the after-effects of a magical healing, Aage couldn't begin to guess.

"You're wasting precious time," Jenil said.

Defiance drained out of Aage. Twenty-four hours ago his life had made sense. Outlandish monsters had surrounded him, the distrust between kingdom and kingdom and between Keeper and Shaper had been growing, but other than that, everything was fine. Best of all, the gods had granted him a child.

Now his king was dead and the whole world was collapsing around them.

And the gods were liars.

"Jeyn," he whispered. He leaned across the table and touched her pale hair with his fingers. When she did not respond, he turned toward Jenil. "You're sure about the baby?"

"There's nothing there, Aage. Life, but no spirit. It's the woman we have to help. It's still not too late for her."

He closed his eyes. It was a last, pitiful denial, he knew, but he couldn't help himself. "What do you need me to do?"

There was no triumph in Jenil's voice. "She'll have to drink this. Then we'll take her in the other room. I'd prefer privacy, Jordy."

"Tob!" the carter called. There was a sound of light footsteps. Aage opened his eyes and looked over his shoulder as one of the girls poked her head through the curtain.

"He fell asleep, Daddy."

"Well, you'll have to wake him. All of you have to come out here, now. Tell your mother."

"Yes, sir," the child replied solemnly.

Aage picked up the mug and coaxed Jeyn to drink. After the first few swallows she trembled and looked at him. "Is it time, Aage? I want to go home."

"Soon, love. Soon."

CHAPTER 28

The thick glass of the east-facing window shone rose with the impending sunrise. Aage sat up, away from the side of the bed, and twisted round to peer at the motionless queen of Sitrine. "Any change?" he asked over his shoulder.

"You keep asking me that." Jenil pushed herself out of the carter's deep chair, moving slowly to be certain that her weight was properly balanced over her feet. She was so numb with power bending that she couldn't guess what her body might do if she didn't pay close attention to it.

"You keep not answering."

"I keep saying, 'no.' "

"That's not the answer I want."

Jenil didn't have the strength to get infuriated again. "She's resting peacefully. That's something. She's capable of surviving this."

Aage bent his head, his face disappearing into shadow. "With no more interference from me."

Jenil walked over to the bed and touched the sleeping woman's throat. Jeyn's pulse beat steadily, and no fever radiated against Jenil's sensitive fingertips. Beside her, Aage got to his feet. Jenil took his arm and steered him across the room. "We'll discuss that later."

"If there is a later. Never mind, I'm joking. I hope. Gods, I feel so useless." He glanced bitterly toward the curtained doorway. "Jordy will enjoy being vindicated. He has considered us useless for years. Or at least, more trouble than we're worth."

Looking at their surroundings from the carter's point of view, Jenil shuddered. The queen of Sitrine slept in her borrowed bed. A litter of jars and bowls covered the bedside table, soiled cloths overflowed a basket near the hearth, and the wood box was empty. Jenil could hear the family beginning to stir in the next room. Jordy and his wife had slept on a spare mattress, brought down from the attic and laid in front of the kitchen fireplace. Tob, after moving furniture and drawing water and fetching firewood without complaint until well past midnight, had brushed aside Jenil's thanks and gone to his own bed. "Useless?" Jenil repeated. "I'm tired of that word."

"All of your healing skill, all of Savyea's fertility magic, won't help any of us survive Damon. He's going to ruin the whole world."

"His sister will stop him."

"What hope does she have? Don't you understand? He killed Sene. How long do you think he'll allow Vray to live?"

Jenil burrowed her hands into her sleeves. The authoritative posture wouldn't impress Aage, but it made her feel stronger. "Damon's not invincible. He's only a Shaper."

"The only Shaper in the world in secure possession of his throne!"

"He failed to kill Jordy. That was a mistake. He'll make others." She wasn't aware that she swayed until Aage reached out to steady her.

"You're drained. Go back to the inn and sleep. I'll stay with your patients."

"They don't need either of us. They're as healed as power bending can make them. The boy can bring a Brownmother after he takes us to the inn."

Aage shook his head wearily. "If I truly cannot help here, I should return to Raisal."

"Go, then."

The bending lines of power that whisked him away screeched against Jenil's stressed senses. She took one more look at Jeyn, then went into the living area. The girls watched her as she knelt beside their father. He was still in the deep sleep his body needed. Cyril, working at the hearth, never turned.

Outside, Tob was crossing the yard on his way to the stable. Jenil soon found herself in a high two-wheeled cart, a rug over her lap, the horse's glistening haunches working rhythmically in front of her. She dozed, jolting awake with each new worry that crossed her mind. At the inn, Herri bustled her solicitously up to her favorite room.

The moment she lay down, her eyes closed and she slept.

It was mid-afternoon when Lim poked his head in the stable door. "Tob?"

"What?"

Lim came inside, leaving the door ajar behind him. Gray daylight caught Tob where he leaned against Stockings's shoulder, the still-unused currycomb in his hand. Lim wouldn't know how long he'd been standing here, or that he needed the comfort of physical closeness to the only living thing he still trusted far more than Stockings needed grooming.

"Jaea said I'd find you out here." The older boy's eyes flicked uncomfortably over the bowl and mug sitting on a stool. "She said you wouldn't come inside to eat."

Tob turned and ran the comb over Stockings's shoulder. "There's a lot of work to do."

"Can I help?"

"Thanks, Lim, but no."

"Herri wants to talk to you." At Tob's swift glare, Lim's voice rose. "Stop that! You have a right to be upset by what happened to Jordy, but you're not going to make anything better by turning against your friends!" More calmly he added, "Herri's going to call a meeting for sunset. Jenil will tell us how to make Broadford ready for whatever is coming."

"What does he want me to do?" Tob asked levelly. "Help spread the word?"

"No. I'm doing that."

"I thought you offered to help me around here."

Lim flushed. "I have time for that, too. Herri wants to see you right now."

"Why?"

"How should I know? Why don't you go and ask him?"

Tob grunted. He could guess what Herri intended to talk about. He didn't want to be interested—but too much of his hurt was the agony of noncomprehension. Maybe any kind of knowledge would be better than the desolation he felt now.

"Right," he said. He grabbed up his cloak and walked to the door, shoving the currycomb into Lim's hand. "Don't let her step on your foot."

Lim waved him away, his expression relieved. "See you later."

Tob trotted out of the yard without a glance at the house.

The main room of the inn was dark and empty. As the door closed behind Tob, Herri appeared in the kitchen doorway. He came and sat down at one of the larger tables, indicating a seat across from him.

Tob sat. "All right, I'm here," he said bluntly. "Say what you want to say."

The innkeeper's black beard bristled as his chin jutted forward. "I may be willing to speak. I may not. Are you willing to hear?"

Tob clenched his hands together. "Yes. I need to hear why you know more about me than I do."

"Fair enough. But don't expect every detail. Only Jordy knows that. I'll start at the beginning, or as much of the beginning as I've heard." Herri leaned back in his chair until the wood creaked.

"You know that Jordy was born in Dherrica. Farren was king there in those days, and not nearly as senseless as some of the Shapers have become. When Jordy was about your age, he thought it was a good idea to join the king's guard, and his parents approved. He became an archer. I imagine you know him well enough to guess he was pretty good at it."

"I don't know him at all!" Tob contradicted the innkeeper bitterly.

"Are you going to listen?"

"Not if you're going to try to tell me what I know or

don't know! If you say he was a guard, I believe you. Yet all my life, the way he always criticized—" Tob broke off, unable to put his emptiness into words. "Just don't tell me how well I know him!"

A grimace twisted Herri's mouth. "Sorry, boy. I wasn't thinking about it like that. Let me continue." He stroked his beard. "I grew up right here in Broadford. Damon's father wasn't as attractive a master as Farren of Dherrica, but at least he was better in those days than he is now. Was," he corrected himself. "A few years after Jordy started making a name for himself in the Dherrican Mountains, King Hion's soldiers came to Broadford looking for possible recruits. I didn't go. I already had my eye on this inn. But a friend of mine, only child of a farmer just north of here, had an urge to see the world. So he left the land to become a guard in Edian."

In spite of his intention to remain skeptical, Tob's mind leapt ahead of Herri's words. He leaned forward. "That was Reas?"

Herri nodded. "A few years passed. We didn't see much of Reas, but we did hear word that the border situation in the southeast was getting worse. The horse people were on the move. Then, one day, a team of carters came through with the unlikely story that Hion and Farren had made an alliance. That was in the fall. In the spring, what should we see one day but Reas riding into the square with a Dherrican archer at his side?

"The two of 'em, Reas and Jordy, stayed for a few days, telling tales and doing their best to drink the inn dry before they went back to their duties. They kept arguing the relative merits of Dherrica and Rhenlan. Reas was showing his friend our best, and the plan was for Jordy to return the favor on the next long leave they could manage in the west.

"Now this next part I've only heard once, Tob, and then not all at the same time, so you'll have to forgive me if it's brief. That same summer, the combined guards of Farren and Hion went south to deal with the horse people. After ninedays of travel and minor skirmishes, they got within

279

striking distance of the tents of a leading horse chief. I said Jordy was an archer. He had one assigned place in the battle. Reas, who was a swordsman, had another. For three days they didn't see each other, until the horse people were in retreat and the village of tents a smoldering ruin. The order finally came for the guards to set up camp. Jordy discovered that Reas had captured a girl." Herri paused.

Tob didn't understand the innkeeper's hesitation. "He took a prisoner during the battle," he reiterated to encourage Herri to continue.

"No. She wasn't one of the fighters. He told Jordy he'd found her in the tent of the chief, and that he intended to keep her. He didn't go so far as to make Jordy find himself another place to keep his gear, but he made him pretty unwelcome at certain times."

"Keep her? In their tent? I thought prisoners would be kept under guard somewhere, until they could be exchanged for—" Tob stopped, shaking his head, but the horrible certainty wouldn't go away. "No."

Herri also looked horrified. "You didn't know? Jordy said I should explain to you—I thought this was what you'd found out somehow—"

"That my father forced my mother!" Tob cried. "That's what you're saying, isn't it?" He found the word somewhere in his memory, spitting it across the table. "Rape. Broadford's Reas turned Abstainer and raped a girl he found on the battlefield—"

"Not Abstainer," Herri objected sharply.

"Who else commits rape?"

"People lose control for other reasons. I'm not just saying that to make you feel better. He was wrong. He never gave Cyril a choice. She certainly hated him. But somehow, for some reason, he loved her. He considered her a prize he'd won, a precious jewel.

"Three or four days later, the horse people returned, with help. The battle started all over again, and this time the kings' guards were the ones who had to retreat. During the first of the renewed fighting, Reas was killed. Everyone knew Jordy had been his closest friend," Herri continued relentlessly over Tob's bowed head. "By tradition, he was given first claim on Reas's belongings. He chose to keep the tent and remain without a comrade in arms for a time. A not uncommon decision. He kept Reas's sword, although as an archer he really didn't need it. And he kept the girl.

"There was no way to return Cyril to her people. That was Jordy's first intention, but a few of the fighters who had also been captured told him that the horse people didn't exchange prisoners. A captive became the slave of the captor. They were also the ones to tell him her name. As Reas had guessed, she was one of the daughters of the chief. With every day that passed, the guards retreated further into Rhenlan—further away from Cyril's home. She continued to hate all of them equally, Jordy included.

"By the time it became obvious that she was carrying Reas's child, the troops had reached Edian. Edian, whose people hated and feared the horse people. She could go nowhere safely, except in Jordy's company. So he kept her by him, and they kept traveling. By autumn, they were back in Dherrica. Jordy vowed that he would find a way to return her to her people as soon as the border became settled, and it was safe for travelers to enter horse people lands.

"You were born in the spring. Other things were happening in Dherrica, things involving Jordy's family, but I've never learned what. That was when he decided to leave the guards." Herri spread his hands apologetically. "There's more to the story, boy. I wish I knew it, and not just for your sake."

"Never mind," Tob said quietly. "Go on."

"Jordy acquired Walnut and began his carting. Horse people weren't well known in the west or north, so no one bothered you and your mother. Eventually, Jordy brought you and Cyril back to her father's country."

Herri looked uncomfortable. "The long and the short of it was, they wouldn't take her back. Her uncle had taken the chieftainship, and her reappearance was the last thing he wanted. Has something to do with horse people honor.

Jordy seems to understand it, but I don't. The point is, they wouldn't have her. In fact, I think Jordy had some difficulty getting the three of you out of there alive. He did it somehow, and then he did the only other thing he could think of under the circumstances. He brought you here to Broadford.

"Now I can give you details out of my own experience, but from this point on there's not much to tell. They arrived with Walnut and a small blue wagon—I don't know if you remember it."

"It broke an axle on a muddy road the summer I was eight," Tob said. "I remember it."

"I was innkeeper by then. Jordy came here, identified himself as Reas's archer friend. We recognized one another from that visit they'd made on their last leave together. Jordy asked after Reas's family, and I had to tell him that there was none. His parents, your grandparents, died in a bad winter storm. There was nothing left but an empty farm.

"Well, that's when Jordy told me most of what I've just told you. He was at his wits' end. He and Cyril had been living an uneasy truce for two years and now he could see no possible resolution to their dilemma."

Herri lifted his chin and glared at Tob. "I told him he'd done all that any man could expect to do, and that he should take you and your mother to Edian or Garden Vale and leave you to find your own way. I admit it and I'm not ashamed of it. Your mother was a healthy young woman, and to this day I don't believe she's simple-minded. She could have set up shop as a weaver, or found support from a Brownmother house. But Jordy wouldn't have it. Stubborn Dherrican. He may have considered it as far as Cyril was concerned."

The innkeeper's broad face twisted ruefully, and he surprised Tob by reaching across the table to punch him on the arm. "But he'd let himself get hopelessly attached to you, you young fool! And since you weren't weaned yet, he had to keep both of you."

Herri sat back in his chair. "No one objected to his set-tling on Reas's land. No one's been disappointed. Having a carter's been good for the village. What else can I say, boy?"

Too many images whirled in Tob's head. Kings he'd never heard of, battles and retreats and two people he'd never met wandering the kingdoms with a baby he couldn't quite identify as himself. Jordy and Cyril hadn't even liked one another? Yet Tob, growing up, had never doubted their mutual affection and regard for one another. Another missing story. Another part of his parents' lives that he wanted desperately to understand.

Tob caught the thought and examined it. His parents' lives. He met Herri's eyes squarely. "Do I look like Reas?"

"Do you mean do I think someone will suspect?" the innkeeper misinterpreted bluntly. "No. Reas was broad in the shoulders, as you are, but in both your cases that's the result of your work. His face was more angular than yours, and, if anything, he was an inch shorter than Jordy. No, you look like Cyril's son, one of the horse people, that's all."

The short autumn afternoon was ending. Somewhere be-hind gray clouds the sun sank toward the horizon. The only light in the inn was a ruddy flicker from the fireplace. Herri's unkempt hair and bushy beard gave a wild appear-ance to the shadow his profile cast on the wall beside them.

"They should have told me," Tob said.

Herri nodded somberly. "This wasn't the best way to learn about your past. But you know your—" He stopped and corrected himself. "Jordy has to do things his own way. He raised you as he thought best. Believe that, Tob."

Outside footsteps thudded on the wooden stairs. Herri pushed himself to his feet and stepped over to the window. "Here's Kessit. I'd better go up and get the Greenmother."

Tob wanted to be left alone. He remained sitting in the darkest corner of the main room and tried to be unobtru-sive. Unfortunately, as the leaders of Broadford and Garden Vale arrived, each seemed to feel it necessary to stop by his table and say hello. Tob gritted his teeth and accepted the inquiries and concerns of friends and neighbors with terse, one-word replies.

No one scolded him for rudeness. If anything, their expressions of sympathy deepened, adding to his already acute unease. What was he doing here? He didn't belong in this council. He would be accepted under false pretenses, accepted because he was Jordy's son. But he wasn't.

He wasn't even sure he wanted anything more to do with Broadford. Did he still care what happened to any of them? To Cyril? Or Pepper and Matti?

He was so lost in his own miseries that he missed the first few minutes of conversation. When he began paying attention, Herri was rattling off a list of the names of farmers living east of Long Pine.

Lannal interrupted. "And if the guards come, what will that buy us? A few more days? That's postponing the problem, not solving it."

"A few days might be all we need." Jenil's voice was thin and brittle. The strain of two difficult healings and the extensive magical traveling she'd done had hardly been relieved by her day's sleep. Dark smudges under her eyes marred her usually pleasant face, and Tob could have sworn that more of the red of her hair had faded to gray.

"Damon's situation is desperate," she continued. "He doesn't recognize that yet, but when he does, he's going to strike out in whatever direction is easiest, to eliminate whatever danger he thinks he can reach."

Kessit fiddled glumly with his belt knife, lifting it a quarter inch out of its sheath, then dropping it back in again with a snick of metal against leather just audible enough to be irritating. "You're saying that Broadford's within easy reach?"

"Isn't it?" Lannal returned quietly.

Herri gestured with one large hand. "He'll expect to have some say in the matter himself."

"And we all know what he's likely to say." Canis's remark produced a ripple of laughter.

"We'll just have to convince him. Tob can help."

"Sir?" Tob asked, startled and confused by the sudden

shift of attention toward him.

"Convince your father," Canis explained patiently, "that he should get away from Broadford for a nineday or two."

"How long will it take Damon to notice that those guards he sent haven't reported back?" Kessit asked.

"I have no idea," Jenil admitted. "We may be worrying unnecessarily. With Edian in an uproar, he may not have time to think about rebellious Keepers a hundred miles away."

"You don't believe that," Lannal said.

Jenil considered. "I don't believe Damon is easily distracted."

"It's getting late," Canis announced. "What do we need to decide tonight?"

"We're agreed we need to protect Jordy from Damon?" Herri asked. Nods and muttered agreement answered him. "Who's willing to travel with him? And who can spare horses for riding and packing supplies?"

"Take a wagon," Lannal suggested.

"Not if they're heading south," Kessit argued.

Herri added, "And not if they want to be free to leave the road."

More opinions were offered. Tob rested his chin in his hands, thoughts churning uselessly as he listened.

CHAPTER 29

Feather left the too-quiet breakfast room. At the first junction of corridors she paused, reviewing the day's work ahead of her. She had too much to do. She had delegated the routine tasks, freeing herself to hear reports from the border and compose replies. A council to advise her would have been nice, but she hadn't yet had time to choose one. Of Sene's usual court, only she remained in the capital.

That wasn't strictly true. The wizard had returned yesterday, pleaded exhaustion, and retired to his room.

Feather considered her options. A sleeping advisor wasn't much use. She only had one choice. Balling her small hands into fists, she marched stiffly to the wizard's quarters.

"All right," she said as the door swung open. "Wake up."

There was no response from the black hump curled amid the rumpled bedcovers.

"I need you," Feather murmured, then cleared her throat and called loudly, "Aage!"

The hump shifted, revealing a drawn face near the edge of the bed. Not a peaceful sleep, she noted. Good. She longed to claw at something or someone, verbally or physically. She wanted to hurt as much as she was hurting.

Instead of giving in to her rage, she sat on the edge of the bed and gently touched the wizard's shoulder. "Aage," she said quietly, shaking him just a little. "Please. Talk to me."

A pale eye cracked open just a little, with no recognition in the look. He mumbled something.

Feather pushed hair off the wizard's wide forehead. The skin beneath her fingers felt dry. Feverish? Did wizards get fevers? She didn't think so. Jenil had never had so much as a sniffle in the years Feather had known her.

Sene was always getting ill. He didn't sleep enough, and went swimming in his ocean when the water was too cold. Sene. She gulped back tears, and thought instead of the recipe for herb tea she always made for the king. The late king.

Perhaps Aage could use a cup. Jeyn wasn't here to take care of her Dreamer. Feather knew about taking care of Dreamers. She needed to take care of someone. Not a kingdom. Kingdoms were many people. She needed a single person.

"Aage," she said again. This time he focused on her.

"Filanora." His voice was rusty. At least he recognized her.

"Wake up."

He closed his eyes instead. "I'm tired."

"I know. Talk to me."

His shoulders hunched up protectively. "Go away. Just go away."

His exhausted petulance almost amused her. "No. If I can't go away, neither can you."

"I want to be left alone," he said clearly. "By everyone. You and kings and Dreamers and gods. Especially gods. I will be left alone." His eyes opened, full of anger and pain and horror. He sat up and pushed Feather off the bed.

She barely kept herself from landing on the floor. She steadied herself and stood before him, hands on hips. "What's the matter with you?"

Aage threw the covers aside and surged upright to tower over her. He wasn't as tall as Sene, but anyone could tower over her. She refused to feel threatened, even though the Dreamer looked quite mad.

"Get out of here," he said softly. "Go away."

"No."

"I won't talk to you. I'm not going to talk to anyone."

"You're going to talk to me. You're going to listen to me, and you're going to work for me," she answered angrily. "You're the Sitrinian wizard, and I'm the ruler of Sitrine."

"Are you?" he asked, voice dangerously quiet. "Do I care?"

"You're talking to me," she pointed out.

"I'm leaving," he announced.

She expected to have to stand by and watch him vanish. Instead she saw his face turn a sickly gray. The next instant he staggered against the bed and fell onto his back. He groaned and flopped one arm over his eyes.

Feather started decisively for the door. "Something's wrong with you. I'll get my herb box."

"That won't help. I don't need your healing. I don't need any healing." His voice came muffled and dull from beneath the arm shielding his face. "I told you, I'm tired."

She returned slowly to the bedside. "All right. I've seen how power bending tires Jenil, but I've never known her to refuse to talk to us. You need more than sleep. You need to eat and to take some gentle exercise."

"Leave me alone!" The words were an almost soundless breath.

"And to talk," she finished, annoyed that he hadn't noticed she was being patient. "People in pain need to talk. Emotional pain," she guessed, as the Dreamer seemed to shrink away from her words. "What is the matter with you? Sene's death? Damon? Jeyn?" He'd told her that Jeyn would be all right. She touched her abdomen. "The baby?"

He sat up, glaring fiercely. "There isn't any baby! There never was a baby! The gods lied!"

"Oh." It was a dull-witted thing to say, but it was the only sound she could manage at the moment.

The wizard looked at her contemptuously. "Do you feel better for hearing that? It didn't make me feel better for saying it. The gods lie. They lied to me. No prophecy is true. Nothing is true. Now, go away and leave me alone!"

Feather backed away. Her legs connected with the edge of a chair and she gratefully fell into it. "Gods don't lie." She touched her abdomen again and felt her child stir in response. "Of course there was a baby. I'm sorry it died, but—"

His blue eyes bored into her. "No child. I never fathered a child. I may have destroyed Jeyn. I could have destroyed the world. I believed. I listened. I obeyed. I was a fool."

"May have, could have," she mocked back at him. "Whatever happened, it's over. And gods don't lie."

"They did."

"Nonsense," she shot back.

"I was there!"

What would Sene say? What would he do? Sene could handle anyone, even a hysterical Dreamer. "Maybe you misunderstood them somehow. What did they say?"

His words were clipped and harsh. "I did not misunderstand. Their instructions were perfectly clear. They lied."

Feather considered hitting him. A Dreamer in a rut was an aggravating thing. "What did they say? Tell me," she insisted.

He shrugged irritably. "Visions can't be put into words. I knew what they wanted me to do. I eventually found a way to do it."

She thought about that for a moment. It seemed to her that miracles shouldn't require any great effort from the beneficiaries. "Eventually? What do you mean, 'eventually?' If they were going to have you father a child, why didn't you just father a child?"

Aage scowled at her. "I couldn't just father a child. Dreamers can't do that."

"Why not?"

"Because the gods won't let us!" he yelled furiously.

"But they told you to."

"They lied."

"GODS DON'T LIE!"

"I'm not lying, either! I didn't imagine the vision. I know what a vision feels like. Jeyn did get pregnant, but it was insane. An insane Dreamer could destroy the world."

Feather studied her hands. "Doesn't sound like something the gods would arrange. Our gods don't want to destroy us, or the world. Your and Morb's monsters are the only ones who want to do that."

She hoped that guess was right. She reviewed everything she'd ever been told about the monsters that existed outside the net of power maintained by the wizards. "The fire bears nearly destroyed us. The monsters sent them. Haven't you claimed that Damon is influenced by them? And the Abstainers? The monsters send dragons and demons and plagues. Perhaps they sent a vision to a wizard. What if they used you, Aage? Tried to make you make a monster?"

The wizard looked shocked. He blinked, and stared hard at her.

She went on, speaking the thoughts as they came to her. "A weapon. You use them, their remains I mean, to make weapons. They're made out of magic. You're made out of magic." He snorted loudly but she went on. "Magic. You use them to make weapons to fight them. Maybe they found a way to use you—to use your magic—to fight you—us."

She stopped, and looked down, staring at her own clasped hands. The room filled with thoughtful silence.

"It wasn't the gods," Aage mused at last, testing the words. "It wasn't the gods?"

"That is what I said."

"I hadn't thought of that."

Dreamers are essential, Feather reminded herself, but they are so slow. They live so long that they forget how to think quickly. She patted her unborn child again. *I'll have a few things to teach you about using your brain, I see.*

"Well, think about it now," she commanded Aage. "I'll give you an hour. Then come to the council room and help me."

She stood and went to the door. Before leaving, she looked back, lifting her head regally. "That's an order from the Regent of Sitrine."

His wide-eyed stare turned briefly from anguished to startled.

"We have work to do," she concluded, and swept out as grandly as someone unpracticed at being a queen could manage. Unpracticed, but not untutored. *Oh, Sene,* she

thought, but did not let the pain show on her set features.
Do you know how much I miss you?

Pirse stood beside his horse, staring at the twinkling fires
that traced the outer edge of the Dherrican camp. To his
left, almost a mile to the east, another line of faint light
marked the location of the nearest Rhenlan guard troop.
The sentries of both groups prowled within their chosen
boundaries, silent and cautious in the pre-dawn darkness.
The white-coated ground and low clouds caught and dimly
reflected every tiny fire glow. The air was damp, threatening more snow.

To the south, only Dherrican watch fires marred the
night. Beyond them lay empty wilderness. To the north, the
lights of Bronle glittered against the black bulk of the
mountain.

Pirse knew the paths among the foothills that surrounded the city. He knew the farms and villages from years
of boyhood rambles, and had come to know their inhabitants during his visits with the minstrel Ivey.

The only thing he didn't know was what to do next.

He had ridden from Juniper Ridge, gathering supporters
along the way, with every intention of confronting his uncle.
He had not anticipated having to confront a force of
Rhenlan guards, as well.

One comfort was that Palle had been equally caught by
surprise. According to every report, and Pirse had listened
to many on his way along the border, the new guard captain, Tatiya, had turned the surprise to her advantage. The
defensive guard camps bristled with discipline, determination, and the best sort of stubborn immovability for which
Dherricans were renowned. Tatiya, supported by a certain
Juniper Ridge dyer who was surely giving her a great deal of
canny advice, was not about to let the Rhenlaners stroll un-
challenged into the mountains.

Of course, from what Pirse could see, none of the
Rhenlaners had shown any desire to enter the mountains.
Like Pirse, they seemed torn between two desires. Enter

Bronle, or deal with Palle?

Pirse wrapped and unwrapped the ends of his horse's reins around one gloved hand as he tried to make sense of the situation. A sizable body of guards remained loyal to Palle. With Rhenlan forces poised on the border, Pirse could not in good conscience set his Dherrican followers against other Dherricans—fighting among themselves would only serve to leave the kingdom defenseless against Damon.

However, unless all of the Dherricans united under one leader, they would not be able to hold off the kind of full-scale attack that Damon was likely to mount as spring softened into summer.

Palle had gone into hiding. A king who could not, or would not, lead his people was worse than no king at all. Rumors were spreading up and down the border that Queen Dea's grandchild was in residence in the castle, but they weren't sufficient to give Captain Tatiya the unquestioned authority she would need to defeat Rhenlan.

Pirse had to find his uncle, and settle the differences between them once and for all.

The momentum of his thoughts carried him into the saddle. A final, rebellious craving to go to his wife stomped through his mind. He ignored it, and picked up the reins. An encouraging cluck started the horse moving, footfalls muffled by the snow. At least he was familiar with the shapes of the land, snow or no snow. His years as a fugitive had not been without their lessons.

Pirse guided the horse past the outskirts of the guard camp, into the dawn.

CHAPTER 30

"This way," Vray said.

She reined her horse off the road onto the familiar, goat-cropped turf of the northern pasture. Behind her she heard the creak of saddle-leather, and a horse's snort as Nocca and Peanal followed her. From the top of the ridge they'd been able to see all of Broadford. The inn had been brightly lit despite the lateness of the hour. From Jordy's field halfway down the ridge, the disturbing signs of activity in the village were no longer visible, but Vray continued to worry. She didn't know why she had expected to find things as calm as they usually were in Broadford. How could they be? Nothing was normal. It seemed quite possible nothing would ever be normal again.

The thought only increased her anxiety. She urged her horse forward. Sheyn was high enough to light familiar landmarks. She heard Peanal's voice, the guard murmuring reassurance to her horse as they picked their way down the steep slope just north of the fenced pasture.

They passed through the necessary gates and emerged finally in the yard near the stable. The house was not entirely dark. Vray dismounted and handed her reins to Nocca. "You'd better wait here."

She felt a curious sense of disassociation as she walked across the quiet yard. The sleepy rustling from the direction of the chicken house and the smell of the stable belonged to another woman: Iris the village Redmother, Iris the apprentice carter, Iris the needle crafter. She had relegated those days, those memories, to a back corner of her mind. The reality of her return, and the intensity of the emotions revived within her, left her shaken. She'd spent so little time here. Her reality was Edian, the castle, her Shaper's vows, Dael. Yet nothing had changed from before. She was still a fugitive princess.

The wooden porch was smooth and solid beneath her boots. Her hand closed on the door latch. She schooled her thoughts sharply. Damon had reached this far, and farther. Happy memories were the insubstantial dream. This was not her home.

She pulled the door open and stepped inside. The only source of light in the room was a lamp sitting on the chest beside the door. She put out one hand to block the glare, and squinted uncertainly toward the hearth. "Cyril?" she called softly.

In the shadows of the curtained doorway leading to the other room a bow was trained on her.

Vray saw it and stopped breathing. The carter's voice, muffled but recognizable, said, "Vray?"

"Yes." The bow didn't waver.

"Who's with you?"

"Friends." Her heart pounded in her throat. "Damon's out of control. I'm running again, Jordy."

The curtain moved. Cyril stepped through, lowering the bow. Jordy appeared out of the shadowy room behind her, dressed in his nightshirt. "Come in, lass," he said. "By the gods, you gave us a scare. We expect the worst of a mounted party in the night."

"I wasn't thinking. I'm sorry. Jenil came to the castle and told us what happened. Did you know that?"

"Aye." He moved unsteadily to the near side of the table and sat down, cradling his right arm against his chest. Cyril stayed beside him, expression watchful. "When she came back from Edian she said you didn't seem to be in danger. What happened? Are ye all right?"

"Yes, I'm fine. You know who I married. You knew all along," she added, but kept the accusation pleasant.

"Not the day you left us," he protested immediately. "Dael never spoke of you. He was protecting you."

"Well, he's still protecting me," she grumbled. "He sent me away."

"To Broadford?" Jordy said skeptically. "I'd've thought

there are safer places for you to hide."

"We could sleep in the stable tonight. Damon won't expect a report from the men he sent to kill you before tonight or tomorrow. We should still have a few days before he makes a move in this direction."

Jordy sighed. "Let's hope you're right." Cyril slipped quietly into the other room. "Tell your friends to make themselves comfortable. Tob will be back shortly. It won't do for him to find them lurking about the yard. Come back when you've seen to them. You'll want to hear what Tob has to say."

"Where is he?"

"At the inn. Herri called another meeting. Jenil is still here, too."

It took Vray only a moment to go outside and confer with Nocca and Peanal. Peanal went to stable the horses, and Nocca followed Vray back to the house. When they entered, the lamp had been placed in the center of the table, and Cyril had draped a blanket over Jordy's shoulders and across his lap. She took the cider pot from the back of the fireplace and filled four mugs as Vray seated herself at the table. Her brother-in-law and the carter exchanged nods as Nocca sat beside her.

Unable to think of an easy way to begin, Vray said bluntly, "The same night you were attacked, Damon tried to have Dael killed. And me."

The lines creasing Jordy's forehead deepened. "Dael thought that he was safe. Damon trusted him."

"Not anymore. At least, not enough to be sure he wouldn't act when I was killed. Dael didn't know you knew me. Just as I didn't know he was working with you."

Jordy brushed the matter aside. "His position in Damon's court was too important. He's had to keep his true loyalties a secret for too many years. As you've kept secrets in your day, Princess Vray."

"True. At least we haven't been working at cross purposes." She took a sip of the cider, and looked at the mug in her hands. It was the one Jordy had brought from Sitrine especially for her at the end of her first summer in Broadford. She traced one finger around the outline of a purple desert flower. Fragile. Why was beauty so fragile? Like happiness, it seemed too fleeting to ever be fully appreciated until after it was gone. Fragile and fleeting and all too easily destroyed.

Dear Mothers. Will Damon destroy everything I love?

"Don't worry so, my girl." She looked up into sympathetic blue eyes. "Dael can look after himself. We're not beaten yet."

She managed a rueful smile. "Oh, I'm just tired. I shouldn't even have come. You don't need me here." Firmly controlling her worry, she concluded simply, "You look tired, too. All I've done is pull you out of bed."

His eyebrows assumed a reasonable approximation of their familiar, bushy ferocity. "None of that, now. It's news I need, not sleep."

Vray twisted around on her bench at the sound of the door latch. Tob had changed, subtly yet significantly, in the time she'd been away. He had added weight across his chest and shoulders, and the shadow of stubble darkening his jaw suggested that his beard had finally thickened. The lines of his face were hard, and unmistakably mature. She wondered if that last change was another result of the passage of time, or his response to the stress of the assault on Jordy. He stopped in mid-stride when he saw her and her companion.

"Vray? When did you get here?"

"Just a few minutes ago."

"Well?" Jordy demanded.

Tob straddled the other end of Vray's bench. "There was hardly any discussion. Everyone agrees that we have to take control of Rhenlan away from Damon before he does any more harm. Riders are leaving first thing in the morning to spread the word and see that it's passed on to farther villages. Jenil says she'll help spread the word."

"Over half of the guard in Edian remains loyal to Damon, but the town itself has risen against him," Vray said. A nineday ago she would still have argued against the Keepers taking up arms, but now her outrage was reserved for her brother. "They had no choice. He pushes people beyond all reasonable limits."

"Well, he's pushed too far now," Tob said. "It may take him a few days to notice it, but he's lost his kingdom."

Cyril unobtrusively placed a mug of cider and a slab of bread dotted with raisins in front of Tob. Vray's half-smile at the woman's normal gesture of concern for a growing son's appetite died almost at once. Tob did not so much as glance at his mother, or give any other indication that he intended to show the common courtesy of a "thank you." *Some other source of strain in the house?* Vray wondered. Beyond attempted murder and the all-pervading question of how to stop a king gone mad?

Vray was certain that Jordy was aware of whatever it was she'd just witnessed, but he continued with the original line of conversation. "It may take considerably longer than that. We never expected him to move this quickly, this drastically. He took us by surprise."

"Not entirely," Tob argued. "It came sooner than expected, that's all."

"I agree with Dad."

Tob's head snapped up so quickly that Vray almost forgot what she was saying. She'd never seen him so defensive.

However, she refused to be distracted by her brother's bad mood. To Jordy, she said, "I mean, you intended to have the villages firmly united before confronting Damon. I had hoped to have the loyalty of Edian and the majority of Rhenlan's Shapers. Instead, Damon has taken the initiative. There will be fighting on the borders by now. Edian is already a battlefield. We have to prepare for a long conflict."

"You have something in mind?" Tob asked tightly.

"Conserve our strength. Exaggerate his failures. You, Jordy, are both of those things. You know the villages, what we might expect from different Keepers. You're also proof that my brother is not infallible. He's not going to be able to accept that, any more than he could accept my continued defiance." She couldn't stop herself from looking nervously over her shoulder at the door. "He'll try again. You've got to get away from here."

"And go where, lass? Don't think I haven't been considering it."

Tob scowled. "For what it's worth, Herri and the others have been saying the same thing. There are plenty of people who would take you in."

As weary as Jordy appeared to be, there was no mistaking that stubborn set to his jaw. "Have you considered this, then? How did Damon come to know of me at all? Someone who knows me works for Damon. I've no mind to be betrayed a second time."

"You have to trust some of us," Vray said. She wouldn't let him have his way this time. It was too important. "If you don't, if you give up, Damon has won. You're the one who's said it all along, Jordy. Keepers don't succeed in keeping anything unless they work together."

"I never said I'm giving up!"

She welcomed his irritability. It was the surest indication that he was still listening. "Then I know just what you should do. Come with me. It's the best way to stay out of Damon's reach."

"No. That would only be making it easier for him. If we have to hide, we should go in opposite directions."

"He'll expect that! He's probably already alerted his border guards to watch for me, and it'll be worse as soon as he knows you've escaped."

"Assuming," Tob said, "that none of those guards rebel."

Jordy tapped an admonishing finger on the tabletop. "You're supporting my argument. If we go our separate ways, at least one of us may remain at liberty."

"Jordy, I know a place we can go where Damon will never find us, because he'll never think to look there. No one would think to look there. No one goes there."

Curiosity and obstinacy struggled for dominance on the

carter's features. He admitted at least temporary precedence to curiosity with a gruff, "Where?"

"The Cave of the Rock."

"Nobody goes there," Tob protested.

Vray allowed herself a smug smile. "I just said that." She saw that Jordy was still frowning, but with less assurance. "Please think about it. All we need is to buy a little time."

Some of Tob's odd tension seemed to abate. "When would you go?"

"I don't want to underestimate Damon again. It'll be best to start as early as we can in the morning."

"Which isn't far away." Tob stood. "Where are you sleeping?"

"The stable, with my brother-in-law here, and a guardswoman." She got quiet satisfaction out of watching Tob's eyebrows take quizzical flight toward the line of wavy dark hair falling across his forehead.

"Dael's brother. So, I have seen you before."

Vray yawned. "Gossip can wait for morning." She stifled a fleeting desire to send Nocca to the stable and climb into the attic to sleep with the girls. However, there was no reason to stop herself from saying a warm, "Good night, Dad."

"Rest well, lassie."

Outside, a cold, damp wind scudded low clouds across a lonely Keyn. Vray pulled her hood over her hair and hurried to the stable to capture whatever sleep the gods would send her.

Tob lay awake long after he rolled himself in his blankets, surrounded by the close, comfortable darkness of the attic. As tired, as oppressed as he was in body and spirit, his mind refused to rest. Memories bubbled up, one after another, from years past or days past, according to some unfathomable pattern. Closing his eyes and trying to relax into sleep only made them more vivid. Herri's words, battering away at the already ragged edges of his self-acceptance, threatened to twist each memory into something new and unrecognizable.

The process had begun the instant his mother had spoken to him in their blood-spattered kitchen. His earliest childhood memory was of Jordy in the yard, standing in front of the blue wagon. Its perspective was skewed, a scene viewed from a point near the ground. He could have been little more than two years old. One wheel of the wagon was off, and he had a vague impression of tools on the ground, although the child's-eye perception was fuzzy. Jordy was arguing, stubborn, determined. The woman answering him, her back to his watching child-self, had short, black hair.

He'd always had the memory. He had treasured it for the vividness of visual detail—the bright paint on the wagon, the carter's hair thick on top, worn long, almost touching his shoulders in a style he must have abandoned soon after, for Tob had no other memories of it. He'd never doubted that the woman was his mother. There was no uncertainty in the view of the two-year-old he had been. How then, through all the years of cherishing this early memory, had he missed, as fantasy or fabrication, the sound of Cyril's voice?

Every memory that crowded forward demanded reevaluation. He had been seven and a half when Pepper was born. He could see Jordy at the Fall Festival, holding up a crying four-month-old for all the village to see, too proud to be embarrassed by the fuss she was making. He remembered more recent winters, standing in the snow in the field behind the stable, trying again and again to master the bow. Not even to master it. To have once performed adequately would have been a triumph. At the time, his gnawing frustration had been eased by Jordy's patience, his confidence that Tob had skills of his own, and his conviction that it was unimportant that father and son excel at the same tasks.

Tob examined the memories, poked at them, worried each fragment as a dog worries a bone. Had Jordy's attitude been one of conviction? Or of resignation?

His most recent memories, however, defied reevaluation. They simply were. Himself and Jordy on the road, loading crates in a small village on the edge of Sitrine's desert, building a bonfire to ward off wolves in the lake country, laughing and drinking at the inn at White Water until his head buzzed pleasantly and Jordy had to half-carry him back to their campsite, watching Vray and the Greenmother leave for Queen Gallia's estate, sorrow a tight lump in his stomach, his father's arm around his shoulders.

His father. The words wouldn't go away. Memories churned and sifted and realigned, took on new overtones, shattered him, but the words remained. His father.

He was still awake when he heard the familiar sound of Cyril stirring the fire in the hearth to life. He lay motionless as Jordy's voice drifted up through the ladder hole a few minutes later, and did not respond to his sisters' whispers as they dressed in the dark and left the attic. Mugs clunked on the table, water sloshed, spoon clattered against pot. The outer door opened and closed, cutting off the sound of childish chatter.

Tob got up. He never had undressed. He descended the ladder unnoticed. Jordy was staring thoughtfully into the fire, clothed in his warmest trousers, boots, a woven tunic, and a sleeveless vest of sheepskin, thick wool inward. His traveling cloak lay over the back of a chair. Cyril stood behind him, gently knotting a sling at the back of his neck. Finishing, she stepped around him to straighten the cloth where it supported his arm.

She caught sight of Tob and lifted her head quickly. Jordy looked around as well. Cyril dropped her gaze and sidled away from her husband, vanishing into their bedroom.

"Cyril!" Jordy called after her. When she did not reappear, he faced Tob again. "It's not you she's angry with, lad."

"Isn't it?" Tob replied quietly.

Jordy flinched, but continued to face Tob squarely. "Herri told you about Reas. So you understand what happened."

"He couldn't tell me why she reacted like—" Tob waved one hand vaguely, indicating the room, Broadford, his mother's entire life. "Like this."

"Anger. Rage." Jordy pulled a bench out with his foot and sat down, watching Tob all the while. "Frustration. Shame. Despair."

"Those are reasons to cut herself off from everyone around her? Everyone except you."

"Including me, for a time."

Tob walked over to the table. "Why?" he insisted. "What good has it done her?"

"It enabled her to survive."

"That's not enough!"

"I've never been able to convince her of that."

The rough-voiced admission stopped Tob's next, half-formed complaint. He said simply, "You should have explained years ago. As soon as I was old enough to listen."

"It has to be her decision. Don't you see? If I don't respect her, who will? If I tried to force her to interact with other people, you, Herri, Jaea, anyone, she'd see it as a betrayal. I can't make her life for her, Tob. She has to choose her own way."

"Even when it hurts her children."

"Aye. Even then."

"It's not right!"

"But it happens. I tried to—" Jordy looked away, clearing his throat. "I protected you as long as I could. Too long, maybe. Now it's your turn to choose." The clear blue eyes inspected Tob, weighed his merits and maturity. "Just don't do anything you'll regret in years to come."

"I already know what I should do. I decided before I got out of bed." Tob shook off the last of his doubts. "I'd like to go with you. Please, Dad?"

A few of the lines of strain on his father's face eased. "Then it's about time you got ready," he said. "It's snowing. Dress warm, lad."

"I will." Tob smiled. "As soon as I say goodbye to Mom."

CHAPTER 31

"That's not good enough."

"Forgive me, Your Majesty." The guard's voice shook. "It is what I was told."

Damon dismissed the man with a quick motion of one hand. "Get out." The guard's departing footsteps echoed within the long, nearly deserted room. Torches flared in their holders, the pre-dawn sky beyond the windows still uselessly dark. Damon resumed drumming his fingers on one arm of his throne. His eyes were fixed on the retreating guard, his thoughts hundreds of miles away.

Everything should have gone flawlessly. There was no excuse for these delays.

The messenger escaped from the throne room, and unseen hands pulled the great double doors closed behind him. The iron panels met with a dull, booming noise that reverberated unpleasantly inside Damon's skull. Hion had never used the doors. Hion had never needed them.

Thrusting his chin out, Damon glared at his uncle and repeated, "Not good at all."

Ledo shifted his weight from one foot to another, his sword belt creaking. With the possible exception of a few servants, everyone in the castle was going armed. Another development which Damon had not anticipated and did not like. Ledo said, "Perhaps, Sire, they simply need more time."

"This was not an exercise intended to drag on from one nineday to the next." Sarcasm, like acid, etched the surface of Damon's words. "Let us look to Sitrine. We don't know what's going on there because we've lost contact with the border entirely!"

"The blame for that might lie with the Abstainers, Sire," Ledo suggested nervously. "If you had consulted me, I would have reminded Your Majesty that Soen's so-called followers are undependable."

Damon gripped the arms of the throne and leaned forward. "Do you stand there and dare to repeat those old superstitions to me? To me?"

Ledo stiffened noticeably. "I do not say they are cursed by the gods. But they are different from ordinary people. Unbalanced."

"Their only difference lies in having the self-confidence to defy worthless traditions. If that's unbalanced, fine. The Dreamers put too much emphasis on maintaining balance. A little unbalance is a reasonable reaction to life's challenges."

"Even when disregard for tradition extends to disregard for a king's commands?"

"No," Damon snapped. "That's not reasonable. That's suicide. I've made that very clear to my good Uncle Soen. Any who disobey the orders I give through him will discover that, as soon as I have time to attend to them."

Damon leaned against the velvet-cushioned back of the throne once more. It wasn't entirely comfortable. He was an inch or so taller and not as broad in the waist as Hion had been, and the cushions had molded themselves over too many years to the old king's form. He supposed he would have to have the entire throne rebuilt. "There's no excuse for the lack of news from Broadford, is there? One of the guards should have been able to make the return journey in a day's ride."

"Perhaps the messenger encountered difficulty on his return to Edian."

The uneven tap of his fingernails—click, click, click—against one of the throne arm's jeweled inlays was loud in the silence that Damon allowed to fall after Ledo's remark. After a suitable pause, he inquired, "Whose fault is it that a king's guard might find the streets of Edian unsafe?"

"We are doing our best, Majesty. Your sister cannot remain in hiding indefinitely."

"My dear sister can rot wherever she is! She has never

been of importance, do you understand?" That was a lie, but Ledo would never know it. If she hadn't presented a danger, Damon wouldn't have troubled himself with her at all. Only her death would ensure that a line of his own choosing would rule after him. Now, however, he wanted Dael's death even more. His captain. His loyal supporter. As he had underestimated Vray's ability to scheme against him, so had he underestimated the influence she would wield over his captain.

He refused to examine the more alarming possibility that Dael had entertained treacherous thoughts before his marriage to Vray. The divisions of allegiance among the guards, the eruptions of disobedience in town, the sluggishness of response from outlying troops, the shocking efficiency with which the rebels evaded capture, all pointed to strong, long-standing leadership. Vray could not have arranged everything in the short time since her return to court, could she? The evidence was too widespread, too subtle. Even if she had put every waking minute into encouraging the Keepers to reject his assumption of the throne—and she had not, he had watched her well enough to be sure of that—she could not have accomplished so much so quickly. Someone must have prepared the way for her.

Someone. His own right arm, his captain, Dael.

No. He rejected that chain of reasoning for the hundredth time. A dozen members of Hion's council had gone into hiding at the first sign of trouble. One of them must have been scheming against him for years.

Dael had merely been foolish enough, or unfortunate enough, to fall in love with his pretty little wife. That was why he protected her and fled with her. Inconvenient, but a typical Keeper reaction. Deserting guards shouted Dael's name as a rallying cry because he was known to them. Far better known than a princess who'd been absent from Edian for years.

Why was that scenario so difficult to believe?

Damon regarded his uncle. "The one person I want to see is Captain Dael. I think I've made that perfectly clear.

How long am I going to have to wait?"

"This might be an appropriate time for your interview with the minstrel. You did hint he might know some things of value."

"Ah, yes, Ivey." Damon accepted his uncle's evasion gracefully. "How long have we had him now? Two days?"

"Nearly that, Your Majesty."

"Excellent." Damon stood. He had wanted the minstrel kept alive as a source of information about Sitrine and Dherrica. It was just possible he could tell them something of the local traitors, as well. He'd be useless to anyone if he was left in the cellars much longer.

"Let's see if he's ready for a talk."

Ivey lay on his stomach on the cool stone floor, face buried in his arms, trying to sleep. If he didn't sleep he'd start thinking again, and that he didn't want. How long had he been awake this time? There was no way to tell. No light, no sound, no measure of the passage of time. He would have tried counting his breaths, except he didn't want to think about breathing. It was hard to breathe. It felt as if there was no air in the dark room.

He knew how many times he'd been driven to use the far corner of the storeroom to relieve himself, but that would have little correlation to his customary daily habits. At first, he'd held back as long as he could—a matter of hours, certainly—but after that, he could not guess how much time had passed. Had lack of food or water slowed his bodily processes? Or had growing dread accelerated them? The inside of his mouth seemed to be coated with wool and his throbbing headache had become an unceasing pain. Was headache an early symptom of death by thirst or death by suffocation?

He had to stop thinking. He rolled onto his back, eyes blinking into the blackness several times before he forced them shut. Sleep. Just sleep. There was nothing else he could do.

The smooth stone would not yield to shoulder blades or

pelvis. When he was tired, he could sleep anywhere. Used to be able to sleep anywhere. Not today. Tonight. How long since they'd locked him in here? What was Dael doing? Even if the princess triumphed over Damon, how long would it be before anyone had reason to visit these storerooms?

A century ago, perhaps, they had been full. When the castle, like the rest of the world, had a larger population. Now they were just unnecessary space in a forgotten corner of the cellars. He'd heard no sound of life, any life—not the muted buzz of an insect or the whisper of mouse paws in some hidden burrow. If he died here, would any scavenger find him? Or would some unsuspecting servant, years or decades hence, open the door to reveal his body, dry as one of last year's fallen leaves but otherwise intact?

The faceless image of some kitchen maid, lantern held high in one hand and a barrel full of potatoes in the corridor behind her, was too much. He rolled over again, stretched out one hand until it touched the door, and groped his way upright. He made noise because it was better than being silent. He kicked the door, shouting and singing until strength and voice failed. That happened more quickly than it had before. Perhaps he was growing weaker. Or perhaps it was the concepts themselves he was losing: fast or slow, now or later. Would he know when he was dying? Would he know when he was dead?

Gods, it was so hard to breathe. He had not been this frightened when Sene dragged him off on monster hunts in Sitrine. Hunts at sea or on land, but always under the open sky. He hated this black dark cellar. He needed the outdoors, the open air.

He pressed his back against the stone wall. *Don't think.*

After an interminable time, he heard a sound. A door scraped open at the far end of the corridor outside of his prison. Ivey turned and pressed his forehead against the wooden surface of his door, peering downward. A broad swathe of yellow flung itself into the room through the crack under the door, reinventing the brown of his boots

307

and the gray of the shadows they cast.

The familiar flicker of light and dark snapped Ivey out of his formless nightmare. At last! Dael had gained control of the castle and learned from a defeated guard of the prisoner alone in the cellar.

The yellow light grew brighter and outlined the entire door. The muddle of several peoples' footsteps grew louder. The door vibrated under Ivey's fingertips as someone lifted the outer bar. He shaded his eyes with one hand against the lantern held high by the figure who pulled open the door.

Behind the lantern bearer, Damon remarked, "What a stink. Pull him out here."

Rough hands dragged him into the corridor. He thought a brief, bitter, farewell to his dreams of rescue by a victorious Dael. The transition from terrifying solitude to being the focus of a select circle's unfriendly attention shocked him out of the limited mental and emotional equilibrium he'd contrived for himself. His arms were held firmly by guards, one on either side. The lantern light made his eyes tear, blurring the faces that confronted him.

"You know my Uncle Ledo," Damon continued. Years of experience listening to and telling tales had sharpened Ivey's hearing. His ears interpreted nuances in the new king's speech without prompting from his still-stunned mind. The words were polite condescension, but the tone hinted at uneasiness, even fear.

Perhaps this was not a casual visit to pass sentence on the vanquished, after all.

Ledo, the slightly shorter blur on the right, said, "I'd hardly have recognized him. Such drab clothing for a minstrel."

"Not just a minstrel, Uncle. Ivey's a man of many talents. Aren't you, Ivey? In fact, I was just beginning to tell my uncle some of the interesting things I know about you. You see, the king of Sitrine was not the only one to collect knowledge of affairs beyond his borders. For the past few years I've been something of a collector myself. I admit that I found his choice of informants unusual. Wizards and minstrels and carters are so unpredictable."

Ivey's vision cleared. Damon stood at his ease, his weight on one leg, the other relaxed, his left hand resting on his wide sword belt. The pose suited the confidence of his words. Ledo watched first Ivey, then the young king, with undisguised interest. He, at least, was less than certain regarding the outcome of this conversation. The essential question was, what caused this doubt, and did Damon share it?

"Of course, that's all past and done with," Damon continued pleasantly. "There's room at my court for a gifted musician such as yourself. You're a sensible Keeper. I'm sure you're as anxious as I am to see order and tranquility restored to the three kingdoms. Without your help, I have to admit the disruption might go on for days. Horrible to think of more people dying, whole villages made homeless."

Damon stepped forward and casually touched Ivey's right hand. Ivey had been standing limply between the guards, but at Damon's touch, he flinched involuntarily. The guards tightened their grips, stretching his arms away from his body. He tried to clench his fists, but Damon had a painful hold on his first finger.

"You're trembling. Don't worry. I'm making the choice as easy as possible for you. Perhaps the greater good of three kingdoms or the well being of some unknown Keepers doesn't concern you. I'll give you the chance to consider yourself. If you don't answer my question, I'm going to break this finger."

The words, spoken in Damon's reasonable, melodious voice, made no sense.

"Now, I realize that some people are more susceptible to pain than others. So, before you entertain any heroic thoughts, make sure you understand the implications. You have ten fingers. Perhaps you think I'll ask the question only ten times. I'm more patient than that. I also have a good idea of how you value your musical skills. A finger can be broken in many places. If a bone is not allowed to heal properly—and I assure you, if you delay answering you'll be given no chance to heal—well, then it becomes deformed, crippled.

"I'm not threatening death, minstrel. I won't let you die. I'll take everything else from you. Skill, dignity, reason for living. But I won't take your life."

The guard on Ivey's left shuddered. It was a well-contained response, imperceptible to any watching eye. Ivey was aware of it only because of the physical contact between them. He caught a glimpse of Ledo, staring with sick fascination at his nephew. It flashed through his mind that the entire interview had to be another nightmare. He had cracked under the strain of solitude. That was the only excuse for such horrible imaginings. No real person would make such threats.

A child might. A spoiled two-year old. Old enough to know when its desires were thwarted, young enough to lack the beginnings of self-control. Adults lost control, yes, fought and hurt one another in moments of high stress and passion. Ivey knew all about passion. He was a minstrel. He knew all the old stories and great tragedies. He knew sagas, too, of the extraordinary steps that Shapers would take to protect their people, banishing enemies, or imprisoning them, even killing them when all other solutions failed.

The words of King Damon were like nothing he'd ever heard.

His tumbling thoughts lasted no longer than the guard's swiftly quelled shudder. Damon continued speaking, oblivious to both. "I think that's clear. Now, listen carefully. Captain Dael and my little sister have disappeared." He began pushing backward on the captive finger. "My question for you is quite simple. Where have they gone?"

Ivey could only stare stupidly into the handsome face. Gone? Where could they go that Damon's troops wouldn't find them? He cried out as the pressure on his hand changed and the long bone in his finger gave way with a muffled snap.

"Where have they gone?"

"Wait!" His dust-dry mouth and throat slowed his

speech. Damon gripped his middle finger. "I don't know!"

The pain lanced up his arm, then intensified as Damon manipulated the broken middle finger, supporting the base and beginning to apply pressure between the first and second joints. Only the rock-firm support of the guards' hands under his armpits prevented Ivey from sinking to his knees.

"Where have they gone?"

He writhed, unable to breathe, another bone cracking as easily as dry kindling between Damon's fingers. Through the shock, he struggled desperately for inspiration. After dragging in a lungful of air he gasped, "Loras! Dael's father."

Damon moved to the third finger. "Don't insult me with the obvious."

The pressure began. Dare he name Broadford? Damon already knew about the carter, so he couldn't endanger Jordy any further. But what if Vray sought the security of her adopted family? That made Broadford the last place he should mention. His best answer had to be the last place she would go.

"The Cave," he croaked. "The Cave of the Rock."

Damon shifted his attention from Ivey's hand to his face. The guards were still and silent, Ivey's panting a lonely sound echoing off the stone walls. "No one goes there," Damon observed pleasantly. "The idea of Vray traveling that far south is absurd."

"The Dreamers are on their side. And Aage is a weather wizard," Ivey added desperately.

"Dreamers!" Fury marked Damon's face, and Ivey gulped a sandpaper swallow, his stomach twisting in anticipation of more pain. His entire hand was throbbing so violently that he didn't detect the precise moment that Damon let go. A swirl of cloak, the sound of the king's sword sheath rubbing against his trousers' leg as he turned away, were Ivey's first indication that his lie had been believed. Damon raged coldly at his uncle, "If they interfere now, I will see them dead, and every Redmother in the three kingdoms as well, and stamp out this insolence once and for all!"

Damon faced the guard on Ivey's right and pointed to the storeroom. "Put him back."

They dragged him to the doorway and shoved him through. He staggered into the nearest wall and slid down onto his knees. Ledo's voice penetrated the increasingly loud ringing in his ears. "You believe him, Sire?"

"For the moment. Has he been fed?"

"No, Your Majesty," one of the guards replied. "Our orders . . ."

"Food and water," Damon interrupted him. "Once a day will keep him alive. I expect you to keep him alive. You two are now personally responsible for him."

The murmured, "Yes, Your Majesty," from both guards came promptly but with a certain dread.

A shadow blocked the lantern light, and Damon loomed in the doorway. "I'll be back, minstrel. Let us hope with a tale for you to learn. The story of the death of two traitors should make an exciting song. Why don't you begin work on the melody while you're waiting? I'm sure it will help to pass the time."

The door closed. Footsteps receded, light faded and was gone. Ivey crumpled to the floor, sick and terrified. With deepest loathing, Ivey emptied his mind of every trace of music and tried not to think about the air.

CHAPTER 32

After three days of fighting, it was apparent to the Sitrinian guards that there was something odd about their Rhenlaner adversaries. Chasa rode a half-dozen miles along the border, his suspicion deepening with each confrontation he observed. Corporals in several different troops suggested that the Rhenlaners' unusual behavior might be the result of new training. Captain Dael was known to be an exceptional leader and tactician. But Chasa could hear the uncertainty in his corporals' voices even as they made the suggestion.

He shared their doubts. There was more than inspirational leadership behind the Rhenlaners' attacks. In their one meeting, Dael had struck Chasa as a clear thinker. That clever mind might have devised a method for instilling in practical Keepers the reckless cruelty Chasa saw again and again. Might have. But why?

As often as Rhenlaner viciousness—there was no other word for it—threatened to overwhelm a troop of Chasa's guards, an equally insidious lack of discipline blunted the effectiveness of the attack, with the result that neither side was making significant advances. Such tactics were not the work of a master strategist like the renowned Captain Dael.

That, of course, raised another question. If Dael had not trained these troops and directed their assault, who had? Damon? If so, to what end? If creating confusion and consternation was his intention, he'd found the proper way to go about it.

Chasa rode over the crest of a low hill in time to witness the conclusion of yet another skirmish. Something less than two troops of Rhenlaners were disappearing on foot into a copse of trees three-quarters of a mile west of his position. A half-troop of mounted Sitrinians was cantering eastward, evidently having just given up the chase. A few hundred yards in front of Chasa, on the side of the next low hill, the dead and injured were scattered among the rocks. The rest of the Sitrinians were clustered efficiently off to his right.

He turned his horse's head and rode toward them. Several of the guards noted his approach, watching carefully until, one by one, they recognized him. He and the returning half-troop reached the larger body of men and women at the same time. Chasa acknowledged the welcoming cries of, "Your Highness!" and, "It's the prince!" with a few curt nods, not trusting himself to speak. They deserved to know, but he wasn't prepared to tell them.

Traditionally, he should not have to tell them. It was a Redmother's duty to announce the death of kings, to proclaim that a "Highness" was henceforth to be addressed as "Your Majesty." At the moment, he cared nothing for what they called him. Perhaps he was merely deluding himself. Perhaps, in some back corner of his mind, a very frightened little boy believed that if he did not say the words, "my father is dead," they would not be true.

"Felistinon," he greeted the corporal of the troop. He slid from his horse and handed the reins to the nearest guard. As the corporal turned to face him, Chasa saw a woman in mud-spattered green and white seated on the ground behind him. "Who's this?"

"She surrendered," Felistinon said, as though he were not quite sure of his facts.

The woman contradicted him. "I deserted."

Chasa continued toward her. Something sharp had grazed the side of her face. The place had been cleaned but not covered, and a line of blood glistened along the edge of the cut. She stood respectfully as he reached her.

"Your name?" he asked.

"Janakol, Highness. I was corporal of that poor excuse for a troop you just missed." Belatedly, she responded to his unconcealable flinch. "You are Prince Chasa, aren't you?"

"I am Chasa," he said. "Why are you leaving the service of Rhenlan?"

Felistinon's dark face grew very still, and Chasa stepped between him and the much smaller woman.

Her words rushed onward. "You'd be wrong, because I was the first person attacked. You'd also be wrong, because the attacker was not Sitrinian. I saw him. I don't know whether the gods were protecting me or tormenting me, but I saw him."

Chasa forgot about the corporal who towered behind him. "Not Sitrinian?" he repeated.

"He was one of my own men. He got to the east of us, somehow. A few minutes after your people rode into sight, he took a Sitrinian arrow from his quiver and tried to kill me."

For Chasa, suspicion solidified into certainty. "He was one of the newer guards? The recent replacements?"

"Yes, of course. But it's impossible. Dael wouldn't give orders for a guard to attack his own troop, and even if he did, the guard shouldn't obey."

In the face of Janakol's increasing desperation, Chasa was almost ashamed of his own calm acceptance. However, he was a Shaper. He was born and trained to see unlikely answers to unexpected problems. Keepers hated anything that broke down the normal order of things. He wasn't fond of having his life disrupted, either, but he could detach logistical details from their emotional impact.

He made a mental note to give himself time to be thoroughly revolted when this was all over.

"Janakol," he said, "have you considered that they might not be ordinary guards?"

"Your Highness?"

He enunciated each word with care. "I believe that Damon has completed his king's guard with Abstainers."

There was a very long silence. A few horses stamped restlessly and one shook its head, jingling its bridle. A handful of crows winged overhead from the south and began cautiously circling the bodies at the base of the hill. Chasa watched as they tried to settle in a flurry of beating wings, only to be chased away by one of Felistinon's sentries.

The shifting black mass reminded Chasa of Aage's robes. He needed the wizard. He needed his father. He did not need to be the focus of the stares of a group of horrified Keepers.

"I should have seen it," Janakol said hoarsely.

Felistinon folded his arms over his broad chest. "It's wrong. Even the horse people agree with you on this. Abstainers must be kept apart."

"It's more than wrong," Chasa told him. "It's forbidden. If Damon really has ordered Abstainers to serve in the king's guard, then he's broken a law that is generations of Dreamers old."

Janakol stared at him with icy disapproval. "Shapers are supposed to uphold laws, not break them."

"I know. That's why, if this is true, I'm going to challenge Damon's right to hold the throne of Rhenlan."

The cheering was spontaneous, and a little frightening. Janakol was stunned into silence.

Felistinon waited for the first uproar to die down a little before saying, "You'll need evidence, will you not?"

Chasa took a deep breath. "And witnesses. Send messengers in both directions along the border. Warn the rest of our troops what to watch for."

"Rider approaching," someone in the crowd called out.

Heads turned, and Chasa looked north with everyone else. The horse slowed as the rider stood in his stirrups and peered toward the gathered guards.

"Felistinon?" he yelled.

"Here!" the corporal bellowed, and waded out of the throng.

"Has the prince passed by here?" The rider guided his horse to meet the tall guard. "He was with Karli's troop a while ago, but they're not sure which way he went when he left."

People stepped quickly out of Chasa's way. "What news?" he asked.

The rider dismounted and hurried toward Chasa. "The wizard Aage sent me, Your Highness. He came looking for

318

you. When we couldn't tell him exactly where to find you, he was, well, not pleased. He left a message."

Chasa tensed. What now? Feather? The baby? "Let's hear it."

The rider clasped his hands behind his back, eyes half-closed as he recited the wizard's words. "Tell Chasa that Feather ordered me not to waste energy chasing him across the countryside. I have been to Edian. The town is still gripped by unrest. I didn't speak to Dael, but I did see and hear a well-organized resistance to Damon's assumption of the throne. He's not going to be sending any more troops to our border, that's certain. Hear my advice. If Sitrine is secure, it's time to carry the attack to Damon. Not with troops, but Shaper to Shaper. Now is the moment for Chasa to ally himself with Vray. Jenil sent her to the Cave of the Rock for safekeeping. He can meet her there. I'll be in Raisal. Oh, and tell him his sister is safe with Greenmother Jenil, and Feather is well. And tell him to hurry."

"Did he have anything to say about the Rhenlaner troops?" Chasa asked.

The rider shook his head. "No, Highness. He didn't have a chance to see any of them. The troop nearest ours ran off about half an hour after you left."

"They're Abstainers," Felistinon growled.

The rider looked doubtful, then disgusted. "That explains a lot."

Such matter-of-fact acceptance lifted Chasa's spirits somehow. He caught the corporal's eye. "Get that warning out right away."

"Yes, Highness." Felistinon turned and strode away, scattering the crowd with a rapid series of orders. The rider followed, leading his horse.

"Will you go?" Janakol asked.

Chasa faced the Rhenlaner woman. "In Sitrine, we value Dreamer advice. However, there was an important 'if' behind his suggestion."

"In Rhenlan, we fight against Abstainers, not with them," Janakol replied.

319

"You said you know many of the troop corporals. Will they believe what Damon has done?"

"For the survival of Rhenlan, they'll have to!"

"For the survival," he corrected her, "of all of us."

A light snow fell all day. Small flakes sifted down through the tree branches, gradually depositing layers of white throughout the woods. Their cloaks acquired a sparkling patina of icy crystals, but the moisture evaporated off the horses' warm coats.

Vray was grateful for the secretive curtain drawn around them by the snow and grateful as well that there was no wind. The thickness of the forest would have dulled a blizzard to a mere storm, and a storm to a series of stray swirling gusts. However, even stray swirling gusts would have made travel difficult. As it was, the temperature was cold but bearable, and the snow accumulated so slowly that it was no impediment to the horses.

They traveled in single file along faintly visible game trails, angling south and east wherever the terrain allowed. Vray was in unfamiliar territory. She knew that Broadford lay behind them and the Broad River itself somewhere to their right, receding as they went farther south. This part of Rhenlan had been decimated by the plague. A few villages lay near the main road between Edian and distant White Water; the same main road that they'd left behind the moment they crossed the river outside of Broadford and turned into the forest. The only habitation in the direction they were going was Oak Mill. Jordy and Nocca had consulted briefly in the village square that morning, while waiting for Jenil to emerge from the inn, and agreed to make for a farm outside Oak Mill for their first night's lodging. After that, as far as Vray knew, they would be traveling through wilderness. No villages remained south of the Broad between Oak Mill and the Dherrican border. They would travel more south than east, and meet the mountains in uninhabited lands, small lost kingdoms that had never been claimed by either Dherrica or Rhenlan.

Not completely uninhabited. Savyea, Jenil reminded them before they left, was always at the Cave.

Once they set out, Jenil said little, and most of that directed at Jordy, when he wasn't half-asleep, head nodding to the familiar rhythm of Stockings's long, easy strides. If Jenil moved ahead for a time, then Tob rode close beside his father. The leggy two-year-old colt he'd borrowed looked absurdly delicate next to Stockings's bulk. Peanal led the line, choosing their path, while Nocca rode last, well behind Vray.

Late in the afternoon, they came to a wider trail, with the indentations of wheel ruts visible beneath the snow. Peanal rode a little farther ahead. Jenil moved her horse closer to Stockings, rousing Jordy. Tob slowed, waiting until Vray had caught up with him.

"We must be close," he said.

Vray arched her back wearily. "Doesn't look familiar, approaching from this direction, does it?"

He turned his head from side to side, breathing deeply. "It can't be anything else. Wood smoke. Smell it? That's a nice thought—hot supper."

"Welcome back," Vray teased.

He eyed her warily, and for an uncomfortable instant Vray thought he was going to urge his horse away from hers.

"Don't do that, Tobble," she said, lowering her voice.

The nickname and the confiding tone kept him beside her. "Do what?"

"Go all stiff and menacing. I like it better when you're making normal Tob-noises about looking forward to your next meal."

"Normal Tob-noises?" His voice, a thoughtful rumble, belonged to a man, but the challenging smile hadn't changed from that of the boy she'd first known. "Is that all you remember me for? My appetite?"

"You were insatiable."

When he read her reminiscent smile correctly, he blushed. Vray felt an urge to giggle. Or cry. Did every preg-

321

nant woman have such uncertain emotions? Or only pregnant women who were miles from their husbands and moving farther away with each step, accompanied by their first lover?

"I shouldn't tease you just because I'm tired. I'm sorry."

"Don't be. I never minded your teasing."

"No, you didn't."

On an impulse, she reached out with her foot and gently nudged his knee. "How have you been, Tob?"

"Lately?" he asked, eyebrows arching in surprise.

"I meant before . . . all this."

"Fine. You know, a life full of the usual things. Unlike yours. How do you like being married?"

"It's nice."

"Is your guard captain all you expected?"

The hostility beneath his casual words reawakened Vray's awareness of the tension that had surrounded Tob all day. He'd been tense when she first saw him the night before, too.

"Is that what's bothering you? My marrying Dael?"

"I can't say I'm surprised, after all the stories you used to tell about him."

She studied his face for a long moment. "That's not an answer. You're not jealous, and you're not worried about me, but it is something about Dael. Is it because he served Hion? Didn't Dad tell you? They've been working together for years."

"I knew."

"Well, I didn't. Of course, I didn't tell Dael I'd lived in Broadford, either. But if you know how long he's worked against Damon, what is it that bothers you about him?"

Tob gazed straight ahead, eyes focused somewhere beyond his mount's pricked ears. "He's a guard. All my life, I've been certain that it isn't acceptable to be a member of a king's guard."

The trail emerged from the forest. A half-mile of stubble-covered field separated the trees from a cluster of farm buildings. Peanal cantered toward the fenced yard. Behind her, Jordy and Jenil were already a good distance into the field. Vray couldn't hear Nocca, though she was confident he was somewhere behind them.

"A lot of people have thought that in recent years, with good reason. Dael would even agree with you."

"He still kills people."

"True, but only when he has to."

"Dad killed those men."

Vray frowned at the coldness in Tob's voice. "Jenil told us. What else could he do? He was lucky to survive."

"Not lucky. He knew exactly what he was doing. He used to be a guard."

Vray paused, waiting for her emotions to become identifiable. Her first reaction was, "That makes sense."

"It does, does it? Maybe to you it would. Shapers!"

His disgust stung her, but she held herself to a mild taunt. "You sound just like your father."

Instead of being embarrassed or amused, Tob clenched his jaw so tightly that the tendons stood out on his neck.

Alarmed, Vray reached one hand toward him. "What did I say? Tob? You're scaring me. Or am I scaring you? Is that it? It's still too close, almost losing him like that. Believe me, I understand."

He interrupted her. "Not just that. I can't explain."

He ran one hand through his hair—the gesture another sharp reminder to Vray of the connection between father and son—and gave her an apologetic half-smile. "There's too much I still don't understand myself. Yes, I was scared. Still am. And I'm angry at the men who did that to him, and angry at him for doing and saying all the things that would attract such men, and angry at . . . oh, at finding out about . . . things . . . That he'd been a guard, for instance. It's as if all my life I've never really known him. Or known myself." He shrugged helplessly.

Vray smiled at him. "Poor Tob. At least you know one thing."

"What?"

"Confusion makes you irritable."

"Thanks a lot!"

Several people had come out of the farmhouse. Jenil dismounted while Peanal stood at Stockings's head, talking to someone in the yard. Nocca came trotting out of the woods a few yards to Vray's left.

He waved to Vray. "No one's nearby. Let's get inside."

"You ready?" Vray asked Tob.

"Maybe I shouldn't have come." He was looking uncomfortable again.

"Why not?"

Tob glanced toward Nocca, but the guard wasn't paying them any attention. "I'm not feeling well. I think I might be getting sick."

"It's the strain. You're just tired," Vray told him firmly. The last thing they needed in the group was another invalid.

"I hope you're right."

"Of course I'm right."

He managed a grin, and kicked the colt into a trot. "Whatever you say, Princess."

"Much better," Vray approved, and proceeded to outrace him to the farmyard fence.

CHAPTER 33

"Has he been seen, or hasn't he?" Damon demanded.

"Not seen, Your Majesty," Demaris replied reluctantly.

Damon turned his head briefly to look at the corporal. They were standing on the outer wall on the south side of the castle. Although the sky was clearing overhead, clouds lingered in the west to mask the sunset, and only the pale glow of blue Sheyn lit Demaris's dark face. That was enough, however, to reveal her uncertainty, and more than enough to anger Damon.

"Then he is gone," he insisted coldly. "As I have said from the beginning."

Demaris continued to look out over the town. "The defense is too well organized, Sire. We haven't regained control of a single street since midday yesterday. They have opened the road west along the lakeshore, and this afternoon either captured or recruited another of my troops. That has to be the captain's doing."

"No. It is my captain's training. The moment he betrayed me I knew we would face difficulties."

He betrayed Damon by surviving. One of many betrayals. Another was killing the men Damon had sent to kill Vray. By that act, Dael had robbed him of the pleasure of killing them himself, in payment for their incompetence. Betrayals and frustration, one after another.

"He taught his followers well enough for the short term, but their resistance will begin to fall apart soon. We have the advantage, Corporal. I'm not going to sit here and let that advantage slip away."

"Sire?"

Having caught her attention, Damon smiled and resumed his own contemplation of his city. The streets of Edian fell away below his feet. Few lights were visible in the buildings nearest the castle, many of which had been abandoned. Down toward the market square, one of the areas temporarily closed to the king's guard, there were signs of normal evening life, such as glowing windows and the drifting murmur of people's voices.

Damon said, "I could wait. They will give up their rebellion once the heroic Dael and his charming wife are no longer encouraging them. The passage of time would prove to the fools that they've been deserted, that Dael and my sister ran away out of fear, with no intention of returning. But waiting would be unfair."

The lie was as easy as it was automatic. "I have to think of the good of Edian. Therefore, we're not going to wait. We're going to go out and bring Vray and Dael back, to be properly judged and executed for their crimes."

"But, Your Majesty, we don't know when they left. Or even in which direction."

Damon gave her his best look of wide-eyed innocence. "Yes, we do. We'll leave in the morning. Put together eight troops, Corporal. Use as many of the new guards as you can. Uncle Ledo never liked Uncle Soen, and he likes Uncle Soen's friends even less. The lack of respect is returned. This would tend to interfere with Ledo's ability to rule in Edian in my absence."

"Your absence?" she repeated blankly.

Damon moved away from the edge of the wall, turning his back on the town and its ungrateful citizens. "I said *we* are going to catch the traitors. We, Corporal. You and I, and a force of guards suitable to the task. Don't burden us with too many provisions. We'll gather supplies from the villages along the way. If we travel light, and travel fast, we'll be on them within the nineday. Go. Inform your people."

Demaris hesitated only an instant before nodding her acceptance of his orders and hurrying past him toward the stairs. Damon followed at a more relaxed pace.

He was doing the right thing, of course. Ledo would be pleased to be in charge of the town, even if it was only for a few days. He would be honored by the chance to earn the favor of the king. The thought that Ledo might try to assume power for himself was laughable. Even if he retained any ambitions after his years of obedience to Hion, he didn't retain the courage.

Ah, the debt that Damon owed to the plague. It had restructured their society, exhausted the leaders who had devoted their best years and last strength to conquering it, and thereby given Damon his opportunities. Another subject he should suggest to the minstrel: the honor and appreciation owed to the late, lamented fire bears for all they'd done for Rhenlan.

Eager and confident, Damon descended into the courtyard and went in search of his uncle.

Tob crossed the unfamiliar farmyard slowly. Keyn hung high in the west, and her yellow light should have enabled him to find the latch on the barn door easily. Instead, Tob had to reach for it three times before his fingers closed on the cold metal. Maybe Sheyn had risen over the trees. A second, bluish shadow occasionally fooled the eye.

Tob looked up at the night sky. No, it was still too early for Sheyn to be up. The tiny, distant, half-circle of Dreyn was near the zenith, but it could cast no detectable shadows when either of the larger moons was in the sky. Tob shook his head once, and tried to blink away the blurriness in his vision. No, he absolutely refused to be sick!

He felt a little better after he entered the barn and began moving among the horses. He located the grain bin at the end of the aisle, but the pail was not where the farm's owner, Loid, had said it would be.

"Stones," he muttered resentfully. Inconsiderate. That's what it was. They were taking advantage of him. Always expecting him to do the chores so they could talk and talk and talk was bad enough. The least they could do was give him instructions that made sense.

Tob paused in his rummaging among the implements next to the grain bin and pressed his fingers over the bridge of his nose as his vision blurred again. He felt worse than sick. Everything was turning inside out. He lost his balance, staggered, and cracked his left elbow against the top of the grain bin.

"Ow!" he cried angrily.

The grain bin burst into flames.

Tob leaped back. The flames were terrifying. Not just oranges and yellows, but blues and greens, writhing toward the rafters. The horses began to scream and dash themselves against the walls of their stalls. The thud of hooves and the splintering of wood added to the din. The grain bin vanished as though it had never existed and the flames licked greedily at the barn wall and upward into the loft. Tob took another lurching step backwards.

Water. He had to get some water.

Wind shook the barn as the wall and an edge of the roof collapsed, eaten away by the flames. Thunder and a torrent of water arrived simultaneously, drowning out all other sounds, and sending the fire back into nonexistence.

The rumble of the thunder faded and the rain became a regular downpour as Vray, Nocca, and Loid rushed into the barn and hurried toward the still-hysterical animals. Jordy was only a few seconds behind them, his clothing, like theirs, drenched through. His expression lightened somewhat when he spotted Tob.

"What happened? Are ye all right?"

Tob didn't know what to say. The blurred vision, the internal twistings were gone. He stood frozen, appalled at whatever it was that was filling him, threatening to overflow and rage out of control again.

"I set the barn on fire," he said, and watched a bewildered frown begin on his father's face. "Then I put it out again. I'm sorry, Dad."

Jordy reached his side. "You put it out?"

Stockings gave another whinny of protest. Nocca left his horse, quivering but silent once more, and went into Stockings's box, making soothing noises. Vray began to help Loid lead two of his animals out of the stalls nearest the fallen wall, where wind and rain were buffeting them, and back toward the undamaged section of the barn.

"Dad, I'm scared."

Jenil arrived in a flurry of wet black cloth. She pushed her hood back as she came down the aisle and didn't stop until she was directly in front of Tob. "Oh, Jordy, how could you?"

Tob's father turned the full force of his worried confusion on her. "How could I what?"

"Be so stubborn! Social revolution is one thing, but this is sheer irresponsibility."

"What?"

"Hiding Cyril's true nature, denying your son his proper training!"

"Cyril's nature?"

"She's a Shaper."

Jordy went so pale that Jenil's healer's instincts overcame her anger and she quickly grasped his arm.

He didn't seem to notice. "She's not. All of the horse people are Keepers, you know that!"

Jenil touched Tob's shoulder lightly with her other hand. "There's no arguing with this, Jordy. Don't you see what's happened? He's come of age. He's one of us now."

Tob understood everything. His newly awakened senses tingled and throbbed in response to the lines of power that focused on Jenil.

Vray came up behind Jordy, expression incredulous. "Tob's a Dreamer? A wizard?"

Jenil gave a decisive shake of her head and gestured at the devoured portion of the barn. "No wizard. Not yet. He can bend the power, that's obvious, but a person needs training to control it. Not all Dreamers have the same gifts. He should have been preparing for this moment for years!"

Vray's eyes grew even rounder. "That means Pepper and Matti . . ."

For a moment, Jenil ignored her. "Tob, try to relax. Believe me, I know you feel as if you're going to explode, but it won't happen. I promise."

Jenil turned her head back toward Vray. "The girls should go into Savyea's care at once. She's been working with Sene's niece and nephew in the Brownmother house in Sitrine."

"No! You'll not take them," Jordy said in a choked voice, and pulled away from the Greenmother.

"By Rock and Pool, carter, they're Dreamer children!" Jenil cried angrily. "If you'd told us about them at birth, arranged regular visits so that we could begin teaching them, it wouldn't be an emergency now!"

Tob found his voice. "Dad, it's all right. No one will take the girls."

"Tob," the Greenmother began.

Tob paid no attention to anyone but Jordy. "Don't you see? You're right. Dherrican or horse people, you're all Keepers. It's Reas."

"Who?" Jenil and Vray demanded in unison.

Some of the anguish left Jordy's face. Tob nodded once in reassurance then faced the Greenmother. "The man who fathered me."

"What?" Vray exclaimed.

"You heard me."

"Reas? The swordsman from Broadford?" Jenil said sharply, then blushed. "I didn't know."

"Everyone assumed he was a Keeper. What if they were wrong?" Tob suggested.

"Do we know his parents' names?" Jenil asked. "Vray, you're the Redmother. Is there a 'Reas' in the Shaper lineage of Rhenlan?"

Jordy abruptly moved over to the nearest storage chest and sat down. Vray went with him, putting a worried hand on his shoulder.

He gazed up at Tob. "What am I going to tell your mother?"

"Don't worry about it. I'll tell her."

"I only met them once," Jordy continued. "Herri told you about the time we visited Broadford? They were nice people. Their names were Thanic and Souvi."

Vray nodded. "I know the names. Thanic was a Dherrican Shaper, cousin or second cousin to King Farren's father. He and Souvi married and settled on her Rhenlan estate. Started having babies and losing them to the plague. One of the border battles overran their property. The recitation as I learned it doesn't say what happened to them, only that their line was ended."

She gave Tob a fond but definitely exasperated smile. "We were wrong."

Nocca came out of Stockings's stall. "It's still raining," he reminded them.

Jenil cast an irritated glance at the ceiling. "I don't do weather magic. It should die out quickly once Tob is gone."

Tob stiffened. "Gone?"

His unease tried to express itself in another surge of power bending, but he caught and stopped it before anything happened.

Jenil took his hands in both of hers. "I felt that. We're getting you out of here, now. We'll go to Morb. He'll know what to do with you."

"But I—Dad?"

"Go on, laddie. It'll be all right. Just take care of yourself."

"This is Morb," Jenil said. Then she began to communicate directly to his new senses, and he lost track of the barn and the animals and the people in it. On this new level, the world was both larger and smaller than he had ever guessed it could be. Larger, because he sensed so many more levels to it than he'd ever suspected before. Smaller, because he could cross it in an instant, simply by bending the power just so . . .

"Hello. I knew you were coming."

Tob snapped his eyes open at the sound of the unfamiliar voice. The barn was gone. The air was hot and humid. The sun was just setting behind the shoulder of a foliage-shrouded mountain.

The owner of the voice was a short fellow, face rounder and skin even darker than Tob's. "So, you're one of our children."

He turned his mild brown eyes on Jenil. "Where have you been hiding this one?"

Jenil dropped Tob's hands and sat with a sigh on the boulder next to the path. "It's a long story. Tob, this is Morb. Morb, meet the first of the new generation of Dreamers."

"He smells like violets. That suits Tobble. Earthy and gentle." Vray sniffed at the wisp of smoke that hung in the barn's cold air, then sighed and turned to Jordy. "Don't you think so?"

For another moment he continued to look stunned. Then he rewarded her comment with a pained grimace, his typical expression when discussing Dreamers.

The normalcy of his reaction reassured her. From some-where, she heard a stifled giggle, and realized the sound came from her. Nocca came up behind her and touched her shoulder. She put her hand over her mouth, trying to keep the mirth inside. It was hopeless. Sinking down on the lid of a tool chest, she threw her head back and laughed.

"What's wrong with you, lass?" Jordy demanded. "What's funny?"

Nocca, concerned, said, "Are you all right?"

"Oh, Dad!" Another peal of laughter caught her.

"What is it?" Through blurring eyes, she saw him sit up straighter.

"You're a fine father," she managed at last, holding her sides and struggling for control.

"That's funny, is it?"

"Mm hmm," she squeaked, nodding weakly.

Nocca stepped in front of her, fists on his hips. "That's enough, Vray. Calm down. This can't be good for you."

"There's nothing wrong with laughter," Jordy intruded at once, as protective as her brother-in-law. That set her off on another round of giggles. She had to be over-tired, to be reacting like this. But it was funny!

As if he'd heard her thought, Jordy said, more sternly than ever, "What's funny?"

"You are," she admitted. Nocca shook his head in disapproval, and Jordy eyed him with agreement.

"Don't mind her," Nocca told him. "She's just—"

"I know what she is!"

"No you don't!" Vray announced brightly.

He glared at her. "Are you finished now?"

She pulled herself together and folded her hands in her lap. "Yes, sir."

"Why am I funny?"

"Because you're such a good father."

"Vray!"

She chortled once, then contained it. "Of Shapers and Dreamers. It's a knack you have. Not everyone can do it, you know. Not with such skill, such understanding, such sensitivity to the special needs and concerns of—"

"All right, lass," he tried to interrupt her.

"—of your daughter, the Shaper who may soon be queen. Your son, the wizard."

Slowly, Jordy's dour expression softened. "A wizard, and a queen. I suppose I did something to deserve this."

She got up and went to him, taking his hand in hers. "Yes. You've been a good man. The best man I've ever known."

His blush was fleeting, followed instantly by a gruff, "So this is a reward, then. It's nothing I expected."

"I don't think Tob expected it, either."

"Can we go back inside now?" Nocca said. "It's cold in here, and Vray, you should get some rest."

Jordy gave the tall man an exasperated look as he got to his feet. "Why is this lumbering ox always hovering over you?"

"My brother told me to," Nocca replied calmly.

Vray linked her arm through Jordy's. "Ignore him. I do."

She smiled over her shoulder at Nocca to take the sting from her words, then returned her attention to Jordy. "You're the one who needs to sleep. Come back to the house. I promise not to laugh any more."

Jordy looked at her doubtfully. The way he always

looked at Shapers, she admitted to herself. Her smile widened.

"Oh Father of Wizards."

"Aye," he grumbled. "Wizards and royalty. I don't suppose I'll ever make proper carters out of the pair of you now."

"Doubtful," she replied. "Come on, let's go in before Nocca hovers to death out here in the cold."

CHAPTER 34

"It's got to be a trick," Dael grumbled under his breath.

No one was near enough to hear his complaint. He urged his horse to a trot along the empty street. A trick. What else could it be?

The street ended in the market square. Dael stopped in the shelter of the last building. The mix of rain and snow that had fallen all night and into the morning was finally slacking off, but gusts of wind continued to tug at his cloak. The only guards he saw were his own, watching the approaches. One acknowledged his arrival, and waved to someone on the northward street. A moment later, a messenger galloped across the muddy field toward him.

"Report," Dael ordered as soon as the rider was close enough to hear him.

"It's definite, sir. He went west."

"Why?"

The messenger shrugged. "Does it matter? He's certainly not going to bother us from there."

"I wish I agreed with you."

"But, Captain—"

Dael gestured the man to silence. He started his horse moving into the square, the messenger following. Dael ignored him. There had to be a trick here somewhere. When word had come in the middle of the night that Damon was gathering the bulk of his forces, preparatory to leaving the castle, Dael had hurried to organize his people for the attack. He had stationed most of his best fighters on and near the road leading south out of Edian, on what seemed the reasonable assumption that Damon had learned of Vray's escape and was preparing to give chase. The fleetest runners had drawn near the castle, hiding in the shadows to wait and watch.

Just after dawn, the gates had opened and Damon's troops had emerged. One by one, the messengers had come to Dael, positioned in what he'd thought was the most critical area, to say that Damon was not coming in his direction. With each messenger, Dael sent new orders around the town to shift his troops, maneuvering again and again to block any attack he could imagine Damon making on the town, any drive the king could begin to reach the road south. Again and again, his moves proved useless, because again and again, Damon's troops attacked no one.

Damon's troops did not circle Edian and turn south. Damon's troops turned their backs on the only threat within two hundred miles and went marching obligingly off onto the broad reaches of the Atowa plateau.

It had to be a trick! Didn't it?

Dael rode up to the corporal at the north entrance to the square. "Who's at the castle?" he asked abruptly.

"The same as have been there all day," the corporal responded just as tersely. The oddness of the day's events, or lack of events, was preying on everyone's nerves. "What's left of the household staff, and maybe four troops of guards, with Ledo in charge of it all. What are they playing at, Captain?"

"A game they're about to lose."

The wind carried Dael's decisive pronouncement down the square, and heads turned in his direction. He raised his voice, eager for it to carry now that he'd made up his mind.

He turned to the waiting messenger. "If King Damon is kind enough to vacate his castle, we have to be gracious enough to accept the gift. We'll post sentries around the town. Damon will find that leaving was a lot easier than returning will be. Everyone else is to gather here. We take the castle in one hour."

If, he reminded himself one last time, the whole thing wasn't some sort of a trick.

"They haven't moved?" Doron asked.

"They haven't moved," the messenger repeated. He

336

sounded sure of his facts, as senseless as they were.

Doron, perched on the forward edge of the throne in the castle's great hall, kept her hands clasped firmly together in her lap. She had no idea if a Shaper queen would fidget or pace during an interview such as this one. For lack of instructions to the contrary, she had decided that part of the job of running a kingdom was to appear calm.

Besides, this was an encouraging report. At least, it sounded like an encouraging report.

"That's encouraging." She offered the comment in a firm voice and watched for the messenger's reaction. His nod of agreement wasn't quite as enthusiastic as she'd hoped it would be, and he fidgeted with one of his riding gloves, pulling it off, then on again.

"Unless they're preparing a surprise elsewhere on the border," he said.

"No," Doron replied immediately. "There aren't that many guards in Rhenlan."

She put all the confidence she could behind the statement, and hoped that she was correct. She did not want to think about how many lives were affected by every decision she made in this room. So far, her advisors assured her that her choices had been wise. Captain Tatiya had the military situation under control, and Redmother Neffera was exercising her subtle but considerable influence to organize the citizens of the town. Every hour, it seemed, another few guards defected from Palle's forces to join one of Tatiya's troops. The Rhenlaners, meanwhile, continued to launch sporadic attacks along the border, but failed to sustain them. At this rate, Doron could hold the castle and the city in safety for ninedays, long enough surely to give Pirse time to settle matters with his uncle, once and for all.

If she only had Dherrica to think about, Doron wouldn't have been so worried. However, two nights before, the wizard Aage had appeared in the throne room and, in a hurried conference, ensured that she would not fall prey to complacency. Damon was meddling with the affairs of the Children of the Rock in every kingdom. Aage implied that the disturbance might even extend to the web of power and its monsters.

There was some positive news, at least. Aage was able to tell them how many of Damon's troops were skirmishing against Sitrine and how many were in Edian, and Tatiya knew the positions that Rhenlaners had held along the Dherrican border last summer. Damon had counted on the element of surprise, and the deaths of Sene and Palle, to throw his opponents into disarray. He did not seem to have anticipated the possibility of failure, or complications, and if he had back-up plans, they had not yet been set in motion.

The messenger tugged at the fingers of his glove. "They really won't attack Bronle without a direct order?"

"A direct order that should have come from here." Doron moved her hands to the arms of the throne and gave them a pat. "That would have been the murderers' first act, if they'd succeeded in taking command of the castle guard. Thanks to the captain, they failed."

"What if they receive orders from elsewhere? From Prince—I mean, King Damon, himself?"

"They may, but they haven't. Not yet. And every day they delay strengthens us, not them. We'll continue as we began. Inform your corporal to hold your troops' positions unless attacked."

"Yes, ma'am." The messenger pulled his glove on for the last time, inclined his head politely, and started down the long hall. As he approached the double doors, the guard there swung one open, allowing the next person to enter and approach the throne.

Redmother Neffera trotted forward a few paces, then stopped and beckoned to Doron, the sleeves of her shabby robe flapping against her wrists. Her round face was flushed, and she seemed short of breath. "You'd better come down, ma'am."

Doron stepped off the dais. "Down where?"

"You remember that some of Palle's troops were still in possession of the bake house and some of the storage cellars? Well, Tatiya finally flushed them out, the clever girl."

As she spoke, Neffera bustled Doron out of the great hall. One guard left his post near the door to accompany them, and a second joined the procession as they passed through corridors and descended into what had been, for several days, disputed territory.

The Redmother continued, "I don't think they were guarding it on purpose, and I don't even know whether or not it's still of any importance. It must be, though, or else why would King Palle have kept it? Prince Pirse would know what to do, of course, but until he comes I'd rather err on the side of caution, if you see what I mean."

Doron sorted through the torrent of words. "Palle left something important stored in the cellar?"

"You're from Juniper Ridge, so you probably know the minstrel Ivey."

Not wanting to encourage what sounded like a digression, Doron held her answer to one word. "Yes."

"He has always supported Prince Pirse and expressed doubts about King Palle. He also collects information from a wide range of sources. Carters, merchants, innkeepers, members of the guard."

"Redmothers?" Doron guessed.

Neffera lifted her chin. "We've had a word or two together over the years, yes. I haven't always agreed with him. Once the man gets an idea in his head, he worries it like a dog with a bone."

They descended a final staircase, a tight spiral of stone cut out of the mountainside, and entered one of the oldest parts of the castle. Torches flared in brackets along the walls. A short corridor led to several square rooms. Glancing through the open doorways, Doron caught a glimpse of wine racks in one room, and smelled the cool, musty odor of turnips and onions drifting from another. At the third doorway, a guard stepped aside at Neffera's approach and allowed them to enter.

Two sturdy trunks nestled against the back wall. Their worn, wooden sides and the rusty metal caps that reinforced the corners were as familiar to Doron as the dye vats in her shop. She stumbled to a halt in the center of the room, her gaze fixed on the closed lids.

"Betajj," she whispered.

Neffera, hand poised to open one of the trunks, turned to look at her. "You knew him, too? I don't know why I'm surprised. In a village like Juniper Ridge, I imagine everyone knows everyone else. So you've heard that he was killed during his last trip to Bronle's market?"

Doron nodded mutely.

"Ivey had a suspicion that his accident on the river wasn't an accident. To be fair, he wasn't the only one who had his doubts, not least because Betajj's cargo was never recovered. Until today."

The Redmother rested one hand briefly on the domed lid of the trunk, then bent and opened it.

The contents of the trunk were exactly as Doron remembered them. Bolts of cloth and skeins of colored yarn lay in neat bundles, cushioning a few pieces of pottery and wood carvings that Betajj had agreed to carry to market for their neighbors.

Although she didn't remember moving, she found herself standing beside Neffera in front of the trunk. She touched one of the skeins, lambs wool dyed a soft, spring green. Betajj had praised this particular dye lot, sure that it would fetch a good price.

She blinked rapidly, anger pushing aside her grief. "Palle! By all the gods, why would he kill a man over a few chests of wool?"

"Not the wool, ma'am. This!"

The Redmother slipped her hand beneath a bolt of sumac-red cloth and pulled out a small, square bag of tightly woven linen. Doron groped for understanding. She had never seen the bag before in her life. Obviously, Betajj had acquired additional cargo after he left Juniper Ridge. The fine weave of the bag suggested precious contents, but what? Spices, gold dust, gemstones?

"What is it?"

Neffera looked up from the bag, her expression hard. "Dragon powder, ma'am. Six bags, in all."

The answer only raised more questions. Mind whirling with confusion, Doron asked, "But why? Why would a Keeper carry dragon powder? And why would a Shaper steal it? It makes no sense!"

"Excuse me, ma'am, but to my mind, the dragon powder explains everything. If Ivey were here, I believe he'd agree with me. Don't you know what dragon powder can do?"

"Dreamers use it in their magic, don't they?" Vague fragments of some of her brother's songs whispered through Doron's memory, but they had never been relevant to her life, so she barely remembered them.

She thought they had not been relevant. Dreamers had been absent from most of Dherrica for most of her life. What did she care about dragon powder?

How could she have guessed it would cause the death of the first man she loved?

"It is essential to the working of any powerful Dreamer magic," the Redmother said with a stern frown. "Without dragon powder, Dreamers could not bend the power to heal life-threatening injuries, or cure disease, or forge the weapons that slay monsters."

Lifting the lid of the second trunk, Doron pushed aside yarn until her fingers brushed the smooth surface of another bag. She pulled it into the light, and stared helplessly at the seemingly insignificant object. "Very well. I concede that it has value. The question remains: what did Palle intend to do with it? Ransom it to one of the Greenmothers? And why, oh why, was Betajj involved?"

Neffera sadly shook her head. "As I told you, ma'am, I wish Prince Pirse were here. Or the minstrel. One of them could tell us what to do. I was taught that the powder is harvested from the bodies of slain dragons—and other monsters, too—and processed by a Dreamer for future use. We all know that the prince slays dragons."

The Redmother lowered her voice and bestowed a knowing wink on Doron. "Now, this isn't common knowledge. Some people think that Queen Dea banished all Dreamers from Dherrica. It's not true, and I'm guessing that His Highness could confirm what I'm saying. A Dreamer still lives in our mountains. I believe that he still bends the power, in spite of royal decree, and makes dragon powder, out of dragons slain by the prince, and sends some of it east, to share with the other Dreamers. Only this time, Palle found out, and decided he wanted it for himself."

Doron had no doubt that Betajj had known exactly what he was doing when he agreed to carry dragon powder in his baggage. The idea would have appealed to him—to be part of an enterprise that would eventually lead to the healing of a sick child, or the forging of one of the almost-mythical dragon swords.

How much harm had Palle caused, by preventing the cargo from reaching its destination?

"Do you know how to contact this Dreamer?" Doron asked.

Neffera's eyes widened. "With Palle at large and enemies lurking behind every hill? I wouldn't advise it."

"Then, for the moment, we don't have much choice. We'll have to keep it." Doron replaced the bag of dragon powder in the trunk in front of her, closed the lid, and motioned for Neffera to do the same.

"If the wizard Aage returns, we can deliver the powder to him. Otherwise, we'll wait for Pirse. Until then, guards will be posted, and the room locked. Unless you have a better idea?"

"No, ma'am."

As they left the room, Doron took one more look at the trunks, her heart hollow with old grief. So, Ivey had been right—Betajj's death had not been an accident. One more incident to add to the list of injustices for which Palle was responsible.

She would honor her memory of Betajj by ensuring that, this time, Palle did not win.

Shutting the storeroom door, she firmly shut aside her memories as well, and returned to the throne room and the demands of the present—how to hold off Palle until Pirse could arrive.

"Captain, you'd better come!"

At the sound of the hail, Dael looked down from his place on the castle wall. As soon as the young guard in the courtyard was sure he'd seen her, she disappeared into the building again. With an exasperated growl, Dael ran for the nearest stairway.

The city outside the castle walls was quiet, basking in peace. The peace of exhaustion, as Dael had told his father in one of his cynical moments during the afternoon. It had been seven days now since Hion had taken to his deathbed and Damon became king. Seven days of uncertainty, followed by terror, were enough to tire even the most stoic and unimaginative of Keepers.

Not that Dael objected to the calm that had descended. They'd had no trouble taking over the castle. Ledo had run for the shelter of his estate outside town as soon as Dael's people began to take control of Edian. Dael just wasn't sure that the peace would last long enough. He needed a quiet Edian. He needed all of the uninterrupted time he could get to prepare the city's defenses against Damon's return.

He did not need a mysterious, urgent summons from an anonymous messenger.

Dael entered the castle. He paused briefly, hand resting near his sword, until his eyes adjusted to the dimness. He saw the guard waiting at the top of the cellar stairs. Before she could run ahead again, he called, "Wait!"

"Ruudy said to hurry," she objected, poised on the balls of her feet.

"Where is he?"

She pointed down the stairs. "The west storage cellars."

Dael caught up with her. "I know the place."

"Then I'll go to find a Brownmother."

"Someone's hurt?" Dael asked sharply.

"The minstrel." An instant later, she was gone.

Dael rushed down the stairs. After a few twists and

turns, he saw a line of light at the base of a door. He entered the long-unused hallway and approached the gleam of lamplight.

Ruudy stood next to an open doorway. The air issuing from the dark room stank of human waste. Ivey leaned weakly against the wall next to Ruudy. He was unshaven and covered with dust, and cradled his swollen right hand, mottled purple and red, against his chest.

"Is it over?"

Dael would never have recognized the harsh voice if he hadn't been standing right in front of the minstrel. "Not yet. What happened to you?"

"Damon. Said you'd gone. Insisted I knew where." Ivey's left hand tightened around his other wrist. He was in shock, Dael judged, brought on as much by disbelief as by pain. "Dael, he enjoyed hurting me."

"Well, I'm here, and he's the one who's gone. He led most of his troops out of the castle this morning. We thought he was set on recapturing Vray, but he acted as if he no longer cares about Edian at all. As soon as we were sure he'd left, we took over," Dael concluded, summing up the preceding hours of chaos succinctly.

Ivey gave a shaky sigh. "So Vray's on the throne where she belongs?"

"Vray left for safety's sake days ago. That must have been after Damon captured you?"

The minstrel nodded.

"We sent her off with Nocca, in a different direction than Damon took. He'll never come near her."

Ivey rested his head back against the wall as the messenger led a pair of Brownmothers into the corridor. One began gingerly examining the minstrel's hand while the other took two poles and some heavy canvas and, with the help of the messenger, constructed a litter.

"We need more light," the first Brownmother announced. "Upstairs, please."

Dael helped Ivey to lay back on the litter. "When was the last time you had something to eat?"

"I don't know. Once, I think, since Damon talked to me."

Ruudy and Dael picked up the litter and began to walk carefully toward the stairs, the Brownmothers and the messenger following behind.

Dael muttered, "Insane. Each thing he does is crazier than the last."

"Damon?" the minstrel interpreted his complaints. "What did he say when he found out you knew nothing about Vray's escape?"

Ivey indicated his misshapen hand. "This. He refused to believe me. I had to make up something just to get him away from me."

They maneuvered the litter through the narrow doorway next to the wine room. "So, he was following your advice when he left? Did you tell him we'd gone to Dherrica?"

"No. I was afraid you might have."

They paused at the foot of the stairs, and Ivey braced himself with his uninjured hand. "Sitrine seemed more likely, though. So I sent him the other way. I sent him to the Cave of the Rock."

Dael almost dropped his end of the litter. The Brownmothers rushed forward to support it, and him.

"Gods, no!" Dael gasped.

Ivey's face was ashen. "What?"

"That's where she's going. I convinced her that it would be the safest place in the world. The one place her brother would overlook."

"The Cave of the Rock?"

"The Cave of the Rock."

CHAPTER 35

The day following Tob's coming of age was clear and cold. The bright sunshine provided the only note of cheer. They left Loid staring morosely at the blackened ruin of his barn wall and set off cross-country with the knowledge that they would be spending their nights outdoors for the remainder of the journey.

Jenil, wretchedly exhausted, paid minimal attention to her companions. The two young guards rode at the front of their tiny column, soberly discussing the amount of successful hunting they'd have to do to extend the group's rations through the wilderness. Vray took Tob's former position riding at Jordy's left side, leaving Jenil to bring up the rear alone. They spoke little. Jordy concentrated on anticipating his mount's occasional lurching missteps on the uneven ground, while Vray stared toward the horizon for long stretches of time, her expression thoughtful.

Jenil had intended, in another day or two, to bend the power and transport herself to Edian for a brief visit. She had hoped to carry news to Sitrine, as well, or at least bring back reassurances to Vray as to the welfare of her husband, and the kingdom.

Now, all of those options were gone. She had expended the last of her strength in the completely unexpected trip to Dherrica with the new Dreamer. Any contact with the people they'd left behind, friend and foe, would have to wait until they reached the Cave of the Rock, and Savyea could be induced to travel to Edian for news.

The snow cover lessened as they traveled through the wooded lands southeast of Oak Mill, out of the area of the storm that had passed through Broadford. Under the trees, dark fell early. They made camp in a sheltered hollow at the foot of a hill and Nocca built a fire for their evening meal while Peanal gathered wood. Jordy, forbidden from exerting himself by Vray at her most commanding, left her to groom the horses by herself and wandered toward the low lip of the hollow.

A half-frozen creek at the foot of the hill provided Jenil with water for her tea. She sprinkled in herbs, then set the pot to heat by the slow, unmagical method of Nocca's wood fire. Vray finished tethering the horses and went to stand beside Jordy. Jenil, grateful to stretch her cramped limbs after the long hours on horseback, strolled toward them.

The last daylight had faded from the sky. All three moons were up, their glow washing out all but the brightest stars. Keyn hung closest to the western horizon, a wide orange crescent. A tree branch overhead partially blocked blue Sheyn, still slowly waxing toward full. Tiny Dreyn hung between them, an unblinking point too small to show a phase. They were a pretty sight, the only spots of color against the blacks and whites of sky and shadows and snow.

The forest was very quiet. Behind them, a piece of wood cracked on the fire. Peanal said something in a low voice and Nocca chuckled. Vray slipped her arm through Jordy's and stood close beside him while Jenil leaned back against the rough bark of a wide-girthed pine and breathed in its fresh scent. For a few moments, they watched the night sky together in peaceful, if not companionable, silence.

"I know a story about the moons," Vray offered softly after a while.

"Redmothers have a story for everything," Jordy replied gruffly. "I don't mind, lass. You can't help it."

Vray shifted her weight and kicked him lightly on the leg, saving Jenil the trouble of doing something more drastic.

Jordy grunted. "None of that, now. I'll hear your story, seeing as your brother and sisters aren't here. Centuries of centuries ago—" he prompted her.

"This one doesn't start that way." She craned her neck to look up at Sheyn, and Jordy followed her glance as she gazed briefly at each of the moons.

"Before the beginnings of the Children of the Rock," she

347

said, "when the world was still young, the gods were lonely. They had knowledge and strength in the bending of power and a great desire to fill the world with self-sufficient life. But there were many obstacles, and many dangers, here as well as outside. With all their strength and wisdom, the gods could not decide how to proceed.

"They looked everywhere for inspiration. The oceans were vast, but too changeable, too unstable to be a model for life. The mountains had endurance, to the point of stagnation. The sun's great energy was unconquerable, but it was also uncontrollable, as capable of destroying the world as were any threats from the outside.

"Then the gods studied the moons. The moons endured, year upon year. Like the mountains, they were rock, dependable. But the moons also knew change. Like the waters, they were always in motion, sometimes growing, sometimes diminishing, presenting new sides to the world with each passing day.

"The moons lacked the inner fire of the sun. Their glow depended entirely on the light that fell on them from another source. But the gods were not disappointed by this.

"Instead, they watched the moons in their dance around the world. They saw how closely each moon touches the others. They noticed the push and pull among the moons, constantly changing but never absent. Each moon, even tiny, distant Dreyn, is equally important in its effects on the entire pattern. Each moon moves independently, according to its chosen path. Each moon depends on the others.

"The gods watched the moons, and learned from them, and remembered them when the time came for the beginning of life.

"That is the story of the moons."

"Insignificant Dreyn," Jenil commented. "Not my favorite part of that particular story."

Vray glanced at Jordy with a smile. "Since we're heading toward the mountains, I was thinking more of the Keeper's moon. Like rock, enduring but inflexible."

"I'm not inflexible," he protested mildly. "You're confusing inflexibility with reasonable caution."

"Then you like the story, carter?" Jenil asked.

"I'll remember it. Especially the moons' dance. Thank you for that, lassie."

"You're welcome," Vray replied.

From the fire Nocca called, "Supper's hot."

"Coming," Vray called back.

They turned their backs on the moons and went into camp to eat.

"And that's another example of Damon's madness," Dael stormed as he pulled winter clothing out of his chest.

His father stood in the doorway of his room, arms folded, face set with the disapproval that usually made his children pause to reconsider the wisdom of their actions. Dael had no time for parental warnings. Maybe the only way to fight madness was with madness.

Dael continued his tirade. "Insisting Dreamers are useless. If we had a Dreamer in every court, in every village and town as we should have, we'd have some chance of keeping up with events."

"Aage brought you some news—" Loras began.

"And then went off to collapse somewhere. Their magic is powerful, but not inexhaustible. He can't do the work of five wizards. Jenil can't heal an entire kingdom."

"You're sending Ivey to her."

"He wants to go. The Brownmothers can do nothing for his hand."

Dael fastened the straps on his bedroll with tight, jerky movements, then leaned it against the saddlebags on the floor. He confronted Loras stubbornly. "I need to be with Vray."

His father did not move from his doorway-blocking position. "Why? I understand that you're afraid of what Damon's planning to do, but you can't stop him alone. Not with several troops of guards at his side. You're good, son, but you're not that good."

"Vray needs me."

"Vray needs you here. Edian's your first responsibility now. Ivey's leaving for Garden Vale in the morning. He'll warn Jenil, and she'll reach the others in the blink of an eye."

"If she's recovered her strength," Dael countered. "And if she hasn't left already."

"None of which explains why you have to be the one to go galloping off after Vray. Edian—"

"Edian is my responsibility. Vray left me with full authority, right?"

His father nodded.

"Then it's my choice where and how to delegate that authority. Everyone in town respects you, Dad. You're perfectly capable of helping the Brownmothers run things."

"That's not the point. We shouldn't have to be running things. That's your place."

"My place is with Vray."

"You're indulging yourself."

"We're talking about my wife. And baby."

"Baby!? You didn't tell me there's a baby!" Loras exploded.

"We didn't tell anyone. It was safer. Except Nocca," Dael added truthfully. "Just before I sent him with Vray."

"An unborn baby. An unborn Dreamer."

"Your grandchild."

Loras winced as though Dael's final word had been a physical blow that had caught him unprepared. He dropped his arms and stepped out of the doorway.

"Get out of here," he said tiredly. "Go on. Go to your family. If the gods are merciful, we won't have to make any decisions while you're gone."

Dael snatched up his bedroll and packs. "I'm sure I'll catch up to them in a few days. We'll turn around and come right back. Everything will be fine."

He left quickly, before Loras could change his mind. Behind him he heard his father grumble, "Fine way to find out I'm about to be a grandfather."

"You want what?" Dimin demanded incredulously.

"A quarter of your grain," the guard corporal repeated. "Your village can spare that easily."

Dimin looked at the rest of the half troop. Their arrogance was infuriating, and frightening. Two women and three more men, mounted like their leader on tired horses. They were positioned on the frozen earth before the inn in a loose semicircle. Two of them, one of the women and the youngest man, seemed vaguely uncomfortable with the situation.

Dimin moved on to her next objection. "What do you intend to trade for it?"

A guard laughed. The corporal's contempt grew more obvious. "I didn't offer to trade. This is a requisition. Supplies for the king's guard. It's your duty to do as I say."

Maintaining her air of puzzled noncomprehension, Dimin said, "Atade sent its support to Edian after the Fall Festival. As always."

"Your support has increased, innkeeper."

His impatience did not impress Dimin. On this of all days she was not going to allow herself to be hurried. This day, which Kerrie had insisted would never come.

Even when word had reached them of Hion's death, followed a day later by the arrival of two farmers' sons with their news of violence in Broadford, Kerrie had not wanted to heed the warning. He had repeated the same arguments he'd tried against the carter for years, insisting that Atade was far enough from Edian to be out of danger, reminding any who would listen to him that other villages might go looking for trouble, but that anyone with sense would keep quiet and avoid attracting the new king's attention.

Dimin kept quiet. Yelling at Kerrie wouldn't have changed his mind. She went straight to Tagara instead. And together—quietly—they implemented their plans.

She wondered if Tagara was in position yet. Dimin wasn't supposed to see or hear the villagers gathering. Anything she could see might be as easily noticed by a guard.

She wondered why the weird silence of the deserted square didn't arouse their suspicions.

She wondered how gracefully Kerrie was accepting the fulfillment of Jordy's direst predictions.

None of the guards had their weapons in their hands. Dimin chose her next delaying tactic. "You can't pack that much grain on those poor horses, even if the six of you walk."

"You'll give us the wagons we need," the corporal informed her.

Dimin slowly shook her head. "I'm not sure anyone around here can spare a wagon. I suppose, given a few days, our carpenter could build something for you. We'd have to consult the wheelwright."

"That's enough," the corporal snapped. "We're not wasting days here, and no one's building us a wagon. Now go get our grain."

Tagara came around the side of the inn. He raised his hand in casual greeting to Dimin. His fingers, cupped together rather than spread, were the signal she wanted.

While a few of the guards, distracted, watched Tagara approach, she said to their corporal, "No."

The man's hand went to his sword hilt. "What?"

"I said no. I won't give you any grain. The grain is not yours. We have no duty to give you anything."

"You'll lose more than grain if you force us to take what we need for ourselves."

Tagara arrived beside her. "We force nothing. You've asked something unreasonable and unfair. We've denied your request. Leave it at that."

Behind the corporal, a brown-bearded man said, "They're fools. Get rid of them. We'll talk to someone else."

Dimin's hands, hidden within the folds of her cloak, balled into fists. Jordy never said it would be easy, but Rock and Pool, she was frightened!

"I speak for Atade," she said to the corporal. "Atade refuses you. If you honor your vows, that ends the matter."

He handed his reins to the woman on his right, jumped to the ground, drew his sword, and advanced on her. When she didn't cringe or cower or turn to flee, he was surprised. For the first time since his arrival, Dimin felt a glimmer of sympathy for him.

When he was still three paces from Dimin, four arrows from the nearest rooftops pierced him, and he died.

Two of the guards, the man with the brown beard and the woman who'd been holding the corporal's horse, immediately screamed and kicked their mounts toward Tagara and Dimin. Dimin snatched up her skirt and ran. Arrows whisked through the air, a horse squealed, and something hit Dimin's leg from behind. Her foot touched the ground and crumpled uselessly, tripping her before she knew she was falling. The pain followed. First the sharp slap of her hands and forearms as she landed on the ground, then a belated, rapidly spreading heat in her calf.

She slid to a stop, gasping, and rolled onto her side. The woman's horse pounded past her. A half dozen yards away, the woman lay motionless on the ground. The bearded man and his horse were both down. Tagara slashed the throat of the feebly struggling horse as Dimin watched. Then he stepped back and turned toward the remaining three guards.

As far as Dimin could see, they hadn't moved, except for the youngest man, who was leaning over his horse's neck, vomiting. The other man was talking rapidly to his mount, which shivered as it eyed the nearby dead horse. The young woman simply waited.

Lightly running footsteps caught Dimin's attention, and someone called her name. With several pairs of hands helping her, Dimin sat up, then insisted on standing.

A voice said, "Where's Brownmother Ottyl?"

Dimin leaned on the nearest strong arm. "Help me. I want to hear what they're saying."

They wouldn't allow her to hobble halfway across the square. Kerrie detached himself from the small crowd that had gathered around her and hurried over to Tagara, waving his arms. After a maddeningly inaudible exchange, Tagara gestured to the guards, who dismounted. The one who'd been sick trailed shakily after his companions as Tagara brought the entire group over to her.

"Do you still want our grain?" she asked them.

The older of the men said, "We never wanted it. We came on the king's orders."

Tagara voiced the important question for her. "Where's the rest of your troop?"

"They were supposed to get provisions in Hillcrest. They never came back."

The young woman said, "Now we know why."

Dimin's leg hurt. She wanted to lie down. She said, "What will you do now?"

The man chose his words carefully. "If the king wants that grain, he can send more than six guards to fetch it. He can destroy every building. You couldn't fight off two or three troops. Or a dozen."

"Is that what you'll do?" Dimin pressed him. "Go back and tell him to destroy us?"

The younger man pushed forward suddenly, face still pale. "I want to go home. It's winter. Guards are supposed to be home in the winter. I have family in Fairdock. A wife and parents. I should be helping them get ready for the spring fishing."

"It may be too early for me to reach Long Pine," the woman said quietly. "The roads will still be closed by snow."

"You should be safe as far as Broadford. Good people there, if you need to stay over a few ninedays," Kerrie offered grudgingly.

The older man shifted slightly so that he could look back at the bodies of the corporal and the other two guards. "He would have killed you for the grain. I can't see how that could be right. Obedience to the king and the honoring of basic vows aren't supposed to contradict one another."

"Which is in error?" Tagara asked. "The vows, or the king?"

After a long silence the man said, "I'll go to Edian. I don't understand any of this. My cousin works for the law reader. Maybe he can get me in to see him and ask a few questions."

Dimin relaxed, and leaned the rest of her weight on the man on her left. "Good. That's settled. Our Redmother will lead the Remembering for your friends before you leave.

"Now," she concluded wearily, "somebody take me home."

CHAPTER 36

Abandoned villages normally saddened Chasa. As he raced across southern Rhenlan, he welcomed the appearance of each snow-dusted ruin. The road he followed had probably not felt the weight of a merchant's wagon in twenty years, but it provided an adequate path through the empty lands for a single horseman. One night, wolves howling in the pine woods kept him awake for hours. The next day, he crossed the broad, level road that had to be the link between Long Pine and Whitewater. As the miles sped by, the southern mountains drew closer on his left. Riding directly toward the imposing walls of rock and ice, which were the dominant features of southern Dherrica at this time of year, made Chasa feel very small and totally insignificant.

The solitude also made him careless. Ordinary people stayed home until well into spring and besides, the road he traveled connected no living towns. He knew that the dangerous encounters between forces of guards were taking place far to the north. He didn't expect to see a single person before he reached Savyea's cave.

When a wiry body dropped from a tree limb and knocked him from the saddle, he thought he'd been ambushed by a mountain lion. He twisted as they hit the ground, one hand going for his knife, the other forearm raised to fend off the fangs that might rip out his throat.

Strong, slender fingers caught his wrist and flipped him onto his stomach.

Nearby, a voice said, "Wait. He isn't one of Damon's."

The knee digging into the small of Chasa's back didn't move. "Stones, Nocca, who else could he be?"

A woman. Agile, no doubt, but perhaps not massive enough to hold him down. He would shift, get one leg under him, and heave her into her friend.

As soon as he tensed his muscles, the toe of a boot slid roughly into the space between his legs. He stopped moving again.

"This is a Sitrinian saddle," the man named Nocca said.

"What does that mean? The carter's horse wears a Sitrinian bridle."

"There's Jenil. Maybe she'll know."

Alarm tightened the woman's voice. "Maybe this one has friends."

Chasa cautiously turned his head, until he caught a glimpse of black robes on a trotting horse.

"Greenmother?" he called as well as he was able.

"Let him up. He's not working for Damon," Jenil said.

His captor released him. Chasa got stiffly to his feet and found himself standing next to a very tall young man who looked down at him curiously.

"You know him?" young Nocca asked the Greenmother.

"I recognized him as soon as you knocked aside his hood."

Jenil did not dismount, but turned her face toward Chasa. "Please tell me you're not fleeing Damon, too."

"Fleeing Damon? No. Sitrine is in no immediate danger. Neither is Dherrica, according to my wizard. I'm on my way to meet with Princess Vray at the Cave of the Rock."

Behind him, the woman asked Nocca, "His wizard?"

Chasa shook the snow out of his cloak and walked toward Jenil. "You said 'fleeing Damon, too.' He threatened you? As much as he hates Dreamers, I didn't think he was a danger to you."

Two more riders had emerged from their hiding place behind a low hill fifty yards north of the road. The man rode a lumbering, barrel-chested carthorse, but the woman cantered ahead of him on a mount as well bred as any Chasa owned.

Jenil said, "No. He can't directly harm a Dreamer. It's Vray we have to protect."

The approaching rider pushed back her hood to reveal red braids. "Who is it?" she asked Jenil.

"Hello, Princess Vray. I'm Chasa."

"Rock and Pool, Peanal," tall Nocca exclaimed suddenly. "You've flattened the king of Sitrine!"

Chasa turned to get his first clear look at his attacker. He was not surprised to see a guard's tunic beneath her cloak. Although she looked like a pretty child standing next to Nocca, she was actually of average size. "I won't hold it against you. Seeing that we're on the same side."

"Thank you, Your Majesty," she replied.

He looked to the princess and found her exchanging a knowing glance with the man on the carthorse. "Damon, I suppose," she told him. "Why else would anyone travel toward southern Dherrica at this time of year?"

The man beside her grumbled, "Northerners, the lot of ye. This weather's not so bad. It's close to spring."

The princess shivered. "Whatever you say, Dad."

She beckoned to Nocca, who brought Chasa's horse forward. Chasa accepted the reins from the tall guard and swung into the saddle.

Jenil said, "Do you still wish to accompany Vray to the Cave?"

"Yes!"

"Then let's go on."

"West again?" Vray asked.

"West."

Dozens of horses, mounted and pack animals, left a conspicuous trail. Dael had no difficulty following Damon and his force despite their head start. The difficulty would be in catching up to them. Despite their numbers, they were moving quickly, and Dael couldn't risk making any assumptions about their ultimate destination until they were much closer to Dherrica.

He didn't stop at any of the farms he passed, despite the ruin Damon was leaving in his wake. Nothing moved in the pillaged farmyards. Dael hoped that the inhabitants were simply hiding, unwilling to face another stranger in the uniform of the king's guard. Each fresh evidence of Damon's methods for supplementing the troops' supplies added to Dael's loathing and fear. He had to find Vray—but he also had to keep track of Damon's movements. He did not know how fast Vray and Jordy were traveling, or what route they would follow. They could be anywhere in the wide lands between Broadford and the Cave. Damon's intentions were even harder to guess. Had his scouts already located Vray and put Damon on her trail, or was he moving blindly toward the Cave of the Rock? What if Dael had misjudged him entirely? Damon cared nothing for the gods. He might view Vray's retreat to the Cave as an admission of defeat, and could therefore be focusing his attention, and troops, on the battle with Dherrica.

Just east of Atade, the main body of troops left the road and turned south. Dael came to the place an hour before sunset. He hesitated, precious minutes speeding by as he tried to anticipate Damon's next move. There were several reasons he might have chosen to bypass Atade, although consideration for the town's citizens was probably not one of them. If it was simply a temporary bypass—the convenience of picketing the animals in more open country, for instance—then Dael could make up some of the time that separated him from the troops by remaining on the main road through town. However, if Damon was intent on the Cave of the Rock rather than the disputed border country, he would not be returning to the westbound road.

If Dael stopped following them now, he might never rediscover the trail.

Dael followed the trampled path south. By the time darkness forced him to stop for the night, he was convinced that Damon was not simply avoiding Atade. Throughout the next day, the trail led south and slightly west as Dherrica's snowcapped mountains began to rise higher above the horizon.

By late afternoon, he had entered uninhabited lands, a stark wilderness of low hills and insufficient rain. Hardwood forests, gray and leafless, spilled upward out of sheltered valleys, never quite encroaching on the brown, grass-covered hilltops. The only sound was the hiss of the wind and the thud of his horse's hooves.

The trail dipped into a valley and up again. Dael slowed, sparing his mount. The complex rhythm of echoing hoof beats continued unchanged. Dael looked at the landscape around him, intrigued. Such clear echoes were more common in rockier terrain than this.

They weren't echoes.

Five horses burst over the crest of the hill, each bearing a uniformed rider. They yelled hoarsely at the sight of Dael, drew their weapons, and raced toward him. Despite the Rhenlan colors they wore, Dael recognized none of them. Their behavior, however, was familiar.

He'd faced Abstainer ambushes before.

He didn't wait to be surrounded. Digging his heels into his horse's flanks, he leaped forward to meet them. First he swerved left, and whipped out his sword in time to decapitate the rider on that end of the line. Another rider was on him at once, parrying his first thrust and slamming his horse sideways into Dael's so that the two men were knee to knee. Dael dropped his reins, grabbed his knife with his left hand, and stabbed his assailant in the gut. He kneed his horse away before the man could topple over, then kicked the animal forward once more.

A woman cut in front of him. He stuck his knife in his boot top and grabbed for his reins. She was too fast. Her light sword whizzed through the air, slicing across his horse's face. The blinded animal screamed and threw itself sideways.

As Dael jumped clear, the last thread of his restraint snapped. Blood smell filled his mind. He was aware of movement, of the need to block and slash. There were other screams, and a brief distant pain down his back. Later, the only visual memory that remained was of a man with hair the color of straw bearing down on him with his sword raised over his head, wild-eyed, matted beard flecked with foam, laughing.

Dael blinked sweat out of his eyes. He stood alone on a

corpse-littered hillside. More moisture trickled down his back. He touched one hand to the spot, felt dampness, looked, and saw more blood. The pain became noticeable then, a hot line across his left shoulder blade.

He sighed and removed his metal-ringed vest. The back was gouged diagonally from neck to waist. Without its protection, the blow might well have gutted him from behind.

He couldn't travel farther that day. First he climbed the hill to make sure that no other unpleasant surprises awaited him beyond. Then he found his maimed horse and put the suffering animal out of its misery. Finally, he built a fire and tended his wound. Although awkward to reach, it was only a shallow cut, irritating but not dangerous. He lost another hour tracking and catching one of the surviving horses and riding it back to camp. For the rest of the afternoon, he gathered firewood. At sunset, he started burning the Abstainers' bodies.

In the morning, with a few hours' sleep, some additional supplies, and the new horse, he resumed the chase.

"We found her," Tatiya said.

For a moment, Doron didn't remember what could have put such a pleased expression on the guard captain's face. Doron had taken a break, in the middle of another long day of reports, conferences, and decisions, to eat lunch and play with Emlie. For a while, questions of troop movements, food rationing, supply lines, and personnel problems had been far from her mind.

Personnel problems. Abruptly, Doron remembered the orders she had given to the captain. She handed her sleepy daughter to the maid and followed Captain Tatiya out of her quarters.

"Is she all right?" Doron asked

"Fine. They're waiting for you in the throne room."

"They?"

"I thought it best to bring the whole family."

The doorkeeper of the great hall announced Doron as she entered, but she barely heard the by-now-familiar

361

words. Five people waited at the foot of the dais. Three were gray-haired elders, the other two a year or so younger than Doron.

Doron stared at the young woman. She was rather short, but shapely in a well-padded way that Doron could never hope to imitate. Her yellow dress was heavily embroidered in blues and greens, and her pale blonde hair hung in loose waves about her shoulders. The bulge of her pregnancy had just begun to show.

As Doron came to a halt in front of them, Tatiya gestured the introductions. "The Shaper Kamara, her mother, her escort Beayo, originally of Galla Mouth, and his parents."

Doron greeted each of them with a nod. "You had a pleasant journey?"

"It was uneventful," Kamara replied politely.

"Unexpected," Beayo added. He glanced around the hall with familiarity rather than awe. An empty scabbard hung from his belt.

"The captain explained the problem?" Doron asked.

"Quite vividly," Beayo said. "Until matters are settled, it's best that we stay out of Palle's reach."

"We do understand," Kamara said.

"We also hope to return home as soon as possible. No offense meant to your hospitality, of course." Beayo had a deep, pleasant voice and, Doron noticed as she inspected him, a dimple in his square chin.

"You're a conscientious escort."

"And husband," the man replied. His smile revealed two more dimples.

Startled, Doron looked to the woman for confirmation. Kamara stepped closer to Beayo.

"I have tried to inform Pirse," she said, blushing.

The stocky Shaper put an arm around his wife. "Not that Pirse has anything to say about what Kamara does or who she chooses to marry. She agreed to bear Farren, and we'll give the boy a loving home for as long as he needs us. But we know that his real life will be here, in Bronle. Our

362

lives, and our children, belong to Live Oak."

"Naturally," Doron agreed, feeling slightly dazed. From the moment Pirse announced his intention to father a Shaper heir to Dherrica's throne, Doron had dreaded this meeting. She had been certain that she would be replaced in Pirse's affections by the beautiful, wealthy Shaper woman he had chosen to bear his child.

It hadn't occurred to her that the woman would have no interest in Pirse.

Kamara frowned prettily. "Will Pirse be offended, do you think? Please don't misunderstand me. I respect Pirse and he was very kind to me, but I hope he wasn't considering having more than one child with me, because I just couldn't." She blushed again, redder than before. "It was too obvious that he did it only for duty. He sent a message when he learned about the baby, and it sounded so relieved that when Beayo asked me to marry him, I knew I had to accept."

The last of Doron's tension vanished beneath the other woman's nervous gush of words. "Of course. You did the right thing. Pirse and I wish both of you nothing but the best." She smiled as she recognized the truth in what she had said. "Tatiya, have the housekeeper arrange quarters for Kamara and her family. Then you and I need to talk about the latest reports from the border."

"Yes, ma'am."

As Kamara and the others turned to go, Doron asked, "Will you join me for supper?"

"Thank you, we'd enjoy that."

Doron waited until they were gone, then mounted the dais and collapsed onto the throne. One more crisis passed. How many left to go?

Pirse, when are you coming home?

Ivey reached the top of the ridge to the north of Broadford late in the morning of their fourth day since leaving Edian. One of the youngsters Loras had sent with him suggested a halt, but Ivey impatiently insisted they continue.

They'd gone too slowly as it was, camping and getting full nights' sleep when he would have preferred to press on. Time spent resting was time spent worrying about Jeyn. Unfortunately, his companions had taken the Brownmothers' instructions regarding his welfare as law and he had, especially on the first day, been too tired to argue with them.

Today was different. He felt better, almost his usual self. Today he had accepted no delays.

Ivey knew Jordy's land well enough to recognize the upper pasture. They jumped the fence and soon arrived in the stable yard. Ivey dismounted, expecting one of the carter's daughters to appear in response to the sound of horses, but the yard remained deserted and silent.

"Pepper! Matti!" Ivey sang the names with considerable volume, not waiting for worry to ruin his vocal control. It was the middle of the day, the girls could be anywhere. Just because the world was turning upside down, he didn't have to assume the worst.

The front door of the house opened. Cyril stepped onto the porch, her dark, indecipherable stare as troubling as always. She was the only unsolvable mystery that Ivey had ever encountered. He wasn't comfortable with her because of it, and he had the eerie, completely unsubstantiated feeling that she knew it.

He pushed his hood back on his shoulders. "Good morning. It's me, Ivey the minstrel. I've come from Edian, from Dael and Vray." Not strictly true, but he doubted that the princess would begrudge him the use of her name.

"May I come in? I'm looking for Greenmother Jenil."

Another form moved in the shadows behind Cyril.

"Ivey?"

He took the steps in a clumsy leap, ignoring the dull ache of his jostled hand, ignoring Cyril's quick retreat, aware of nothing until he reached Jeyn. She wrapped her arms around his waist and leaned into the hug as though she would never let him go. Without releasing her, he urged her gently back inside.

"Am I here?" she asked. "Are you?"

"Yes, I'm here. How are you? What are you doing here?"

"Aage brought me here, but he couldn't bring me home."

Ivey stiffened. All Dael had been able to tell him was that Aage had mentioned being with Jeyn and Greenmother Jenil at Jordy's house. The lack of further explanation had filled Ivey's thoughts and troubled his dreams during every moment of his journey from Edian. "I'm here now. I'll take you home. Jeyn, I'm so sorry about your father."

"Dad?"

Ivey guided her to the table in front of the fireplace, and sat down beside her on the long bench. Cyril, in typical fashion, had vanished. Had Jenil gone away with Vray and Jordy? Surely the Greenmother, or Aage, would have broken the news to Jeyn before they left.

"Did no one tell you, lass? Your father's dead."

For a second her eyes filled with anguished shock. Then her shoulders sagged. "Yes. They must have," she agreed in a strained voice.

"Don't you remember?"

"I remember several things. The hard part is knowing what to feel about them. I've been so numb for so long."

She shifted on the bench until she was facing him, and combed her fingers through the curls that hung against the side of his face. "You are really here, aren't you? What happened to your hand? Did Chasa take you dragon hunting again?"

He shook his head. "Let's start over. Jeyn, why are you in Rhenlan? You should be home. You're Queen of Sitrine."

"I remember them telling me that. I'll be queen later." She spread her hands over her flat stomach. "There wasn't a baby. There was something, but it wasn't a baby. They took it away."

"Oh, Jeyn." He stroked her shoulders as helpless grief rose to block his throat. How could Aage have been so wrong? The thought that Jeyn had suffered for nothing pained him more deeply than his terror-filled imprisonment in the castle, or the damage to his hand.

She moved her hands to her lap, then changed her mind and gently touched his face. "Jenil told me it's impossible. We won't try again. I'm glad, Ivey."

"So am I." He drew her close again, and cradled her head against his shoulder with his good hand.

"When do you want go home, lassie?"

She snuggled against him. "Tomorrow?"

"Tomorrow."

CHAPTER 37

"There it is," Jenil said.

Vray urged her horse up the last few feet of the path to join the Greenmother at the crest of the hill. Brown, brittle grass crackled beneath the animal's hooves. Snow lay in the shallow valley before them, piled in drifts against bushes and tree trunks, but wind had swept the hilltop clear. A quarter mile away, the valley floor sloped steeply upward, shedding grass and shrubs to become the rocky skirt of the mountain that towered like a wall across their path. To north and south, more mountains rose, huge expanses of black rock and white snow.

These mountains had seen the birth of gods. Or so Vray's memories told her.

The early afternoon sun, reflecting off so much whiteness, made Vray's eyes water. She removed one glove, rubbed the tears away, then peered under her hand, in the direction indicated by Jenil's pointing hand.

The black rocks and their hardly distinguishable shadows were angular. The opening at the foot of the mountain, framed loosely by trees, was unmistakably circular. In the valley between their hilltop and the mouth of the cave stood a small cluster of low buildings devoid of any motion—chimney smoke, animals, people—that would have indicated habitation.

Vray put her glove back on and rubbed her fingers, chilled by the few moments they'd been bare. "Quiet, isn't it?"

"Most of Savyea's visitors prefer warmer weather," Jenil agreed.

They separated to make room for Stockings's arrival. The flood of sunlight after an hour spent climbing the shaded south face of the hill didn't trouble Jordy. He squinted, bushy eyebrows drawing down to provide all the protection his sharp eyes required.

He gave the cave opening only a single glance before nodding southward. "Do you know where we are, Vray? Follow this valley—four days' travel in the summer for Stockings and the wagon—and you'd reach the old road connecting White Water with Three Spurs. Follow that a day to the east, and you're on the road we traveled from Juniper Ridge to White Water."

"I remember. That explains the snow. We're farther south than I thought."

Jordy snorted. "This is nothing. You should see it in midwinter."

"I hope we won't have to," Chasa's voice said behind them. Stockings switched her tail irritably but stepped aside at Jordy's insistence to make way for the king's mount.

"I don't think you realize what road you're on at all." Jenil's disapproving voice was barely audible, and she didn't wait for an answer before she started down the hill.

The carter had rested his reins on the back of Stockings's neck and was stiffly flexing his left hand. He caught Vray watching him as he fumbled to pick up the reins.

"Not a word," he warned her softly.

"I worry."

"We're almost there. Another hour." Jordy nudged Stockings forward with his heels.

Peanal and Nocca urged their horses onto the hilltop.

"So this is it?" Nocca asked.

"We should scout the area," Peanal added.

Nocca gestured northward, where the valley swung to the east and passed between their hill and the base of the next mountain. "If we're going to be here more than a few days, we'd better start thinking about our supplies. What if we follow the valley for a mile or so, and see how the hunting looks?"

"Good idea," Chasa agreed.

Vray said, "Don't be long. The sun will set early behind those mountains."

As Vray followed Chasa down the hill, Nocca said, "Be thankful you don't have a big sister, Peanal. 'Be home before dark, eat all your vegetables, pull up your hood.' "

Vray looked back at him over her shoulder. "You should pull up your hood. Your ears are getting pink."

She savored her big little brother-in-law's look of surprise and his girlfriend's gleeful laugh as she rode down the hill. She knew that Dael would be proud of the pair. The two of them were carrying responsibility enough for an entire troop of guards. Once she was queen, she would strongly recommend that her captain-husband give Nocca and Peanal the choicest posting he could find for them. Preferably something quiet. It was time those two got married and started a family.

You, woman, she chided herself silently, *are thinking entirely too much about babies.*

Of course, it was a natural topic to think about, for a pregnant woman. Besides, she was about to enter the Cave of the Rock. Without effort, she could hear the opening phrases of the Story of the Beginning stir in her memory. If any spot in all the kingdoms should make a person think of babies, this was it.

Maybe that was why Greenmother Savyea was known for encouraging people to get pregnant. She had lived here so many years that some of the Cave's influence must have rubbed off on her.

The snow was not too deep and the horses had no difficulty finding the path that wound across the valley toward the mouth of the cave. As they drew closer, Vray saw that the opening was not a perfect circle, but was slightly wider than it was high. Two horses, she thought, could enter side by side, if the riders ducked their heads a bit. The level space directly in front of the cave was large enough for all of their animals to graze comfortably, assuming that they could find last year's dried grass beneath the snow.

Within the opening, all was blackness. Savyea was supposed to be expecting them. Vray did not find the thought of a dark, cold, empty cave particularly welcoming.

369

Jenil dismounted in front of the opening, Chasa beside her. Stockings stopped halfway up the path. When Jordy did not immediately urge her on, Vray leaned sideways, trying to peer around them. "Is something wrong? Why did she stop?"

The carter didn't reply.

Alarmed, Vray slid down from her horse and crunched through the snow, keeping well clear of Stockings's powerful back legs. She put a tentative hand on Jordy's knee. "If you're going to fall off," she told him calmly, "fall this way. There's a drift you can land in."

Jenil's voice above them complained, "Oh, Mothers. I thought you'd be over that by now."

Vray twisted round and shouted, "Don't scare the horse!" just as Jenil vanished. She started to reach for Stockings's head and Jordy, gray-faced but aware of the danger, gripped a handful of mane.

Jenil took form immediately next to Vray. Her puff of lavender-scented smoke drifted downhill and never entered the horse's field of vision. Stockings twisted one ear in Vray's direction, but otherwise paid none of them any attention. Jordy relaxed his grip and closed his eyes.

Jenil pulled something out of her bag. "The worst effects of healing magic usually dissipate in a nineday or so. Otherwise, I would have warned you."

She handed a small ceramic cup to Vray. "Fill this with snow. Pack it down."

Vray knelt away from the trampled path and pressed clean snow into the little cup.

"Warned me?" Jordy asked, voice tightly controlled.

"The power of the gods is very strong in the Cave of the Rock. That's what you're feeling."

Chasa came to the edge of the ledge above them. "I don't feel anything."

"You haven't been sensitized to the power. He has."

As Jenil accepted the cup from Vray, the snow within transformed into water. She sprinkled a glittery powder into the cup from the pouch in her other hand.

"The power bends throughout this valley. You should have said something sooner," she told Jordy.

He took the cup carefully from Jenil's upstretched hand. "I thought I was just tired."

"Well, drink it," the Greenmother commanded.

He finished the contents in two swallows. Almost at once, the tension left his expression and he exhaled softly.

"Aye, that's better." He met the healer's eyes. "Thank you, Jenil."

"You're welcome. Now come inside."

He straightened his shoulders and said, "Walk on." Stockings continued up the path.

Jenil waited until the horse was moving before she vanished again, leaving a scent of iris behind her.

Vray returned to her horse and paused a moment to study the snow-shrouded valley. Like Chasa, she felt nothing special in their surroundings. The old tales gave the place meaning, yes, but it was nothing tangible, nothing that would have warned her, for instance, if they'd approached in the dark.

She passed her hand lightly across her abdomen. Unless she someday needed a Greenmother's healing, which she sincerely hoped she would not, she might never feel the power of the gods. Not the way her baby would. The thought that magic surrounded her, invisible and undetectable, made her skin prickle. She quickly swung onto her horse and hurried it up the path.

Jenil had not reappeared on the ledge. Jordy dismounted and walked over to the black opening in the side of the mountain, leading Stockings.

"There's a stable here," he exclaimed.

Vray and Chasa brought their horses and Jenil's into the cave. Beyond the opening, the walls widened considerably and the ceiling vaulted away out of reach of the light filtering in from outside. Wooden partitions marked the dimensions of twelve generous loose boxes arranged in two rows of six near the middle of the cavern.

Jordy left Stockings in one of the boxes and set off to explore beyond the stalls. With a "why not?" shrug to Chasa, Vray followed his example. Just before the wall receded entirely out of the light from the mouth of the cave, they found a rough, oval gap, four feet wide and seven in height, neatly filled by a framed wooden door. Chasa, a hand on his sword hilt, stepped past Jordy to take for himself the privilege—or peril—of being the first to enter. He eased the door open.

They stepped across the threshold into a flood of light and warmth. As her eyes adjusted, Vray gasped. They were standing in a sort of room, no larger than the front half of the carter's house. The heat and much of the light came from the fire that crackled merrily in a hearth set in the wall to their right. The long wall behind them, on either side of the doorway, was a mass of shelves. A table filled most of the left half of the room, its surface hidden under a riotous clutter of objects.

Vray was only peripherally aware of these commonplace details. Beside her, Jordy rested his hand on her shoulder. A comforting gesture, but for her, or for himself? All of his traveling, all of her Redmother stories, and they'd still been caught unprepared.

There was no fourth wall to the room in which they stood. A few steps past the table, the floor fell away in a stepped series of ledges. The cavern beyond was as remotely similar to the cavern in which they'd left the horses as the great hall of Edian castle was similar to a rabbit's burrow. The further wall was hundreds of yards away. Vray found the distance difficult to judge, until she spotted a black-robed figure walking along the sand far below them. Jenil's head was bowed and she walked slowly. A few yards to her right, the sand ended at the shore of a small lake or pool of motionless, dark water. In the midst of the pool was a rock, dome-shaped, perhaps twenty feet across, rising five feet above the surface of the pool.

"Mother of us all," Jordy whispered.

"Is that a curse?" Vray asked shakily. "Or an observation?"

Clearing his throat, her wonderful, skeptical, maddeningly practical, adopted dad asked, "Where is the light coming from?"

Vray took a step forward and peered more critically around the cavern. Of course it wasn't daylight, nor was there any evidence of torches or fire of any kind. Now that she was really looking, she saw that there were no shadows, either. The pearly glow that gently illuminated the entire cavern seemed part of the air itself.

"Jenil's doing?" the carter guessed.

"Hardly," said a new voice.

The black-robed woman must have been standing behind the table near the gray rock wall the whole time, unobtrusively observing their reactions. She nodded graciously at the diffusely lit scene. "The power bends easily here. I thought you children would prefer that to a great empty mysterious hole in the wall."

Coming around the table, her face brightened, and she clapped her plump, shapely hands. "My dear, you're with child!"

Chasa looked at Vray. "You are? By Dael?"

"They are married." From his dry tone, Vray could not guess whether Jordy was pleased for her, annoyed at not having been told, or simply refusing to be surprised by anything anymore.

The Greenmother said, "I'm very proud of both of them. In case you haven't guessed, I'm Savyea. Make yourselves at home. Jenil's told me all about Damon's nasty behavior. Now that you're all safely here, everything will be fine. Would anyone like some hot cider?"

"Oh, yes. It makes perfect sense," Pirse told Captain Tatiya.

They stood next to their horses at the edge of a farmer's field, twenty miles north of Bronle. Behind them, the seventeen men and women who made up the core of Pirse's loyal followers, armed and mounted veterans of the last nineday's scramble through the countryside around the capital, were flanked on both sides by the members of three of Tatiya's troops of guards. Two days of mild temperatures had melted most of the snow, and gray mud spattered the legs of people and horses alike.

On the other side of the field, the encampment of Palle, King of Dherrica, stretched in disciplined, orderly ranks from the base of a wooded hill on the west to the outskirts of the village of Stillwell on the east. In addition to the troops of guards that remained loyal to Palle, representatives of the majority of the Shaper landholders in Dherrica had ridden to the defense of their king.

Pirse smiled grimly. Numbers meant nothing, now that he knew the truth.

Tatiya glanced curiously at the bag that lay in the palm of her hand. "I always thought that only Dreamers could make use of dragon powder."

"My uncle, as you'll soon see, thought differently."

"What if he doesn't agree to meet with you?" Tatiya asked.

"He agrees. Look."

Pirse gestured across the field, and was gratified to hear the captain's sharp grunt of surprise. A party of approximately twenty men and women had emerged from the king's encampment and was riding toward them across the short stubble of the field. Palle, dark head bare in the slanting afternoon sunlight, was just visible toward the back of the group.

"He has no choice," Pirse continued. "You know how unpopular he is, even among the Shapers who have profited most from his reign. His entire claim to the throne has been based on the law, and the assumption that he's a better ruler than a vowless mother-killer like me. If he ignored my declaration of lawful challenge, he would risk destroying the keystone of his authority."

As Palle and his escort drew closer, Pirse noticed a stirring in the camp behind them and felt a twinge of unease. If he was right, Palle, for all his posturing, cared no more for the law than did his friend and ally, Damon. An attack launched now, in defiance of the declared truce, would decimate Pirse's smaller force.

Fortunately, Palle had always been better at posturing than at strategy.

Pirse took one last look at the sheaf of papers in his hand. Kamara's father-in-law had taken it upon himself to act as scribe for the kingdom's Keeper regent. His detailed description of the discovery of Betajj's missing cargo chests, accompanied by the solid proof that Tatiya held in her hand, was more important to Pirse than all the troops in Dherrica.

Thoughts of troops reminded Pirse of his other responsibility. He took the bag of dragon powder from the captain, and tucked the folded papers into his belt. "These reports agree with what you've told me about the situation on the border. The attacks from Rhenlan have all but stopped."

"The Rhenlaner corporal I spoke to claims that he didn't know that the troop below the ford was made up of Abstainers."

"What matters is that he believed the evidence of his eyes, and cooperated with you to bring an end to the fighting."

Palle and his escort had come to a halt. Pirse, with a gesture to his people to hold their places, walked onto the field and lifted the bag of dragon powder for all to see.

"Hear me, Keepers and Shapers! I, Pirse, son of Dea, lawful heir to the throne of Dherrica, claim blood debt against my uncle, Palle, for the murder of my mother, his sister, the queen!"

A wave of murmurs washed through both groups of people, like the first inrush of the tide. Palle's curses carried above the other comments, and a moment later his horse shouldered its way through to the front of his escorting party.

"What did I tell you?" he sputtered. "The boy speaks Abstainer madness! A dragon sword killed Queen Dea, and the only man in the kingdom—"

Palle stopped as abruptly as if a knife had sliced off the

words. He had seen the bag of dragon powder.

Pirse addressed his uncle's companions. "Is there a law reader in the camp?"

Toward the end of the line, on Palle's right, a well-dressed man touched his horse's flanks with his heels and joined Pirse in the open space between the two factions.

"I'm the law reader of Stillwell. Make your claim, Pirse of Dherrica. We're all listening."

CHAPTER 38

By mutual consent, Vray and her companions accepted
Savyea's invitation and devoted their first hour at the Cave
of the Rock to basic housekeeping chores. There were many
alcoves in the upper walls of the great cavern, thoughtfully
furnished by generations of Dreamers with all that a visitor's comfort and convenience might require.

Vray stayed longer in her hot bath than she'd intended.
The warmth seemed to wake the baby, and she became en-
grossed in the mysterious kicking and squirming inside her.
That led to thoughts of Dael. He loved to put his ear to her
abdomen. She was waiting for him to receive a sharp little
elbow in the jaw for his trouble.

Dael would not be pleased if the child was born while
she was hiding here. She vacillated between pessimism and
impatience with her own self-indulgent fantasies. They
were on the edge of southern Dherrica. It would be all too
easy to find themselves snowed in for the remainder of the
winter.

No. Better to adopt Savyea's confident attitude. Now
that they were safe, she and Chasa would pool their ideas
and resources and devise a way to challenge Damon within
a few ninedays. Assuming, of course, that Dael had won
control of Edian and the guard.

He couldn't have failed. He was Dael.

When she finally returned to Savyea's chamber, Chasa
was waiting for her at the table. Savyea was seated across
from him, on the side nearest the cave, picking over a
mound of tiny dried berries by the light of a pale, foggy ball
of luminescence that floated a few feet above her head. The
carter, comfortably established in one of the large chairs in
front of the fire, was asleep.

Vray kept her voice low as she sat down next to the

377

young king. "What are you doing?"

"Wishing Sene were here." He traced one finger across the scrap of parchment on the table in front of him. "These were his maps."

"Maps of Sitrine?"

"Maps of the world."

Vray glanced at the intricate charcoal lines on the nearest corner of parchment. "The entire world?"

"The part we inhabit. Specifically, the boundaries of the Eighteen Kingdoms as they existed before the plague. Of all the kings and queens of his generation, only Dad understood that the consolidations would be unstable."

"You brought maps all the way from Sitrine to the Cave of the Rock? Why? We haven't forgotten the old kingdoms."

"Who remembers them? The Dreamers? Scattered village Redmothers?"

Chasa spread his hands wide, blocking Vray's view of the map. She looked up and met his intense gaze.

"From the first arguments between King Farren and the wizard Morb, Dad knew we were in trouble. He almost convinced Hion to see the danger. At least Rhenlan didn't banish its Dreamers. But with so many deaths from the plague, there was only so much he could do. He knew he'd have to wait until the population began to grow again before suggesting that we return to the old regional divisions."

"If Sene knew all this, why didn't he stop it?"

"Stop Damon, you mean?" Chasa snapped with more than a touch of bitterness. "What could he do as long as Hion was alive? Hion, who couldn't see reason where his son was concerned."

Vray firmly pushed his hand away from the drawing. "What do we gain by reminding everyone of the boundaries of the old kingdoms? Yes, all knowledge is valuable, but I don't see that this is particularly relevant just now."

Chasa looked at her thoughtfully. "You insist on calling them old kingdoms. These aren't the old borders. These are the only proper borders."

"I would agree, except that fine sentiments won't get us

anywhere. Let's discuss something practical. The details of my challenge against Damon, for example."

Behind Savyea, the glow in the Cave of the Rock had faded almost entirely away. One of the horses in the outer cave nickered softly.

Chasa said, "There'll be no difficulty in challenging Damon now. You've been organizing evidence and witnesses in Rhenlan, and I'll have something to say about his use of Abstainers as part of his troops. We've got Damon. What's important is what happens afterward."

"We all go home," Vray said firmly.

"To rule three kingdoms?"

"There aren't Shapers enough to rule eighteen."

"There are. Ivey has been collecting names for Dad for years. Shapers in every community, where we belong. Maybe not every small village," he conceded. "But we're not as limited as some have pretended."

A clattering of hooves echoed loudly in the outer cave. Jordy woke with a start. "Eh? What's that?"

Chasa rose calmly from his chair. "Vray's guards, I expect. She gave them permission to explore the valley."

"They didn't take long," Vray said.

Nocca, deep voice muffled by intervening stone and wood, was calling Vray's name. She pushed back from the table as Jenil entered the room from the Cave beyond, hands tucked in her sleeves, eyebrows raised in curiosity.

With a grunt of effort, Jordy heaved himself out of his chair and went to open the sturdy wooden door. "By the sound of him, the lad's found something. Nocca, we're in here! There's a rack of hay in the shadows there on the south wall. Stones, man! Watch where you're going."

The last words rose in stridency as the carter staggered back a pace, pushed aside by the large and usually gentle Nocca.

Peanal exploded into the room behind her comrade, anxiety as sharp in her every movement as it was in Nocca's. "Where is the back door? Is the passage wide enough for the horses, or will we have to make walking packs?"

"This is the Cave of the Rock, dear." Savyea stopped sorting berries long enough to bestow a rather amused smile on the two young guards. "It has no back door."

Nocca jerked one thumb over his shoulder. "That's the only way in or out?"

Jenil did not share the other Greenmother's equanimity. "What's gotten into you two? Why do you want a second door?"

Nocca, expression almost comically appalled, couldn't answer. Peanal gave his arm a rough shake before venting her anger equally on Jenil and Vray. "That's terrible!"

"We are in serious trouble," Nocca added solemnly.

Annoyance and growing fear increased Vray's disbelief. "Is that supposed to be a report? So much for the marvelous Captain Dael and his training of the Rhenlan guard! If this is the way you two react under stress, I'm only grateful that we didn't encounter anything really dangerous on the way here."

Peanal's face slowly reddened. Nocca blinked and pulled back slightly, as if trying to duck the stream of caustic words.

"Would you like to go outside and start this whole conversation over from the beginning?"

"Vray," Jordy scolded her.

She snapped her mouth shut.

"What trouble?" the carter demanded, catching Nocca's eye.

Wide shoulders lifted and fell in a helpless shrug. Even before he spoke, Vray saw that her brother-in-law didn't expect to be believed. "King Damon's outside."

"No," Vray protested.

Jordy ducked nimbly around Nocca and disappeared into the stable, Peanal and Chasa close behind him.

"It doesn't seem possible," Nocca agreed.

Jenil, exasperated, threw up her hands and collapsed into a chair to glower at Savyea. "Why didn't you tell us?"

Jordy was right, Vray thought as she watched the placid smile that was as unchangeable a part of Savyea's appearance as the shape of her nose. Dreamers were hopeless. Utterly, insufferably, hopeless.

"I knew it would only upset the children. Besides, he can't do any further harm."

Vray fled. The outer cavern was cool. Beyond the cave mouth, the afternoon shadows of the mountains covered the valley. She came up beside the others, who stood just within the opening, gazing toward the northeast. Nocca loomed close behind her. Undoubtedly, he meant it as a protective gesture, but it only made her feel trapped.

". . . a quarter mile beyond," Peanal was saying.

"You're certain it was Damon?" Jordy asked intently. Savyea, her robes making her all but invisible in the black shadows, emerged from the inner cave.

Vray appealed to Nocca. "It should be Dael. He said he would come to tell us when it was safe to return to Edian. It must be Dael."

"It's not," Peanal said firmly.

"We know the difference," Nocca said. "Believe me, we checked and double-checked."

"We counted five troops of guards," Peanal added.

Chasa said, "As many as half of them might be Abstainers."

"They are," Savyea said. "I can feel their madness from here."

"You weren't seen?" Vray asked. Peanal shook her head.

"Is there a chance we could slip away? In the darkness, perhaps?" Jordy asked. "I wonder who told him we were coming here?"

Gloomy silence fell as they each considered this new uncertainty. Damon's appearance here and now with nearly a hundred guards at his back had to be more than coincidence. Vray fought an abrupt, verging on hysterical, desire to giggle.

No one comes to the Cave of the Rock.

Gods, how could she laugh at a time like this? Because the entire thing was absurd, that's how. They shouldn't have underestimated Damon. They didn't underestimate

Damon. They thought of everything.

Except this.

"Do we run?" Peanal asked. "Follow the valley south before they come into view?"

Nocca rubbed his hands together, breath steaming in the cool cave. "To go where? There's no other haven for miles."

Chasa somberly met Vray's gaze. "Perhaps no haven at all."

"There's one chance." A defensive undercurrent to Jordy's tone of voice warned Vray that he was about to say something he knew would be unpopular.

The carter nodded at Chasa. "We can split up. You and Vray are the most dangerous to Damon. Take the guards and double back the way we came, then make your way to White Water."

"He'd follow us."

"Not if I delay him here long enough. It's a chance."

"It is not," Vray insisted. "How long would you delay them? The mighty archer who can't even string a bow, much less draw it?" Jordy flushed, but Vray didn't relent. A little hurt pride wouldn't kill him. Damon would. "Against all those troops of guards? What kind of a chance do you call that?"

"Do you have a better idea?" Jordy demanded.

"No!" she shouted back at him.

There was a pause, until Nocca broke the strained silence.

"What can Damon do, exactly? It would have been different if he'd caught us in the open. If you think about it, this cave is pretty defensible." He left Vray's side to step onto the broad area in front of the cave mouth. "No troop corporal is going to want to put more than six people on horseback up here. Not and leave them any ability to maneuver. They could only enter this area a few at a time. Will they risk it?"

"Do they know how many of us are here?" Peanal asked.

"If they don't, they'll find out soon enough," Nocca said.

Jordy ran his hand over the top of his head, a gesture that only served to muss his hair and betray to Vray how worried he was. "It's no good, lad. Sound, sensible strategy, I'll give you that; but we can't expect common sense from Damon. Not from a man who'd work with Abstainers. Not from the Abstainers, either."

"How many could come through on foot, do you think?" Peanal said to Chasa.

The pale-haired Sitrinian moved back from the cave opening and eyed it speculatively. "And have room to fight? No more than four."

Peanal rested a meaningful hand on her sword hilt and jerked her head toward Nocca. "There are three of us. Acceptable odds in a defensive position."

Vray shuddered violently. This was wrong. This had nothing to do with a Shaper's vows. She had to swallow against a mouth gone dry as dust before she could get any words out. "Does every answer require death?"

"They are Abstainers," Chasa said quietly.

"All of them? I doubt it. How many Rhenlan Keepers will you kill as well, four by four? That solves nothing."

"It might save our lives," Nocca said, growing angry. "I think that is the idea."

From the shadows, Savyea said, "Your lives are in no danger, children. Damon cannot harm you."

Chasa and Nocca exchanged startled glances, but for a moment no one could think of a response to the Greenmother's serene insistence on ignoring the obvious.

Jordy gave a dubious snort. "Dreamers! You can't recognize a crisis even when it stands up and stares you in the face."

Savyea's smile never wavered, but there was a glint of iron in her eyes when she answered. "The gods live here, carter. You may believe or not, as you wish, but they will not let you come to any harm. I know."

Vray's voice shook. "Well, I've got another question for you. Why is Damon here? What about Edian?"

"What about it?" Chasa remained calm.

"Who rules there? Dael? Would Damon turn his back on such a threat? Even for the sake of chasing any of us? Or has he won? Does he control all of Rhenlan now? Will he simply replace these troops with more? Who'll be left alive to care even if I do eventually challenge him for the throne?"

Peanal put her hand on Nocca's sword arm and drew him swiftly within the shadow of the cave opening. "Look."

Tiny figures were moving at the northern end of the valley. Riders appeared by threes and fours. If any of them had been trained to move in Dael's orderly columns, they weren't practicing that discipline here. From a distance, it was impossible to recognize individuals, but when Vray spotted a lone rider moving to the left and a little ahead of the larger body of guards, she knew at once that it was her brother.

Chasa had apparently come to the same conclusion. "Coward. If he had any honor, he'd face you himself."

Jordy watched the slowly approaching troops. "He won't face you. He won't fight you. He'll let others do the work until the very end."

Vray hugged herself. The baby within her squirmed, restless. *Dreamer child, you're in danger, too.* Why couldn't Hion have lived just a little longer? She had wanted to stop Damon without more waste of lives. Instead, he'd never been more dangerous than he was right now.

More dangerous. A danger to the Children of the Rock. A danger to all Keepers.

The words echoed in Vray's mind, mocking her. She darted a swift, guilty glance at Jordy. There was the one ancient, practiced Shaper response to danger. She'd considered it once before, and with far less justification.

Jordy turned his head, reacting to her stare, or her shiver. "You shouldn't be standing out here without your cloak. Best go inside, my girl."

"I'll take her," Nocca offered.

Vray allowed herself to be escorted into the firelit warmth of Savyea's chamber. The older Greenmother followed her.

Jenil, still seated at the table, asked, "Is it your brother?"

Vray nodded, wordless.

"He won't harm you," Savyea promised again.

Nocca slipped out unobtrusively. Vray left the Dreamers and descended several levels into the Cave of the Rock. Except for a few faint reflections in the still surface of the pool, the huge cavern was completely dark. The glow of the single candle in the room where Vray had taken her bath and left her pack beckoned her to the right along the gently curving path of rock. There, she slipped on her cloak, but left her gloves.

She wouldn't want gloves.

CHAPTER 39

They had stopped at a bend in the valley. Had they lost the trail, or was the Cave nearby? Gods, Dael prayed, don't let it be the Cave. If it was the Cave, he was too late.

He drove his horse up the ridge, forcing the animal through a chest-high drift of snow, most of his attention on the guards a half-mile away. As the captain who had theoretically trained them, Dael seethed at their incompetence. No watch kept to their rear, no flanking scouts. The troops following Damon were little more than a mass of people and horses held together by their leader's purpose.

As a man who needed to evade their notice, Dael supposed he had to be grateful.

Where was the Cave? On which side of which mountain? Was it near a summit, or easily accessible from that valley? Easily accessible to Damon? Dael continued south and east, ruthlessly demanding more speed from his exhausted horse. He put a fold of the hills between himself and Damon's troops. Perhaps they were lost. Perhaps they were stopping because the afternoon was nearly over. Would any of the men or women who followed the new king of Rhenlan recognize the Cave of the Rock, even if it was right in front of them? Would Damon? Redmother stories described the Cave clearly, and Dael knew the stories. Now, faced with endless miles of snow-covered rock and roadless valleys, uninhabited and unnamed, that knowledge seemed less than practical.

When he thought he must have passed the main body of Damon's force, he veered cautiously westward. Despite his contempt for Damon's tactical arrangements, he dismounted below the crest of the hill. If he had gotten ahead of them, he didn't intend to offer an easy-to-spot silhouette of horse and rider against open sky. He left the horse a dozen feet short of the top and scrambled, crouching, the rest of the way.

He had succeeded in circling around Damon's guards, but with only a few hundred yards to spare. Damon sat in front of a few almost organized troops near the middle of the valley. From Dael's position, the sun was still visible, poised to vanish behind the shoulder of the mountain. Below, the valley was already in shadow.

Dael shifted his gaze and searched the far side. The dark, almost circular opening stared back at him, too large to miss, too obvious to mistake for anything else.

There was movement in the black opening, a tall figure briefly visible against the gray rock at one side. Dael sagged with relief at the sight of his long-legged little brother. If Nocca was here and safe, Vray had to be, too.

Vray returned to Savyea's chamber. Jenil had joined the older Greenmother in sorting berries. Would Savyea offer her perpetual, placid smile to Damon's troops as they broke down her door and threw her basket, and her, into the fireplace? Vray walked around the big table without speaking and crouched down to loosen the binding on Jordy's pack.

The quiver of arrows, a long, carefully padded bundle, came away in her hand. She stood and lifted the bow out of the corner. Unstrung, its tip threatened to scrape the ceiling. She angled it downward, rested it carefully against a chair, then bent to rummage in another pocket, looking for the coil of gut that must be there.

Out of the corner of her eye, she saw the bow begin to move. Thinking that it was slipping from its position, she gave a little cry of annoyance and reached for it. It lifted away from her outstretched fingers. Vray straightened.

In front of her, the bow firmly, comfortably, in his left hand, stood Jordy.

"This won't be an archer's battle, lass. Even if it were, you can't risk yourself."

"There'll be no battle at all." It was a relief to say the words. To say them with the firm conviction that she was doing the right thing. "Give me that bow."

The carter only stared at her, suspicion deepening. "What were you going to do?"

"I'm going to defeat Damon. Give me that bow."

Surprisingly, it was passive, good-natured, ineffectual Savyea who understood. "You really mustn't, dear. One in the family is quite enough."

"One what?" Chasa strode into the room. "Did you tell her? Have you seen my pack? I need my whetstone." He stopped, scanning their faces. "One what?"

Savyea picked up a wrinkled berry and deliberated before placing it on one of the smaller piles. None of the others were going to say it, either. Vray hung the strap of the quiver over her shoulder.

"Abstainer," she answered Chasa. "The Greenmother was reminding me that it will be forsaking all vows to kill my brother."

Chasa said, "You don't really believe he'll participate in the battle, do you?"

"There won't be a battle if he's not alive to order it."

Her intention finally became clear to Chasa. "No, Vray. Not your brother."

"He's an Abstainer. Weren't any of you listening out there? He defiles his vows. We've seen it, but we were afraid to recognize it. I failed to recognize it. All my life, I've known of his cruelty. But he was always so clever. Clever, and the heir to a ruling family. If he'd been a Keeper of Broadford, he would have been killed as an Abstainer before he was ten. Or run off to die in the wilderness, or on a guard's sword, by the time he was twenty." She flung the words, almost an accusation, at Jordy. "Well, it's not going on any longer. Give me that bow."

She stepped nimbly around the chair and put out her hand. The stubborn carter turned, and placed the bow farther out of her reach. As he did so, he somehow slipped his right arm out of its sling, then caught her wrist and pulled her hand down between them.

He spoke urgently, roughly, with distress that had little if anything to do with the pain such abrupt motion would have caused in his half-healed arm.

"Wait awhile, now, lassie. I won't argue with you. You know I think Damon more vowless a Shaper than any other, present or past. That's why he deserves to be challenged. That's the law. Law you've vowed to guard and protect. Law that separates us from Abstainers."

Seething with fury, she wanted to jerk away from him, but couldn't bring herself to hurt him. "Rock and Pool! Don't quote law. He wants to abolish law! He's going to kill us all, and then who'll challenge him?"

Savyea gave a very small sigh. "I've told you before; you're perfectly safe here with me."

No one paid her any attention.

Vray glared at Chasa. "He killed your father. Why don't you claim blood debt against him? Because you know he'll have you murdered where you stand by one of those abominations pretending to be king's guards."

Jenil rose from the table. "Vray, stop that. It doesn't help."

Chasa said, "Yes, it does. You're right, Vray. We'll challenge him, here and now. Claim the throne that's rightfully yours."

"You can't be serious! Facing him at court was one thing, but here? He'll never listen."

"Savyea can carry the message. He can't harm you, can he, Greenmother?"

"Of course not. I keep telling everyone, Damon is powerless here."

"If he still refuses to face you before the law readers, if by his words and actions he is proven to be without honor, a despiser of vows, then by law, with Nocca and Peanal and as many of his troops as are still loyal king's guards to witness, and Dreamers to hear the judgment, you and I will declare him an Abstainer." In a single fluid motion, Chasa drew his sword, its edges glittering blue and yellow in moonlight that wasn't there. "And with that lawful judgment, I'll strike him dead."

The Redmother in Vray spoke before she could stop herself. "You need three Dreamers to sentence a ruling Shaper."

Peanal put her head in at the door. "They're coming," she said, and vanished back into the darkness.

Jenil said, "I can try to reach Morb's cave. Savyea, don't let them do anything foolish." The scent of drifting lilac told Vray she had gone.

Vray turned frantically back to Jordy. There was doubt now in his troubled blue eyes. "Please. There's no time. You don't want more people to die. Give me that bow."

"We'll stop Damon," Chasa said. "But it shouldn't be by your hand. Let me face him. As you pointed out, I have a rightful claim against him. Those troops can't all be Abstainers. They'd never have had the organization to come this far. When the other guards see the truth, they'll stand with us against Damon. Watch if you have to, but let me do what has to be done."

Vray could find no words to answer him. After a moment, the king left. The closing of the door cut off the chill draft that had been creeping around Vray's ankles.

Jordy relaxed his grip on her wrist, but refused to allow her to look away. "You want him dead. I sometimes wonder if Shapers don't make laws only so that they can later break them."

The door opened again. Nocca's voice said, "Savyea, can you come out now?"

The Greenmother paused beside Vray and Jordy. "Don't quarrel. He's right. Generations of Shapers have designed the law. It deserves far more respect than some people give it. She's also right, carter. Sometimes it's necessary to improvise. That's why, like it or not, we need Shapers. It's their gift and their curse, to be able to think the unthinkable."

Jordy broke their locked gaze to watch Savyea depart. She left the door ajar, but when she spoke to Chasa, Vray could not quite make out the words. Chasa's plan was good, up to a point, but Vray wasn't satisfied.

She didn't trust Damon.

She stepped to the side and placed her hand on the bow, above Jordy's.

"Vray—" he began.

"I have to be there. I have to be ready, just in case. Please, Dad. Give me the bow."

He wanted to argue further, Vray could see it in the spark in his eye and set of his jaw. She could also see the bone-deep weariness, as much emotional as physical. So much had happened, and was happening. Through the door to the outer cavern drifted other, fainter sounds, more distant and ominous than the buzz of conversation among their friends. The muffled rumble of many horses as Damon's troops moved up the valley was punctuated by occasional shouts, harsh and vehement.

"Hark to that," Jordy said. "When I was a boy, you never saw more than twelve guards from one year to the next. It's best that way. I think you understand that. The killing should have stopped when the last fire bear died. Mind what the lad said. You have to use the law now."

"Damon won't."

He relinquished the bow. "For protection, then. I've never been one to deny the value of a simple precaution or two," he added, with the ghost of a smile. He grew serious again. "But not murder, lass. It doesn't have to be murder."

"I don't want to hear it," Damon snarled.

The corporal, a brown-skinned northerner, black eyes resentful, tightened her grip on her reins as she rode beside him, but remained silent.

"The troop is yours to command," Damon reminded her. "Therefore, its members are your responsibility. They are not to question my orders. They are to take their position."

"They won't."

"They'll do as they're told."

"Abstainers," she insisted without troubling to lower her voice, "do as they please."

"I've told you. Such labels no longer apply."

The corporal's eyes widened. It had been a slip, then, rather than deliberate insubordination. However, she did not beg his forgiveness.

"Your Majesty, they believe in the vows they have chosen to . . . to defile. Whatever the reality or illusion of the old tales, they hold great meaning for the—that portion of your guard. They're terrified of the Cave and of the Dreamers—" At his scowl, she amended hastily, "—the magic workers who traditionally live there."

"Superstition."

"They're useless like this, Sire. Give us a Dherrican village to fight and I'll be able to control them."

Two riders galloped toward them from the south, snow spraying in all directions from the horse's hooves. They had the sense to slow before coming close enough to splatter the king.

"Well?" Damon demanded as soon as they were near enough to hear.

"Recent hoof prints, Sire. Crossing the valley from east to west, directly toward the cave."

"How recent?"

"This morning, perhaps even early this afternoon. Five sets of tracks."

"Not ours?" Damon asked sharply. Several groups had managed to lose themselves during the journey from Edian. That was in addition to those who had never returned from their foraging expeditions to various villages. The numbers involved weren't important, because the force that remained to him could still overwhelm anyone that crossed their path, but he despised cowardice.

"No, Sire. Absolutely not."

Damon smiled. "Then I have them. Well done. Report to your troop corporal."

So simple, after all. If his recent recruits wished to hold back at the final moment, it was no concern of his. Let them make fools of themselves. All the easier to be rid of them later. As much as he hated to admit it, it was evident that their usefulness was more limited than he'd hoped. After he finished here, perhaps they'd win a few more battles for him on the Dherrican border, but he would not invite them back to Edian. Soen's rabble could live off the border villages.

He waved a dismissive hand at the corporal. "Reform the troops if you wish. Leave those unwilling to continue here, under guard. The rest—"

His horse danced to one side, almost throwing him from the saddle. Damon jerked the creature cruelly to a standstill. A frightened murmur spread from the guards nearest him, alarming those who could not see the large, black-hooded shape that materialized out of nowhere, or smell the wisp of warm, earth-scented smoke that hung briefly in the air a few feet in front of the king before it faded to nothing.

"Stop that!" the figure scolded Damon. "A horse's mouth is too sensitive for such treatment."

Damon turned his mount so sharply that it nearly sank back on its haunches. "Quiet!" he bellowed.

In an instant, the nervous clusters of guards fell silent. A few tried to slink toward the back of the loose column, but sharp-eyed corporals and less-fearful companions blocked their attempts to escape.

Damon spun his horse again, taking savage delight in the flecks of bloody foam that fell from its mouth onto the woman's dark robes. She was not Jenil. Damon had almost forgotten that any other Greenmother existed. This one pushed her hood back, revealing a plain, broad, rather flushed face beneath a thatch of unattractively short hair the color of dead grass.

"What do you want?" Damon demanded of her.

"I want you to marry and have several children," she replied promptly.

Before he could convince himself that he'd actually heard such a ludicrous statement, she was continuing.

"It's not too late. You're young, and I know of one or two women who might take you in hand. A very firm hand it would have to be."

"I know of more than two," Damon said with a leer.

She was not impressed. "You shouldn't ask someone what they want if you're not prepared to listen to the answer. However, I didn't come here to give you lessons in how to be respectful, though it's obvious you need them. I have a message. King Chasa of Sitrine and your sister, Vray of Rhenlan, challenge your right to rule."

A stir of barely audible comment behind Damon did not deserve acknowledgment. He laughed his disdain of the woman and her somber pronouncement. "Challenge? Am I supposed to be concerned with the meddlesome opinions of some distant Shaper and a spoiled child?"

"Yes. You must."

She stared at him, her expression unpleasantly cool. Very well, he too could play that game.

Coldly, he said, "A challenge by law must be presented one person to another, with proper witnessing. Your kind do not participate in such affairs."

"I do not challenge you. I merely inform you that the challenge is to take place."

"The message is irrelevant and you waste my time. My sister ignores the law, not I. She has refused to obey the just commands of her king, not only my own but our father's before me. As for Chasa, he has enough to concern him in Sitrine."

"Chasa is here." The woman said the impossible words matter of factly. "Three Dreamers will hear the challenge. There are sufficient Keepers present to represent their kind in the witnessing."

"And Dael? Does my traitorous captain take no part in this quaint ritual?"

"Dael is not here. His role is to father Vray's children, which is far more important than this distasteful exercise. Now, will you and some of your companions come to the Cave of the Rock? Or do you prefer to hear the challenge here?"

Dael was not here. The words hit Damon like physical blows, threatening his every assumption. Dael was still at large—where? In Sitrine, searching for sympathetic support? He'd be disappointed. Sene's son was as much a fool as his father had been, to think that an appeal to law or kingly honor would change his mind. Theirs was exactly the sort of intellectual blindness Damon despised most. Superstition from ignorant guards he could at least understand.

Vray had always been a fool, too. Now she was desperate as well. Fools and desperate people make mistakes. This would be their last.

Damon faced the black-robed woman, covering his fury with brittle charm. "Here. I have nothing to hide from my guards. I am their king. You will learn their opinion of anyone who dares to challenge that basic truth."

"Basic truths can be misleading."

The typically nonsensical statement was almost lost in the wash of noise that followed the magician's abrupt disappearance. Riders transmitted their consternation to animals that would otherwise have remained oblivious. The corporals hurried to separate out the panic-stricken members of each troop from the merely nervous, and position them furthest from the Cave. Damon looked at the guards that remained nearest to him. Seven people, out of what had once been three troops favored for their efficiency and obedience.

The failure in Edian had been a fluke. Damon still wanted to know who could have forewarned Dael. Not that it really mattered. There would be no warning here. He singled out three men and a woman and beckoned them forward.

"This proposed challenge threatens the security of Rhenlan. I think we can imagine their accusations without hearing them, can't we?"

His four listeners nodded dutifully.

"Wait for my signal. I'd be very surprised if my sister came out with the others. If she does, be ready. If not, ride for the Cave the moment Chasa falls. I want to finish this tonight."

They left, vanishing into the partially formed troops now

taking up their positions on either side of the narrow creek. Efficient, unquestioning obedience. With supreme confidence, Damon dismissed them from his thoughts. He called one of the harried corporals to him and began to explain that he suspected a trap. As he spoke, he kept one eye on the mouth of the Cave.

CHAPTER 40

Dael watched the Greenmother vanish in a puff of smoke. Damon conferred briefly with several guards, dismissed them, turned to a troop corporal, and issued more orders.

Nocca reappeared on the shelf of rock in front of the cave opening. A man whose pale hair gleamed against sun-darkened skin accompanied him. They led horses into the open and prepared to mount. Clearly, they were aware of Damon's presence, and the fact that he was watching them.

Dael slid back toward his horse. Whatever they were about to try, they could probably use his help.

"But, that's easy."

"I believe it is, for you," Morb replied.

Tob continued to hold his bowl, with the miniature replica of the Rock and Pool that were the source of life. Tob was aware that the bowl itself had nothing to do with bending the power. It merely helped him to focus his concentration. Despite that, he couldn't bring himself to relax his eager grip on the humble wooden object, even when Morb set his bowl on the floor beside him and leaned back against the rock wall of the cave.

"You've constructed an admirable barrier on your first try," Morb said. "We'll test its endurance now."

"Yes, sir."

Tob felt the giddy exuberance sneaking up on him again. So much to see, so much to learn! He was glad of Morb's approval. In the space of a nineday, the strange old man had become more than a teacher or guide. Morb didn't just recite pedantic rules and issue instructions. He participated in Tob's discoveries and self-exploration, and shared memories from his rich lifetime of experience.

To be honest, Tob had to admit that he did not need the

wizard's words of praise or support or reassurance. His ability to bend the power required neither justification nor explanation. It was right. The deep satisfaction reminded him of how good it had once felt to outsmart Stockings on a mountain road, or pack delicate ceramics in Atade and uncrate them in perfect condition at their destination, or take simple, physical pleasure in the routines of loading the wagon with his father, or setting up a camp.

Bending the power produced that same challenge and exhilaration. Not only to his body and will, but to the newly awakened part of himself, his Dreamer gifts—his magic. He had control now, and understanding.

So much to try, so much to do! Would even a Dreamer's lifetime hold years enough?

Lines of power quivered and twisted, tugging at Tob's awareness. The world turned beneath his feet and rushed around the sun. Outside Morb's cave, rain fell steadily, as it had fallen with little interruption for many ninedays. Tob wasn't sure he liked a winter without snow. He would ask Morb for more traveling practice. A change of scene—different climate, company instead of solitude—was only a step and a thought away.

The web of power jerked around him. The Others!

Immediately, Morb was with Tob. The Other pushed against Tob's barrier, its strength massive, its will implacable. Without an exchange of words, Tob sensed what Morb had already detected, other monsters, pushing close, arrowing toward Sitrine, assuming form and substance in the sea.

The Other was too strong. Morb deflected it into Dherrica, and bent a summons of power toward Aage.

Another tendril quivered near them. Tob recognized the pattern, and followed Morb out of the web, back to the world.

Rain pattered on leaves and dripped from the overhang above the entrance to Morb's cave. Tob opened his eyes to see the old wizard rise nimbly to his feet.

"You felt that, did you?" Morb asked.

Jenil materialized on the sandy floor between them.

"One of you must come to the Cave of the Rock," she announced.

Morb indicated Tob without hesitation. "Take him, then. He's talented, but he's not ready to be alone here."

Tob looked quickly from one Dreamer to the other. "What is it? What's happening?"

"Vray and King Chasa are about to challenge Damon. Which is more difficult than it sounds. We must be the witnesses."

"Where is Vray? And my father?"

"They're at the Cave," she told him shortly. "Everyone's at the Cave."

Tob didn't mind being confused. He didn't expect to understand his fellow Dreamers immediately. A century and more of shared experiences separated their generation from his. What he disliked was the tension within Jenil. Her short temper was not a response to his ignorance. The Greenmother was afraid.

Jenil continued, "There's no time to waste. Pay attention."

Tob followed where Jenil led, turning himself along the lines of power. So many of the lines came to a focus at the Cave of the Rock that he sped ahead of her, drawn inexorably onward, as he had once been drawn to his mother's kitchen by the smell of fresh-baked bread.

Energy flooded him, buffeted him, sated hungers he hadn't known he possessed. It was an effort to gather himself to locate the hard reality of the Cave interior, and recall how to resume his body.

Fighting for coherency, he thought, *This is how a moth feels, drawn to the flame.*

At the last second, he sensed that the Cave itself was empty, and shifted to the entry chamber that lay closer to the face of the mountain. Jenil puffed into existence beside him, but mercifully made no comment about the erratic course he'd taken through the web.

A wide cave mouth opened onto the gray light of early

evening. The cold air smelled of snow and horses. Vray, standing straight and still in the shadow of the entrance with a familiar, tall bow in her hand, did not look around, but Peanal noted their arrival with a distracted frown.

Savyea was unmistakable—black-robed, serene, and brimming with power. She smiled sadly at Tob. "It will be lonely for you, but I sincerely hope you're the only one of your generation of Dreamers to see what you're about to see."

Jenil left him to stand near Savyea. Tob searched the deepening shadows for his father, and found him crouched within the opening of the cave, on the side of the entrance opposite Vray. As Tob took a step toward him, Jordy stood. At his feet he'd collected a small pile of stones.

Tob had so many things he wanted to tell Jordy, so many experiences he needed to share. Face to face with his father at last, the only thing he could think of to say was, "Hello, Dad."

"You're looking well, laddie." The trace of roughness in Jordy's voice cleared. "You know what's happened?"

"A Shaper challenge. Maybe it's not how Vray planned it, but it's what we need. Damon removed from authority, I mean."

Tob moved closer to the cave mouth to peer outside. The number of guards ranged across the valley shocked him. "We're not going to be lacking for witnesses to the decision, are we?"

Jenil sighed heavily. "That is one way of looking at it."

Everyone watched Damon, and the two riders approaching him. Tob recognized Nocca by his size, and deduced that the other man must be the King of Sitrine.

Tob's eye was drawn to movement on the far side of the valley. He drew his father's attention to a lone horseman, galloping to intercept Nocca and Chasa.

"Who's that?"

Vray spared a single glance for the newcomer, and heaved a deep sigh.

"My husband."

★ ★ ★ ★ ★

"Nocca, wait!" Dael shouted.

His brother pulled his horse up sharply and stared at him in astonishment.

"Stones, Dael, what are you doing here?"

"What am I doing? What are you doing? Two swordsmen against a horde of Damon's Abstainers?"

The blond man also reined his horse in. "We're here to talk, not fight. Hello, Dael."

Dael gave a curt nod. "King Chasa. No disrespect intended, but do you really think this will work?"

Chasa stood briefly in his stirrups and scanned the mass of guards ahead of them.

"No," he growled as he resumed his seat.

Nocca finished the young king's thought. "But we have to try."

They were close enough to see Damon's smiling face. The smile was cold, confident, and triumphant. The ruler of Rhenlan lifted a gloved hand. A half-dozen guards surged out around Damon and sped toward them.

With sweet satisfaction, Dael drew his blade. The sword Sene had given him glittered fiercely against the last reddish glow of the sunset sky. A sword for killing monsters. At last, Dael understood what Sene had intended. This was the moment that the Sitrinian king had foreseen.

"No time for talk," Dael shouted. "Split up! We don't stop until Damon dies!"

The rush of hoof beats over frozen ground swallowed his words. The first guards were on them in seconds, and two more troops galloped forward to join the attack. Dael furiously beheaded one rider, slashed the hand off a second, and goaded his horse into the midst of the rest of the guards.

He looked up, and found Damon staring directly at him, his face a mask of blazing hatred. Dael grinned his defiance. With a gesture, Damon sent another dozen guards out of the formation behind him, directly toward Dael.

"Loan me your sword, and I'll prove it," Pirse said.

401

The law reader of Stillwell studied Pirse for a long moment, his expression unreadable in the flickering light of the torches that had been brought forward as twilight deepened around them. Without a word, he dismounted smoothly and drew his blade from its scabbard.

Behind him, Palle cried, "Don't be a fool! This man has twisted the truth! He is the outlaw, not I!"

Pirse ignored his uncle, and was pleased to note that a few more of the man's supposed allies had surreptitiously put a little distance between themselves and the, gods willing, soon-to-be-former king. As Captain Tatiya had given her statement, the sheaf of papers containing the report from Bronle had been passed from one hand to the next among the Shapers in Palle's retinue. The law reader, and others, had raised questions. Pirse answered them, and took pleasure in watching comprehension grow, not only among the landholders, but in one initially skeptical Keeper face after another.

He accepted the offered sword, and lay it on the black dirt. Two guards bearing torches started to move closer, but he waved them back.

"That won't be necessary."

Pirse's sword, forged with dragon powder and Dreamer magic, slid eagerly from its sheath and sent a tingle of power up the length of his arm. He tightened his grip on the hilt and thrust the blade skyward. On all sides, men and women murmured as tongues of yellow and green flame whispered along the edges of the blade, and lit the faces of Pirse and the people closest to him as if they stood within the glow of hearth fire.

When he was certain that everyone's attention was focused on him, Pirse lay his sword on the ground at Tatiya's feet. Then he raised his other hand, and opened the bag of dragon powder that Palle had somehow stolen from the unfortunate Betajj. Pirse wished, fleetingly, that he could talk to Ivey. The minstrel might already have discovered, or be able to figure out, what had inspired Palle to steal dragon powder. A tale from some half-trained, disgruntled

Redmother, perhaps, or a scroll in the castle library, over-looked when Morb was first banished from the court.

Ironic, if Dea's rejection of the Dreamers and their guidance had led, however indirectly, to her murder.

He shook powder into the palm of his hand, and addressed the silent Stillwell law reader.

"Dragon powder focuses the power that can be bent by a Dreamer. Its very substance is magic, shaped and concentrated into a tool that can be used to serve the Children of the Rock. Unfortunately, as with any tool, what can be used can also be abused."

Pirse knelt, and carefully tipped his cupped hand over the law reader's sword. The powder glimmered in the dusk, firefly specks in shades of turquoise and aquamarine. A few sparks, landing on the ground, flickered and went out. The rest clung to the blade, innumerable as grains of sand, until both edges of the weapon were outlined in glowing blue.

"Take it. Go on," Pirse insisted, when the law reader hesitated.

"It's a trick!" Palle said.

Without warning, Palle kicked his horse and trotted directly toward Pirse. He had drawn neither knife nor sword, so Pirse cautiously stood his ground. At the last second, the horse shied away from running him down, and came to a quivering halt.

His uncle was breathing heavily, his eyes wild. Glaring at Pirse, he said, "A clever tale, but none of it can be proven! Who knows what's in that sack? Cheap glitter dust from some unscrupulous gem cutter, no doubt."

"See for yourself," Pirse said, and tossed the sack into Palle's surprised hands.

With quick, jerky steps, the law reader shoved in front of Palle, bent, grasped the hilt of his sword, and straightened again, the gently shining blade held as far from his body as he could manage. After a moment, when nothing happened, the tense lines of his arm and shoulders loosened a little. He lowered the sword tip and faced Pirse.

"Your Highness, which is it? A pretty deception, or do I

now possess a magic sword?"

"Neither. The weapon is unchanged, as trusty as the sword smith who forged it for you, but no more capable of slaying a dragon or phantom cat tonight than it was this morning. A simple cleaning will wipe away the glow, and every trace of the powder that causes it.

"However, I am willing to wager my kingdom, and my life, on a single test. You and I will go to your camp butcher, now, alone, and slay two animals, you with your blade, I with my dragon sword. Goat, pig, fowl—it doesn't matter. We'll return here with the carcasses, and allow any experts you choose to examine the wounds. I guarantee that they won't be able to tell them apart.

"Queen Dea was not killed by my hand, nor by my sword."

A bellow split the darkness. All around Pirse, horses squealed with terror and bolted in every direction, carrying cursing guards and merchants with them. A black shape blotted out the last embers of the fading sunset, and the rush of oncoming wind made the torches flare and gutter.

In the group behind Pirse, one of his comrades shouted in excitement, though the warning was hardly necessary.

"Dragon!"

Palle fought his terrified mount long enough to turn the animal's head toward Stillwell, then bent over its neck and raced for shelter.

Pirse swept his gaze across the sky in search of the winged shape. It was already lower than he had expected, neck outstretched, skimming over the heads of fleeing animals and people, as if focused on a single target.

Snatching up his sword, Pirse gave chase.

The silence in the Cave was not expectant, as Tob had first thought. It was grim. He frantically reviewed his new strengths and skills, but found no answer, and no inspiration.

Seeking reassurance, he said, "Damon won't ignore the law."

"He can't be allowed to ignore the law," Jenil corrected him.

Tob's eyes were drawn back to his father's collection of stones. Just the right size and shape, piled ready to hand. Jordy saw the direction of his gaze.

"A precaution," he said with a calmness Tob couldn't understand.

"Half a dozen people can't fight off an entire king's guard! And Dreamer magic is useless in this kind of fight. Useless!"

Jordy put his hand on Tob's shoulder and squeezed gently. "Not entirely. If it comes to fighting, you'll be safe. The three of you can get away. Sooner or later, you'll find some way of controlling Damon."

"Dad!" Tob protested.

"They're almost there," Savyea interrupted. In spite of his anguish, Tob could not help responding to her decisive tone. "Watch."

CHAPTER 41

"Not yet," Jordy warned.

"I know," Vray replied. She stood just within the opening to the cave, holding Jordy's bow upright in front of her, its foot resting on the solid earth. The arrow was nocked, her fingers lax on the shaft. She wouldn't take aim yet. The melee below surged irregularly, mounted guards passing between her and Damon. The troops on foot didn't concern her. They were staying back, away from the horsemen, and therefore out of her line of fire.

The battle shifted slowly to the west. Damon moved with it, changing his position to better observe his troops as they continued to fall under the onslaught of Dael, Nocca, and Chasa. Another few seconds passed, and Rhenlan's king turned his horse, trotting up a low rise, waving more guards forward. Never once did he glance at the Cave.

Perhaps he didn't realize that he'd drifted so close. Perhaps his lifelong disdain of all the Cave stood for clouded his judgment. Otherwise, how could he forget such a basic precaution as keeping himself and his troops out of bowshot of the defending forces? If, that is, he had ever thought of his despised sister and her Dreamer friends as a force.

She saw the clear target and stepped through the arched opening. No cold wind touched her, no sound reached her. She felt the earth beneath her boots, felt the mass of the mountains behind her, supporting her, lending her their stone surety. The bow weighed nothing in her hand as she lifted it.

She would get only one shot. One chance. Damon wouldn't wait for a second.

Besides, she thought as she drew the arrow back toward her ear, *I'll never be able to pull this bow more than once.*

Her fingers caressed the string. Calmly, she adjusted for

her height above her brother's position. He seemed frozen in place. The world had stopped. Nothing moved, waiting. She was ready.

Light.

Achingly clear radiance.

The hill became a second sun, and the stones blazed too bright to have color.

"What is it?" Ivey asked.

Jeyn turned a puzzled gaze toward the window. They were alone in their room in Garden Vale's Brownmother house. Through the wall, Ivey could hear a reassuring jumble of noises as the dining hall was cleared after the evening meal.

She said, "I don't know. I felt something, but now it's gone. I think it's gone."

Ivey started to swing his legs off the bed. "I'll go get someone."

"You'll stay right there!" Jeyn commanded. From her seat beside the bed, she pressed him firmly back against the pillows.

"If you're feeling unwell—"

"I didn't say that. It was just a touch or a whisper. I thought Aage was about to appear. I must be imagining things."

Jordy squeezed his eyes shut against the sensation that surged through him. An instant later, light seared his eyelids. He turned his head and raised a shielding arm, even as he realized that such meager gestures would offer no protection at all. The light intensified.

It wasn't directed at him.

Heart pounding irregularly in the storm of forces that were coalescing so close at hand, Jordy groped for the wall at his side and peered with growing awe into the valley.

"No!"

Dael roared his protest against the coherency that

crashed through him. His sword stroke continued on its own momentum through the empty space where his target should have been. The guard, too terrified to hear him, sprawled face down on the cold ground and covered his head with his arms.

Dael almost overbalanced from the force of his unimpeded swing. The dazzling light didn't help any, either. It made his awareness too sharp, mercilessly illuminating the people around him. He saw the beginnings of panic in nearby faces and felt his horse stiffen with terror.

Not a trace of his battle concentration remained. His one hope of winning through the throng around Damon was gone.

Morb's summons snatched Aage away from the council meeting. He heard the first syllable of Feather's startled inquiry as he twisted his body away from Sitrine, but he couldn't stop to answer. The compulsion to enter the web left no room for other considerations.

He sensed the monsters and reached desperately to block them, though his limited strength made the gesture meaningless. Elsewhere, other forces entered the world. The writhing taste and clangorous flash of phantom cats, sea monsters, and a huge Dherrican dragon battered Aage's senses.

A new presence entered the web. The pulsations of power were flawless, unlike anything he'd experienced before.

No. That wasn't true. He knew them, but never this close, never this strong.

Aage hovered, torn between outrage and ecstasy. In the distance, the other Dreamers were also present, poised, watching.

Innocent.

Dael pivoted his horse in a tight circle. The chaos of the battle vanished before his eyes, replaced by a ripple of unanimity that rushed outward with the light. He saw the desire on the faces of strangers, then saw it catch and immobilize Nocca. He felt it in himself as the glare of the light filled him, overwhelmed him, and still kept on growing.

Weapons fell from inattentive hands. On all sides, riders cried out and transmitted their terror to their mounts. The animals, responding to the same desire that flooded their riders, raced in every direction, out of control.

None of them could be expected to concentrate on a battle when faced with such an overwhelming desire to hide.

The Others fled in uncontrolled panic. Morb's senses swam as the increasing power surrounded him. Quickly, but with more wonder than fear, he withdrew from the temporarily impregnable web.

A cool breeze stirred the shrubberies around his rock. The rain had ceased. Morb stood and walked outside, where he could look to the south. Too many mountains, too many miles separated him from the place. He couldn't expect to see anything.

But he could feel it.

Oh, yes.

He would feel it.

"Look out!" Pirse called.

Surrounded by the shouting of men and the screaming of horses, Pirse knew that his warning would never be heard. Even so, he drove himself on, legs pumping, as the dragon closed the final distance between itself and Palle.

The great jaws gaped, snatched, and closed. The horse shied sideways and escaped with one disembodied leg still dangling from a stirrup. When the dragon landed, the ground shook under its weight with a force that almost jolted Pirse off his feet.

He caught his balance and staggered forward another few paces. The burning brightness of his sword was mirrored in a fiery glare that shone from the open mouth of the dragon. For a moment, it was as if the flashes of a hundred dragon swords lit the belly of the monster from within. Its body swelled, and its roar flattened the tents in Palle's camp and blew the roofs off half of the buildings in Stillwell.

Pirse ignored the noise, and the size, and the blinding glare. It was still a dragon, and he was still a dragon slayer. He charged forward, both hands gripping the hilt of his sword.

The dragon threw its head back. In the blink of an eye, it expanded from the size of a house, to the size of a hill, to the size of a thundercloud. With a flicker like summer lightning and a pop no louder than a soap bubble, it was gone.

For Tob, the light was a physical force that impacted his senses, the way a strong wind might buffet his body. He leaned into it, vacillating between eagerness and alarm. Moth and flame, indeed. He was a moth with just enough knowledge to know the danger, not enough experience to know how to react.

Beside him, Jenil stiffened. Her caution held him in place. Nearby, Savyea's waiting patience shielded him, too.

The web had become so pure, so full of power, that it was no effort to touch Morb and Aage as well. He felt them feeling him, and knew that they, too, were aware of the light.

Light. Growing light.

The light should have blinded, but Vray could see clearly through it. She saw the horse rear in terror. She saw the man's face, filled with fear, filled with disbelief, filled with death.

Light streaked up from the ground. Ignoring the people around him, ignoring the animal, the jagged spears of light reached directly for Damon.

Vray sagged, cheated of her target. He belonged to the light.

She watched him writhe, fall, then twist, pinned to the

ground. He burned, for one heartbeat a shaft of white-gold, in an instant charred black. A single scream stretched over the valley.

The light sank back, dimmed, and was gone.

Damon remained, dead.

"The gods' way," Savyea commented in Vray's ear.

The Dreamer gently folded her hand over Vray's and helped her lower the bow. "I told you everything would be all right."

Vray tore her gaze from the corpse on the hillside to gape at the serene woman and, beyond her, Jordy.

For once, the carter was speechless. He dropped the rock he'd been preparing to throw and turned slowly to stare at Tob.

Slightly breathless, Tob said, "Dad! Did you see that? That was the gods!"

"If you say so, son."

"It was the gods," Savyea confirmed. "They come here often. We are their children, remember. They take care of us. Damon was an offense to them."

"I have to sit down," Jenil said weakly, and went toward the inner room without waiting for anyone's reaction to her statement.

"You shouldn't forget to consider the gods," Savyea continued to Jordy. "It's been difficult, I know. With so few Dreamers, too many of the rest of you have had too little magic in your lives. But it was only we who diminished, never the power itself. The gods are always here." She sighed. "You don't look for them, so you don't see them. Except when they insist, of course."

Vray leaned against the cave opening, suddenly freezing. She didn't care what she had seen, or how it had been accomplished. All that mattered was that Damon was dead.

As the light ceased, Dael found himself sitting in the cold dirt. He stared at an ordinary hill of stone and snow-dusted grass, and wondered why he wasn't blind. Then he wondered why they weren't all dead.

411

Around him, a few men struggled to control their panicked horses. Most of the Rhenlaners were on the ground,
either thrown by the horses now fleeing up the valley, or
fallen in sheer terror and a vain attempt to hide from the incomprehensible.

Dael flinched as a foam-flecked horse loomed over him.
Chasa dropped from the saddle, one hand on his mount's
bridle to keep the animal still. "He's dead."

Nocca limped up to them, the hair above one ear matted
with somebody's blood. His horse had evidently joined Dael's
in the general stampede. "But I was going to kill him!"

"So was I," Dael replied, climbing to his feet.

Chasa said, "It seems that the gods took the matter out
of our hands. It's probably for the best."

"Gods?"

"What else comes out of the earth to destroy evil?" the
Sitrinian king replied with philosophical calm.

"Oh. Right."

"We should have known," Nocca agreed helplessly.

Chasa looked around. On every side, dazed people were
beginning to sit up.

"Do you think we still have a problem here?" he asked.

Nocca said, "Dael, you're the guard captain. Take command of your troops."

"In the name of their queen," Chasa prompted helpfully.

"Where is Vray? Is she all right?" Dael looked toward the
black opening above them, but saw no one.

"She will be once you disperse this mob," Nocca said.

More guards were recovering as they spoke. Quite a few
stumbled to their feet and immediately turned to run away.
A smaller number stood where they were, looking stunned
and increasingly uncomfortable.

Dael jumped up on the nearest boulder. The thought of
Vray, nearby, cleared his mind wonderfully. "Corporal!" he
roared. "Report!"

Jordy emerged from the warmth of Savyea's cave into the
outer cavern. Peanal, dimly visible in the moonlight,

glanced back at him from the ledge just outside the opening, then resumed watching the valley. As his eyes adjusted to the darkness, he saw that Vray was still sitting in the archway, staring into the night. He came up behind her and pulled her hood over her hair.

She tilted her face up to him. "I'm fine, Dad."

"Come inside. Supper's ready."

"In a little while. I want to wait for Dael."

He sat down next to her. "I'll wait with you."

The cavern was quiet, except for Stockings, who snuffled contentedly in her sleep. Vray slipped her hand out from beneath her cloak and laced her fingers through his.

"It's over. It's really over."

"It is that," he agreed.

"I wasn't even frightened."

"Of Damon?"

"Of the gods. Not when it happened. But now, I am."

He squeezed her hand. "Nonsense. It's all worked out for the best."

"Has it? What about you? What about freeing Keepers from Shaper rule and Dreamer foolishness?"

He sighed, unhappy but unable to express it. First a Shaper daughter, now not only a Dreamer son but a coming Dreamer grandchild. Whatever he had experienced and seen this past nineday, he couldn't dismiss any of it as Dreamer foolishness. As much as he hated to admit it, the gods were real.

"From Shaper misrule," he corrected the girl gruffly. "You'll not misuse your authority. I won't allow it."

She gave a tired chuckle. "We'll probably fight about this tomorrow."

"And the next day, and the next. But not tonight."

After a moment she whispered, "I'm still afraid."

"Of what?"

"I've lived so long in Damon's shadow. Spent so much time scheming to be rid of him. I thought I was ready for what would come after he was gone, but now I'm not sure."

"You're ready. You're just tired. It's been—"

He groped for a word. At last, he offered the inadequate, "An unusual day. You shouldn't do so much when you're pregnant."

She didn't respond to his attempt at normalcy as he'd hoped.

"It would have been easy to kill him. I would have enjoyed killing him. That makes me just like him."

"No!" Jordy snapped at once. He pulled his hand out of her grasp, reached up, and firmly turned her face toward him. Her eyes glittered faintly with moonslight and moisture.

"You'll never be like him. I won't let you. Tob won't let you. Dael won't let you." Jordy trusted the Rhenlan captain, more than he had trusted any guard since his years of friendship with Reas. If any man could watch over the girl, it was Dael. "We'll all take care of you, lass. All you have to do is take care of Rhenlan."

Peanal came into the cavern. "They're coming," she said.

Vray put a hand on Jordy's shoulder, leaned forward, and kissed his cheek. She rose smoothly and looked toward the cave entrance. The sound of voices and bootsteps reached them. Jordy got up just as the three large men loomed against the night sky. Towering Nocca draped a long arm over Peanal's shoulders, and the two young guards followed Chasa into the inner chamber of the cave.

Vray and Dael came together in the middle of the arched opening. They gazed into one another's eyes for a heartbeat. Then Vray buried her face against Dael's chest. Dael looked over her head, finding Jordy in the shadows. He nodded once, in acknowledgment and dismissal.

Jordy turned away, satisfied. *You'll be fine, lass, he thought. We'll all be fine, now.*

CHAPTER 42

Aage paused to rest at the bend in the path. Flowers of a hundred shades and scents overflowed the bushes and trees on all sides. Summer had arrived with enthusiasm in the lush valley. Even the tiny plants that clung to the bare rock on either side of Morb's boulder bore their own profusion of tiny white blossoms. Above them, Morb's round face and bare brown shoulders glowed warmly in the sunlight.

The lines of power shifted again, shattering the peace of the moment. Aage climbed swiftly the rest of the way up the path. The Others had been quiescent since Damon's death, and the respite had freed Aage to concentrate on the everyday needs of the new kings and queens. He had been so busy that he hadn't noticed exactly when Morb resumed his defense, but eventually the battle intensified enough to catch his attention. He got back in the habit of keeping track of Morb's progress, and eventually felt the time approach when the old wizard would need assistance.

Soon the dragon sightings would begin, and phantom cats would reappear on the plains north of the Broad. At least all of the kingdoms now had ruling Shapers—and consorts—prepared to deal with that part of the threat. Aage felt confident that he could leave that work in their capable hands.

As a wizard, he belonged here.

The power quivered and shifted as Morb opened his eyes. He turned his head toward Aage.

"What are you doing here? Not trouble again?"

Aage clasped the other Dreamer's hand and helped him to his feet. "No. No trouble. The queens are in good health. Jeyn and Ivey wed at the Spring Festival."

Morb drank his bowl of water, then wiped his chin with

the back of one hand. "You didn't have to come all this way to tell me that."

"I didn't. I came for the battle."

The vines in front of the upper edge of the cave opening rustled as a figure stepped into the light. Morb never had to stoop to enter his cave, leaving the vines' growth undisturbed. But even though the young man ducked as he stepped through, a few leaves caught at his dark hair as he passed.

Aage blinked. Of course. Jenil's new Dreamer.

Unlike Morb, who as usual was protected only by a loincloth, Tob wore lightweight shorts and a pale, loose shirt liberally decorated with his mother's embroidery.

He smiled quizzically at Aage. "I thought I heard voices. What are you doing here?"

"He came to help." To Aage, Morb continued, "Savyea said she told you about the boy. Weren't you listening?"

Tob walked along the ledge and stood behind Morb, betraying no discomfort at being the subject of their discussion. The confidence, combined with his height and weight and the knowledge held behind those dark eyes, belied Morb's use of the word "boy."

Aage answered the other wizard. "She said he showed promise. She didn't mention he was a monster slayer."

"Promise? He's already stronger than I am. He needs to develop some tactics and refine his approach, but that will come with practice."

Aage pressed his lips together, disgusted with himself for not seeing the obvious sooner. "You don't need me anymore."

"Not this time." Tob made the correction gently.

"He has five times your endurance," Morb said. "This is his primary skill. Just as Savyea's is fertility and yours is weather magic. Now that I've found a proper apprentice, you can relax. Go back to doing what you do best."

"Unless something unusual happens," Tob added. "I expect there'll be times we'll need your experience more than my clumsiness."

Morb shrugged. "Sometimes I'll want both of you. I also expect you to find some time to teach him what you know. The quicker he learns all the ins and outs of our defense, the better."

A clear image returned to Aage from his last conversation with the gods. He hadn't thought of it in ninedays. In the portion before the disastrous misdirections concerning Jeyn, he had seen a dark-haired Dreamer. Aage had not recognized him, and the gods had told him that the newcomer was not a child of any of the known Shapers.

A knot of bitter pain within Aage melted. Feather had been right. The gods had not lied. They had spoken clearly to him—until the Others slipped past him, and took over the conversation. If he had known what to look for, he might have sensed the difference. That was why the Others had battled him so vigorously, so that he would be too exhausted and distracted to detect their interference. He would never be misled like that again.

He smiled in honest relief. "Of course. Whatever I can do to help. Just say the word."

The power bent delicately as Morb tested the web.

"Better get to it," he told Tob.

"See you later," the youngster said, and returned Aage's smile.

Tob took his place on the boulder without further instruction from Morb, bowl and rock already in his hand. He bent the power and slipped away faster than Aage could follow.

"He's a good boy," Morb said. "Knew nothing when I first got him, except how to listen, thank the gods. He flits about more than I like, but it doesn't seem to tire him, so I can't complain. I wasn't sure I could get used to having an apprentice again. However, there are a few advantages."

"Oh?" Aage prompted.

Morb winked slyly. "He likes to visit his family. Comes back with little gifts. His father is a carter, you know."

"I know."

"Last time, it was a keg of the richest beer I've tasted in

417

years. Would you care for a drink before you go?"

"Thanks, I would."

Morb went into his cave. Aage stopped in the archway a moment. He looked back at the person who sat where he had expected to be. It wasn't comfortable to be dispensable. Then again, he'd been freed from a frightening responsibility.

Advantages, indeed, to this apprenticeship. Aage bent the power just a little, testing the web as Morb had done.

He sensed the world of the Children of the Rock, its inhabitants at peace—and a young man sitting on a rock, holding the universe at bay.

ABOUT THE AUTHOR

Marguerite Krause and Susan Sizemore have been friends since their days writing and editing for a Star Trek fanzine. In fact, they met through writing. Marguerite was Susan's first editor and publisher . . . long ago in a galaxy far far away.

When they decided to give up fan writing to try their luck in the world of professional publishing it seemed only natural to collaborate on a fantasy novel together. The results are *Moons' Dreaming* and *Moons' Dancing*.

Susan has been published in the romance and dark fantasy fields, both in paperback and by electronic publishers. She has won the Romance Writers of America's Golden Heart award. Susan is the proud mother of a spoiled mutt with a remarkable resemblance to the ancient Egyptian god Anubis.

Marguerite has become a freelance editor, and her fantasy novel, *Blind Vision*, was published by Speculation Press, in August, 2000. Marguerite is married, and the mother of two brilliant, award-winning children . . . who are both finally in college!